By the same author

Praise for *Loser Baby*

"Jason Bovberg's *Loser Baby* is a beautiful noir novel for the 21st century! It's a wild, frantic ride through shady Southern California, a desperate drug-fueled search for a girl who only wants to escape a sordid life."
—Scott Phillips, author of *The Ice Harvest* and *That Left Turn at Albuquerque*

"*Loser Baby* is one cool book! Bovberg writes characters who get into your head and under your skin. You won't shake this one easily: It'll stay with you long after you read it!"
—Terrill Lee Lankford, author of *Shooters* and *Angry Moon*.

"Jason Bovberg's *Loser Baby* is a high-octane thriller that moves like greased lightning! The beauty of this book is its motley collection of despicable characters whom you come to love by the end. *Loser Baby* is Bovberg's greatest book and one of the best of the year."
—Gary Phillips, author of *Blood and Asphalt* and *Birds of Fire*

"Steps on the gas and never lets up. *Loser Baby* is a modern noir work of art full of tricky twists and turns. But Bovberg remembers what makes the genre tick—it's all about the characters, baby."
—Kirk Whitham, author of *Attack of the Flying Spiders* and coeditor of *Skull Full of Spurs*

Praise for the *Blood* trilogy

"An epic addition to the genre, *Blood Red* delivers a nonstop, real-time experience of the End Times—replete with visceral terror, buckets of gore, and, ultimately, a redemptive humanity."
—Alden Bell, author of *The Reapers Are the Angels* and *Exit Kingdom*

FOLLOW ME!

facebook.com/jasonbovberg.author

twitter.com/jasonbovberg

REVIEW ME!

www.amazon.com/Jason-Bovberg/e/B00JJ36NNW

Wherever you buy my books, they can be reviewed!

LEARN ALL ABOUT ME!

www.jasonbovberg.com

JASON BOVBERG

Author of *The Naked Dame* and the *Blood* trilogy

A DARK HIGHWAY PRESS book
published by arrangement with the author
ISBN (trade paperback): 978-0-9662629-8-8
ISBN (ebook): 978-0-9662629-9-5

Cover Art by Michael Morris
Design and Layout by Kirk Whitham

This one's for Harper and Sophie,
a zany glimpse of where Dad came from
before he journeyed to Colorado
to be your father.

The only constant in life is change.
—Heraclitus

Time is a piece of wax falling on a termite
that's choking on the splinters.
—Beck

0
JASMINE

Smack in the middle of Santa Ana on a Friday night, gang-funk psychedelia, the animal snarl and faint butane odor of nitrous-juiced import cars, the streets undulating and ratcheting like a grungy arcade game—*rumble, whoosh, clickety-clack!*

The city was still new to Jasmine Frank, this sprawling expanse of damp concrete, swaying palms, salty beach sweat, and steaming antifreeze. The japchae and the spicy fish tacos and the pulsating afro grooves, the cackling Chicano rap, the cacophony of indecipherable shouts coming at her along Westminster Boulevard—*yes!* She got off on the staccato ghetto thrill of it all, closing her eyes, lost in the jagged rhythms, the music and the traffic, crisscrossing like a spastic radio dial. A constantly moving mobile night life.

Sooooo different from what she and Jordy were used to back home in that deadened whitebread cul-de-sac, north Garden Grove. In their new life, it felt as if there were raging pool parties around every cinder-block corner, drugs and condoms handed out like candy, cool kids as far as the eye could see. Plenty of assholes, too, but who cared about them? You just ignored them, and they went away, bothered someone else.

Jordy's voice whispered hot in her ear, but he wasn't in the car with her now, he was back at Tommy's party. She couldn't catch her brother's words. It was as if they were buffeting on the humid wind outside her window. Or maybe she didn't *want* to hear him. She tuned him out, left him back at Tommy's house. She laughed at that, then felt a little bad. Just a little.

The inside of the car looked new—it even had a spiffy aftermarket audio deck with a touchscreen—but it was an older ride, some kind of Volkswagen according to the steering wheel. The driver (*what was his name, again?*) had let her thumb down her window to let the night in. She'd made him turn off his USB stick full of sugary pop right away, in favor of the nightsong. The hazy world swirled, and her body with it. She grooved in the contoured seat.

Jasmine glanced over at the dude, caught him ogling her legs, which she knew looked fabulous beneath the hem of her blue dress. His gaze both mortified and delighted her. Dude was OK looking but nothing special, and of course she knew what he was after. But she aimed higher, deserved better. Deserved more. That's what Jordy told her, and that's what her mom used to say, too.

Hell, the guy was good for a ride, anyway.

"How much farther, my duuuuude?" she sang out, full-throated, and she swore she could see her voice splay out colorfully and blast out the window into the night.

LOL, she thought, like actually conjuring the individual letters. She giggled, loving it. *What's wrong with me?*

"Few miles," he said, smirk-voiced.

He was wearing a silly dark fedora that he thought made him look sophisticated or something, but she knew it was only there to hide his thinning hair. She remembered him from the vitamin store a few days ago, when this all started. He was harmless, like a puppy dog. If you'd told her then that she'd end up alone with him, shotgun in his VW a few days later, high as shitballs, rushing through the late-late Santa Ana night in search of burgers, she'd have laughed in your face. Nice eyes, though. A good set of blue eyes could take a guy a long way.

She found herself balling up her fists and drumming the dash and screaming, *"Fuuuuuck iiiiiiiit!"*

Holy crap, something was in her system, gooey and euphoric, making her feel as if her head was twisting up and away like some fancy warm firecracker. Everything exaggerated, everything spinning out, like just now this hopped-up neon-yellow Toyota ahead of them, its tires chirping on the concrete of the intersection, couple of teenagers' hands waving frantically out the sunroof. Heading toward the beach, probably, the bonfires, the giddy drunken dancing at the shore. Jasmine squealed laughter, wanting to go with them.

But she was hungry, *Jesus Christ! Whooaaa hooooooo!*

Food first.

"Well, hurry up, then!" she said nonsensically, realizing after she said it that she was responding to whatever the driver said a few minutes ago.

They were stopped at a light, and she was tapping her foot.

"This probably isn't the greatest idea, you know," he said, right hand resting on his short-throw gearshift. "Tommy's gonna be pissed. At *both* of us."

"Jeez, man, you're bringin' me down."

"You don't want Tommy pissed at you."

"Awww, he's a big ol' softie."

"I'm serious."

"He's cool."

He gave her a look. "Girl, you're thinkin' of someone else."

"Sheesh, I've known Tommy *forever*."

"Be that as it may, you don't—"

"Hold up, did you just say, 'Be that as it may'?"

A pause. "Shut up."

Jasmine started laughing so hard that she could barely breathe. After a while, her leaking eyes opened blurrily on the car next to them, and she saw a large Hispanic man staring at her as if he couldn't figure her out. That was fine with her. She waved goofily at the dull-faced man, and then he pulled away when the light turned green. A few moments later, someone passed them in an underlit red Subaru WRX, sound system booming, windows tinted so black that it was like looking into the devil's eyes. The rally car swerved liquidly around the traffic ahead of them and was gone as if it had never been.

"*Oooooh*," she breathed.

Her laughter had run its course. It seemed like they were hitting every goddamn signal, and it was harshing her chill.

"What's your name again?" Lolling her head toward the driver.

"Mark." He looked annoyed, and that made her start laughing again. "It's Mark."

When she caught her breath, she said, sighing, "Let's fetch those burgers and then go right back to Tommy's, all right, Mark? Sound like a plan? If I don't get something to eat, I'm gonna faint dead away."

Jasmine hardly knew what was coming out of her mouth. She sounded like her mom, she realized distantly. Every once in a while she'd blink hard and fall into a clarity gap in which she could curse Tommy and that guy who'd given her the pills, Derek, the weirdo with the tats. She was surprised Jordy'd let that guy get within twenty feet of her. But shit, who cared, she felt *gooooood*. Although now she could sense that she was approaching the end of it—*fuck!*

She gripped the straps of her purse tightly, like holding on to the lapbar at the top of one of the insane rollercoasters at Magic Mountain, way up I-5, north of Los Angeles. That's what she felt like right now. She remembered her mom taking her and Jordan up there to Valencia years ago, blitzing on so many goddamn coasters and so much candy and funnel cake that they'd felt nauseated and lightheaded for days after. That was before Karl came into the picture, before the fun drained out of the world.

The purse straps felt funny. Slippery. She glanced down and found she was holding on to a Safeway grocery bag. It was heavy.

Whatever.

But then all of a sudden, beneath the chemical bliss of whatever she'd ingested, her throat was raw, and she felt like crying. It was as if she were catching intermittent glimpses of an abyss that had been there beneath her always. The sensation was all wrapped up in Jordy, her twin brother whom she both loved and hated, and what they'd done months ago. Sometimes she knew *for sure* that they'd made the right decision and were on their way to a future that meant something—like, *absolutely*. Other times, she was just as certain that there was no future, at least along this path ... and nothing but doom lay on the horizon.

And now she knew she'd done something *extra* stupid, and she was heading toward a horizon that she wasn't prepared for at all. She knew these things, but her body wouldn't let her feel their full import. It left her fingers sweaty and shaking, barely holding on to this slippery Safeway bag. She pictured her mother's face, and then the tears were closer than ever. She felt as if her lips were on the verge of murmuring—*Mommy*.

"Here it is, coming up on the left," Mark said. "Yeah, I can definitely go for a Double-Double. This was a good call."

Jasmine perked up, leaned forward, took a look around, wanting to squeeze every last drop of whatever was vibrating in her veins.

Westminster Boulevard seemed abruptly empty now, desolate almost, and it felt like seven hours had passed since she'd gotten in this stranger's car.

"Where'd everyone go?" she whispered. "I mean, where'd everyone go?"

As the car slowed and eased into the turn lane, Jasmine felt a twitch of hollow nausea, and the eternal abyss—the one that was always beneath her—began to widen. She turned back to the open window, sucked in the night air in huge gasps, forced a beatific smile, tried to lose herself again.

It wasn't working.

Mark turned into the dark, empty parking lot and immediately began shouting.

Jasmine's head felt like a gob of Hubba Bubba. She sensed Mark's frustrated temper like a soft pummeling up there, and she brought disembodied hands to her face to massage her temple. Without realizing it, her head had fallen against her door, and she was idly watching the dead-of-night traffic continue to drift down Westminster Boulevard toward the 405 overpass. It was an endless procession of vehicles even at this ungodly hour, and why was she even out here at the edge of nowhere with this Mark person? The Safeway bag was even more slippery now, and it felt wrong in her grip, unnatural, and somewhere deep down she knew she was in trouble because of it.

Mark was still yelling, and now he was asking her a question, a repeated question, but all she could do was listen to the lonely night, the cars and vans and trucks *whooooshing* past. She closed her eyes, locked onto the repetition, the endless mournful sighs and howls of tires on asphalt, rising and then fading into the distance, one by one.

That was really what Santa Ana was all about—a bunch of restless people on the move, all the time, on their way to *anywhere else.*

Except her.

Except Jasmine Frank.

She would always be here, trapped in SoCal amber, looking outward and yearning for the other side. Even if she found someone to take her to Santa Ana's edge, like Mark had just done, she'd always be left gazing out into a great unknown, like a fish staring out of a murky bowl, and there'd always be someone yelling at her and telling her what to be or where to go.

As exhaustion began to press down on her, as well as increased nausea, Jasmine's awareness fractured, and Jordy's voice came into the mix, and then her mom's, and she just wanted to go home. *Home!* Not the little anonymous hovel in Santa Ana that she shared with her brother, but her real home, where her mom was, when the world was good and promising.

She lifted her heavy head from the door, and she turned toward Mark.

He stopped yelling abruptly.

"Hey, are you all right? Are you crying?" His expression was one of genuine concern, and she felt a sudden warmth toward him.

"I don't feel so hot," she said, smacking her lips with distaste.

"Let's get you home."

Every once in a while, someone said just the right thing. Today it was this guy's turn. *Mark*. That was his name. The man with the hat.

Jasmine smiled at him.

"Really?"

1
JORDAN

Jordan Frank, on edge.

Standing on Tommy fucking Strafe's porch.

Jesus Christ, how was it possible he was here again? His hands were shaking. He cracked his knuckles and snapped his fingers, hopped up and down a few times. Glanced at the curb, at his 'Vette, wishing he could hop back in and drive back home, crawl back under the sheets.

Goddammit, Jasmine.

He didn't want to knock on this door.

Fuuuuuck.

Twice in ten hours.

The tiny blue house, just off Bristol, looked no less crappy in the hazy morning light, planted in its row of clapboard shacks in the middle of Santa Ana. Front awning crooked like a sneering brow, windows barred, siding thrashed. Everything dead, what should be green all brown.

Last night, the Santa Ana winds had buffeted the neighborhood, forcing everyone inside the shlumpy little shack. The gusts had rocked the place with a long series of angry wallops, like a punishment. It had been like that for three fucking days leading up to last night. Should've taken all that as a warning.

This morning, everything was eerie calm.

Jordan remembered arriving at the party around twilight, standing right here on this porch, on edge for other reasons. He'd been watching a woman across the street drag her daughter from an old Subaru across a brown front yard, kid flailing. Little pasty kid, hair so blond it was almost white. He'd recognized himself in the kid. Then Tommy's door had opened, and the music had blasted out, and Jasmine had preceded Jordan inside, all smiling and flirty.

They shouldn't have come to the party. Jasmine had insisted, itching to get juiced, aching to live a little, and shit, man, his sister was probably right. That's what he'd thought on the drive over. He couldn't remember the last time they'd hung with real people, laughed, grooved. So, yeah, like he could blame her. Younger than him by minutes, and yet nowadays she always had to remind him how to live.

But Tommy Strafe?

There was still a brutal thump of music coming from the other side of the door. That kind of hate rap that brings you low about everything. Like the world is so full of venom and anger, there's no hope at all. That was Jasmine talking, right there. She preferred the light over the dark.

It was the same music from last night, still playing, and that just made him more nervous.

Oh, hell, might as well knock. Get it over with.

Distant slam of a door somewhere down the street, and he jumped a little.

He still felt the mucus-like liquid stretch of the drugs inside him, pulling him in weird directions like Silly Putty. The dregs. Dregs of the drugs. He wasn't sure what he'd ingested toward the end—must have been around three this morning when Tommy's candyman Derek with the shaved eyebrows and the bar through his nose dropped it into his palm like crumbling gravel and drawled one drawn-out expletive. Huge goofy smile undulating like a taffy machine.

Jasmine was already gone by then, in one of the rooms somewhere, or maybe despite the wind she'd tried venturing into the back yard, to the makeshift fire pit, the railroad ties and the broken-down chairs. A few hardy souls had braved the wind, but not for long.

Jordan growled in his throat.

He didn't want to knock on this door—wasn't sure what he'd find. Ignorance was better. Sleep was better.

Everyone *inside this house* was probably asleep, slung over the rancid sofas and that one squalid bean bag crisscrossed with duct tape. (Hell, he was *banking* on the probability that Tommy was still unconscious, despite the hate music still throbbing the windows.) Jordan remembered the afro girl who camped out in that deflated chair all night, chain-smoking those nasty hand-rolled gorts or whatever. She'd kept flashing him buttcheek, winking. All sweaty. You'd have to pay him to hook up with that bag bitch.

His right hand snuck out and knocked hard three times on the door. His heart went *yow.*

The music went on.

No one came to the door.

Jordan dug out his phone and checked it for calls, texts, IM, voicemail, snaps. Nothing new since the last text, the one from Jasmine at 3:16 a.m.

Jor, where are you?

He'd been gone, baby, gone, that's where he'd been. Jordan couldn't even remember going home. Morning had come, and his 'Vette had been out in front of their apartment, bumper kissing the rear of a nasty Ford (no damage), but he had no memory of the drive, the route, or, shit, man, leaving this porch. Everything was a blank, grey cloud. He figured he knew now what it felt like to be dead.

On impulse, he reached for the doorknob.

Unlocked.

He twisted it open and pushed, peering in. Stale smoke made him squint, strong as incense, and the music battered his skull. The front room lay in chaos. He saw two bodies right away. A shiny jet-black dude he didn't recognize, blotto on the couch, head back and mouth open so wide that his toothy jaw appeared unhinged. And white afro girl on the bag, yep, skirt yanked up to her thighs, revealing the origin of the world, densely hirsute, dry ragged lips. A bad tattoo of a blue butterfly adorned her way-upper-thigh.

Jordan closed the door behind him, then stepped through the front room to the hallway.

To the left was the blasted kitchen, replete with glass empties and pizza boxes and Chinese takeout containers and plastic bags and dirty dishes and two large overflowing trash cans, one of them the brown curbside type. He plodded the greasy, threadbare carpet and approached the first of two bedrooms. The door was half-cracked. He nudged it further open with his knuckle and saw that the room was full of boxes. A few of them were colorful containers apparently meant for Tommy's supplement store—the store Jazz had told him about, the one where she'd run into the fucking goon again, after all these years. Most of the boxes were still sealed, filled with vitamins or powders or snack bars. But most of the boxes were generic cardboard, labeled with black marker: *Kickers, Oils, Fillers, Binders.*

He let the door whisper shut.

"I don't care if it's at Tommy's," Jasmine had said yesterday afternoon, delicately applying her makeup. *"He's nice to me. He's all right. Just because he treats you like shit doesn't mean he's all bad. Hey, maybe bringing me over there will soften him up for you."*

Tommy'd always had it out for Jordan, ever since they'd come up through seventh and eighth grade. That was the highest grade Tommy had gotten to, but at least Jordan kept going, made it through half of high school, in fact. Tommy was just one of those assholes that got rubbed wrong at first sight. He had a flat face with soft round edges and dull eyes that went sharp when he was incensed, which was always. And that could be about anything. Kids either feared him (the boys) or loved him (the girls). A bad boy, destined for badder. He'd once broken a boy's arm in the middle of a school hallway, twisting it up behind the poor sixth grader's back until—*snap!* Jordan had seen that shit himself, the boy screaming like an animal on the ground, Tommy hustling away blameless, shrugging and laughing. But a teacher saw it, too. After Tommy's suspension, he'd stopped lurking the school halls altogether, never came back. That was, what, eight years ago? And now somehow Tommy was a fixture in his life again.

Jordan passed a rank bathroom, muttering *holy shit*. It was empty but probably a crime scene of some kind. Needles on the sink edge, empty packets of who-knew-what, dried vomit in rivulets on the toilet, the side of the tub, the peeling vinyl floor. Someone had written an ugly word on the mirror in either blood or lipstick. Something dark filled the toilet to near the brim. The smell was otherworldly, reaching its tendrils into his brain and daring him not to hork.

The bedroom door at the end of the hall, which led to Tommy's bedroom, was closed. *Oh Jesus please don't let Jasmine be in there, please please please ...*

He inched toward the door, cocking his ear. Couldn't hear a damn thing over the rap behind him.

Jordan touched the cold metal knob, tried turning it.

Locked.

"*Motherfuuuuuuuuhhhh ....*" he whispered.

Then he heard some kind of clamor from the other side of the door. He jolted as if struck. He made his way back to the front room, stepping lightly. The two bodies there were in the same position. He nearly tripped over afro girl's anklet leg. He took the opportunity to reach down and cover her business with a dish towel that was draped on a barstool.

More noise from the hallway. The door opening.

Jordan held his hands by his side in tight fists, then loosened them, tightened them, loosened them.

Footsteps.

A woman rounded the corner out of the hall, dragging her feet like she didn't care about anything. Skin like coffee, black hair kinky and unkempt, face looking the worse for wear under last night's makeup. Clothes too tight, wrinkled. Otherwise, she was beautiful. Jordan remembered her darting around the party, looking spiffier than now, and he never got her name because it didn't matter then. She was Tommy's girl. Like Jordan was gonna talk to her.

"Oh shit," was all she said on seeing him—a kind of greeting, he guessed—and she went straight to the beatbox, shutting it off with the stab of a long nail. She glared at him, as if he'd been the one to dial into that thunderous crap so early in the morning. "That's not creepy at all."

"Hey," Jordan managed, hands on hips, restless.

"What are you doing there, weirdo?" She stomped to the kitchen to find food, opening one cabinet after another until she found a half-empty box of Lucky Charms. "Didn't you leave?"

Jordan came a little closer, cleared his throat while the woman rooted around in the fridge for milk. Finding none, she began taking handfuls of cereal from the box and crunching it dry. She leaned back against the fridge and took his measure.

"I'm looking for my sister," he told her.

Simultaneously, something occurred to her, and she choked out a laugh that sprayed a little sugar dust on the counter. "You're the one that cried!"

He frowned. He had awakened in his bed that morning, finally somewhat lucid, and felt that telltale burn in his throat, that at some point he'd shed tears. Like, a lot. Had no memory of actually doing so, obviously. Till now.

"You were tweaked, baby," she purred, chewing. "Perma-fried."

"I'm looking for my sister," he said again. "Jasmine? Blue dress? She had the funny laugh? I mean, that's what—"

"The pretty flirty one, oh yeah, I remember her."

He felt his lips twist. He still had trouble seeing his sister beyond the little twirler she'd been when she was young. Impish pigtailed girly-girl. He felt as if her whole adolescence was gone to him—she'd jumped from high-strung round-faced grade-school tyke to bouncy high school cheerleader in a leap that still left him bewildered. And now she was living with him, they were on their own, a way to pool resources and escape their duplicitous mother and the Asshole of all Assholes, who still loomed like a black shadow on the other side of Orange County.

"I guess."

"You left that bitch here, right? Fuck, man, she was lookin' for *you!*" That set her off on another choking round of laughter. "*She* didn't cry, though! She held it together."

"So she's not here?" Jordan put in, dead-eyed. "She's not back there somewhere—?" He gestured with his chin.

The woman's face darkened, her mascara smears becoming malevolent. She swallowed a dry lump of cereal cud.

"What are you trying to say?"

"She's not back there with—?"

"You're still saying it? You watch it, little twerp. There wasn't nobody back there but me."

Jordan chewed his cheeks, watching the hallway. No sound coming from back there. Tommy was probably passed out, hard belly flopped, snoring out of his flat face. Jordan's eyes flicked back to the woman. She was telling the truth. Jasmine wasn't here.

Then where the hell *was* she? *Shit, shit, shit.*

"OK."

"You need to get on outta here."

"Look, I'm sorry, I didn't mean anything by it."

"I know you didn't, fool, that's what makes it worse." Sour scrawl of an expression, mouth working on more cereal.

"But you saw her leave?" Jordan squinted under a migraine pang. "Did she say where—"

"I didn't say a word to princess the whole night."

"Yeah, but did *she*—?"

"Get on outta here now, or I'm gonna wake up Tommy, and he's not gonna appreciate that shit. He's not gonna be as happy to see you as I am."

Jordan put up his palms. "Fine, fine."

He definitely didn't need to see Tommy.

The woman waited for him to leave, watching him with her bitch face.

He about-faced and started for the front door. By pure chance, a flash of glitter caught his eye, over by a mammoth tweeter-exposed speaker in the corner, beyond afro girl. The blue glitter on Jasmine's purse, sorta matching her dress. He stopped, stunned, and went to it, picked it up. He held it out to the woman.

"This is hers."

"So?"

"So, I really don't think she would've just *left* it."

He unzipped it and rifled through it. Her cash, her cards, her ID, and Jesus there were condoms in there. Lipstick, everything. Her phone! He pulled it out and tried powering it on. Dead. That explained why all his calls earlier went straight to voicemail. He dropped it back in, zipped the purse, reeling. Irresponsible as she was, Jasmine wouldn't have left this place without her purse. At least, willingly.

"I don't see how this is our problem," the woman said from the kitchen. Meaning her problem *or* Tommy's.

Jordan squeezed his temples with one hand, closed his eyes. Gritty. He could fall asleep and have twisty nightmares for hours—he could feel it. He could still feel the taffy pull.

"I guess it's not," he said.

"Right, now get the fuck outta here." The last word tilting into an off-key like she was tired of saying the same thing three times and why wasn't he gone already. "Your sis ain't here. She's probably in her jammies back home."

Jordan took the purse out to the porch. He squinted around, taking in the dead grass and the junk. He wandered to the side fences and checked out both of the narrow side yards, peering over the weathered slats to where the fire pit was. There was no one back there. Just cans and old barbecue supplies, landscaping shit left by the previous owner, unused in ten years, infested with spiders and shit. Back yard looked deserted and cold.

He trudged to the street and fell into the 'Vette, ran his fingers through his hair. He tossed the purse to the passenger side. The anxiety came back hard, fluttering in his chest like a coke shudder.

Jasmine could be anywhere, then.

Anywhere.

"Goddammit, Jazz," he whispered.

2
LORI

Lori Holst opened the door to find Jasmine's brother in the hall, looking like a beaten puppy. Dude looked obliterated in his stretched-out tee-shirt and coat, carrying a blue spangly purse, of all things. His typically louvred hair was clinging to his skull. Bad skin with a sheen of moisture, hair stringy, eyes sunken in darkness. His usual poor posture enhanced by what appeared to be a foul mood. The blue of the purse the only color on him.

"What are *you* doin' here?"

"Is Jasmine here?"

"Why would she be here?" She finished her Marlboro, stepped forward to grind it out on the concrete floor outside her apartment door, blew smoke out the side of her mouth. "You OK, man?"

Jordan's shoulders sagged. He looked about to cry.

"I don't know where she is," he said.

Lori hadn't seen Jasmine since the previous weekend—well, wait, there was Wednesday, when she'd caught sight of Jasmine on the sidewalk, moseying home from shopping in her too-short-shorts and red halter. The apartment that Jordan and Jasmine shared was below hers and to the east. Lori always had an easy view of either of the twins when they hit the pavement toward the strip mall on Flower. Jasmine'd had a couple of bulky grocery bags in her hand Wednesday afternoon, and she'd looked atypically content. Lori remembered that striking her. She hadn't talked to the girl that day.

Last time the two of them had actually spoken was when Jasmine had come up smiling wide for a little of that sweet weed that Lori was scoring these days from Shaun, the idiot at work with the killer dealer. (Lori was sure Shaun was losing money selling to her, because he wanted in her pants, and Lori wasn't above using that to her advantage.) That was last Sunday night, after dinner.

"She at work, maybe?"

Lori watched Jordan try to process everything. He looked tweaked on something, or the vestiges of it. He kept blinking, and shaking a little. A sad blinking puppy.

She was sure Jasmine was fine somewhere, no doubt nursing a hangover somewhere, sipping coffee at a restaurant maybe. Lot of the time, also, Jasmine just needed to get away from Jordan, who rarely liked to do anything, only work and save money and watch over his sister like a parent, even though they were the exact same age. Lori wasn't sure of anything else the dude liked to do, recreation-wise. He probably just sat downstairs watching TV or reading his sci-fi paperbacks. Like, that was his life. Jasmine had complained to her about it—why live in Orange County if you were just gonna sit in your apartment all day? One time, Jasmine told her that Jordan fucking hated SoCal. That seemed on the verge of criminal.

"She doesn't work weekends," Jordan mumbled.

"I don't know, picking up an extra shift?"

Jasmine worked at a day spa waxing unwanted hair, yeah even down there, and applying facials to rich women from the nicer parts of the city. Lori had been considering a Brazilian for Steve, but he was a distracted asshole most of the time and didn't deserve it. Plus, she'd known him for all of, what, two months? She wouldn't go to Jasmine for that, anyway. Too weird. She and Jasmine had laughed about that, imagining it. Lori upending her puckered asshole and Jasmine peering in, searching for strands of gold. One of the other girls, maybe.

But Jasmine had an actual set-in-stone weekday shift, and proud of it—9 to 3.

"No," he said on a groan. "She's been gone all night."

"You wanna come in?"

He strode in, and Lori closed the door behind him. He shrugged out of his ratty jacket and hung it on an empty peg next to the door. He went straight for the couch and perched on its edge, setting the purse beside him against a pillow. He immediately checked his phone. He scrolled through a few screens while she watched, then let out a kind of bark as he dropped the phone and clutched his skull.

"Where is she?" he asked the floor.

"So, did she just take off? Was she with someone? I'll get you an Advil."

Jordan didn't say anything until she came back with two little green capsules and a plastic cup half-filled with tap water. He nodded, drank them down, and told Lori about a house party at the home of an old friend. Jasmine had dragged him there. In all the crowded, smoky melee, he'd lost sight of her, and now she was gone, like *poof*. His word. While Jordan talked, he gesticulated helplessly, eyes bloodshot.

"It's not like I can keep watch over her all the time!" Gaze darting. "I can't be responsible for her, like, her whole life!"

That seems like exactly what you want to do, she thought.

"Did you have an argument?" she prompted.

"No."

"Well—"

"We shouldn't have gone to that fucking party."

He stood abruptly and began wandering around the room, absently studying things, not really seeing them. He had that way about him, standoffish, remote—kind of dickish, if she was telling the truth.

The Frank siblings had arrived at the Sunset Vista apartments the year before, September or October, late at night, carrying a bunch of shit in big Hefty garbage bags and that was it, except for Jasmine's shoulder-slung backpack, making her look like a schoolgirl. Lori had watched them from her window, smoking. First impression: Jordan was a bit of an ass, pushing his sister around, telling her to hurry up and get the fuck inside. That impression had only been verified over time.

Lori'd felt an immediate protective gravity toward the girl, who from the window had looked gawky and lonely and sad. Reminded Lori of herself when she was younger, finding her way in a world that owed her no favors.

The first time she'd actually met Jasmine, out by the trash cans one afternoon, she invited her over for beers or, hell, even sweet tea. Just her. Wanted to get to know her, maybe be a friend. Jasmine was shy and wary back then, eyes mostly hidden by a curtain of hair. Like she'd been beaten down. Kinda like Jordan, actually. Like she'd been through some shit. Hard to believe now, the girl shined so bright.

"You sure she's not here?" Jordan made a left toward the hall.

"Hey, come on, man, she's not here, I'd tell you."

"Where else would she go?"

"Jasmine has other friends, you know."

The guy peeked in the bathroom, then into her bedroom, layered with laundry, bed a disaster, bottles on the dresser. He stepped into the room.

"Hey, fucker, out!"

Lori rarely got pissed off, but Jordan was pushing her buttons. She didn't know him well enough for this kind of bullcrap. She grabbed his meager bicep, cloth-wrapped bone, and made him face her. She let go, backed up. There was a cross-eyed intensity there that he immediately shook off.

"Sorry, sorry, I'm sorry, OK?" Palms up.

Lori ushered him out, closed her bedroom door.

"I'm telling you the truth, she's not here. You need to lighten up, man, seriously. Jasmine probably just hooked up with someone, that's all."

Jordan didn't answer, merely glowered at her. As they emerged from the dim hallway, he took out his phone and swiped up the last message he'd received from his sister at 3:16 this morning. Showed it to her.

Jor, where are you?

Lori felt a scrape of dread like heartburn. She glanced over at the purse on the couch, then up into Jordan's bloodshot eyes. She had never seen him this intense in the entire nine months she'd known him. It was like she was seeing him for the first time, like he'd been in hibernation and now was awake.

There was only one other time he'd shown a tiny glimmer of it, and it came to her now, that time Jasmine got a date through work that she didn't tell Jordan about until the last minute. After finally informing him of her impending night out—with a massage tech, no less—Jasmine had run upstairs to gab with Lori about the dude, all hyped and juiced for him, and Lori had even helped her put some pizzazz into her hair. Jordan had come up at one point and knocked on Lori's door, first time ever, and when she opened it he'd had a look in his eye, an anxious seethe like he was holding something back. He'd asked to talk privately to Jasmine, and Jasmine had walked out the door like some dutiful spouse caught in a moment of impropriety. The girl had touched Lori's hand, a silent thanks, and then she hadn't seen her again that night. The date happened, but Lori always had the feeling that Jordan maybe escorted them or at least followed them. Jasmine was twenty, they both were (although they looked younger), so that felt sketchy.

Lori guided Jordan to the front room.

"Well, where were you, then?" Lori asked him. "She asked where you were, so where were you? Were you still at the party? At the house?"

"What?" He glared at her, angrily pocketed his phone. "I was asleep, OK?"

Lori was confused. "Asleep at the party?"

Jordan was shaking his head.

"Why do you have that?" she asked, gesturing at the purse on the couch.

Jordan went blank-faced for a second, then, "I went back there. To the house. OK?" He unzipped the purse and held it open. "She left her purse, her phone, her wallet, everything."

Lori pawed through the purse, starting to breathe faster. Lipstick, compact, condoms, tissues, pepper spray, phone. She tried the phone—dead. She lifted out the wallet, found her ID, all her credit cards intact, some small bills.

"You went back to the party house and found this, but she was gone?"

He nodded, miserable.

"Jordan, this is serious."

"That's what I've been trying to fucking tell you!" Spittle came flying out of his mouth.

"Don't yell at me!" She stared him down. "You can check that shit right now."

Lori glanced at her watch—10:13 a.m. Jasmine had been out of communication for just about seven hours. Christ, that was a long time. Unless she was just asleep somewhere.

"What did you find out at the house?"

He looked suddenly impatient. "Listen, I gotta go."

"Now hold on, I'll help you. Jesus." She closed her eyes, thinking. "Have you called the hospital? She doesn't have her ID with her, so if she ended up at a hospital, they might not know who to call. You know, if she's unconscious or something."

"OK." He seemed to ratchet his intensity down a notch. "OK, that's good."

"I'll do that. You go back to your apartment, write a note for her, in case she comes back. Put it somewhere obvious. I'll make the call to the hospital. Then I'll throw some clothes on, and we'll go look for her, all right?"

Jordan looked at her with a peculiar expression, balancing between suspicion and relief. She'd never fully taken his measure before, she realized. Surface impression was still dick, but maybe there was something deeper inside, something better. He always kept his distance, whether out of mistrust or because of his own problems. And it wasn't like she'd ever encouraged anything, given the way he looked at her, or didn't look at her, when they passed each other. But, hell, he was Jasmine's brother. There had to be some good in him.

"Thanks," he mumbled.

"And plug in her phone!" she called to him as he dashed out of the apartment. "Do you have a car charger?"

"Yeah," he called.

Lori closed the door, held her palm flat against it. She performed several calculations in her head, going through her schedule.

The most pressing thing was Sarah, with her dad at the fucking beach house he shared with the rich redhead in Laguna. Lori was due to meet Sarah at noon, at their park, where Daniel would drop her off. Depending on how long this Jasmine thing lasted, Lori could easily be late. She didn't want to be late. She hadn't seen her girl in a week. They had plans. Some playtime and picnic at the park, followed by as much shopping as Lori's hoarded tips would allow, then an early dinner at TK Burger. Later some of Sarah's favorite ice cream at Baskin-Robbins, where her dad would pick her up again.

That was the plan, anyway.

Lori let her head fall to the door for a moment. Sometimes she missed her girl so much, it was like a missing limb. Or a missing heart.

And it was her own fault.

"OK," she said, pushing away from the door. She went for her phone on the kitchen counter. She knew she wouldn't find anything from Jasmine, but she checked again anyway. Nothing.

Great.

3
KAYLA

Kayla Jennings dug into the cereal box for another stale handful. She chewed while she watched the creep drive off in his old yellow Corvette. Weird kid turned out of the neighborhood and was gone.

Gone again.

A low moan behind her. She turned.

Alicia was stirring on the bean bag. She opened her eyes and stared at Kayla like she'd never seen her before. Blank owl eyes.

"What time is it?" she slurred.

"Girl, cover your parts."

Alicia glanced down at the dishtowel draped over her nethers. "I'm covered, sheesh. Why you lookin' down there anyway, lezzo?"

"No way I'm lookin' down that black hole."

"More like glory hole." A self-guffaw followed.

"Didn't see you reaching any glory last night."

Alicia yawned, stretching her miniskirt down, covering herself, tossing the towel aside. "I'm hungry."

"Want some of this?" Extending the box.

"Naw, that's just sugar." Alicia smacked her dry lips, frowning with distaste.

"Hell, I know that."

"I need some eggs or somethin', get me some protein." Alicia wobbled, found her sea legs, held out her arms for balance. "Jesus."

"Well, IHOP's up the street." Kayla dug in for some more cereal, crunching away.

"Maybe I'll do that. I know Todd over there, works in the kitchen."

Kayla looked at her. "Not the Todd that was here last night, I hope. Derek's neighbor or whatever?"

"There was a Todd here?"

"Good."

They both paused to consider Marlon on the couch, sprawled and slaughtered. If Kayla let him sleep, she probably wouldn't see the whites of his eyes until the afternoon, or tomorrow even. His breath was a deep, snorting wheeze, almost agonal.

"Should we wake him up?" Alicia pondered.

Kayla ignored her. "Hey, you remember that one dude last night, the one with the sister, both of 'em looked too young? Sister had that blue dress on, all spangly?"

"Sure, baby, yeah." Alicia squinted, scratching her head. "Shit, what was that girl's name?"

"Jasmine."

"Bingo." Cocked a finger at her. "That's right, yeah. Girl *loooooved* to get low. Beggin' for it. Didn't want to have anything to do with me, though."

"But that dude she was with—"

Alicia was rubbing her face. "He wandered around a lot. Creeper maybe. Who were they?"

"Fuckin' Tommy invited her—of course. From his school days, up in Garden Grove. He ran into the girl the other day, at the shop I guess. They're brother and sister. Twins, actually."

Alicia swayed. "Uh huh, so what about 'em?"

"Sister disappeared. Dude was just here lookin' for her."

"Oh. Huh." She made her way to the window, squinting at the dull sameness of it all. "I don't remember anything after about midnight, shit."

"You're a big help." Kayla smirked, watching Alicia with her kinky hair all crooked from the beanbag. Below the reddish afro, the girl's face seemed stunned to be conscious. There were stark lines along her thighs from beanbag folds. "You need to go on home, girl."

"I need to get some eggs."

"Well, go get 'em somewhere else."

"You up for a grocery run later?"

Kayla shrugged. "Probably. You'll sleep the rest of the day, though."

Alicia acknowledged that that was true. She was soon out of the house, after borrowing a coat. Kayla watched her walk a crooked path to her rusty Toyota and plop herself in. Took an epoch for the little car's door to rust-scream shut and the motor to fire up. Kayla watched thick vape smoke twist out of the cracked window and rise in a humid cloud. Girl could hardly breathe without smoke of some kind going in and out of her lungs.

Kayla turned from the window and started cleaning up bottles, knuckling them and depositing them in one of the cans in the kitchen. She dropped them in carefully, not wanting to wake Tommy, the big bastard. Marlon she didn't give a shit about, that gangly motherfucker, but Tommy could snore all day for all she cared. Like, would it kill the asshole to be a human being now and then?

On her second round through the living room collecting bottles, she caught a small glint of blue, half submerged between the couch cushions, next to Marlon's leg. It was a sparkly barrette. She picked it up and studied it. Yeah, it was the girl's. Kayla pocketed it.

"*Jasmine, Jasmine, Jasmine,*" she whispered, even the name making her gag.

Kayla ache-bent to the floor to grab a half-open pizza box. It contained a single hard slice of pepperoni.

She went about her cleaning, thinking of that spastic girl—the way she'd arrived on the porch in front of her brother, instantly out of place, too colorful. They'd looked like jailbait, the both of them. Everyone giving Jasmine looks, like she was a cheerleader in full uniform jumping about. Kayla remembered her more than the brother, who sort of faded into the wallpaper. Jasmine'd made an impression, that was true. All giggly, a jabbering little girl invited to the big kids' table. And she'd kept repeating something, what was it? Kayla must've heard her high voice six or seven times, asking the same inane question, bubbly and insipid.

Are you kidding me right now?

That was it. Earned her some eyerolls by 1 a.m. or so. From Kayla, too.

The girl had gotten herself high on something punchy early, care of Derek, and her voice rose in volume and pitch as the hours passed. Kayla stayed away from her, but Jasmine drew a crowd. Like, infectious. She was the one that started dancing, like actually dancing to that horrible gangsta rap Tommy liked to throw on. And, fuck, even Kayla had to admit that Jasmine made it work. Fucking princess.

Tommy had his eye on her all night, you bet.

It's why Kayla had pretty much stayed grounded, eyes and brain clear to keep tabs on her man. Tommy'd wandered the house like a gorilla, growling out his bass-heavy chortle at any provocation. Fucking flirting right in front of her, and Kayla *psshawing* like she didn't give a shit, like given the opportunity Tommy wouldn't bend half the girls in the room over the arm of the couch and go to town like some TV cowboy. *Heeeeyaahh!*

Kayla stopped herself from hate-smashing the plates she was dunking in the sink.

Stood there and closed her eyes.

She remembered falling for Tommy, yeah, she could still remember that. Last year, that kegger at Derek's. Oh *Jesus* that had been a throwdown, that crank-balls night, appalled even her by the end when the cops broke it up. There'd been a by-God orgy happening in one of the rooms, door flung wide for all to witness, seven or eight people. She'd never seen that kind of shit before. Sweaty tattooed limbs roiling like exotic snakes. Genitals enflamed, splayed out. Tommy'd been in the kitchen, lording over the stolen booze. He'd recruited some local bartender to do fancy shit, some twerky girl, of course. He kept lifting the little cutie into the air, effortlessly with his big arms, making her squeal while she two-fisted cheap tequila and a mixer of her own making.

Tommy's muscles, his broad frame, all of that had made Kayla vibrate across the room. That mountainous chest. Face like an ocean cliff, like a cartoon thug, almost comical but in a hot way. Piercing eyes that finally caught hers, and it was all over—like *bang*. She knew she'd have him, and have him for the long term.

Tommy's first words to her, as she'd angled up to him?

Well, you're somethin'.

His gaze ravaging her like big, beefy hands—which would actually happen not much later, and not in the orgy room, *ha!* Tommy was always able to commandeer a space, any space. While they were fucking in some back room, some kind of office, in a big fancy leather chair, Derek had apparently brought out his samples in the front room, like some Tupperware party. She learned that later from Derek himself. And the house went gradually apocalyptic on all the product, most of it wildly mysterious, homemade pills and this grey crumbly stuff like old concrete. Violent shit started breaking out around 2 a.m., hate-screaming, face smashing, guys brandishing knives. Couple assholes got cut, bad. Whole place went *mwwaaaaahhh!!!* Kayla would always remember the way Tommy wrapped her up and shielded her from all that, took her outside and they'd walked casually away as the sirens shrieked, a stroll over to that little kid park on Hennessey like nothing was happening. Nothing except the full moon and the increasing night-quiet and murmured laughter and those big muscles, pushing her in a lopsided swing while she recalled the crammed-full sensation of him inside her, back in that office chair, like he was all she'd ever need.

Kayla coughed out of the memory. She felt herself juiced up down there, shook her head a little, smiling despite herself. Then she let the frown come back.

She started washing dishes. The place was a fucking disaster. Why'd she always let this crap happen at her place? Pigs is what they were, rootin' around in filth of their own making. And she always stood there and watched it happen, even in her own home.

She paused and took the blue barrette out of her pocket, placed it on the counter in front of her, watched it as she went on washing.

"*Jasmine, Jasmine,*" she whispered.

The girl wasn't *her* problem. Hell, it was Jasmine's own fault for waltzing in here all innocent last night. The girl had attracted a crowd all evening, there was no way Kayla could remember every individual creep who'd taken an interest in her. She couldn't visualize any guys hanging too close, starting to obsess. Probably a few of them did that. Jasmine was a dick magnet—including Tommy's dick. Kayla could tell. She wasn't an idiot. Big stupid fuck all but salivating, sneaking looks.

Truth was, Kayla remembered Jasmine twisting googly-eyed into the living room at some point late, still tweaking on something she'd never experienced before but coming down just enough to start thumb-texting someone, and Kayla guessed that someone was Jordan. But Jasmine hadn't seen her brother twitching and crying in the corner earlier, hadn't seen him stumble outside into the misty black wee-morning, hadn't recognized the 'Vette's rattling motor as it coughed to a semblance of life and roared off to wherever. No one else had really paid much attention to all that, but Kayla had, clear-eyed as she remained. She just hadn't felt the need to tell Jasmine about it.

The girl had started asking about her brother in her sing-song voice, bouncing out onto the porch and back, peering into rooms and into clots of people, hair in disarray, clothes rumpled from all the dry-humping, and then finally Kayla had tuned out of that particular drama, and it was as if neither brother nor sister had ever crossed her threshold. Good riddance.

Kayla cleaned most of the place before Tommy woke up. As she tackled the last of the dishes, Marlon woke up and couldn't stop smacking his dry-ass lips, so she kicked him out. At the sink, with her fingers wrinkling in the dishwater, she stared at the barrette again and said, "Shit."

4
JORDAN

"Jazz?"

The apartment door banged against the wall, and Jordan Frank cocked his ear, listening.

No answer.

Fucking Tommy. He did it. He did something to her. Jordan had no doubt in his mind.

He slammed the door shut, muttering.

Tommy knew *exactly* where Jasmine was, goddammit. She was in another room in that filthy house, or tied up in a closet, or a different place altogether, or the bed of his idiotic jacked-up black Chevy truck—whatever, he had Jazz somewhere. The asshole knew precisely where she was, and probably so did his skank, Kayla (he remembered her name now).

"*Fuck!*" he gritted.

Jordan checked the rooms of his tiny apartment again, nothing. Poked into the bathroom, empty. Checked behind the shower curtain. Nope. The small counter was cluttered with Jasmine's makeup and shit, the room still reeking of her cheap perfume. On her side of the bed, she'd tossed three dresses, the ones she'd decided against for the party. They were three of only seven that she owned, most of them picked up at Goodwill over the past few months, except for the tight yellow one and the blue spangly one she wore last night. Those she'd paid good money for at Kohl's with her first paycheck from the spa. The bed looked like a sloppy painter's color palette.

Jordan bent to peek underneath it. Nothing but dusty carpet.

He felt a sob forming, hocked it back.

"*Jazz!*" he cried, voice cracking, wrenching open the closet door in the bedroom.

Desperate. Tired and miserable and desperate.

He fell backward to the edge of the bed, breathing hard. Glanced around, searching for *something*. Anything. Then he glared at his phone, battery almost gone. He clambered to his knees, reached over and plugged it in. He remembered what Lori'd said. He dug into Jazz's purse, found *her* phone, and went over and plugged it into her charger on her side of the bed. He waited for the display to power up, urging it, screaming at it. Finally, it came to life—password-protected. He tried a few of Jazz's passwords, none of them worked. He tossed the phone onto her makeshift nightstand, where it clattered. He pounded his knee with his fist.

If only he could go back in time—just hours! When she was here, right next to him, prettying herself up for that asshole. Jordan had told her it was a mistake, *repeatedly*, going to this party, reconnecting with Tommy. Story of his existence, this happening. One of three or four people he'd ever known that he wouldn't mind seeing dead, skull blown open, guts churned out, limbs cracked in awful directions. That thug, back in his life. It wasn't fair, but then what was?

He thought they'd gotten away, him and Jazz.

He'd been the one to architect their escape from the armpit of Garden Grove. Not only family *(fuck them!)* but also the slimy web of low-class trashies that Karl brought to the house, the lowlives who he and Jazz ran into every day on the streets, in the schools, at the markets, in the neighboring homes. Bringing them down, every day. He and Jazz held more in their destiny, he was sure of it. Or, at least, *she* did. She shined, man! Maybe he was just tagging along, waiting for his opportunity to catch some residual glow, but she definitely had bright things ahead of her. So why did she always manage to fall backwards?

It drove him batshit when she batted her lashes at every browneye who blew a kiss at her. All she had to do was twerk that cheerleader butt, practically inviting the creeps to grab hold like her ass cheeks were handlebars.

It worked in the neighborhood, and it worked at home.

And it worked last night.

But *Jesus*—Tommy Strafe?

The worst.

Jordan couldn't recall *anything* he'd ever done to Tommy except exist. The first day Jordan had ever seen Tommy at Alamitos Intermediate, the dough-browed goon with the inset eyes had stared at him over a book during individual reading time, gathering a baseless grudge. Jordan had watched it happen out of the corner of his eye, wondering what the fuck he was doing wrong. Finally, Tommy had wandered over to his table and soundlessly taken Jordan's book right out of his hands—some stupid old book that Mr. Crane had let him borrow. Jordan hadn't said a word, just gave in.

That's who he'd been then, a fucking coward. No backbone. And it had put a target on his face from then on. Tommy would sucker-punch him, he'd spit on his clothes, he'd press gum in his hair, then hate-laugh with his dawgs.

Tommy fucking Strafe.

Christ, the balls on God!

Jordan hadn't seen Tommy in years—had tried not to even think about him—and then Jazz bounces straight into him at a Muscle Mesa outlet, for chrissakes. At least, that's what she'd told Jordan. And all he'd been able to say, repeatedly for days, was *What the fuck?*

He could imagine the way Tommy drank her in, like a slick vitamin smoothie, and she went down easy, no doubt. Next thing Jordan knew, he and Jazz were knocking on the front door of his sad little tenement a mile away on Santa Ana's even-uglier side.

He couldn't help but think the meeting was more than fate, that Jazz had sought it out somehow. That she'd looked Tommy up, asked around, talked to an old friend and found out where the dicksnot worked. Shit, he hoped he could give Jazz more credit than that.

Jordan felt skittery exhaustion yanking at him, pulling him under the surface, straight into Tommy nightmares. He pushed himself off the bed, went to the bathroom and splashed tepid, rusty water in his face. Dried off with Jazz's towel, could smell her on it. He stepped back into the bedroom and changed his shirt for something dry.

He went to the kitchen and found paper and Sharpie, scrawled out a note.

Jazz, where were you? Lost track of you at the party. Out looking for you with Lori. Stay put if you come back!—J

Left it in the center of the counter.

Jordan planted himself against the Formica, willed his heartbeat to stop hammering. Slammed a glass of water. His head felt cleaner, less slimy now. It was clearing out. He focused on the memory of his sister's face, last night. The bright eyes, eager and naïve, not askew like his own murkier ones. The perky, slightly upturned nose—hers turned up while his turned down. The prominent cheekbones were the things they shared, cute and jaunty on her, awkward and gaunt on him. The dirty brown hair that she was always trying to coax the light out of, like she *wanted* to be a dumb blonde. Then her figure, that tight golden gymnast body that he desired only to protect. He didn't want *anyone* to touch that, it was too young and innocent, would *always* be young and innocent. Would always belong to his little sis (younger by seven minutes), too pure and perfect to be touched by anyone.

These thoughts always funneled back to Karl. Karl Granger. The scumbag their mom brought home from the OC fair, from his setup hawking lighters and flasks and glass pipes, years ago now. Jordan still felt the memory like heat, like something stinky and boiling. Karl was the reason why he and Jazz had high-tailed it out of Garden Grove, but Jordan blamed their mom just as much, for allowing that shitstain into their lives. A lot like Tommy, was Karl Granger. Why were there so many monsters in the world?

Jordan hadn't spoken to Gloria Frank since late last summer, when they'd snuck away. He was pretty sure Jasmine hadn't, either. Their mom probably didn't even miss her kids.

"Where are you, Jazz?" he asked the empty kitchen. "Come back."

At that moment, a sharp knock sounded at the door. Jordan jumped, went to it, opened it.

"Ready?" Lori said, standing there with her big purse.

"Lemme get my phone."

"You plugged hers in? Anything on it?"

"Couldn't hack the password."

"Shit."

Lori followed him to the bedroom, where she looked around, irritating him. Judging him.

"No luck at the hospital," she said, flipping idly through Jazz's dresses on the bed. "There's a few hospitals in the area, but you only need to ask at one if anyone has come in with no ID. They're all connected. Did you know that?"

"No."

Lori was glancing around, searching for clues or whatever.

"Is this her room?"

"Uh huh," he said, "that's her phone over there, if you want to bring it. Just grab the cable, I have a USB thing plugs into the cigarette lighter in my car."

She didn't go to the phone, but he saw her eyes flicking toward the bed.

He didn't really want to get into it, that he and Jazz shared a bed. Hey, it was about cash, man, simple as that. In the early months after leaving Garden Grove, when they'd had less than nothing between them, he'd slept on the couch out in the front room, but the fucking thing stank like feet. They'd found it in an alley behind the apartments, and who knew how long it had been sitting out there? And also his back had begun to ache, ever since the trunk. Jazz didn't care how it looked, sleeping in the same bed like they did when they were kids. So, they split the bed, nothing weird. She was working now, and a second bed was on the list, after a TV.

Jordan ushered Lori out of the bedroom after grabbing his own phone.

"Let's go," he said as she paused to read the note he'd scrawled.

Even that felt personal.

"Come on!"

He felt her irritated look, hot on his back as he went for the door.

"Hey," she snapped, "I'm here to help you, OK? Knock it off with the attitude."

"I just want to get going—*fuck*, I don't even know where to start."

"Well, the place to start is *right here*, you know? You need to calm down a little and make sure you're thinking right."

"What the fuck does that mean?"

"It means settle down and focus, dude! Jesus. What's your deal?"

She left the question in the air.

Jordan stopped at the door. Eyes closed.

"My *deal* is Jasmine is gone." Voice coming back to him sharply, echoing off the door. "Missing. Vanished." He turned back to Lori. Exhaustion made the room tilt. "This is the one place where I know she's not."

"I get that, I do, but look—she could be anywhere, OK?"

"I told you—"

"That you were sleeping, yeah. And that you have no idea where she is. I think those were your exact words."

"Lori—" Felt his breath moving too fast, felt his teeth grinding.

Jordan hardly knew this woman, this busybody that seemed to coax gossip out of Jasmine as effortlessly as breathing. Deep down, Jordan harbored a suspicion that Jasmine had told Lori *everything*. Who knew what Jazz had already told her during one of their endless bitch sessions? His sister went upstairs for drinks and gabfests sometimes twice a week, and she'd always come back bossy and crabby and giving him the stink eye, like she and Lori had talked about Jordan most of that time. Complained about him, more like.

Well, maybe he *hoped* she already knew everything. He couldn't imagine filling her in on Tommy and their whole sordid association with that mouthbreather. That conversation would flow into confessions about home, and all those oceans of shit, almost against his will. He always ran his mouth off when he shouldn't. Who knew, maybe that had been a problem last night at the party, too.

"All I'm saying is we need to be thorough, right?" Lori said, already turning to let her eyes rove the small kitchen. "So before we leave, is there anything out of place, anything—I don't know—anything unusual about the way she left something? Like, any indication she came back this morning at some point? You have to look around with something besides panic."

Jordan took a deep breath, balled his fists. Truth was, he needed Lori's help. Left alone to look for his sister, he was sure he wouldn't do anything right, would simply flail out into a shitstorm of nerves and helplessness. He knew that about himself. He wasn't delusional. A sweaty leftover sheen of drugs had swept him back to Tommy's place this morning, on the nervous hunt, but now he was in a state of disbelief that he'd gone back to that house alone. The thought made him shudder.

"Humor me," Lori said, glancing around. "Give the place one more sweep, look for anything. Like, does she keep any kind of calendar?"

"On her phone, maybe."

"Let's bring it then, in case you figure out her password."

Jordan about-faced stiffly and returned to the bedroom. He gathered up her phone—no new texts on the lock screen, just the low-battery indicator—and pocketed it. He took a moment to glance around, in case Lori was watching him. He opened Jazz's dresser drawers, rifled around a bit. There was nothing there. He knew pretty much her whole life, it's not like they kept secrets from each other.

"Nothing here!" he spat, already on his way out.

"All right, let's go."

Jordan stopped at the bedroom door. Jazz's backpack caught his eye, flung into the corner, forgotten. She'd carried the worn-out thing through high school, and it had become sort of a fixture on her, almost a security blanket. He had never looked inside it; it was her private stuff. He had a quick-flash image of tattered-edge notebooks from her sophomore year—that was how far she'd gotten in high school, just like him. It was possible she'd used one of those as a homegrown journal, but he doubted she'd actually touched anything in her notebooks for years.

On impulse, he picked up the backpack by its straps and headed for the kitchen.

"Might be something in here, we can check it out on the road," he said.

Lori nodded, already at the open front door. "When we get in the car, keep working on her password."

"Fine."

5
TOMMY

Tommy Strafe woke like a smear, his brain grinding and dripping. His big mouth hung open, drooling into the pillow. His jaw felt separate from the rest of his head, like by three feet, and his skull felt like a broken Etch-a-Sketch.

"Oh fuck," he murmured.

Oh, right, the party. There'd been a party. His memory sent out feelers, but for the moment, those ended in blunt nubs. He couldn't remember much of anything.

He lay angled across his bed for long minutes, trying to open his gummy eyes. There was some kind of racket coming from the front room, making him annoyed and then paranoid. When he finally heard the sink disposal, he groaned and cursed Kayla. He swung his bulky legs over the edge of the bed and heaved himself up. The world went askew. He sat motionless until his brain corrected itself.

It was all coming back now.

Derek with his spider hands had hooked him up with something new and profound around 11, something special, a mixture of dope and pharmaceuticals that even Derek couldn't precisely source. Derek was always trying new things on his customer base. He liked to brag about it, the way he did business. He was a drug whisperer, a trip scientist, tinkering and toying. For this one, though, he'd given Tommy a laughing warning, and Tommy'd shushed him, and Derek had simply watched Tommy's eyes as he shot up—the flat widening, the drop. Derek's expression intense and curious until his face imploded away on a jittery song. Tommy didn't remember much after that.

Except Jasmine, the girl from way back.

Out of the blue, week and a half ago, she'd come into the store looking for supplements, wanting to kickstart a new regimen—"start a new life," she'd said. He'd checked out her yoga-pantsed ass through the storeroom window as she'd talked animatedly with Mark Pellegro, the cashier with the silly hat hiding the receding hairline, not recognizing her at first, but then something about the way she cocked her head sparked a memory. He barreled out onto the floor to get a closer look and—*wham!*—there she was, Jasmine Frank. She didn't even look any older. If anything, she looked *better* with some years on her bones, features a little sharper, body still kickin' it (if the slightest bit heavier, in a welcome way), eyes a little more piercing, like there was more behind them. Man, those eyes had always got to him somewhere deep, those blue orbs flecked with stardust. Even when she was young. Too young.

She'd caught him looking, and he'd caught the barely-there sneer when she placed him.

"Holy shit," she'd said, turning away from Pelly to face him.

"Look at you," was all he could come up with. "You're all grown up."

"Never thought I'd see *you* again." That same voice but pitched lower. She was holding a canister of the shop's green tea energy powder that he himself had cut with baking soda and corn starch and newspaper ash.

"Good luck happens all the damn time."

"Guess it depends on your point of view, huh?" She cocked a hip.

Time to change the subject.

"What are you doin' here? You need something?" He shooed Pelly away. "Maybe I can hook you up." Voice softer, conspiratorial.

Jasmine had stood there eyeing him warily. But he softened her up like he always could. He had a gift. Turned out she was living with her brother around the corner, southwest off Flower, she didn't specify exactly where, seemed like she didn't want to. Cautious.

But yeah, her brother. Jordan Frank. The asshole with the eyes slightly askew, always looked like he was scoffing. And that lanky way of walking, all skin and bones, little twerp. Tommy'd gone to Alamitos with both of them, but it was Jordan that he'd noticed first, the prick. Dude was just one of those chickenshits that had it coming. He'd given Jordan merry hell for a year before crashing out of Alamitos. Toward the end there, though, Tommy remembered Jordan hanging more with his twin sis, who just felt younger, purer, ran in different circles. He'd see her biking through the streets, the fine features, the posture, the face and body that would become something someday—the potential. Perky middle-school pumpkin, all vital and shit. Something about her.

And the way she looked at him. Even then. Like, seeing something in him.

The fact that Jasmine was that runt Jordan's twin sister pissed Tommy off. One day out on the Alamitos commons, he passed Jordan among the lunch tables and sent a fist into his gut, a vicious piston, and sauntered on by laughing with Eric and Stoolie, didn't even look back as he heard Jordan stumble *ooooph*ing to the ground unable to breathe. Kid no doubt blubbered about it later to his mom or someone, could never just man up and take it.

"Jordan, right?" he said to Jasmine. "Your brother?"

"Oh, he'll *love* that I ran into you."

"Aw, that dude's all right. We're grown now." He stepped over to the counter, lorded over it, made himself even taller. "The past is past."

"So you work here?" Yeah, she was warming up to him again.

"In the back mostly."

"And you—" She got all coy. "—you can really hook me up?"

"Maybe."

It had gone on from there. She said she'd finally been inching out of the red, thanks to a spa gig in Orange, near the Block, and felt like it was high time to knock off the ramen and bologna sandwiches and get back to her cheerleader shape. She'd started some body weight routines at home (couldn't afford the gym)—pushups, sit-ups, lunges, those kinds of things—and she wanted to get back into the powders, the shakes, the fasts. The more they talked, the more she loosened up. He could bullshit alongside the best of the shop's sales staff, even Pelly, and so he was able to sell her on some diluted crap, gave her his "employee discount." Way he figured, it was all placebo powder anyway.

He made the discount look like a big deal, glancing around like he was taking some big risk, doing her this favor. Made it a secret between the two of them, winked at her.

"Any time you need more ..." he said.

"Really?"

"Hey, you busy next Friday night? Having a little party at the house."

"Homeowner, huh?"

"Yeah, it's not much, but it's home." Kayla's home, anyway. "So, you'll come?"

She'd waffled on him, biting her lower lip.

"Shit, girl, bring your brother. I don't care. It'll be fun. We'll kiss and make up."

She didn't give him a hard answer. But he managed to score her number, promising texts about deep deals on product, keeping it light, and he watched her go. She glanced back, watching him appreciate her ass. Then she finally smiled—still a dazzler.

You just had to give them more attention than they got anywhere else. It wasn't a tough equation. And he could tell she wasn't getting it anywhere else, at least at that point in her life. He knew he'd fuck her, probably during the party. Foregone conclusion. Jasmine liked boys like him. Shit, he saw it when she was thirteen years old, with the promising shape and the braces, the lingering glances. She'd have ended up in his lap way back then, at least eventually, if her family hadn't moved her to a different part of town.

Damn, that was so long ago. A whole lifetime between then and now.

Tommy finally managed to get out of bed and find the bathroom. He planted himself at the sink and stared at his reflection in the mirror—dark eyes beneath his broad brow, nostrils enflamed, teeth going yellow. He still looked sort of like a linebacker who smoked too much, and whose face had been smacked too much. His dad had told him that the last time he saw him, before he'd gotten into his old Ford and got himself killed on the highway. *People gonna blame me for that face,* he'd said. Fine last words.

Tommy gave himself a parting gaze, chuckling. A shining specimen in the morning, for sure. But he still had the raw material. He just used to have everything put together better. Maybe he should join Jasmine for her workouts. He could show her how to rotate those hips, yeah.

He went to the toilet and let loose with a firehose piss, then scratched his belly and lurched back to the bedroom, where he found some clothes in the dresser that Kayla kept tidy. He unplugged his phone, checked it for messages while he lit an unfiltered Camel from the nearly empty pack lying there. Nothing on his phone, everyone still asleep. The time was 10:17 a.m. He shoved the drawer shut with his dick.

Tommy went out into the front room and found Kayla, sure enough, scrubbing the damn sink.

"What the fuck, girl? You have to do that shit now?"

"Haven't cleaned house in too long." Voice clipped like she was irritated. "People are pigs, Tommy."

"It's Saturday," Tommy announced as he approached the barred front window. "We should be doin' something."

"Yeah, no shit."

He glanced over at her, squinting. "Sounds like you should've got low last night. You'd be easier on the ears right now."

"I don't want to hear it, *babe*."

"What in the hell is wrong with *you*?"

"You had your paws all over that girl last night, that's what's wrong. What did you think? I'd just laugh it off?"

"What girl?"

"You trying to get me to throw this pan at you? Because I will. I will throw this pan at you."

Tommy took a last lingering look at the patchy sky, scratched his belly again, and sucked in two large lungfuls of smoke. The nicotine clarified things for him, cleared away the effects of last night's ingestions. He balanced the half-smoked cigarette on the purple glass ashtray sitting on the windowsill. Then he walked to the kitchen. Kayla watched him come, twelve-inch skillet in hand as she dried it. He could see the muscles in her jaws clenching. She started shaking her head a little as he got close. He calmly took the pan and towel from her grip and set them precisely on the counter. Finally, she looked down at her feet, and her shoulders sagged.

"I'm sorry, I shouldn't have yelled," she said.

Tommy let his face go slack. Gave her the look. She trembled beneath him, turned her head away. He brought his big gnarled-knuckled hand to her chin, brought her attention back.

"You remember last time?"

He stroked her cheek, and she nodded, and a tear leaked down her cheek, a sudden drop.

"I don't want it to go like that," he said, "and you don't either."

"Tommy—"

"I want you to shut your fucking mouth and go to the bedroom now. Position yourself like I told you, and keep your mouth shut. Do you understand?"

She seemed about to say something. He tensed his upper body and arms so the muscles twitched, and she receded into herself. She wiped her damp trembling hands on her jeans and gave the kitchen a sad, appraising look. Then she backed away like she was melting, and moved soundlessly out of the kitchen and into the hall toward the bedroom.

He watched her go.

So, she was upset about Jasmine. Of course she was. Couldn't blame her, really.

He opened the fridge and found a beer in the produce drawer, where he kept his bottles. Popped the top, drank a long swallow. He spied a pizza box angled out of a trash can and took it out. There was one slice of pepperoni left, and he munched on the stale thing thoughtfully.

Tommy'd actually been surprised to see Jasmine and her brother walking through the door last night—the girl looking delicious in her blue dress, showing off bounteous gam, and the boy looking cagey and meek. He might as well have been still walking the halls of Alamitos.

Tommy had pointed the two of them out straight away to Derek, telling him to be creative with the two new arrivals. Describing to him the result he wanted. Even on the spur of the moment, Derek was a spindly magician, wielding his substances like a mad scientist in one of those old black-and-white movies that Tommy's dad used to show him on weekends, feet up in the front room of the trailer, which actually swayed as the big man laughed. Tommy'd watch Derek at work sometimes, studious in the back of the store, and the weird dude was captivating in his expertise.

He'd set the brother, Jordan, spiraling with some of his gray dirt, and the sister had become crazy submissive, giggly, and blissed-out on pills of some sort. Perfect. Tommy'd used Alicia and Freddie to set Kayla on a subtle distraction course over by the kitchen, and then he'd managed to corner Jasmine a couple times. Got his hands under her dress as she mind-peaked. She'd batted him away, playfully zoned. When he'd nudged her toward the bedroom, she insisted in a whisper that Jordan go with them, and Tommy allowed it, faux-cheerful. Jordan was barely standing at that point, looked like he was about to collapse onto the bed. Tommy wouldn't have minded. But the asshole stayed conscious, the small part of his brain that was alert watching Tommy and his probing hands. Protective to the last.

Tommy'd ended up showing them his collections in the bedroom, all innocent. Nostalgic almost. The coins and the books and the sports cards in the corner case. He was proud as hell of all that shit, never passed up an opportunity to show it off.

Soooooo, he hadn't nailed Jasmine last night, but he'd come close. He'd finally managed to separate the siblings and had started up new moves on the blitzed girl, but then he'd noticed Kayla watching him aghast from the doorway. Then it all fell apart, and Jasmine danced away, disappeared into the hallway. He didn't know what happened to Jordan after that, didn't care.

He finished the beer and dropped the empty into the trash. He walked back to the bedroom and opened the door. Kayla was in position.

"Let's get this over with," he said.

For the first time, he noticed the broken pane of glass in the corner cabinet, and the glimmering shards on the worn carpet.

Tommy Strafe let out a strangled, furious cry.

6
JASMINE

Jasmine Frank massaged her temples beneath the red awning of the In-N-Out Burger just off the 405 on Westminster Boulevard, of all places. A loud clank had awakened her in the humid shadows. It had taken her a full half hour to come to almost-full consciousness and stand on wobbly legs. She was jelly-eyed and confused, listening to vehicles zip by on the interstate a block away.

She was nine or ten miles from home, she guessed, due west, and she had no earthly idea how she'd gotten here. Well, strike that: She had a fog-swirly aural memory of someone yelling at her as she stumble-fell out of a small car onto the pavement of the parking lot. And as the car sped away, gathering herself and hurrying over to the building. Into a secluded corner. In front of a dark business that she hadn't realized, early this morning, was an In-N-Out Burger.

A gaggle of employees were now inside the joint, performing their prep work for the day—stocking, loading up condiments, greasing the grill. They kept giving her odd looks.

Jasmine didn't have her phone or her purse or her wallet or her ID—Jesus, what had *happened* last night?—and she had no clue what time it was. She was too embarrassed to knock on the window and ask someone. What time did In-N-Out start getting ready for the early-lunch crowd?

She didn't think there'd been any rain last night, but everything was moist. She went over to a gross bench that was permanently affixed to a stone wall, alone in the gray morning. The bench was slippery with dew and grimy with who-knew-what. She found an unsticky area, wiped some moisture away, and placed her ass on it.

Sighed.

In one hand, she held a wrinkled, plastic Safeway grocery bag full of something solid and heavy, like a brick. It sagged to the cement. All she knew was that it didn't contain her belongings. Those were nowhere to be found. Her murky mind envisioned her purse on the floorboards of an Uber, or some stranger's pickup, and she felt a distant panic. She shook her head like a dog, trying to clear it, trying to make things make sense.

She wiped her eyes, pressing her fingers in deep as if to massage her brain. Everything felt like mucus, or as if her fingers were pressing into clay.

God, she was starving. The hunger hit her like a gut punch.

She glanced back at the In-N-Out service window to find two employees staring out at her. They turned away and got back to their work. She wondered what her face looked like, her makeup, her lipstick, her eyes. Probably a horror show.

What was the last thing she remembered? Trying to pursue that thought gave way to paralysis; her brain ground to a halt, the synapses refusing to fire. She tried to push past the blankness. It took a moment, but she finally found her way to fractured images of Jordy whining at her in their bedroom.

Of course, Jordy yelling. He could be so *controlling*. He never wanted her to have any fun. She couldn't exactly *blame* him, after everything that had happened in Garden Grove, but there was such a thing as overdoing it. Especially considering that she was an adult now—like, a real adult with a job and responsibilities and shit.

(Well, almost. Her very effective fake ID, which Jordan had managed to secure for them through his friend he'd made at Home Depot, said she was 20, but she was actually 17. That fake ID had a far better picture of herself than her real one, and she loved that. It made her feel more like an adult than the false date of birth printed on the card.)

Hell, man, Jordan didn't even have a real job. *She* was supporting *him*. So get the fuck outta here with that shit.

He'd been yelling at her about *everything* last night—what she wore, where they were going, her perfume, bumping into Tommy in the first place.

Tommy! Oh Christ, she'd dragged Jordy to that party last night.

Had Tommy done something to her? Had he dumped her here? Why?

There was a scrape behind her, and she jumped. It was the service window sliding open.

"Ma'am?" came a young man's voice.

She twisted around. A teenager was poking his head out the window, his nose scrunched beneath his black glasses and paper hat.

"Yeah?" she managed. Her voice was hoarse.

"We won't be open for another forty minutes or so. Would you like some water or ...?"

"I would kill for some water." She approached the window, brought her voice down just for him. "And look, I'm not homeless or anything, I just lost my purse. If you can spare anything like an old bun or whatever, I'd kiss you."

He smiled at her. "I'll see what I can do."

A cute girl with braces, standing behind Jasmine's new buddy, gave her the once-over, then turned back to stocking cups and lids. Before the kid could slide the window shut, Jasmine leaned toward him.

"Hey, what time is it?"

The boy slid out a plastic cup full of ice water. "Coming up on ten."

"Thanks."

As he ducked back away, she tried to get a better look at herself in the smudged glass. Her mascara had run a little bit, but nothing alarming. She wiped at it, tried to smooth it out. Her lipstick looked faded but stable. She used her fingers to manage her hair, fluffing it, contouring it. Then she grabbed the plastic cup gratefully and took long, thirsty swallows, nearly draining it. The water invigorated her, clarified her.

She leaned back against the high, filthy counter and looked out on the traffic of Westminster Boulevard.

How was she going to get home, with no money, no phone, no nothing? How had she even gotten here? Did buses run that late? Even if they did, mass transit required a fare, and by the way, how could she have covered that without her purse? Unless she'd left all her shit on the bus. Goddamn it!

She needed to cancel cards, she needed to call her bank. She guessed it was finally a good thing she was dirt-poor. The largest piece of currency she had in her wallet was probably a five-dollar bill—a below-the-table tip from one of her customers. Jake something. He'd gone back for a massage from Wendy, but he'd given Jasmine the tip afterward. The only tip she'd ever gotten—so far. He'd said he wished she was the one massaged him, and gave her a wink. If Jordan had known about Jake's blunt come-on, he'd have thrown a hissy fit, but there was no denying it: A compliment like that made a girl feel good.

She'd wanted to keep that tip for a while. Now it was gone, along with everything else.

She experienced a flutter of deeper panic then, fearing today was a workday and she was an hour late for work, but no, it was Saturday, she was sure of it.

Yeah, Saturday.

That probably precluded the notion of the bus, too.

Relief came with dizziness. She went back to the grimy bench, swinging the brick in the bag.

Her thoughts returned to Tommy. Tommy Strafe, from back in the neighborhood, back in Garden Grove. Well, hell, now she'd never hear the end of it from Jordan, who'd already gone into full-on rage and disbelief when she'd told him she bumped into Tommy at the vitamin store, and that he'd invited her and Jordy to his place for a party. What were the odds, Jordy had wondered, that that hemorrhoidal asshole had ended up blocks away from the apartment where he and Jasmine had ended up in Santa Ana? It wasn't fair, it wasn't right. *God has played a cruel joke on us!* he'd gone on. Jordy'd practically been in tears, hanging his head while planted on the edge of their stinky couch, and Jasmine had stood there watching him, not knowing what to say.

Yeah, Tommy was an old-school bully—there was no other word for the big lump. And it's not like Jasmine would ever admit this to Jordy, but she'd had a hot thang for Tommy Strafe since hormones had first begun coursing through her glands. And that shit was against all odds. Tommy was twice as big as she was, he was a total lunkhead, and let's face it—he was kind of repugnant. That had become more and more apparent as she grew older.

She remembered one time, probably a year after Tommy crashed out of Alamitos, when he and a few of his cretin friends parked themselves on the lunch benches at the edge of the playground. They were just outside the fence, taunting the middle-schoolers as they endured Phys Ed. Jasmine had been among their ranks, dribbling a basketball half-heartedly in her white school uniform, and she'd felt Tommy's eyes on her the whole time. A couple of her friends had sneered with disgust and given Tommy the evil eye while they played, finding him revolting with his smelly black clothes and his unwashed hair and his scraggly gross half-beard. But to Jasmine, it came down to those eyes—that cliff-like brow and those piercing eyes checking her out. Well, that and his size.

Jasmine—at just over five feet, and rail-thin for as long as she could remember—had always thought of herself as a bit of a runt, mostly because that's the exact word that not one but *two* of her mom's boyfriends had called her twin brother. *You fuckin' runt!* And the way she saw it, words used to describe Jordy could just as easily describe her.

So the thought of this giant of a boy squashing his thick self against her? It had sent her into convulsions of secret slick delight. And if she were being honest with herself, she'd have to admit that it still did. The fact that all her friends looked on him with distaste? That only fed into it. Yeah, he projected that creepy-older-boy vibe. But she saw through it. She knew there was something interesting there. It spoke to her.

She wasn't stupid, though. The dude had a flicker of danger in him.

Maybe that was part of the appeal.

"Ma'am?"

Jasmine brought her head up, frowning. This dude was calling her *ma'am*?

The kid at the window gestured her over. Jasmine stood, still lightheaded, and tried to walk a straight line to the shadowed window. The kid had prepared her a hamburger.

"This one's on me," he said.

"Oh my god," she said, suddenly besotted with this paper-crowned nerd. "I love you."

He couldn't hide a blush. "Don't tell, OK?"

"I won't. Thank you *so much*. I promise to pay you back later!"

"Don't worry about it." He nodded at her. "Just be sure to come back."

She smiled flirtily at the suggestion, then took the burger to her stone bench and wolfed it down as if she hadn't eaten in days. Which wasn't far from the truth. She'd starved herself for the past half-week, subsisting on tea and lemons to fit into this stupid junior dress she found at Kohl's. She'd quickly dropped five pounds and managed to squeeze into it, like that video of sausage-making she'd seen on YouTube. Then yesterday she'd fasted in anticipation of the party.

When she'd stirred this morning, the dress had actually felt loose on her bones. So, she felt fine shoving this greasy burger down her gullet.

She washed it down with the rest of her water, glanced over at the window to find her new boyfriend in the window. She gave him a thumbs-up, and he looked all goofy, and she knew the kid had one of those instant crushes on her.

She was used to that kind of thing.

Just like she knew that when she showed up at Tommy's party last night, she'd rile him up so much that all the years would melt away and maybe they'd finally consummate whatever had been between them for five years, or however long it had been since she'd first glimpsed him.

She knew she drove Jordy bugnut crazy with that kind of thinking. He could sense it. Sometimes he overheard her talking about those kinds of things with Lori. Like she did with some of the spa clients over the counter. She couldn't help it. Some of them were downright yummy. Yeah, she was close to Jordan and always would be. Twins were that way. It was psychic, and it was physical sometimes. She'd read about it; it was natural. But she felt like she was growing away from all that. She couldn't imagine having that conversation with Jordy and telling him straight-out that she wanted to be on her own, experience other things. Jesus, he'd go mental.

She gathered her trash and went over to dump it in the can at the edge of the small patio area. When she returned to the stone table, she felt much refreshed. Invigorated. Funny what actual food could do to your worldly outlook.

How was she supposed to get home? She thought about asking to borrow a phone to call Jordy, but she realized she didn't actually know his number. She thought maybe it started with 5-something, and the end was 2304 or 2314, but the middle part was hopelessly lost to her. Hell, she didn't know any phone numbers. They were all programmed into her phone.

Sighing, she looked down at the grocery bag that she'd placed next to her. It was an old Safeway bag, heavily wrinkled, and it was wrapped tightly around what seemed to be a brick. A single piece of yellowed Scotch tape held the package together. She had absolutely no memory of it.

What's your story?

She unfastened the tape and unwound the plastic. A heavy plastic container fell into her palm. There was a small mechanism on the side that kept the box closed. She clicked it open, and the lid came open. Inside the rectangular box were rows upon rows of paper envelopes, each of which had words written on them in a tiny, cramped hand.

"What the—?" she started, and then the memory came flooding into her.

7
KAYLA

Tommy never hit Kayla in the face, of course. He usually focused on the ribs and the belly. The areas no one ever saw. That was his thing. The abdomen was his favorite—the shock gut punch that took her breath away. He liked the effect of that kind of jab. She knew that all too well. Taking away her voice, delivering a crashing quiet into the room, watching her wilt, ending the argument, exerting his dominance. He mostly did it when they were alone, but he wasn't above doing it in front of people. She'd never once seen it coming, that powertrain arm.

And that was true this morning.

When he entered the bedroom, he let out a cry of rage, and just as she twisted atop the bed—braced in position for something else entirely—he punched her from the left, landing a blow to her lower ribs. She curled naked into a fetal position on the sheets. The impact left her breath shallow, and with it she emitted a sharp mewl.

"What did you do?" he growled. "What did you do?"

Kayla barely heard him, but when his words made it through, her thoughts twisted in confusion. What had she done? Her short breaths came in and out on little grunts. Her left side felt like a stab wound, and she could hardly form a coherent thought.

"Where are they?" Tommy bellowed.

Coiled on the bed and squinting through abrupt tears, she watched him rifle through the cabinet in the corner. He seemed larger than usual, like an aggressive ape or something, the muscles in his back bulging, his neck massive with cords.

Oh Jesus, she thought.

She rarely saw or heard him so upset—and over what? She tried yanking her breath back, in short gasps, and finally was able to say something.

"What are you looking for?" she squeezed out.

He ignored her.

Kayla scooted back to the headboard, cradling her side. Watching Tommy. A crazed man searching frantically for ... something. At first—gritting her teeth in sharp agony—she had no earthly idea what that something could be. But as she watched, it dawned on her that it had to be one of his collections.

She tried to assess the state of the corner cabinet as he moved left and right. It was this ornate triangular fixture that he'd had forever. She remembered him moving it in. Derek had helped him. It was like they'd been carrying in the Ark of the Covenant or something. Story was, he'd actually paid for the thing. The items it would hold were that important to him. He'd had it custom-made at a high-end furniture joint specifically to hold his collections, something that he could use to display the stuff and also keep it all secure. It had thick drawers and two locked glass doors.

"*Goddamn it!*" Tommy thundered.

"*What?*" she cried, getting her shit together.

He half-turned to her, glaring. "I swear to god, Kayla, if you—"

When he shifted his massive thigh, Kayla saw the broken pane of glass. Behind that pane was a key-lock drawer where Tommy kept his father's coins. At the thought of the coins stolen, her stomach twisted hollowly.

"Tommy, I'm right here," she said, reaching for a sheet to cover herself. "I've been here all morning. I live here. I didn't take anything. What do you think I'd do? Break into our own bedroom and take something?"

"Then who did this?"

"What's missing?"

"The coins, Kayla, the *fucking coins.*"

Kayla winced, grasping her ribs on the left side with long-nailed fingers.

That coin collection was really the only thing Tommy had kept from his dad. Tommy'd told her the story on their first real date—a week after Derek's insane kegger. Dinner at Paulino's in Orange, care of one of the servers who owed Tommy a favor. Kayla thought about that night a lot. Tommy'd been at his best then—early days, just a little cranked (or trying harder to hide it back then), expounding on all things Tommy. He'd flashed a gentle side then, too, actually showing interest in her stories. Hard to believe now. She remembered opening up to the big brute about her brother's crippling autism, her best friend's suicide in high school (which had very nearly prompted her own), her mom's early and torturous death to throat cancer. It was that last conversation, actually, that had led to Tommy's long story about his dad, told over four slow Heinekens.

Tommy's mom had been out of the picture early—one of the things she and him sorta had in common. *His* mom had succumbed to breast cancer. As a result, he'd been pretty close to his dad. Kayla had gotten the impression, since then, that his dad didn't completely deserve that closeness. In fact, she got the distinct vibe that the elder Strafe was something of a prick—a would-be absentee dad who only stuck around because no one else was there. But Tommy's memories of his father were overall not bad. Hanging together, working on jobs as a father-son duo, two big men getting work where they could, and all of that only occasionally marred by the belt or the long, drunken absence.

Gordon Strafe had worked construction—drywalling, in particular— but he'd also had, somehow, a small stake in a rare/vintage coin shop in Fullerton. The way Tommy told it, he and his dad would belly-laugh over beers about the owners' naïvete, the way Gordon had maneuvered himself into a position of trust at the shop and often took in new coins for himself on the cheap without the store ever recording the transactions.

There wasn't a business out there, Gordon once told his son, that had less educated customers, except maybe the stock market. Coin shop customers would blithely haul in their family treasures and hand them over for pennies on the dollar—literally! Gordon would fill out a fake receipt from a book he got at a dollar store, and send these idiots on their way with his own fronted cash. He would then trade most of the coins at another store a few counties away in Riverside or Pasadena or even San Diego for full value, sometimes achieving what he believed to be fiftyfold profit. But he kept the cream of the crop as an investment. Kayla remembered the way Tommy had wistfully sounded off on the rarest coins in his inherited collection, boasting of values in the tens of thousands—if he could one day find the right customer. She didn't remember any of the specifics, but she'd loved the way he'd talk about those little rare pieces of bronze, copper, silver, and gold. It was as if Tommy was laying out his dreams for her, and inviting her in.

So anyway, yeah, that coin collection was Tommy's sole inheritance, apparently, following Gordon Strafe's violent death four years earlier. Tommy was still raw about that, all this time later. Couldn't talk about it.

Staring at the broken curio, Tommy let loose with another cry of rage. *"Fuck! Look at it!"*

"It must have been last night," Kayla said, cowering.

"Oh, you think so?" His fists were clenched, white-knuckled. *"Shit!"*

She gathered the sheet more firmly around herself and stepped off the other side of the bed. She clutched the sheet in her own fist, felt her heart pounding.

"Who do you think—?"

"I kept that door locked last night."

"Tommy," she said cautiously, "I saw you bringing people back here."

He stared hard at her. "You think I wasn't careful?"

"Who'd you show it to? I mean, think of everyone who had an opportunity."

He didn't answer at first, just stood there with the stupid look he got on his face when he was confused. Kayla would never, ever say it to Tommy's face, but damned if he couldn't look like a big retard sometimes. And this time it was all tinged with black rage.

"You brought that girl back here, right?" Her voice was shaking only a little bit. "That girl and her brother?"

Something dark dawned across Tommy's face. "Fuckin' Jordan, man. *Are you kidding me?*"

"Would he—?" She let the question hang, steering herself away from blame.

"You think it was that little fuckin' weezer?"

"He was here at the house this morning, you know."

Tommy was still confused. *"What? Who was here?"*

"That Jordan kid." Kayla swallowed the last word. "Seemed upset. He said he was looking for his sister."

"When?"

"I don't know, an hour ago?"

"You're shitting me." He glanced around, his face flushed, bulging. "Did he come in this room?"

"No way, there's just no way. You were asleep. I closed the door. I wouldn't let anyone back here."

There was a beat of ferocious silence.

"Why would that piece of shit come back to this house if he stole it last night?" he said.

"I don't know—trying to return it?"

"Why would he steal it and then come back to return it?"

"Guilty conscience, who knows?" She weighed her words. "He was fuckin' tweaked last night, you know that, maybe he woke up sober and realized what he did. That dude is scared to death of you, right? The question is why would he take the coins in the first place. The answer is ... he was out of his skull." She almost added *thanks to you and Derek,* but no frickin' way was she going to directly implicate Tommy.

"Shit yeah." Tommy rubbed his chin savagely, fingers gnarled. "Was he carrying anything? Did you see him carrying anything?"

"Not that I saw. He found his sister's purse, though."

Confusion bloomed across Tommy's features.

"What the fuck? That doesn't make sense. He came into this house? This morning?"

"Yeah."

"And he found Jasmine's purse here?"

"Uh huh."

"So they stole my shit, but they accidentally left her purse, and he came back for it and found it, and you let him leave with it?"

She stared at him.

"Oh my fucking Christ." Shaking his head menacingly.

"It ... it wasn't like that, Tommy. He was really looking for her, you know? I'm sure of it."

"Shit, Kayla, you're gullible."

She tried to picture Jordan again—like, in a new light. Had he really been pulling one over on her?

"I mean, maybe ..." she said, "... maybe it was both of them, maybe they were working it together."

Tommy exploded with profanity, and she felt it all raining down on her head. She backed away.

"Fucking hell, I brought them in here!" He gestured at the broken glass. "I showed them the whole goddamn collection, just one after the other! *'Here, look at this one, don't forget to take this one when you rip me off! Oh, and this one too!'* Jesus fucking Christ!"

"You didn't know." Meekly.

"My dad was right, I am a fucking *idiot.*"

"It's not your fault, Tommy." Pleading with him. "It's their fault, *their fault*, don't blame yourself. Blame those assholes! He's a loser, baby, and so is she. Come on."

"I need to get Rennie on this. Charlton, too. They'll know what to do. Fuckin' Jordan, man. But *Jasmine*? I can't believe ..." He jerked his head back and forth, almost like a tic. "I showed them the coins, I remember that, but when did they come back in here? How? *Fuck!*"

Kayla knew how. Oh, yeah, she knew how. The bitch must've distracted him, must've pulled one over on him. Kayla had no doubt. She couldn't say that to Tommy, though. Accuse him of being swayed by pussy. It was bad enough, Tommy standing in the middle of their bedroom holding his dick like a fool, but tell him those two had got him to willingly turn his back while they jacked his inheritance right out of his fucking bedroom? He'd fucking murder her.

She felt her lips moving, trembling, wanting to say something, wanting to implicate the blue-jangly slut who stole the coins but forgot her fucking purse. Kayla felt her throat fattening with dreadful emotion, felt something coming, felt pain on the immediate horizon.

Tommy got a determined look on his face and went straight for his phone, still plugged in at the bedside under the lava lamp. He whipped the charging cable away and began swiping. He stabbed at something, put the phone to his ear, went back to staring at the broken cabinet. Then he took the phone away from his ear again.

"It's not ringing." He let loose with an angry grunt. "Fucking phone."

He tried again.

Kayla could only watch Tommy from the bedside. He was breathing heavily, and his entire body was tightened like a torqued wrench. She felt a tear spill onto her cheek. She wrapped the sheet around her body, tighter, tighter, doubling it up as if it might serve as armor.

Please work, she prayed to the phone, or whoever was listening. *Please, and then someone please answer.* She knew what would come after he ended this call; she never wanted this call to end.

But the call never started.

Tommy made to throw the phone against the wall—and held back at the last microsecond. He turned his attention to Kayla and screamed a full-throated howl as he leapt in her direction.

8
LORI

Lori Holst scooted into the passenger seat of Jordan's rusty, dinged-up yellow 'Vette and watched Jordan fall into his bucket seat, driver's side. He tucked Jasmine's pack behind Lori's seat, then cranked the ignition with a shaking hand. His whole body was tense and edgy.

"Dude, take it easy, you're gonna flood it."

"I'm not gonna flood it, Jesus."

"Yeah, you are."

"I know my engine, OK?" Loud in the closeness of the car's interior.

"Apparently not."

"I see, you're an expert on performance cars?"

"Performance car!"

"Oh, shut up, you fuckin'—!"

"We're not gonna get anywhere if we're yelling the whole time!"

"Then stop yelling at me!"

Lori went quiet. She held her purse in her lap and tried not to laugh at the whole situation. Despite her initial unease with the fact that Jasmine was without her phone and other essentials, she still suspected everything was going to be fine, and she was out here on a Saturday with this paranoid doofus when she should be getting ready for her time with Sarah. There was a precedent to this, after all—of Jasmine managing to sneak away from her overprotective brother and enjoy a little time to herself.

Lori was thinking of that one night maybe two months ago when Jasmine had arrived at her door, a sheen on her cheeks. The girl had grabbed at her, imploring her to take her out, go to a bar, somewhere, anywhere! Suddenly Jasmine had been *this* close to tears, and Lori had seen desperation in her new friend's eyes. Lori'd had to beg off, though; she was on her way out to see Steve at the restaurant and hopefully get some after that. Jasmine had grudgingly understood, whispering away down the hall in her hasty, too-tight outfit. A few moments later, as Lori grabbed her car keys, she'd watched from her kitchen window as Jasmine had jog-walked south along the broken sidewalk toward the corner shopping center, where a low-key bar called The Spot was nestled. Obviously, Jasmine had returned home just fine from *that* secret outing, and later she'd laughed about Jordan's bug-eyed shouting as she brushed her teeth.

Just as she'd return fine from *this* one.

So, Lori refused to panic. Well, at least, she wasn't going to succumb to *full-bore* panic, like Jordan here. That wasn't going to accomplish anything. She knew from experience that it was important to stay clear-headed in high-stress scenarios. Too often, Lori fell off the cliff in those situations.

Jordan cranked the ignition again, and this time she noticed he wasn't even touching the gas. The engine groaned and finally fluttered to life.

Jordan gave her a look that said, *See?*

Now Lori did smile. "All right, let's move."

"Where?"

"Do you want to try the spa? Just for kicks?"

"They're not open today."

"You want to go back to party central?"

"Hell no!"

"All right, how about Disneyland?"

"Why would she—?"

"Dude, I'm yanking you, come on."

Jordan gave her a look as the 'Vette idled. "Are you gonna be any help at all?"

"Jordan, if you're this worried, why not just go to the police? That should be our first stop."

He was shaking his head immediately. "We can't go to the fucking police, all right?"

"Why not?"

He looked at her evenly for a long moment, seeming about to say something.

"We just can't. You're gonna have to take my word on that."

His eyes were rimmed with an alarming red, and his face was ashen, almost sunken. Man, he had come down from something hard. Like, *just* come down. Or was still coming down. The dude smelled sour, he was jittery as hell, and his whole face looked hollowed out—yeah, probably not the best idea to walk into the local precinct.

"Should I be driving?"

"I'm fine."

"You don't look fine."

"Thanks."

"I'm serious, man, let me drive. You're in no condition."

"No!" Punctuating the word by banging the steering wheel.

"OK, you're making me nervous. The only way I'm helping you is if I drive."

"Look, no one drives my—"

"Oh, come off it, it's a fucking car. Put it in neutral. We're switching."

"Jesus *Christ*, you're … you're driving me *crazy*. Fine! Whatever!"

Jordan shifted into neutral and made a big deal out of opening the door and climbing out, exaggerating every stomp. Lori took in an even breath, stowing her purse behind the driver's seat. She gracefully removed herself from the passenger seat and walked around the front while he glared at her. He took her place, and she smiled at him as she glided into the driver's seat. She settled in, shifted into reverse, and fiddled with the mirrors. He was staring straight ahead at the apartment building's stucco wall, where an abandoned spider's web lay dirty and twisted.

"That's better," Lori said. "Have you thought about where to start?"

"I have some ideas." He didn't look as if he had any ideas whatsoever.

"I think we should start close and then go wider."

"OK."

"So let's start at The Spot."

Jordan ruminated on that for a second, then nodded his shaggy head. "I guess so." The words came out reluctantly, as if he didn't want to acknowledge the reality that Jasmine liked to drink. "But they're not gonna be open either."

"There could be people there. I think they serve lunch. Let's just check it out."

He nodded as she pulled out. He opened the glove box and removed what looked like a small car battery, heavily scuffed and emblazoned with slashing scrawls of white paint, like zebra stripes.

"What the hell is that?" she said, getting the hang of the soft clutch and heading out onto the road.

"Charger."

"Jeez, man, looks like a home-made bomb."

She could see the USB ports now, along with other less discernible ones. She half-watched him plug in Jasmine's phone and his own. When his phone's cracked screen came to unenthusiastic life, he checked his notifications. Even she could see that there was no recent activity.

"Nothing," he confirmed, making a ragged sound in his throat. He began scanning the street.

They passed a hunched old woman walking an extremely small dog along a crumbling sidewalk. A congregation of Hispanic teens surrounding a car, every one of them silently watching them motor past. A house painted neon yellow, next to a dilapidated, condemned tenement with notices plastered all over its front door. The small, cramped lot it sat on was a muddy brown square.

It was a typically quiet Saturday morning in Santa Ana, and the sun was straining through scuds of cloud, giving the air a gray, humid haze. It felt like a day when something would probably go wrong.

Lori came up on the shopping center quickly and turned in. The Spot looked deserted—lights out, locked down. She cruised through the parking lot and turned into the back alley. She found the rear door to the bar; someone had scrawled SPOT across the metal with black paint. Closed. She put the car in neutral and ratcheted up the emergency brake. She took a sec to fish around in her purse behind the seat and finally drew out her half-empty pack of Marlboros. She put one to her lip and offered Jordan one. He shook his head irritably and looked away. She lit up and inhaled deeply. She stowed the pack and hopped out of the car.

She went to the grungy door, knocked sharply.

Silence.

A lonely breeze touched at her face.

She stood there for a full minute feeling increasingly worried. The seemingly abandoned bar amped up her helplessness. *Where are you, girl?* She bit her lip, not wanting Jordan to notice. She shrugged and turned back.

Lori fell back into the 'Vette to find Jordan staring at her and scratching the back of his head.

"OK," she said, "just thought we should start here. Cross that off the list. Where to next?"

"Christ, we're never gonna find her."

There was a whine in his voice. Apparently, he'd felt the same spike of hopelessness that she'd felt at The Spot's rear door. And he was right: Southern California was an incomprehensibly sprawling place, and it had been hours since Jasmine disappeared, apparently. Where would they even begin seriously looking for her?

"That's why I need you to think harder about last night."

Jordan began squirming at the thought.

"I'm serious," she said, taking another deep drag off the cig. "Obviously this isn't gonna work, just driving around aimlessly. We need a better starting point, and it makes sense to go where you last saw her."

"I already went there."

"Not with me, you didn't."

Lori could see him working over the problem, like grinding a hard nut between his teeth. The dude clearly didn't want to go back there, wherever that was, and for whatever reason. Probably something bad happened last night that he didn't want to talk about.

"Tell me where it is."

"She's not there."

"I realize that, but it's where we have to start."

"*Fuck!*"

"Why are you so upset about it? Is there something you aren't telling me?"

"No."

"I'm beginning to think you don't really want to find her, bro."

"*What?*"

"Like, you want to put in some kind of manic effort, but you're scared of actually looking."

"That's insane."

"I *know!*"

"Then go!" Jordan said, gesticulating with his skinny arms. "Start driving! That way!"

Lori pointed the car south and pulled out into light traffic. She passed neighborhoods and restaurants and strip malls—donut joints and bail bondsmen and pawn shops and liquor stores, Yellow Basket burgers and Subway sandwiches. Then the park where she took Sarah most of the time. It was like a little oasis; the landscaping looked like someone actually cared. It had a clean playground and sharp edging. It was maintained by the city, unlike some of the gross neighborhood parks farther west. The benches had bars on them to discourage the homeless from sleeping there. Like that. She hadn't seen any drug deals happening in that park.

She watched it glide past, feeling a tug of longing. She wished she were there now, relaxing with her girl, watching her little body swing from the jungle gym. She'd see Sarah soon, a little bit of soul refreshment, and she certainly needed that. But for now, she had to help this weirdo. Had to find her friend.

"So ..." she said, her voice riding a smoky sigh, "tell me what happened last night."

"It was just a party."

"Doesn't sound like it."

He sneered at her as if he wanted no part of this conversation, but now he had no choice. "Shouldn't have gone to that fucking party, I told her that."

When Lori looked over at him, she saw him savagely wipe at his eyes, exuding self-hatred. He was crying.

She waited for him.

"She always dives right into trouble!" Jordan sniffed loudly. "Like she seeks it out! This is her own fault, you know, where she is, whoever's got her."

"What do you mean, 'whoever's got her'? What did you see last night? You must've seen something."

"Look, there was some shit going around, OK? We both took it. I knew we shouldn't, but we both did. You just get wrapped up in it." He paused, and the road came at them. "She wanted to get out, have some fun. It had been a while, she probably told you that. We've been laying low for so long."

"You mean drugs?"

He looked at her squarely. "Yes, I mean drugs, Jesus. It was everywhere, like candy. Everyone's laughing, feeling good. It's what she wanted, and yeah, she got it. Shit!"

"Do you think someone gave her something ... I don't know ... to knock her out?"

"That's—yeah, that's what I'm afraid of, OK? You need me to spell it out?"

"And you were knocked out, too?"

Jordan shrugged, embarrassed.

"Who gave it to you?"

Jordan gestured with his chin. "Couple more blocks, you're gonna turn left."

Lori repeated her question.

"It was either Tommy or this creepy dude, the one with the drugs. Derek? Pretty sure that was his name. I think Tommy was using him to get to Jazz. He's always had a thing for her. *Despises* me, *loves* her." He made a sound in his throat. "Who *wouldn't* love her?"

"Tommy? Why does he hate you? And why the hell'd you go to his party if he hates you—?"

"Jesus, that's a long fucking story." He was watching the road. "How much time you got? Left coming up."

She changed lanes, shifting to fourth. He was watching her right hand as if making sure she was being careful.

"Tommy's this fucking asshole from the old neighborhood," Jordan murmured. "Just a stupid thug when we were coming up, but now— *fuuuuck*. It was his party last night. Wish I'd never met him. Bane of my existence."

"Why is he here? I mean, in Santa Ana?"

"Hell if I know—our destiny, I guess." Voice a little choked. "OK, here."

Lori made the turn, nearly running over a cat. She veered around it, cursing softly. She entered a sad little neighborhood of drab prefab houses, one after another. Cracked concrete sidewalks connected the rectangle lots like a dense maze, which otherwise held a remarkable spectrum of domiciles, from apparent crack dens to well-kept, even modernized kit homes. At one of those, Lori spied an old Asian man in plaid pants staring out at them.

"OK, *fuck*, left here, and it's down toward the end, on the right. Park over here first. Here!" Pointing crazily, grabbing at the wheel.

"All right, jeez."

Lori slowed to a stop behind an old Volkswagen Beetle on blocks.

"See that ridiculous black truck up there?" Jordan said.

"Uh huh."

"That's Tommy's truck. That's his house to the right." He groaned.

"Can't believe I'm back here."

Hand on the 'vette's knobbed wheel, Lori watched the faded blue house with its stunted porch leading to a ratty screen door. A crooked awning leered over the door like a sarcastic brow. The house was three lots south of them. There was no activity anywhere near it. Lori cocked her head—she did hear unintelligible shouting coming from somewhere, but she couldn't localize the voices. She shut off the engine.

"What are you doing?" Jordan screeched.

"Shhh!"

"Do you hear something?"

"Will you shut the fuck up for a second?"

Jordan went quiet, fidgeting, and now the voices became more distinct. It was a man's raised voice, and it had a distinct, penetrating clang at its top end, like a bell, as if the man were putting hard emphasis on the last word of questions.

"That's him," Jordan said. "Christ, that's him."

"I can't hear what he's saying. I mean, I can't hear any words."

Out of nowhere, Jordan jumped in his seat, staring down at his lap.

"What?" Lori said.

"Jasmine's phone!" he said.

"What about her phone?"

He lifted up the device, still tethered to his bulky charger, and showed it to her. The face of the phone read Tommy Strafe, indicating an incoming call.

"That him?"

"Yes!" Jordan cried, and then rattled off a bunch of words like machine-gun fire. "Why's he calling her phone? What the fuck? Why does he have her number? How—"

"Don't answer it!"

"Yeah, like I'm gonna answer it! It's not even my phone!"

"Don't even touch it, put it down!"

The phone was loose in his hand, his nervous fingers jostling it, and Lori swore to herself. Dude was gonna answer it by mistake.

"Give me that!" She reached over, and he held it away from her with his long arms, keeping it away from her grasping reach. "Goddammit!"

"Knock it off!" Jordan cried. "What are you doing?"

"You're gonna fuck this up, give it to me," she said. "Please."

Jordan looked at her stupidly.

"Give it to me," she repeated.

He handed it over, and Lori held the phone, staring at it unblinking until the ringing stopped short.

"He'll leave a messag—" she started, and then her breath stopped.

Three houses south, Tommy Strafe bashed his front door open so hard that it slammed into the siding. He was a large man, thick and purposeful and clearly dangerous. Lori held her breath, and she knew Jordan was doing the same. Tommy was headed for his truck, holding his phone to his ear.

Just then, he stopped short and began braying into the phone, glancing deliriously around the squalid neighborhood, and at one point Lori was certain he'd spotted them in Jordan's yellow 'Vette, was certain they were dead now, but his gaze flitted right past them as he barked into the phone. Lori had yanked Jordan low, but she could just make out Tommy's shouting.

"Jasmine? Jasmine? Hello? Was it you? It wasn't you, right? Or was it your retard brother? Was it both of you? Hello? You took it, didn't you? Oh my fucking god, you bitch, you took it. You don't think I'll fucking find you? I will. I'll find both of you. And when I do, if you don't have it, I'll—Jesus Christ."

Tommy headed for his truck, climbed up to the door. He settled in and slammed that door, too. The black Chevy let loose with a rattling growl and lurched forward, subwoofer-blasted rap throbbing.

Next to Lori, Jordan looked pale. Shocked and dazed.

"Took what?" Lori asked.

She glanced down at the phone and watched as a voicemail icon blinked onto the screen. She handed the device to Jordan, gesturing as if it were scalding hot. He took it numbly.

"I have no fucking clue."

"Come on, yes you do."

"I'm serious, I have no idea." He put his head in his hands. "Oh Jesus. I'm doomed."

The truck swerved away, out into the narrow street, and Lori had a scary premonition that it would peel into a U-turn and pass right by them, and Tommy would see them, and he would have then cornered, and he would murder them. But Tommy continued forward jerkily until he turned abruptly toward Bishop, waiting to leave the neighborhood.

Lori glanced over at Jordan, smiling as she cranked up the 'Vette. "I'm gonna follow him."

9
JASMINE

Jasmine Frank stepped between two squat shrubs, out of the In-N-Out Burger parking lot. She started walking east on Westminster Boulevard, under sporadic palm trees and blue skies dotted with cumulus, toward Santa Ana. If she had to hoof all ten miles home, or however far it was, then she would do that. She'd walked ten miles before, although never in shoes like these, and never all at once, but hell, she could get it done. She'd do it barefoot if she had to, she supposed. What else was she gonna do? Walk the other way to the beach, find a boat, start a new life on the coast of Mexico?

She laughed out loud in the middle of a crosswalk, taking a sip of water from her small cup.

Moments ago, she'd scored a refill from her bespectacled friend on the other side of the In-N-Out walk-up window. She promised to come back when everything made sense again and order a full meal—and pay for it. She'd even given the kid a wink, earning a blush.

The past few days of wind had given way to sun and stickiness, and every step felt like a trudge. It didn't help that she was carrying—in addition, now, to her dangling heels—what felt like a five-pound brick of rare coins. Her memory of tip-toeing back into Tommy's room and swiping the brick out of the cabinet was such a fractured scatter of images and sensations that she still hadn't stitched them all together into a coherent timeline, but she had no doubt that she'd done it. He'd left the door and the drawer unlocked and practically invited it, for chrissakes.

Her first question for herself, as she gradually emerged from her haze: Was she really *that* stupid? Stealing from Tommy Strafe? Really?

She frowned under a sluggish headache, pondering her reasoning for taking the coins. Somewhere back there, rattling around her skull, was the memory of Tommy grabbing her ass while she leaned against the wall next to his filthy bathroom, and trying to wriggle out of his grip. He'd had her cornered there, and his big body had blocked her from the view of everyone in the living room, including Jordy, who'd been lost in conversation with Tommy's scraggly homie Derek, the guy with the pills. It felt like strategy, that hand on her ass. The memory was shivery, spiked with a fuzzy unreality, and she couldn't yet place it in the timeline of the night. And complicating it all was the fact of their long history—the flirting, the teasing, the yelling, the accusations. Maybe there was a part of her that craved something Tommy had, but not like that.

She knew she really *must* have been *that* stupid, because she also had a clear recollection—earlier in the night—of happily taking a few of those fat pills from Derek, all playful, all in good fun, all in the interest of a fun, hilarious evening ahead of them. And then Derek handing her right off to Tommy while Jordy drifted off wherever—she'd lost sight of him.

So, later, when Tommy acted all gracious as host and walked his two old friends through his bedroom and bragged about his precious collections, showing off his custom glass case in the corner … well, the first thing that she knew she was going to do, given the chance, was grab those fucking coins and find a way to sell them.

And, somehow, she got her chance.

Thinking about that plan soberly, and glancing at the deadweight dangling from her fist, she shook her head.

"*Stupid!*" she hissed at the roaring street.

A bundled-up Asian woman standing next to a baby stroller at the edge of a bus stop gave her the eye and started saying something unintelligible. Her stroller didn't have any baby in it. It was filled with a single fat Hefty bag, probably packed with aluminum cans for recycling.

Jasmine walked past, and the rat-tat-tat mumbling faded behind her.

Westminster Boulevard reached out into infinity, toward the inevitable end of her trek. Tommy. Broken glass. Jordy. Tearful explanations. Already her head was ricocheting with excuses. She envisioned handing over the brick of coins with a shrugging apology, blaming the drugs that Tommy's freak friend had pushed on her, at Tommy's own party. She'd meant no harm, she hadn't been in her right mind, yeah, like she would consciously steal from Tommy, it didn't make any sense. She'd pay for the damage to the cabinet, obviously. But it was Tommy's fault, Jesus!

She stared straight ahead, down the row of bodegas and laundromats and auto-repair outlets and old photomats converted into locksmiths, into the endless line of vehicles scurrying east and west, the horizon line diminishing into late-morning, palm-dotted haze.

She sighed.

To Jasmine, life was a string of disappointments and failures and disasters that she had to overcome, only to face the next one, which was always more dire. Every one of them seemed to involved a monster of some kind. This humiliating perp walk was just the next in a long line. She never much liked to step back and take the measure of her short ridiculous life, it was just too deflating, but what else was she supposed to do, walking ten miles home, barefoot? With each step, she bounced through her childhood, neighborhood to neighborhood, transferring school to school, with a mother who might not have even cared about education had Jasmine not prodded her to do her fucking job and enroll her. Saying goodbye to friends over and over, penpal letters that dried up almost instantly, quiet in the back of class while strangers peered back at her, snickering. A cheerleader disposition, and yet always the outsider. Never invited to birthday parties or sleepovers. Never really part of the team, and just when a connection started to happen—yanked away again.

So she learned to latch on to people quickly.

Lost her virginity at twelve, seemed to *keep* losing it at every new school as she reached for intimacy even as she failed to connect with the people around her at every other level. When she finally got to Alamitos Intermediate, she was ripe and she knew it. Oh, the boys slobbered over her. But goddamn if Jordy didn't have that protective streak, and the streak had only gotten more pronounced the more she filled out her clothes. Where before she'd use the vestiges of her little-girl charm to corral the boys, she found it orders-of-magnitude easier to get even better reactions with her burgeoning tits and hips. Jordy became aware of her as a new being and acted as if he'd staked his claim at birth. *She's mine.*

It wasn't like Jordy had taken advantage of her. Ever! It was different with twins. When they were little, they'd explored each other. They took baths together, they touched each other—yeah, even down there. They practiced kissing—quite a bit, actually. But then all that faded.

It seemed like just as she started attracting the big boys at school, Jordy receded into himself, becoming even more of a loner and actively repelling people. He'd suffered from acne, and he'd started to smell, and she'd pushed consciously away from him. Flirting with people like Tommy to spite her brother. And as the boys flocked to her, Jordy only became more angrily protective, desperate almost, while she dismissed him. She hated Jordy for that, at the time, but the truth was that he was the one constant through everything. He was always there for her, for better or for worse. That's what she had to admit.

And now—almost to the ripe old age of eighteen (don't tell anybody)—she was *still* conflicted about him.

Jordy, I do love you, you fucking weirdo.

Jasmine crossed yet another street, passed another bus stop. It looked recently rebuilt or refreshed, much nicer than anything near her home in Santa Ana. A black kid wearing spotless untied Nikes and huge white headphones sat in the center of the bench, mouthing lyrics, jutting his head back and forth to a beat.

She kept walking.

Every once in a while, she swapped the bagged brick in one hand with her heels in the other hand. The coins were getting heavy. It probably wasn't even a lot of actual weight, but they were becoming a kind of torture. She couldn't remember the stories behind the coins, but the few Tommy had shown to her and Jordy were big, like the silver dollars she and her brother got from their dad when they were young. She wondered whatever happened to those, and whether they were worth anything. Probably not.

Every time she felt tempted to jerk out a thumb and try hitching, she caught sight of a cop car—they were like frickin' mosquitos around here, hovering around, itching to descend and bite.

She crossed a few more streets and reached the next bus stop. It was empty. She ducked under the overhang and sat on the bench, dropping the bag of coins next to her. She was starting to sweat, and she had at least eight miles to go.

She sat there, watching vehicles rev and cough past her for a minute. Life was a relentless surge, rushing from one moment to the next without any consideration of the hapless assholes and monsters taking part in it. Just like the endlessly disastrous trajectory of her own existence, life barreled forward into the future exactly like this unending flow of traffic, everyone trying to one-up each other, gain the upper hand, cut each other off, take advantage of everyone else. *Me, me, ME!* It was all so depressing, just looking at it. For Jasmine's whole life, she tried to put on the brave, happy face. That was her way, to be optimistic in the face of an unremitting onslaught of setbacks and defeats.

That was goddamn difficult today.

After a short rest, she settled down a little bit, even nodded her head as she came back to herself. She turned her attention back to the bagged brick of coins again, and she had a sudden memory of the night before. She recalled stumbling out of Tommy's house—the fear of him catching her, the way her body tensed even as she laughed, expecting shouts and enraged footfalls behind her. But none came. Even as she got two, three blocks away, no one came after her. She got far enough away that she could no longer hear the laughter and the music, and now she remembered the weight of the coin brick swinging from her arm, perhaps confusing it—in her drug fog—for her purse. Yeah, she could see how that probably happened.

Her purse was at Tommy's. Because of course it was.

Well, shit.

Something she'd have to deal with. With every step she'd taken so far this morning, she'd imagined herself finally arriving back at Tommy's house to hand over his absurd collection of coins—somehow so important to that grab-ass ape—and apologizing. It was a disheartening thought, but now all the more necessary with the thought that he himself had her bag, her wallet, her phone.

But again, how had she gotten all the way over here in *Westminster?*

She got on her feet and started walking again. She passed a long row of apartments and then a gas station. And then strip mall after strip mall. Drug stores, banks, fast food restaurants, parking lots. Frenzies of vehicles turning in and out of them. As she walked, she watched the storefronts. Taco shacks, liquor outlets, beauty salons, little bakeries, karate studios, home security frauds, mom-and-pop dental stops, Chinese joints. Rare coins.

Jasmine stopped on her bare feet.

She stared at the aging sign in the center of a string of stores facing a cramped parking lot and a corner café. The small store was mashed between a comic shop, its windows plastered with fading superhero images, and a dry cleaners. The sign read Woody's Coins and Metals.

She stepped into the parking lot and walked over to the store. She pulled on her shoes, then reached for the door handle. It was locked.

She placed her forehead against the smeared glass door and peered inside. A small round man with librarian's glasses and a huge mustache stared back at her from behind a glass case. He pointed at a chunky watch on his wrist, then at an old-time wall clock behind him whose hands pointed to 11:43. Jasmine backed up and found the store's hours hand-printed on a little sign next to the door—12 p.m. to 5 p.m. Tuesday to Saturday.

Jesus, what kind of store is open five hours a day?

She nodded at him, gave him a little salute.

The store's tattered faded-blue awning provided a bit of shade, and Jasmine settled herself on the concrete underneath it. She placed the bagged brick of coins on her lap and waited.

10
TOMMY

Tommy Strafe slammed the truck's door and twisted the ignition. The engine chugged to life, and he gunned it, screaming raggedly inside the closed-off cab, unconsciously harmonizing with the choppy motor. He wanted those fucking twins' throats in his hands, imagined squeezing them just as he gripped the steering wheel now.

Last year, Rennie Mawk—he owned the warehouse Tommy was heading to now—had told him this story about a Mexican kid who'd died at one of his construction sites. The kid was a lazy asshole by all accounts, and worse than that, he'd stolen some expensive ornamental metals from the site that he'd later tried to sell to a third party—and that third party had gone straight back to Rennie to report it, recognizing the items and knowing exactly who did that kind of work. So add *stupid* to *lazy*. Even more so because (purely coincidentally, Rennie'd assured him) the kid had later taken a fall from the fourth story of the half-constructed structure at the site, and he'd landed hard on concrete. Despite the nearly fifty-foot drop, according to the story, the kid *survived*—at least, for a little while. Rennie said the kid eventually drowned in his own blood, unable to move, screaming raw gargling agony.

It was an image that had stayed with him, the way Rennie described it. Sometimes it came to Tommy in the middle of the night.

And it was how Tommy imagined Jordan, after he got his hands on him. Jasmine, too, if it turned out she'd had something to do with it.

Tommy reached over to stab at his phone, which he'd lodged in a tear in the seat. While Rennie's phone rang and rang, he waited to turn out onto Bristol. Finally saw a gap and floored it, off toward Rennie's place near Euclid and Hazard.

No answer on Rennie's phone. It was possible he was busy with a client. Dude was always on the phone.

Jordan and Jasmine's faces hovered in front of him, tinged with red. Derek had jacked Tommy up last night, the way he liked it, but he'd also fucked with the Frank twins—precisely what Tommy had asked him to do. What Tommy couldn't get over was that they'd had the presence of mind after that to do something like this! The way he recalled it, Derek had given Jordan a gray-death concoction of his own design, a little crushed-up Oxy, a little street heroin, whatever synthetic binders he had on hand. Tommy'd seen the needle go in! Then Derek had slipped Jasmine a GHB pill, telling her it was just a low-dose Vicodin, and Tommy had watched her swallow it, all giggly with a plastic cup of beer, and after that she'd mostly been bendy, euphoric putty. Tommy could've had her six ways to Sunday if Kayla hadn't been a territorial bitch all night, glaring at him with her lava eyes.

After all that, they'd *still* had the presence of mind to steal his shit.

Tommy remembered acting the gracious host, giving their dilated eyes a glimpse of all *three* of his collections—the baseball cards and the coins and the couple of valuable pulp books he'd inherited from his grandfather. He'd been all proud. There'd been something about having Jasmine there, and even her cross-eyed brother, that had bloomed some nostalgia in him, some memories of easier times. When his dad was alive and they were doing their thing. For all Jasmine's ditzy gullibility and Jordan's nerdling hopelessness, they were totems of home, when Tommy'd had a real home.

But *fuuuuuuck!* He'd practically *handed* them those coins.

The cards were his own silly hobby, picked it up from Gil Jones in grade school and never really stopped. Tommy'd lifted five or six primo Dodger rookie cards of his dad's favorite late-'70s infield—Garvey, Cey, Lopes, Russell—from a now-defunct memorabilia shack in Pasadena. That was back around the time Tommy (yep, named after Lasorda) had quit school. He displayed the cards in a glass cabinet in the corner, the upper portion, along with the paperbacks in bags, some old Chandlers and Hammetts. They were like mint condition, straight off the spinning rack at the drugstore, back in the day.

It was the coins that were the real treasure, handed down from his father, gathered over a short career of under-the-table coin-shop swindles. Tommy kept them in a drawer at the bottom of the glass cabinet. He'd taken the brick-like box carefully out of the drawer to show the twins. Held it reverently, walked them through the highlights. A Civil War era liberty head gold dollar, a bronze Lincoln wheat penny, a Morgan silver dollar from the turn of the past century. There were a bunch of others, all neatly wrapped and catalogued, his father's precise handwriting spelling out their details and worth.

He always got a contact high, sifting through his collections, but Jasmine took everything in like the items were fireworks in the sky. *Ooooooohhh!* Tommy had laughed right alone with her, massaging her back right in front of her idiot brother. And now Tommy had an acid-jangly memory of Jordan smirking and nodding and sweating while he watched the coins, and Tommy knew he was the one. Somehow, some way, Jordan was the one who lifted his collection.

"Fuck you, you piece of shit!" Tommy yelled inside the humid cab.

He took the right onto Bristol and watched his pace through the popular speed trap. He didn't see any of the usual cycle cops there, so he gave the truck some juice. Streets were sparse, allowing him to get way ahead of himself and muse on body disposal. He'd always had that habit, of getting two or three steps ahead, but he found that the ruminations calmed him.

He suspected that Rennie had never actually *done* these things, but the man claimed to have two reliable methods for getting rid of a corpse. Rennie had never trusted the notion of burying bodies under tons of construction-site cement—too obvious, he thought, too close to home. Plus, the body was still there, begging to be unearthed. No, his first method was to suspend the body over a bathtub, slit the throat, and wait for it to bleed out. Then, over a reasonable amount of time, cut the flesh into small cubes and distribute those around Orange County—hell, even in the upscale neighborhoods—where racoons and coyotes and mountain lions and foxes and even fucking house cats would take care of the evidence.

But that was a lot of work. Rennie's second and favorite way was to wrap the body in multiple heavy-duty plastic bags, after attaching some heavy construction-site disposal to it, take it out halfway to Catalina where the water reached a depth of a couple thousand feet, deeper than the reach of even the most skilled divers, and let it sink.

Tommy was lost in the image of two sinking bag-shrouded bodies when he noticed flashing lights in his rearview.

He twisted in his seat to see a police cruiser tracking him—*fucking hell!*

He pulled his foot off the gas as he turned back forward, and his eyes darted down to the speedometer, which showed his speed drifting down through the fifties. At that moment, he passed a sign that read 40MPH.

"Jesus Chr—"

He braked the truck and pulled over into the bike line, and the cop angled in behind him, lights all spastic. Tommy twisted the ignition off, waited. Sat there boiling with rage, trying to tamp it down. But it was like something bubbling up his esophagus, bile or fire, and he couldn't contain it. He opened his window and took deep breaths, on the edge of black panic. He pounded the seat next to him, narrowly missing his phone. Gradually, he forced himself calm.

The cop approached the truck, and Tommy eyed him through the side mirror. Cop looked wiry and wary.

"Fucker," Tommy breathed.

He rolled down the window, glanced down, tried for amiable.

"Hey officer." Going for obsequious.

"In a hurry?" The man was all mustache and sunglasses, staring up at him.

"I'm sorry, man. Must've got away from me."

"Know how fast you were going?"

"Not exactly."

"Got you doing 58 miles per hour."

"This isn't a 50?"

"It's 40 through here."

"Gotcha. I apologize."

"Can I see your license and registration?"

"Of course."

Tommy dug into the glove box, finally located the crinkled papers, then strained his bulk upward so that he could burrow into his back pocket for his fat wallet. He finally managed to free the wallet and fish out his license. He gritted his teeth and handed down all the items, everything in order. The cop took them and moved back to his cruiser.

As Tommy settled in to wait some more, feeling as if blood was leaking from his eyes, he glanced up into the rearview again to watch the hypnotizing rock and sway of the cruiser's light bar. A sense of urgency tightened his chest, crunched his teeth together until his molars felt as if they might shatter.

Bottom line was he wanted to get to Rennie and hash out a plan.

Rennie Mawk—with his otherworldly calm fronting a diabolical mind —always had the uncanny ability to focus Tommy. That stretched back to when Rennie had hired him for the apartment complex job in Orange. Tommy still maintained that was because Rennie felt sorry for him over his dad's death out on the interstate, but apparently Rennie had seen something in him too. Tommy'd had a gift with drywall, got it from his dad, and even though he hated the work—despised it, truth be told—he'd done it for Rennie for three solid years, apartment after apartment, no doubt ruining his back in the daily grunt-like grind. But in no time, that grunt work had transitioned into more suitable jobs, under-the-table intimidation shit alongside Rennie's asshole son, Charlton. Way Tommy looked at it, Rennie had groomed him and built him up through the ranks until he was as strong and imposing as he'd ever been in his life.

Gordon Strafe and Rennie were old pals. Business associates. If Tommy remembered the story right, his dad had hired Rennie much the same way that Rennie had hired Tommy. *Waaaay* back. Tommy remembered going with his dad to a worksite one time, some cheap suburban tract north of Dallas, godawful early in the morning to avoid the heat, and meeting Rennie for the first time. Flint-faced even then, with the bandana around his angular skull, ever-present unfiltered Lucky Strike hanging off his lip. (Rennie was the first person Tommy ever saw smoking unfiltereds, and it stuck like glue—so badass.) After a bologna sandwich lunch and water out of a hose, a bunch of the yokel help had cornered and grabbed a pregnant-looking spiny lizard inside one of the houses. Rennie had taken it and nailed it with a ten-penny to an upright naked two-by-four. Tommy had watched the lizard squirm and squeak while Rennie chuckled, flipping his hammer. Tommy remembered feeling a kind of nauseated awe.

Hell, Tommy even remembered Rennie coming over to the house when his mom was still around. Like, a lot. He and his dad would smoke out on the back porch, and Tommy would bring them cold Buds every fifteen minutes, and sometimes his dad would let him sit out there with them and—

Tommy coughed and sat up straighter.

Way behind him, beyond the parked cruiser, a yellow Corvette was poking out of a side street two blocks south, its distinctive fiberglass nose looking like it was sniffing Bristol's asphalt.

"*No fucking way,*" he murmured, turning to squint out the rear window.

He couldn't make out the driver from this distance, but it had to be Jordan, right? And was that Jasmine, hunkered down in the passenger seat? Were they *following* him? What in the name of shit? Could it be? Why? Tommy was *sure* that was the 'Vette he'd seen in front of the house last night as he'd welcomed the twins inside—*fuck*, man, he'd even commented on it. *Cool ride.* Again, starting off the night as the goddamn gracious host.

But ... but ... first stealing from him, and then coming to the house again this morning? The prospect of those two malcontents—Jordan fucking Frank and his sister—trying to pull something on him ... well, it boggled the mind.

Tommy dug out his phone and dialed Kayla.

11
JORDAN

When the police cruiser gunned past the 'Vette, lights strobing, Jordan Frank felt as if all his guts had abruptly flushed out his ass in a ropy stream, like *floofooofoooghhh*. But the cop had his sights on someone else—and that someone else turned out to be Tommy! The cruiser zeroed in on the big-ass truck like an illuminated wasp, and he and Lori watched Tommy pull over. His stupid towering truck appeared defeated as it sidled over into the bike lane.

Jordan let out a triumphant yelp.

"Holy shit!" He watched the unfolding scene with nervous energy. "What should we do? Should we go over there? Tell the cop about Jasmine? Tell him what Tommy said on the phone? We can nail him!"

Lori slowed to a stop at a traffic signal two blocks south of Tommy. Then she turned to glare at Jordan, frowning, like he was a child.

"You are the weirdest fucking guy."

"What?"

"One minute you're scared to death of that fucker, and the next you want to run over there and implicate him in a kidnapping."

Jordan thought about that as they sat idling at the signal. He realized he was bouncing his legs obnoxiously, so he grabbed hold of them to stop the nervous movement. Lori was right, he realized. *Goddammit!* He'd always felt this rift between the things he *thought* should happen in the world—things like justice, comeuppance, revenge—and what he actually had the balls to spearhead. It was like he was only his best, most confident self in the scenarios that played out in his brain, but in real life he was more apt to shrink himself into a cowardly, mewling puddle. He'd been called a coward before, even by Tommy himself, and he always tried to snap back, deny it, but right at this moment, he felt as if—given the slightest nudge—fucking *tears* could come to his eyes. What kind of man was he?

"Shit!" he blurted.

Lori looked at him. "Do you have Tourette's or something?"

"Fuck you."

Ahead of them, the cop sidled out of his cruiser and began approaching the tall truck with caution, hand poised calmly at his belt.

"What about the phone call? Tommy's message?"

His voice sounded weak in his mouth. He despised every word coming out of his face, but he couldn't contain their flow. What the fuck was wrong with him?

"What about it?" Lori said. "We can't do anything with that."

"What are you talking about? He—"

"We can't go over there! C'mon, man, think!" Lori glared at him. "That message doesn't prove anything. It doesn't have any real threat in it. It doesn't prove the first thing about where Jasmine is! In fact, all it would do is give Tommy ammunition. Right? He thinks you stole something. Tommy would turn that shit around, and the cop would end up suspecting *you* of something. And besides all of that, the call came on Jasmine's phone, which you can't even access!"

Jordan sulked.

The light turned green, and Lori took a sudden right into a subdivision, nearly colliding head-on with a gardening jalopy full of Mexicans.

"Jesus!" Jordan cried. "Where are you going?"

"Can't just park here in the middle of the street."

She slid into a three-point turn and went back to the edge of Bristol, parking at the curb, nosing out so that they could *just* glimpse Tommy's stupidly tall truck beyond the cop car. Abruptly, Jordan felt entirely exposed. He shrank in the bucket passenger seat, his butt cheeks crawling him low into the ripped and scuffed vinyl. He stared out the window at the flashing cop car, his eyes barely above the edge of the door panel.

Jordan felt Lori at his shoulder, watching right along with him. Tommy was handing papers down to the cop, exchanging words. The cop turned heel and went back to his cruiser.

"Looks like he's gonna write up a ticket," Lori said, sounding resigned. She checked her watch and slumped into her seat.

The world paused, and Jordan fell into a funk of depressed introspection. He knew it was a twin thing, but Jasmine's absence was making him extra twitchy. His hands were shaking, and his teeth were *this* close to chattering. He observed himself from outside his body and felt an intense self-loathing. He was closer to Jasmine than any other human being on the planet, would always be, and he felt a desperation verging on mania. He felt these things and yet was powerless to do much about them. He wasn't stupid, he *wasn't!* But he knew his actions made him look that way.

He had to find her. He couldn't even entertain the idea that something had happened to her. Like, something bad. When his thoughts started inching in that direction, his mind clattered shut.

He checked his phone again. Nothing.

Went back to peering at the scene beyond the flashing lights.

He hated to dwell on the asshole in the asinine black truck, but Tommy was emblematic of everything wrong in Jordan's life. The fact that he'd materialized in Santa Ana, blocks from where Jordan and Jazz had secretly relocated—to get away from everything Tommy represented!—was the stuff of a horror story. It was like the monster had followed them, in an almost supernatural way. A ghost from the past.

It reminded Jordan of a time when they'd lived at the old place off Western—that was the house before the even worse shack on Redstone, that despicable corner of Garden Grove where it seemed the sun was always searing down, no relief, no shade, everything baking atop urine-soaked concrete. Jordan was walking home from school by himself (Jazz usually walked with him, but that day she'd gone over to the yogurt shop with Shelley and Imogen), and he'd suddenly felt the shadow of someone tagging along behind him. He'd grown increasingly paranoid. He started skirting between cars, sprinting across lawns, taking shortcuts, until he felt he was safe, and then he'd slammed straight into Tommy's chest. Five or six doors down from the safety of his house.

"Where's your sister?" Tommy'd said, belligerent, thick-mouthed. "Doesn't she usually walk you home?"

"No."

"Biles said you were being a little pussy out on the field."

Jordan had watched Tommy with uncomprehending fear.

"Who's Biles?" Trying to keep his voice steady.

"Ray Biles, you idiot. Kid with the hair."

"Oh, Ray."

Ray had squinty red eyes and long hair, atrocious acne and a droopy bottom lip that freaked out Jordan.

"Yeah, Ray."

Jordan knew exactly the moment Tommy was talking about. The flag football teams had decided out of thin air to play a shirts-versus-skins game, and Jordan hadn't wanted to take off his shirt. Simple as that. He had a big birthmark across his abdomen that looked like a fucking pig, and no one except his mother and sister and maybe a doctor or two had ever seen it, and nothing was going to change that. He'd rather have walked off the field and off school grounds and out into the traffic crisscrossing Magnolia than take off his goddamn shirt.

"Not much of a team player, huh?" Tommy'd said, coming close. "Why don'tcha take that shirt off now? Let's see that scrawny chest."

"No."

Tommy had snatched at the fabric of the shirt, a hard smile showing bad teeth.

"Come on, let's see it."

"No, Tommy."

Jordan remembered Tommy glancing around to take the measure of the street, and finding a few neighbors in their lawns, on their porches, peering at them out of the corners of their eyes. Tommy gauging how much he could get away with.

"*Fucking pendejo,*" Tommy'd whispered, hot, coming even closer.

Jordan remembered smelling the older boy's sour breath, and maybe that's what made the biggest impression. The acid breath. It seemed to say a lot about Tommy. And then a middle-aged man with a huge beer belly and greasy hair came bursting out of the house they were standing in front of, startling them both, and asked what was going on. Tommy'd stalked off with a murmured curse, and Jordan had stood there stupidly thankful for this meddling stranger until tears had squirted helplessly from his eyes. He'd walked away, ashamed, silent, as the man called out, "You OK kid? Huh? You're welcome."

Watching Tommy's truck now, years later, Jordan knew that—given the chance, given stacked odds—he would kill Tommy Strafe. He would perform the act with relish. He would enjoy it. It wasn't like this was some new kind of insight, some shining realization. He'd held similar thoughts in his skull many times.

Given the chance.

Jordan let loose with grunt choked with self-hatred. To him, *given the chance* meant Tommy'd have to be hog-tied and gagged, utterly powerless on the ground. Maybe a cloak over his head so Jordan couldn't see his face.

Just as Jordan began to sigh, Lori sighed next to him.

He stared at her. He noticed beads of sweat forming on her brow, and her eyes looked a little different, a little wider or something.

"What is it?"

"This is gonna take a while."

The cop was still in his cruiser, writing up the ticket.

Jordan shook away from his thoughts, came back to himself. *I'm sorry my sister possibly being murdered is messing with your schedule.*

"I'm supposed to pick up my kid for lunch."

A long moment passed.

Still watching the scene on the street, he said, "You have a kid?"

But then Jordan remembered Jazz mentioning it at some point. He couldn't recall any details. Usually when his sister returned from Lori's apartment, she was tipsy and abrupt with him, and when he asked her questions, she was evasive. But one time she'd said something to the effect of *Found out she's a mama.* He hadn't cared at the time, wrapped up in his own shit.

"Yeah," Lori said, nodding quickly. "Sarah."

"I've never noticed—"

"She lives with her dad."

"Oh."

"How old is she?" Jordan asked.

"She's six."

He watched her nervous movements for a second, then made a sound in his throat. "That's cool."

"I don't see her enough," Lori murmured, voice thick. "Her dad won the custody battle. Takes a lot to do that in California, believe me. But I did enough." Shook her head. "Judge just looked at me like I was some hopeless crack addict. Dude had pity in his eyes, watching my girl. Sarah all sad, standing next to her worthless father." She sat up straighter. "We're better now, we hang out." She said it in an odd way, like trying to convince herself.

Jordan nodded as he watched her a little more carefully.

The first image to pop into his head, inevitably, was Jazz at Sarah's age.

Pigtailed and sassy, already so different from Jordan in poise and personality. Jazz was never a sad girl, at least on the outside. That was back when their mom doted on them, especially Jazz, her little cutie-pie. New clothes from Target on her first day of school, bright and bouncy. Backpack that still smelled like its packaging, all stiff and shiny, cartoon characters emblazoned across its fabric.

God, he loved her.

Tears threatened to spill out of his eyes, so—on impulse—Jordan twisted around and grabbed Jazz's backpack behind the seat, pulled it into his lap. It was a worn-out blue JanSport, gray-strapped, with two broken zipper tabs. Peering into the small front pocket, he found an ancient plastic baggie filled with orange dust, possibly the remains of old Cheez-Its. He scrunched his nose and checked the next pocket—some dull pencils and dried-out highlighters. In the first of the larger pockets, he discovered a vastly overdue library book (*Flowers in the Attic*, by V.C. Andrews), some dog-eared blank 3×5 cards, and a collection of heavily used block erasers. And from the big, back section—whose zipper he had to carefully pull by its metal nub—he pulled out three crumpled notebooks. As he watched the police cruiser for movement, he randomly flipped through them.

By this time, Lori was glancing from the road to Jordan's finds.

"Anything?" she said, distracted.

"Nothing from the past year or two," he said.

The writing looked old—scrawled by a young hand with a pencil whose graphite was now faded. One notebook was filled with math equations and notes, and another with silly poems and doodles. Nothing there.

But there was something else in the pack, something small but hefty weighing on his thighs. He reached inside and felt something like leather. He grasped some kind of strap and drew out a pink-and-white leopard-print case, and his chest seemed to suck in on itself. He knew exactly what this was. Jordan couldn't help a small gasp from escaping his lips.

"What is that?" came Lori's voice.

Jordan didn't answer.

All he had to do was unzip the pouch fully and lay it open on top of the backpack. Snugly inside the pouch lay his mother's pistol—a 9mm Smith & Wesson Shield.

12
JASMINE

Backed up against jagged, musty concrete, her ass numb on the hard ground, Jasmine Frank watched the traffic flow across Westminster Boulevard. To the east, the boulevard would eventually turn into Westminster *Avenue*, for some reason, and then into 17th Street, and then finally she'd know she was close to home.

Home.

Sometimes it was hard to picture where home was supposed to be. She guessed home was wherever Jordan was—at least, that's the way she'd felt over the past couple years. But, now, when she thought about the cramped apartment they shared, the arguments they had almost every night, the monotony of her once promising new start ... it didn't feel like the home that she wanted it to be. But then it wasn't as if she knew what might make it that way. She felt as if she had no way to articulate what was missing. She didn't even know what she didn't *know*. Someone had said that to her once—*"You don't even know what you don't know!"*—back in school, and it had stuck with her for years. Apparently it was true.

Used to be her mommy that made her feel like she was home. Which was how it was supposed to be, she supposed.

Sometimes she missed her mom so much that her stomach would convulse and she'd curl helplessly into a ball on the ratty couch in front of the TV, or even in bed next to her brother, and he would wrap an arm around her and whisper *Shhhhh* in her ear, and pet her, and she would pretend it was Gloria Frank spooning her and making everything OK, like when she was little, but then she *knew* she was pretending, so it didn't really count.

Then she would remember what her mother had done—or, really, what she *hadn't* done—through those last years, the bad years, and she would fling her brother's arm away and bolt from the bed, disgusted. It wasn't Jordan's fault, she knew that, and she'd always go back to him, apologizing, but she was sick of apologizing. Like she was always on her back foot, on the verge of stumbling backwards.

Maybe it was time to lean forward instead. To start making her own home.

Maybe she was just tired of walking.

Tired of running.

At five to noon, she heard a rattle behind her. A little trill of adrenaline shot up through her chest. She stood up on wobbly legs as the old codger unlocked the grimy glass door and flipped the hanging door sign to OPEN. But instead of opening the door for her, he came out onto the sidewalk.

"I just need to grab my lunch from my car, young lady." He smiled generously. "I'll be right back."

He was a large roly-poly man with a prominently red face. He shuffled out into the parking lot, to its edge. Jasmine guessed his vehicle right: It was the vintage orange Volkswagen Karmann Ghia. It just seemed right. She already liked this guy. She watched him bend laboriously into the passenger side and retrieve a brown-bag lunch. Then he swung the door shut and made his way back to the door.

"Come on in," he said, voice muffled as if filtered through his mustache. "May I ask your name, young lady?"

"Oh, um, Kelly."

"Nice to meet you, Kelly, I'm George."

"Hey there." Going for cheerful.

The round man named George waddled back to his counter perch. "Got something to show me?" He grunted as he sat on his old stool.

"Yeah, I guess I do."

She showed him the brick of coins still swaddled in the grocery bag. He nodded. She approached the counter and dug out the rectangular box, planted it atop the counter with a thump. They both looked at the nondescript container.

"This is my dad's collection," she lied smoothly. "He died recently, and he left it for me. I guess I wanted to see what it's worth … maybe see what you'd offer. I don't know a whole lot about it."

"I see." He had a look in his eye that she couldn't decipher. "I'm sorry for your loss."

"It's OK."

George cleared his throat, and Jasmine smelled something sweet like waffles and fake maple syrup. He eyed her up and down, and she felt a little foolish in her wrinkled blue dress and bare feet. She still wasn't precisely sure of the state of her makeup. It was probable that she looked as if she hadn't changed or bathed in days, and it was even more probable that he could sniff the drugs that were still perspiring out of her. For a split second, she thought he might be poised to call the cops, and she strategized a quick grab-and-dash in her forebrain.

Instead, he made a show of settling himself into his seat and raising his hands, wiggling his pudgy fingers.

Ah, greed.

"Do you mind if I …?" Gesturing with his nose toward the box.

"Sure." Jasmine shrugged.

"I'll just give them a look-see."

She watched him squirt a dollop of hand sanitizer from a well-used bottle to his left, under the wall clock, then rub his soft fat hands together almost sensuously. He meticulously removed the first diminutive envelope from the box, like a card from the top of a deck. He examined the text on the envelope through his bifocals, then carefully removed the coin, placing it on a worn felt mat. After studying it for a time, he trained a large, brightly lit magnifier over it to inspect it more closely. Flipped it over, and again.

"This is a fairly nice Morgan Dollar, although—" Here he emitted a chortle. "—not quite as brilliant a specimen as is detailed on the envelope. The coin has seen significant wear. I see this kind of exaggeration all the time. People tend to be optimistic about their collections, you see." He paused. "Ah! And the year is incorrectly noted."

"What's it worth?"

He peered at her above the rim of his glasses. "A proper grading would take a length of time, of course, but an 1880 coin of this condition would get you … oh … twenty to thirty dollars? The Morgans are always in demand. Yes, I think that would be close to the mark."

Jasmine barked out a laugh. Although her memory of last night was still partly clouded in medicinal haze, she distinctly remembered Tommy sliding out that first coin, all proud and braggy, and telling her and Jordan it could be worth thousands of dollars.

"I assure you, that is a properly educated guess." The little man's face had flushed even redder, and he seemed insulted. "I can walk you through the basics of the valuation, if you'd like. I have a blue book here, and we can do it together. I would insist on transparency in any transaction."

"Oh, no, that's not necessary," Jasmine said. "It's just ... it's just like you said—my dad was ... overly optimistic."

He nodded. "Shall I move to the next?"

Jasmine nodded. She had a feeling she knew where this whole enterprise was headed. She estimated there were as many as three hundred square envelopes in the box, and the thought of George examining each one was abruptly deflating. Maybe she should just gather up the coins and leave. She was sure this odd little man was going to announce that it would take days or weeks to do a proper scrutiny of all of them. Something like that wasn't going to work. It was just another example of the kinds of little fires that were sometimes sparked deep inside her, only to be unceremoniously extinguished. She sighed quietly.

George bent to his task, performing cursory examinations of the envelopes, flipping through them.

"These Morgans all appear to be similar, of decreasing value, if I may be frank," George said. "I'll skip to the next batch, if that works for you."

"Yeah, that's cool."

That made her feel better about things. Maybe George could rifle through the whole box in a relatively short amount of time and at least give her the ol' ballpark estimate, as her dad used to say, *waaaaaay* back before he'd withered away in hospice, when Jasmine and Jordy were all of five years old.

She took a deep breath and began a slow tour of the premises while George worked. Jasmine felt oddly comfortable in the shop, hermetically sealed from the sounds of traffic and the humid chaos of Southern California, surrounded by antiquity and fastidious care and a lived-in sense of old-school passion. She turned to offer George a small smile, but he didn't see her—too absorbed in his study. It was obvious that he was perfectly at home inside this place, and it was equally obvious how out of place he would be, oh, anywhere else.

There was that word again—*home*. She needed to find a place like this where everything made sense to *her*. Where she was an expert at everything thrown at her.

"Your father has a collection of Liberty Nickels here that is quite nice," George announced, still hunched over the coins. "Their condition, I mean. Although, I must caution you, the years all appear to be of high mintage, so value, again, would be comparatively low ..."

"Of course," Jasmine said, just letting the man talk.

She wandered over to the far wall, which was plastered with framed, colorful displays of uncirculated coin collections—commemorative assortments celebrating Mount Rushmore, the Alamo, national parks ... a couple of faded cards holding silver coins with the faces of past presidents, most of whose names Jasmine barely recognized ... a set of dirty World War II pennies. She came to a collection of shiny quarters whose tail sides showed iconic images from all of the United States. A colorful mountainscape in Colorado, the open plains of Nebraska, the pine trees of Minnesota, a picturesque lake in Oregon, and there was Mount Rushmore again. South Dakota. Huh.

Well, why couldn't she turn tail and run? Make a fresh start somewhere? Like, one of these places?

She had never been out of the state—had hardly been out of Orange County—and it was a fact of her life that humiliated her. Just last week, Lindy at the parlor had passed some time with her in the empty lobby, describing a recent trip she'd taken to New York City. She'd gone on and on about the subway and the night clubs and the constant people and the noise and the huge cacophony of everything. Jasmine had responded with great interest but at the same time had inwardly begged the older woman—*please please please*—not to ask her about her *own* travels, which amounted to zippo.

At that moment, she let out a loud, surely inappropriate giggle. George at the counter gave her a long look, then returned to his work.

"Sorry," she murmured, turning back to the wall, feeling her mirth instantly evaporate.

Jasmine hadn't done *anything* in her life that was interesting or unpredictable. Part of her couldn't even imagine taking off on her own somewhere. The idea was ridiculous. She wouldn't even know where to start.

Start right here, a voice whispered. It sounded like her mom, years ago when she was good, when she was kind, when she would hold her and smile with her.

And like an out-of-nowhere recollection of a dream, Jasmine remembered a chunk of conversation from late last night, talking with someone in a car? She'd wanted to go home, she'd pleaded with the driver to *take her home*—as in, to Garden Grove, to her mom, to her house when she was young. To transport her to a time and place that no longer existed. There was the sensory memory of some kind of dreamy techno music washing over her like neon. Storefronts, streetlights, headlamps. The sweep of asphalt under the tires. She felt she could almost recall the driver's face—the glow of the dash, and he was like some nerd or something, wasn't he? He had that weird hat on his head, and he had the look, the look that was the same on all the boys' faces, the look that she always had to be careful about. She could practically hear Jordy telling her that. *Forever* he had told her that. *Watch out for those bastards, they only want one thing.* But the driver was also concerned about her, and open to taking her ... where? How had she ended up in the parking lot of a—?

"These buffalo nickels are fairly typical, I'm afraid to say," George said behind her, muttering as if to himself. "Looks like your father took quite a liking to them! There's just so little demand for these right now, though that could change. Hard to say."

Jasmine had no idea what he was talking about—and at this point, she didn't really care.

She nodded.

Without realizing it, she was rubbing her lower thigh—an old nervous habit that Jordy pointed out to her often. It was her "tell," he said. She knocked it off. She continued perusing the store's wall displays and checked out a number of the high-ticket items in a couple of the cases, but she didn't really see anything. She felt her heart beating faster as she inched closer to the front counter, closer to George. She was having an out-of-body experience, she realized. She felt as if she was about to do something dangerous and life-changing, even more so than when Jordy had secreted them away from Garden Grove.

George glanced up at her, over his bifocals, expectant.

She swallowed.

"How much could you give me for the whole box?" she whispered. "Like, right now?"

13
KAYLA

Kayla Jennings sat smoking in the front room, watching out the window as the cloudy, humid morning gave way to speckled sunlight. It looked like a pleasant afternoon was in the offing, but no way was she feeling it. The street was empty, and so was she.

Her chest was still hitching from the flood of tears, and her ass hurt like a bitch. It felt like she was barely holding it together, just the tiniest letup away from leaking blood and acid. It wasn't funny or electrifying anymore, the way he did what he did, all anger and impulse. Maybe early on, yeah, when they were new, but now it was just humiliating.

Tommy had roared off a whole hour ago in his stupid truck, and there was no telling what the bastard was getting up to. After pulling on his black jeans and faded AC/DC tee, he'd snatched his phone from the dresser and started dialing that reprobate Rennie—*oh my fucking god, that monstrous asshole*—and that's really when she'd started crying. Because then it was crystal clear this thing wasn't gonna get any better. No, a real shitstorm was brewing, she knew it. All because of that twirly spangly girl.

Jasmine.

What an asinine name! Girl was doomed from birth.

After a while, Kayla couldn't take it anymore, lying there across the couch feeling sorry for herself. She was the doomed one, Kayla Jennings, the girl who stayed put. At least Jasmine got out of there, wherever she'd gone. At least she'd had the balls to take off in the middle of the night, to snatch something valuable and never look back. Kayla hated that fucking girl, but goddamn if she didn't admire her a little, too.

Who was the one who got her ass hammered? Who was the girl who just gave it up, like some submissive lamb way down the food chain? Yeah, that was Kayla Jennings.

"*Shit!*" she yelled hoarsely into the empty house.

She ground out her cig in a metal plate balanced on the couch's arm and heaved herself up. She stalked back to the bedroom and stared at the corner cabinet. She and Tommy had shared this house for, what, a couple of years? Never had a break-in, never had an incident—well, except that time her brother took money out of her wallet, but that was, you know, family. She'd taken care of that.

This was an honest-to-Christ burglary, and it had happened directly under their noses. She found it hard to believe that either one of those young kids—Miss Blue Spangly or her weird brother—had had the guts to do something like this, but she couldn't think of anyone else from last night who would even imagine it. Marlon and Alicia had sacked out in the front room, and they were harmless. Derek and Trey were total loyalists who wouldn't even *think* of ripping off Tommy. Riley and Christian were old friends, so ditto. Mark, Lacey, Sid—no fucking way! She counted them all off, shaking her head, bending to examine the damage to the cabinet.

It was a smash-and-grab all the way. The shattered glass was from the lowest pane, the one that led directly to the hidden drawer containing the coins. Whoever it was, he or she knew exactly where to go. Probably used the toe of a shoe to break the glass, and then the inner drawer was a no-brainer if it was already unlocked, just fling it open and take the box. Well, it was Tommy's fucking fault for designing such a terrible cabinet.

The doorbell rang, startling her. She nearly fell back on her sore ass.

When she got to the front room, she peered out the window to find Mark Pellegro on the porch, looking stupid and pale in his dark blue fedora.

"What in the world?"

What was with all these dudes showing up on her porch on a Saturday morning?

Pellegro had worn that silly hat ever since she'd first met him at the store. He was one of the floor guys, one of the good ones, according to Tommy. When she'd met him, he'd had a little more hair on that head, wore it like a white man's afro. Now the hairline was slowly inching back, so he'd cut it short, but the vampire hairline wasn't doing him any favors. Wanted to look sharp, but that wasn't working. Kayla found it oddly funny in a nerdy way. Mostly he hid his dome with the hat. Yeah, he was quite a package—weak chin, spade nose, dopey smile. He did have good eyes—two of the brightest, most piercing blue eyes she'd ever seen on a human. They were what helped him with sales, no doubt. She guessed everyone had their saving grace.

It wasn't just the hat, she realized. He was wearing all the same clothes he'd had on last night. His favorite bowling shirt, old black jeans, black sneakers.

His white late-model Jetta sat at the curb, all its windows open.

Huh.

She opened the door.

"Hey Kay," he said, a startled, nervous look on his face, as if he'd expected—or hoped—no one would be home to open the door. He was unshaven and red-eyed, looked like he hadn't slept all night.

"What do you want? Tommy ain't here." Figuring he needed to make a drop. She didn't have a hand in any of that under-the-counter shit. Didn't *want* to.

Mark stood there fidgeting for a minute, glanced back at his car. As he did that, Kayla flashed on the dude last night, remembered him talking to Tommy, whispers here and there. They'd been up to something, probably. Assholes, all of them.

"Listen, did that—did that one girl come back here?" He had a whine in his voice, and it was also written across his face. "Bitch threw up in my car."

"Wait, what?"

"That girl, the one in the blue dress. You remember."

Kayla stared at him open-mouthed. Then she stood back, swung the door open.

"You best get your ass in here," she said.

Mark looked reluctant, but something was tearing him up inside. He tried digging his phone out of his too-tight jeans.

"Maybe I should try Tommy again."

"Tommy's busy."

He stopped digging.

"Shit, Kay, I screwed up, I think."

"Get on in here, we'll figure it out."

Mark trudged in all slumped and started gesticulating, pacing the front room. He kept licking his lips. Kayla shut the door.

"She threw up in my car, what was I supposed to do? You should smell it Kay, oh my shit, it's—"

"When?"

"Last night ... this morning ... early this morning."

"After the party?"

He nodded. "Tommy wanted me to keep an eye on her, and I did that,

I did, but she wanted a ride, so—"

"Hold up, man, here, sit down." Kayla directed Mark to the couch. "Calm down, huh? You want some water?"

"Yeah, yeah." He kept nodding, licking his lips some more.

She went to the kitchen and found a clean cup, filled it at the tap. She watched him from the sink, watched him fidget. "Take it easy, Mark, come on."

"I don't know, OK, maybe I overreacted, but I'll never get that fucking smell out of there."

Kayla brought over the cup of water, and he took it gratefully, chugging it down. He slapped the cup on the table next to him.

"Where'd you take her?"

"She was just gonna walk off into the night. She'd gotten a couple of blocks, and she wasn't coming back. I was watching her from the porch, right there. I panicked, man! The one thing Tommy asked me to do, and there she went. Can I have more water?"

"Yeah." She grabbed the cup and went for a refill, called out, "Why'd Tommy have you shadowing her?"

He got all shifty-eyed, shrugged repeatedly. Jesus, such a bad liar.

"Fuck if I know, I think he wanted to sell her on something."

She brought him the water. "Uh huh."

He gave her a look, like he knew what she was thinking, and she acknowledged that he knew, and enough said about that. Stalemate, but fine, move on.

"So you picked her up?"

He took another long swig, coughed a little.

"Probably shoulda went to Tommy, but I got in the car and chased after her." Coughed again, set the half-empty cup down. "Pulled up next to her, asked her if she wanted a lift—this isn't exactly the safest neighborhood, no offense—figured I'd at least be able to tell Tommy where she was going. Humor her for a while, see what she was up to, then swing her back here. She was so *high*, goofy as fuck, stumbling all over the place, but she was also sorta crying, kept saying she wanted to go home."

"You took her home?"

"Like, her *childhood* home. Kept going on about her mom. I *know!*"

"Where was that?"

He leaned forward, broke eye contact. "Well, we never got there."

Kayla cocked her hip. "Sounds like you got downright chummy."

"Shit, Kay, he's gonna kill me, I should've come right back after it happened, I was furious, man, I love that car."

Mark dropped his face into his palms so that she was left staring at the crown of the sweat-stained hat.

"So, where the fuck is she? Where'd you take her?"

"We—we—we just drove, we just drove out that way." He gestured toward the bedroom. "West, down 17th. She's fucking cute, OK? She was laughing, and then I was laughing, and she kept going on about being hungry."

"Hungry?"

"That shit Derek gave her, have you tried it?"

"I don't know what the fuck Derek was giving anybody." That fucking weirdo.

"Well, it makes you hungry as hell, must be a little THC in there." He stuttered a short laugh.

"OK, so?"

"She wanted to go to In-N-Out Burger, and fuck, man, you ever get a Double-Double on the brain? Not only that, a brain on dope? It's otherworldly, OK? You can't deny that shit. Come on. So I just kept driving till we got to In-N-Out. Who wouldn't? So we pull in, and the place is fuckin' closed! What kind of place closes at 1 on a Friday night? Thought they were open all night! Bullshit! But it didn't matter because right there in the middle of the parking lot she yakked all over my floorboards, got some on the seat, Jesus Christ, what the fuck, man! They're *cloth seats!*"

"What'd you do then?"

"I kicked her out, Kay, I kicked her out of my car and took off. It was *disgusting!*"

"You left her there in the middle of the night? Way out there? Alone?"

"Hey, I'm not proud of it, all right? But—yes! I got out of there and went to one of those do-it-yourself car washes, got the floormats out of there, sprayed 'em, cleaned the fucking seat, steam-vacced that motherfucker, but it still stinks like a bastard." He let out a strangled cry. "What was I supposed to do? I freaked, OK?"

"So where've you been all this time?"

"Home! I've been home! Cleaning, staring at nothing, wondering what to do. Slept a little."

"Christ, you're useless, aren't you?"

"I'm here now! I mean, I want to—"

"Did she have anything on her?"

Mark gave her a long look, squinting. "*Yes*, she had a bag of something. At first I didn't give it any mind, it was just her shit, but the more I think about it, it maybe could've been dope. I mean, it maybe coulda been dope. Like she grabbed something from the garage? I don't know."

He was eager to shift blame, any blame.

Kayla started pacing, feeling the acid stitch in her asshole with each step. Fucking Tommy. She felt a burgeoning heat flush through her chest, and shook her head angrily.

"So what do I do, Kay? What do I fucking do?"

"Shut up for a second."

That girl was out there, alone, without her phone, without anything except the clothes on her back and a box full of valuable coins. An image sprang into Kayla's head, and it was of that stupid girl removing the coins one at a time and buying burgers and drinks and, hell, taxi rides to her childhood home, wherever the hell that might be.

No doubt, that girl was miles away from that burger joint already, spending Tommy's inheritance like a clueless tool, but—then again—she was also a deliriously naïve child without her phone or her purse or any money that wasn't encased in collectible envelopes. Kayla considered the bright mental image of the blue spangly girl, sitting on her butt in front of a burger joint without any idea what to do or where to go.

"All right," she decided, "you're gonna take me for a drive. We're gonna go find her. She can't have gotten far on foot. Let's go see how stinky your fucking car is."

14
LORI

Lori Holst stared at the gun in Jordan's lap, feeling her eyes bug.

"Holy crap," Jordan mumbled. He was holding the weapon loosely by its barrel, awkwardly, like it was some kind of unknown foreign object. "I can't believe she *has* this."

"Where'd she *get* it?"

"It's our mom's," Jordan mumbled.

One part of Lori admired the pretty little pistol. It was the kind of gun she herself wouldn't mind stowing away in her purse. In fact, she *had* had one a bit like this one before Daniel had convinced the court to take her weapon from her following her half-hearted suicide attempt two years ago. Another, bigger part of her was freaked out by the pistol's sudden appearance in the confines of Jordan's 'Vette, right next to her.

"Like—she took it?"

"I think so."

"Well … put it back, put it back in there." She glanced over at the cop, who'd settled back into his cruiser. "Careful! Don't point that thing anywhere near me."

"I doubt it's loaded."

"You *doubt!* You've never even touched one of those before, have you?"

Jordan shook his head. "Not really."

"Put it away! There's a cop *right fucking there!*"

"She never told me about this," Jordan said, sounding a little numb. "Why wouldn't she tell me she took this?"

"Well," Lori said, "you know, maybe your sister's got more going on inside her than you realize."

Jordan placed the gun back in its case, almost reverently, and then shoved the case deeply into Jasmine's backpack. He clumsily zipped up the pack, stuffing it down toward his feet. Lori continued to glare at him, but he just slumped there, staring out the window toward the truck.

"Do you think the gun has anything to do with—with her disappearance?"

Jordan let out a little *harrumph*. "No."

"Why not?"

He took a quick glance at her over his shoulder. "I don't think she's looked at that since we left. I don't even think she's opened this backpack since then."

"Since you left Garden Grove?"

He nodded, almost imperceptibly.

Lori sighed and checked her watch. It was past 11:30 now, and her lunch date with Sarah loomed. She was already nervous about that, the prospect of seeing Daniel step out of his spiffed-out Highlander, his child bride in the seat next to him, giving her the eye, while Lori sat stiff-backed in her old Tercel trying to look at all confident. Sarah jumping down into the parking lot, dolled up, excited to see her real mommy but a little wary too. Lori always saw the wariness behind her eyes.

And now there was this: She didn't have any idea where Jasmine could be, and the last thing she wanted to be doing was hang with her weird brother while he spazzed out, and suddenly the cops were tangentially involved, and now there was a *gun* in the picture! Lori sensed that the cops were very probably about to be much more involved in this thing, regardless of Jordan Frank's thoughts on the matter.

How did she *get* here?

Lori started unconsciously chewing on her thumb—then became aware of it.

Oh no, she thought.

She slammed her hand down to her lap.

She'd felt it brewing for the past fifteen minutes but had been actively denying it. Just nerves, she'd rationalized. Understandable. But the cuticle chewing was a legitimate precursor. Sometimes if she was self-aware enough, she could head it off, the thing that always sent her spiraling once it dug in. She took in a deep breath, followed it with another. Closed her eyes for a sec.

OK, OK. Don't lose your shit.

She performed an impromptu bit of meditation, felt her heartbeat begin to calm.

"Hey, he's leaving, Tommy's leaving!" Jordan hissed.

She jerked back to reality.

The big black truck was pulling away from the curb slowly, its signal blinking obediently. The police cruiser remained, its lights now dormant.

Lori started up the 'Vette, waited a few beats, and pulled out onto Bristol.

She held her breath as she passed the cop, exposed, as if his laser eyes could pierce directly into the car and see the pistol in the backpack. But he didn't even glance up. She kept her own eyes on the rear of Tommy Strafe's truck, way up ahead, as it remained steady in the left lane. And as she fell into place following him, she felt a dark flutter in her heart.

No, she told it. *Calm down.*

Tommy took the left on 1st, and moments later, a block behind him, Lori took the turn as well, entering a seemingly endless lane of strip malls and beauty salons and old gas stations converted into whatever. She kept breathing, tamping down, focusing on the rear of Tommy's truck, staying back far enough so that he wouldn't see them.

At that moment, Lori's phone started ringing—a loud jangle coming from behind her in her purse. Next to her, Jordan reacted with a full-body jolt.

"Jesus fuck!" he shouted.

It was Sarah's ringtone. Lori frowned at Jordan to calm him down, then reached behind her seat, straining against the belt, feeling as if she was tearing something in her abdomen. Immediately she had a stinging cramp in her side, but at least it distracted her from the other thing.

"Answer it!" Jordan cried.

She found the phone and twisted back into her seat, wincing with the cramp.

"Thanks for the help!"

She twisted the other way to ease the cramp, and stabbed at her daughter's sweet face, emblazoned across her cracked screen.

"Sarah?"

"Hi Mommy," Sarah said languidly.

"Hi honey, hey listen, I'm gonna have to call you right back."

"Do I still get to see you today?" her daughter said, as if she hadn't heard her.

"Yes, baby, we're still on, but—"

"Will I get a prize?" Her voice sweet as candy.

"Oh, I've got big plans for you, baby, don't you worry, but—"

She felt her voice crack a little, and she cleared her throat.

Sarah continued blabbing, and Tommy's truck rolled off into the distance, and the time was headed toward noon, and Jordan was fidgeting next to her—a goddamn pistol at his feet—and suddenly everything was too much.

Everything came crashing down on her.

Her chest seized up, and her jaw seemed to lock.

She looked over at Jordan, felt the phone slippery in her hand. "I don't—I don't—"

He gave her a confused glance. "What?"

"I'm sorry," she whispered.

The blackness took her in its fist.

It was the very thing that took her daughter away from her, she knew it, this thing inside her that shut her down when things amped up. For so long, she'd had it under control. After escaping Illinois and living through the constant self-abusive torment of St. Louis for over a year, Lori'd finally found a semblance of peace after a dismal through-the-night drive over the Rockies with Scotty, landing in Santa Ana at the home of Scotty's niece, Georgia, the girl with all the tattoos who worked at the hospital. Georgia put her up in her attic apartment until she got on her feet. Getting on her feet had taken four months, and in that time Lori had fallen whole-heartedly in love with her adopted city—the climate, the pace, the absence of anyone and anything connected to her former life. In that spirit, she'd also fallen for the first guy who showed her any attention, at the office where she'd found temp work as a receptionist. Sarah's dad had seduced her effortlessly, a first-date encounter on the beach while the surf hypnotized her, bonfires dotting the horizon. That's when Sarah had been conceived, out there in the sand near the Newport Beach pier. Depressing to think her life peaked there, but it was true. The pregnancy went all right, and Daniel had quietly married her at City Hall (she could still see the jaw-clenched reluctance on his face) one rainy Tuesday morning. The birth had been surprisingly easy, and Lori thought the future was open and clear.

Nope.

Within weeks, Lori hated her daughter. Everything about her—her suckling lips, her writhing helpless limbs, her piercing screams, her neediness. Her doctor whispered *post-partum*, but Lori knew it was the reemergence of the thing that had been there since she herself was small, as small as Sarah. A spoiled segment of her DNA, a stain that became uglier as she grew. Mashed down with Zoloft and Xanax, but always there. And every time she tried to cuddle with her girl—feeling unnatural, an impostor—she knew that Sarah must have the black spot deep in her skull that would eventually blossom into the same thing. She hated her little girl for that, if for nothing else.

Then, ultimately, the unforgivable episode.

Lori didn't like to give the thing its name, the name Dr. Yang had given it so baldly. She never wanted to acknowledge it, but it haunted her. Despite the drugs that Yang got for her, the samples and the scrips, she still had the clawed fingers inside her that would clench sometimes. They were always there, waiting.

Unconsciously, Lori drifted the 'Vette into the bike lane, slowing down.

"What are you doing?" Jordan hissed. *"You'll lose him!"*

"I can't—"

"Mommy?" Sarah's voice came through the phone's tiny speaker.

"Bye, honey," she mumbled.

Lori came to a stop in the narrow bike lane, awkwardly and probably illegally straddling the sidewalk. Distantly, she felt herself end the call with her daughter. The phone went blank and slipped down between her legs.

"What's wrong?" Jordan asked.

She felt his eyes on the side of her head. Lori folded in on herself as she clutched the wheel. Her ears were ringing. The darkness felt like a drowning pressure; she imagined it like waterboarding. It was a slow build, and sometimes she could ward it off, as long as she kept the panic at bay. She knew that, she knew it well, and she knew all the tricks to slow the approach of the darkness, but all too often when it happened she ignored everything and simply succumbed. Somehow, merely knowing that she knew how to manage it made everything worse, made her helpless and powerless. It was worst when she was alone in her apartment, with no one there to talk her up, no one even to hold her. Not even her little girl.

She felt it growing, getting worse, and then—

Jarring her back to awareness, Jordan had her by the shoulders, hard.

"Hey," he said, evenly. "Listen! It's OK."

She remained rigid, and she was embarrassed that she was crying, embarrassed that this dude she barely knew had hold of her. But against all odds, he had that thing in his eyes that relaxed her muscles the tiniest bit—enough for her body to reverse course and shrink back from the precipice. She stared at him with open shock. *Him?*

"Are you on meds?" he asked.

She felt herself distantly nodding. "Mostly."

"You can't be irregular about that shit, you know that."

"How do you know—?"

"I've been through this, trust me."

She clenched her entire body, tried to ride it out, and far away she felt his hand firmly on her shoulder, heard his voice coming at her. At first, something in her recoiled, but then she went with it, feeling the warmth of his fingers, the drone of his words. The world pressed down on her as if to obliterate her, and hate seemed to seep from her every pore. She felt she might bark or cry out, but she managed to keep it in. A minor victory. And with each breath, the minor victory became a little bit larger a victory, and then the next breath was the tiniest fraction easier.

"Why'd you have to bring out a goddamn gun?" she breathed.

At length, Lori calmed, and she realized she'd been close to hyperventilating. Maybe she *had* gotten there, maybe she *had* growled. Sometimes she wasn't even aware of how hard the thing was hitting her. But this time, right now, she felt like she had a handle on it, and she realized that Jordan of all people had helped her avoid the worst. Unreal. Not that she'd acknowledge that, of course.

She let out a breath.

After a long moment, she glanced up, wiped her eyes. It wasn't *gone* or anything, but it was under control.

"OK," she breathed.

About three blocks ahead, she saw Tommy's truck. He had pulled over on the side of the road, just like the 'Vette. She felt that Jordan was still watching her, and she met his gaze, gestured forward.

"Look."

Jordan didn't notice it at first. But when he saw it, his whole demeanor changed.

"What's he doing?" he asked, voice drained of all energy.

"He knows we're following him."

"*What?*"

"He's spotted us."

"Fuck! *Fuck!*"

"So, we're done."

"Yeah, no shit?" And just like that, Jordan had returned to his basic nature. "You followed him too close! He knows this car. He knows it's *my* car. What do we do now? *What the fuck do we do now?*"

"Dude, take it easy." Easy words to say, but she herself felt as if her insides had filled with liquid fear.

Abruptly, Jordan was grabbing the backpack at his feet and gathering the phones—his and Jasmine's. He stuffed Jasmine's inside, along with his battery charger, and he palmed his own phone like a weapon, ready to go.

"What are you doing?"

"I'm getting outta here."

"What the fuck are you talking about?"

"He wants *me*. He doesn't know the first thing about you. If I'm gone, he'll just think you're a stranger in another 'Vette."

"Don't you dare leave this car!"

"Sorry."

"Jordan!"

He turned back and gave Lori a final understanding glance as he creaked his door open.

"Hey, listen," he said matter-of-factly. "You're OK. You're OK now. Believe it."

She grabbed at his jacket, clutched at him, tried to stop him, but he slipped out, let the door close, and sprinted straight into an alley behind a line of stores. Fucking gangly weirdo with his slight limp, probably injured by fear, the asshole leaving her here. Dude didn't even look back.

Lori let out a breath and shifted her gaze to the rear of Tommy's ridiculous truck, idling three blocks up.

"Well, shit."

Her phone began ringing again.

15
JASMINE

Jasmine Frank stood immobile at the corner of Tunstall and Belgrave in west Garden Grove, staring up the narrow street toward the home where her life fell apart. The taxi had been gone a full five minutes, and she'd found that she could hardly move. It was as if she was rooted to the spot.

The taxi driver had taken one of the twenty-dollar bills that the weird coin guy had given her, so that was already gone. She felt the rest of cash at her hip, in the same worn-out Safeway grocery bag that had contained Tommy's stupid brick of coins. The paper bills weighed a lot less than the metal coins, and although that was obvious, it also made her anxious. She knew she hadn't been screwed in the deal, she *knew* it, but—well, she didn't know that.

A guy offers you over two grand in cash to take some silly coins off your hands, that's gonna catch your attention, right? It certainly caught *her* attention, especially when the man named George gave her a wink and gestured for her to follow him out in front of the store, where he'd made a show of lighting up a cigarette, offering her one.

"Listen," he'd said, "the owner, Hank, he prefers to go by the book with transactions like these, draw 'em out over weeks, but I'm always open to more private deals, especially for folks like you who want to pick up some cash right away."

She'd nodded, coughing a little as he lit her cigarette for her.

"I take it the coins are really yours? I mean, I can tell you're trustworthy just looking at you, but I need to make sure."

"Well, like I told you, they were my d—"

"Your dad's, right, OK." George took a long drag, blew it out on a string of words. "Look, I'm being totally honest with you when I say that your 'dad' overvalued his collection. Truth is, there's a few good coins in there, but it's mostly low-value stuff because of grade and mintage. Also, frankly, demand. I take these on, it's a long-term deal, 'cause most of those coins have already flooded the market, you see?"

"OK."

"The only way this makes sense for me is to take the whole box from you at a flat rate, try to get what I can for the good coins and make up the difference with low-and-slow sales from the rest. You see where I'm coming from?"

She'd nodded, not at all sure what he meant, but feeling swept up in the looming promise of actual money.

George paused, and Jasmine noticed his eyes darting around behind his glasses. It was the image that stuck with her now.

Weird coin guy had offered her $2,200 cash for the box, and Jasmine had said "Yes!" so fast that the cigarette had tumbled from her lips and hit the concrete at her feet. She'd laughed apologetically and bent to pick it up, feeling a little sandy grit as she returned it to her lips and inhaled, trying to appear natural.

"Very well," George had said. "I'm going to go back inside, and I will wrap up your collection and hand it back to you, with my regrets. That will only be for the benefit of the in-store cameras. Hank is very particular, you see. I want to emphasize that our deal would happen outside the range of those cameras not because of any impropriety but rather in the interest of doing you a favor, OK?"

"Thank you, I appre—"

"At that point, you will leave the store and meet me at this spot again in ten minutes, when I will hand you an envelope containing the agreed-upon figure. I need time to gather the funds from the safe in back. Does that work for you?"

Indeed, that had worked for her.

It was a bigger wad of money than she'd ever seen in her life, the way he'd shelled it out, a mess of tens and twenties. She felt like she'd won the lottery, or like some kind of Vegas machine was spitting bills at her, except all the clanging prize bells were ringing inside her head. Fuck Tommy and his absurd collection, fuck him and his party, and for making her do this.

Fuck her life. Her *former* life.

Her two former lives!

She turned to the quiet little house to her right, on the corner. In her memory, a middle-aged couple lived there, no kids, going about the daily routine of living their lives, not bothering anybody. No one seemed to be home at the moment—curtains open on an empty living room, no activity in there, both would-be occupants away, perhaps at the swap meet or grocery shopping, whatever. She eyed the big window warily for another five minutes from her spot on the corner, watching for any semblance of life, before she finally unrooted herself from the sidewalk. She walked up the narrow path, climbed the steps, and perched on the wooden chair on the tiny porch, between two sun-bleached plastic trees anchored in buckets filled with sand.

The day had warmed up from its morning malaise, but it was humid, and she felt disgusting. She took a moment to remove her heels once more, and her feet seemed to issue twin sighs of relief. But her face and hair, her entire body, it all felt sheathed in grime. She was half-tempted to find a way into this home and use the shower. This money in her hand—it emboldened her.

Maybe the drugs were still running through her. That was possible too.

From her vantage point, she could just make out her old house. Four doors up the street, on the other side. The lawn was mostly brown, compared to its neighbors. That made sense since Jordy had been the one in charge of watering, and clearly Karl wasn't gonna take up the slack. He'd just let it die, like everything else in his miserable life. Or maybe he didn't even live there anymore! The thought detonated inside her—a hot rush. Imagine! After all those years, pulling up stakes from the home he'd destroyed, moving on to the next, leaving Gloria to—

Emotion fattened Jasmine's throat as she pictured her mom how she used to be, only now alone and lost.

Mommy.

A silver Acura turned onto the street, right in front of her. The driver was a small Asian woman—probably a mother herself—and she didn't even give Jasmine a glance, just glided up the street and parked in a driveway in the far distance. But without realizing it, Jasmine had lurched forward to the edge of the chair, her heart in her throat. Christ, she was jumpy! She couldn't believe she was here, really.

She eased back, returned her gaze to her old house. The single garage slot, the short driveway. It was a ranch layout, an aging advertisement for the '60s, that's what her mom used to say. Jasmine could remember moving into that place, how angry she was, her mom gathering shit from the trunk and walking into this foreign, sleek house—a house, not an apartment, Karl demanding Jasmine's and Jordy's thanks for rescuing them from their previous life, that horrible place to the north, but the old neighborhood was where all her friends were. She never saw a single one of them again. She'd cried herself to sleep every night.

Tears blurred her vision now, in sympathy with her younger self, and she blinked them away. The details of her bleary drive this morning—early this morning—flashed back at her, overlaid by this weird yearning for her mom. Like, as if her mom had possessed her, had flooded her with nauseating nostalgia, except it *worked*, and for the first time in weeks, she was missing her mother again. Missing Gloria Frank. *Needing* her.

Especially now.

Jesus, what would Jordy say if he knew she was here? *Oh my god.*

The whole place appeared smaller than she remembered. She looked at it like it was a childhood home, but sheesh, it hadn't even been a full year that they'd been gone. Felt like a lifetime had passed, and that was the truth, in a way. She'd been a kid when she lived here. God, the memories at that house. They'd kill her if she gave them a chance.

She lost track of time.

And didn't even notice at first when the garage door of her old house began to open.

She stopped breathing.

Nothing happened for what seemed an eternity, and then there he was, there was fucking *Karl Granger*, opening the trunk of his gray Buick—*oh, he was so fucking proud of his custom LeSabre*—whose evil trunk Jasmine could barely glimpse at the edge of the garage. No telling what he was putting in there or taking out of there, but who cared, it was really him, that gross scumbag in the flesh. Jasmine and Jordy had been gone from this place for, what, nine months, and the asshole looked exactly the same—the thin hair swept back from a brutally receded hairline, the dark jeans, the big jangly watch. She shuddered at the sensory memory of his rough hands on her thigh, his whiskey face in the hollow of her neck as she murmured in half-drunk sleep. The beer cans he'd given her on her little nightstand.

She heard the familiar hacking of the Buick coming to life, and then Karl backed the vehicle slowly down the driveway, garage door groaning shut behind him. Jasmine watched both the man and the car with revulsion—then felt abruptly exposed on this porch in her blue dress. If he came this way, he was going to see her. She darted her gaze left and right, looking for a spot to conceal herself—nothing at all—but then she saw that he was angling the Buick in the opposite direction, and he was driving off, oblivious to her.

Her heartbeat calmed, and she was left staring at the house.

Was her mom in there? Alone?

Jasmine realized she hadn't adequately prepared herself for this moment. She'd had a long time to try to forgive her mother for what she'd done—what she *hadn't* done—but it never really happened. She never found that forgiveness in her heart. Jasmine had stolen money, she'd stolen other things, and she'd secreted away holding Jordy's hand in the middle of the night, and then her life had undergone a rebirth. The truth was, she'd rarely looked back ... except in lonely dreams and quiet moments when there was no one else around.

After weeks and months had passed, she'd felt free of all those times. She felt like an adult. And eventually she felt a kind of guilt for *not* missing her mother. And *that* had turned into *actually* missing her—to the point where she felt as if she'd been fooling herself all along.

She was shaking. She was actually shaking.

She stood up out of the rigid chair and stepped off the porch, the wrapped bag of cash tight in her right fist. She watched the rear end of Karl's Buick as it turned right off Tunstall. She hurried across the street and up the sidewalk, cutting across the weedy lawn. Her heart was in her throat, *Christ!* She bounded up the front steps without thinking and went straight for the front door. Tried the knob. Locked.

She about-faced and curled around the garage to the side gate, opened it without hesitation. She clicked it shut lightly behind her and continued through the concrete side yard into the back, which was dominated by an empty pool covered by a sun-bleached canvas cover. Jasmine gave it an annoyed glance. In all their time at this house, Jasmine and Jordy had never had the opportunity to enjoy that pool, despite its promise when they moved in. It had never been filled with water.

The back door that led into the kitchen was unlocked. She entered whisper-quiet, shutting the door behind her. She listened for a full minute, hearing only her pulse in her ears. She was still shaking. The kitchen looked just as she remembered it, except more cluttered. Unkempt. There was a line of Bud bottles behind the sink, Karl's brand, left there like nobody cared. She stared at them with disgust, swallowed hard.

Her mom wouldn't have allowed that kind of mess, right? Did she even live here anymore? At that thought, a small hole began widening inside her.

She stepped through to the front room, which was also sloppy. It wasn't like Tommy's place or anything, but her mom's touch wasn't here. Pillows mashed into the sofa cushions, more empty bottles on the big square coffee table, a thin layer of dust over everything. It didn't feel right.

"Mommy?" she whispered.

She crept into the dark hallway, glancing at the door to her old bedroom. Right next to it, Jordan's. There was nothing beyond that door that she needed in her life anymore. Jordy's, either. A part of her was afraid to open those doors, afraid she might find them completely changed, full of junk, with no memory of the lives they'd contained only months ago. No one liked to feel that the ground had dropped from underneath them.

The door to the master bedroom was half-open upon darkness. Jasmine gently pushed it fully open.

Gloria Frank lay in the king-sized bed, coiled and snoring. She was covered by a thin blue sheet, but her arms and shoulders were bare, skin pale and showing age spots. The room stank vaguely of piss. Jasmine gave the whole room a series of half-glances, but she couldn't see much in the dimness. It was untidy, though—piles of clothes, empty drinking glasses, newspapers scattered about. The floor felt rough under her feet.

Her gaze returned to the bed.

A sob escaped Jasmine's throat, shocking her. She brought up her free hand and clamped it down.

Screw that! she screamed inside.

She stood next to the bedside and stared down at the woman who had birthed her. Her brain felt like a blender of images—old photographs of her mom actually smiling, real memories of horsing around on the living room floor of old apartments, stern faces at meetings with school counselors, and then the later screaming, the distant looks from faraway. The more recent memories in vivid, loud color, and the older ones faded and blurry.

Jasmine knelt down, felt her jaw clamp tight, felt the tears threatening again. She let them come.

She studied the lines of her mother's face. Here she was, right in front of her. She was older, for sure. Older than the nine or so months Jasmine had been gone. Gloria Frank was in her forties but looked and smelled much older. Sour breath was wafting out of her open mouth, but she knew that sour breath, had loved it once, found it endearing. It was worse now, though, intensified with age and wear-and-tear. The booze, the benders, the boyfriends. Particularly that last one—the current one. The monster. Same old, same old.

She debated whether to wake her mother, decided against it.

She wasn't even sure why she was here. Earlier, she'd wondered what Jordy would say (or, rather, *shout*) if he knew she was here, but really she was at a loss for words about her own presence here, in this room, at this moment—with a bundle of stolen cash in her hand, and her head filled with thoughts of escape. If walking away from everything was her aim, then why was she standing in front of her mother, in this house of horrors?

Maybe it's a goodbye, she thought. *A real, final goodbye.*

On the nightstand next to the bed, her mother's phone lit up, showing an incoming call. Jasmine stood up lightning-quick and prepared to flee. Heart pounding. But the phone was silent, and Gloria Frank continued to snore. Jasmine craned her neck to see the name on the phone, but she didn't recognize it. After half a minute, the phone went black.

Jasmine continued to stare at it.

Finally she picked it up and powered it on, quickly entering her mother's old password. Same one she used on her own phone. It still worked. The home screen came up, waiting for her. She swallowed and went to the text app, scrolling through the conversations. She saw her aunt's name in there, the old harpie, and a couple of her bitch cousins. Some of her mom's old friends, and a few people she couldn't place at all. Jasmine flicked through them impatiently, then went to the call history—and, yeah, maybe this was the reason she was here. The reason she'd gotten in someone's car and headed east, the reason she'd hopped in the taxi.

She swiped through the first few calls, and there it was.

Jasmine's phone number.

She had called her mother early this morning—there was her new number, with a timestamp of 1:14 a.m. She'd left a message. Jasmine pressed the icon to play it and brought the phone to her ear.

" ... *Hi Mommy, it's Jazz ... yeah, it's Jazz ....*" Jesus, she'd actually been giggly. "*I ... I just wanted to call and ... I don't know ... I ... Mommy, I miss you.*"

Her voice sounded faraway, trilling high like she was in the grip of it. Embarrassing. There was a long pause, during which Jasmine could make out that awful music playing last night. It sounded like she was in a back bedroom, maybe Tommy's, or even outside the house. The back yard? When her voice came back, it was warbly with emotion.

"*I know things were bad, Mommy ... but I know we shouldn't have left like we did.*"

Jasmine watched her mother snore. There were no more tears.

"*I was hoping you could pick me up. I don't want to be here. I don't know where Jordy went. I just want to see you. It doesn't have to be for long. The address is—*"

And now Jasmine had the sensory memory of it, there in Tommy's back yard, spinning around to find numbers somewhere, spinning and giggling through the pain and the shame, only there weren't any numbers back there, there were only strangers, and so Jasmine had spoken the first address that came into her head.

Jasmine stabbed at the phone to end the call.

Shit.

She'd given *her own fucking address*. The apartment.

All those times, Jordy laying out their new rules about their new IDs and documents, their new lives three years older. He'd had to lay down nearly five hundred dollars of their combined savings for all of it, cheap apparently, through the guy the landlord had turned him on to. The new SIM cards for their phones; crushing the old ones had felt so scary good that one day out on the sidewalk, saying good riddance to their old lives, and Jasmine had promised to be smart, to *never call their mom again*, they just couldn't take the chance. Shit, Karl probably had a connection on the Garden Grove police department who could run a number past the carrier and get a location, maybe not exact but close enough, and they'd be screwed.

It had worked for nine months.

Jasmine placed her mom's phone back on the nightstand and left the room. She walked straight through her old house and out the front door.

16
JORDAN

Jordan Frank sprinted up the alley like a madman, skirting the edge of a long peach stucco wall and emitting a long string of expletives. He reached the end of the wall, which gave way to a small corridor leading into a neighborhood, and nearly stumbled headfirst into a jagged edge of exposed cinder block. He hid himself and glared back down the alley, waiting for Tommy's truck to come roaring into it like some demonic behemoth.

Fuck, fuck, fuck!

How did he always screw things up so completely? Look at him, bumbling about, everything going into the toilet. Tommy was on to him, he'd (willfully) lost his fucking 'Vette, and he was no closer to finding Jazz than he'd been when he woke up.

The truck didn't appear in the mouth of the alley.

Still shaking, he glanced around, trying to come up with a plan. Should he keep sprinting up the alley, toward whatever his grim future held, or should he head into this neighborhood, maybe eventually find his way back home? Where the hell was he? Even after nine months living in this godforsaken city, he still didn't know the area all that well. The apartment couldn't be too far away. They hadn't driven *that* many miles from Tommy's, and when they had, it had been in the general direction of their place. He was probably a mile away from the apartment, diagonally. Somewhere to the southeast.

Jordan shifted to the left to get a better view of Bristol. His Corvette was still idling in the bike lane.

He'd given up his 'Vette! He'd actually done that.

He spat out another vivid, multisyllabic string of profanities and considered running back to the car. No! He couldn't do that shit, wouldn't in a million years. He couldn't get back in there with Lori. As he pushed off the wall toward the neighborhood, he caught a final glimpse of Lori's head in the driver's seat.

Goddamn it, he thought miserably. *I'm sorry, OK?*

She was better now, he'd got her through her little episode. He supposed he could feel good about that.

Lori Holst, of all people! He hardly knew the woman except through

Jason Bovberg

Jazz, and yet calming her down from her sudden episode had been like muscle memory. Brought back all those years with his mom, when she'd descend into a twitching mood—early on, her clutching him to her like a teddy bear, she'd been so needy! Seemed like once a week she'd confine him to her room, pressed into her, almost fetal, the sensation of her shivering abdomen against his back, until she was functional again. When he was older, he'd go to her every time he recognized the onset of her symptoms—the pitch change in her voice, the slightly more wide-open eyes, the involuntary swallowing. He was the only one who could talk her down. Sometimes she was too far gone, and he couldn't do a fucking thing, and he'd be left shaking and crying in his own room, under his thin covers, holding on to a nightmare memory of her contorted face and her rage. One time they'd even taken her to the hospital. She'd ended up staying under observation for three days. But most of the time, he could bring her back to earth. He knew the words.

He'd known them for Lori. They'd all come back. And they'd worked.

But doing it had also brought back all those negative recollections of his mom, reminding him of what he'd escaped, of what had come before this new life, for whatever it was worth. And when he was done soothing Lori, yeah, he'd freaked out. Sure, there was the Tommy thing, imminent death and all that, but that wasn't the whole story. He just couldn't be in that car with her anymore.

So sue him.

Shit, man, it seemed like everyone was depressed these days. It was like everyone he encountered had some kind of imbalance going on, whether it was simple ugly moodiness or full-blown bipolar mania. It followed him wherever he went. And the kids today, don't get him started about the kids, they seemed to crave the attention of depression, glomming onto it to elicit fake empathy, cutting themselves or self-medicating or self-immolating by way of social media—and then drowning in real depression the result of self-fulfilling prophecy. He was like ground zero, the starting point, of the depression generation.

All of them except Jasmine.

He never had to help her, he never had to be her crutch.

Jordan caught his breath, sweating. He ambled through the musty corridor and came out onto a boring street in the middle of a '50s-era neighborhood filled with modest bungalows, looked like the street must be populated entirely by seniors, the *Leave It to Beaver* generation. Monotonous, manicured, silent—zzzzzz.

Anonymous.

And that was fine by him.

He walked serenely east, eventually crossing the asphalt onto the north side of the street for the shade from the mature trees lining the sidewalk. He only wanted to lose himself right now. That's all. If only for a half hour. Maybe Tommy hadn't seen him, maybe he could get on the right side of this shitshow if he just gave it some time, some perspective. Let things take care of themselves.

The street sprawled off into the distance, more of the same kinds of squat, diminutive homes. Abruptly, he felt the weight of Jazz's backpack hanging from his left hand—

—*(the weight of the pistol)*—

—and his phone gripped in his right. He cast a fevered gaze ahead, saw a little concrete alley a block ahead. He made his way toward it, taking deep breaths. He felt like the most obvious, desperate junkie shambling along this street, and he imagined the collective distaste of every inhabitant watching from their windows, tapping 9-1-1 on their phones. He kept his head down and moved along, minding his own business.

He got to the southbound alley. It was a grungy deserted path between homes, littered with trash, including a filthy blue mattress that had somehow been torn completely in half. The path seemed to run the length of the entire neighborhood and was bordered by a hodgepodge array of fencing materials—chainlink, split-rail, cedar-plank, cinder block, stucco, some pristine, some dilapidated. He spotted a jacaranda tree hanging over one of the fences and ambled that way. He sat against a cinder-block wall in the shade of the jacaranda, whose indigo flowers always reminded him of his dead father, gone so long now that Jordan couldn't even remember the sound of his voice. A broken tube TV sat across from him, staring at him like an accusation.

"Fuck you," he told it.

He remained motionless for fifteen minutes, obsessively checking his phone for any word from Jazz, growling deep in his throat each time he found nothing. He was also watching for any actual signs of life over the fences around him. Despite his paranoia, no one seemed to be paying attention to him.

When he felt anonymous and safe, he opened the backpack and took out the pink-and-white leopard-print case containing the pistol. He turned it over and over in his hands.

Chrrriiiist, he knew this case all too well.

Fumbling it down from their mom's high closet shelf, giggling with Jazz as they horsed around with it, playing cowboy and squaw prisoner like in that John Wayne movie that played on channel 5. Mom never knew, and they never asked her why she had it—until much later when she actually showed it to them like some artifact from her youth. He could still recall her climbing the stepladder to reach the box it was hidden in. He and Jazz exchanging wide-eyed glances. *Were they in trouble? For stupid games they'd played as kids, with little to no supervision? What was the statute of limitations?* No, this was different, this was about Karl. Of course it was about Karl, the degenerate. Their mother spotted with bruises (even a black eye once), crying in the night, drinking till she almost constantly smelled like whiskey. That one night, a night Karl was gone to Riverside, bringing the pistol down to show them, and it had felt sorta good, the feel of the family, the camaraderie, as if to say, yeah, we got a problem here, let's tackle it together—fucking armed, man! The next week, the pistol was packed deep in the closet again, and their mom was back to watching the monster assault and belittle Jordan.

That was why Jazz had stolen the gun, he knew.

Wasn't like it was a mystery.

Wiping his stupid eyes, he glanced around a final time, then opened the case. He took the pistol from its confines, felt the weight of it in his fist. It had seemed larger, of course, when he was a kid. But it was like a toy now, tiny and blunt-nosed. Fucking thing was *purple.* Looked like a high-end squirt pistol. It appeared brand-new, buried away for so long, free of dust and wear. He rooted around in the case's side pockets and came away with three seven-round magazines still full of ammo. He doubted his mom had ever fired the damn thing. He loaded one of the magazines with a soft click, made sure the grip safety was engaged. He was just about to slide the pistol into the waistband of his jeans—but then thought better of it. Imagine a cop searching him, finding him with that. He quickly stashed the gun back into its case, along with the extra mags, and shoved the whole thing back into Jazz's pack.

Before standing up again, he checked his phone for any texts or calls. Nothing.

Jesus, Jazz, where in the name of fuck are you?

Five minutes later, he'd found his way out of the sleepy neighborhood and onto Bishop, headed east. He figured he'd get to Flower and then cut straight down home. He wasn't sure now why he'd ever left the apartment. Obviously that's where Jazz would go the moment she woke up or whatever. Now that his head didn't feel like it was swaddled in a wet turban lined with spikes, he could imagine—without gritting his molars—that his sister had gone home with some asshole and was now waking up to realize that she'd left her shit behind at Tommy's. *She* was probably worried about *him*, knowing that he'd be beside himself.

He stuck to shadowed sidewalks, feeling safe on the residential streets. Took him twenty more minutes but he was finally in sight of the apartment building. He paused, watching it for a few minutes. Looked as normal as any other day.

He walked nonchalantly up the crooked path to the front entrance, his eyes darting this way and that. A bored Asian kid on the top floor, the third, was watching him from a window. Jordan had seen the boy around a couple times. Fat sullen kid. The rest of the flat façade appeared empty of life, just messy mismatched curtains and twisted blinds and clear glass looking in on stained, shadowed popcorn ceilings.

Idly checking the mailbox, Jordan paused in the mildewed foyer, feeling at ease. Jazz was probably upstairs right now.

After a moment, he went to the dark stairs and began climbing them. His footfalls echoed back at him. He reached the second floor and stepped into the hallway leading to their apartment. No life whatsoever. All he could hear was a TV, probably on the floor above him, Lori's floor. He kept walking until he came to their door. It was exactly as he'd left it—unlocked in case Jazz came home.

He pushed the door open, his right hand touching the backpack where the weight of the pistol case was. Fat lot of good it would do him, but it gave him a bit of comfort.

"Jazz?" he called, hoping against hope.

Utter silence.

The door clicked shut behind him.

He stopped at the kitchen, found the note he'd written to his sister. Backpack still hanging from his shoulder, he checked his phone again. Despair settled over him again. He aimlessly stabbed at his phone, wanting it to do something more helpful.

What now?

Seized by an idea, he brought Jazz's pack to the counter and dug out Jasmine's phone. He typed in their mom's birthdate for the passcode—a passcode he knew his sister had used years earlier—and the home screen appeared as if by a miracle.

"Oh my god!" he blurted.

He ran quickly through the texts, stuff from people at work, mindless crap from Lori, nothing much there—nothing from today. Then the calls. Nothing there either. He stared blankly at the screen, all that promise so suddenly dashed, and he was left with nothing again. Fuck, what was he supposed to do? Would he have to go to the police after all? Was it worth it, to expose themselves to everything they'd done to get away? To take that chance? It had only been a few hours since she'd disappeared, right? Or at least since he'd become aware she was gone. Did it make sense to risk everything? If not now, when?

Wait, he thought.

He clicked through to her outgoing calls—and there it was.

Jasmine had called their mom. Early this morning.

1:14 a.m.

He stared at the call log without breathing, then stuffed Jazz's phone back in her pack.

Before he could even flinch, someone grabbed him from behind.

"What the fuck!" he screamed before a hand clamped over his mouth.

The weight of his assailant crushed him to the ground, blasting the breath out of him in a *whuuffff!* He grunted a glottal cough, tried to suck air. Panic engulfed him. A knee pressed hard on his spine, and he writhed like a bug.

"I got you, you rat bastard," a voice whispered at his ear.

Jordan tried to reach for the pistol in its case, but it was no use. The last thing he saw before his life ended in a wet slap of blood against the gritty hallway floor was the worn strap of Jazz's backpack.

17
LORI

Lori Holst forced a smile as she watched Sarah swing on the monkey bars. Daniel in his Acura SUV had glided out of sight ten minutes ago, and—to her relief—the drop-off had gone much better than usual. No tears, no yelling, no acrimony.

Her muscles were relaxing.

The day looked good.

Right?

Her daughter was wearing bright primary colors, dark yellow-ribboned pigtails bouncing playfully. The girl kept screaming, *"Mommy, look!"* and Lori kept smiling and nodding from her perch on the bench. She praised Sarah over and over again, and she was trying *so, so hard* not to be annoyed as fuck. And she *hated* feeling that way! She had a love in her heart for Sarah that was stronger than anything else in her life. Beyond Sarah, what else was there?

Lori was still processing everything that had happened with Jordan an hour earlier. Jesus, that guy, what a disaster, and yet she was as conflicted about him as she was, at this moment, about Sarah. Jordan was petulant, impulsive, and idiotic, but he'd also—in the moment her episode threatened to seize her—calmed her like a drug. Another way of looking at it: This morning Lori had been absolutely fine, relaxing in anticipation of a few hours with her girl, and then Jordan had come in like a wrecking ball and laid waste to her day, eventually propelling her toward a manic episode.

Either way, he'd abandoned the 'Vette at the perfect moment, whisking away into that back alley and essentially vanishing—precisely when the thug in the black truck might have pounced on them. In the immediate wake of Jordan sprinting away from the car, Lori had taken the call from her daughter and—somehow—spoken smilingly with her girl as she cruised on past the truck, feeling Tommy's eyes on the side of her face as she moved along. She'd watched the truck in her rearview as it pulled out to follow, and then, when she'd made the pulse-pounding right turn onto 17th, he'd made the *left*, his big tires screeching away, and she'd let loose with a *whoop!* that left Sarah speechless and giggling on the other end of the sweaty phone in her hand.

"I'm just so excited to see you!" Lori had squealed.

And now she was here.

She kept an almost constant eye on Flower, which ran adjacent to the park. Jordan's yellow Corvette stuck out like a sore thumb in the little parking lot that fed off the street. Lori predicted that her dreams for the next few years would be haunted by that Tommy character's monstrous truck returning, spying the 'Vette, and rolling right over her, squashing her beneath its stupid tires. She'd had barely a glimpse of Tommy himself as he'd stalked from his home to his vehicle, and her lips still curled with distaste, recalling that thick hoodlum.

"Mommy, look!"

"I see, sweetie."

"Mommy, come push me!"

"Not right now, sweetie."

She fished around in her bag and brought out her cigarettes—shit, only three left. She put one to her lip and lit it, inhaling bountifully. Christ, what a morning. She didn't need this kind of crap in her life. She had enough on her plate with Steve, seeing if that developed into anything despite his seeming inability to enjoy anything they did together. She had plans to take him to see some funk band at Malone's later tonight, after he finished at the restaurant, see if she could get him drunk, see what might happen. Total role reversal, she knew, the girl pushing alcohol on the guy. But goddammit, she was *looooong* overdue to get laid, and the past couple hours were the straw that broke her vagina's back. Unfortunately, given the opportunity, Steve would usually rather toss himself on her couch with a beer and turn on a game. Any game. Didn't seem to matter to him which sport, which team. The infuriating, clichéd reality of her life.

Lori felt like she'd kept herself together over the years. The way into her pants wasn't exactly like an Agatha Christie mystery. She liked to think she made it a relatively simple process for would-be suitors. She was fucking attractive, for chrissakes.

On top of all that, it was the goddamn weekend! A woman with a shit job—data processing at a waste-disposal company, of all things—is going to need to let off a little steam now and then. She's going to want to be treated like a lady. Take her out on the town, open doors for her, buy her a treat, smile at her like you crave her, share some wine with her, and then at the end of a nice evening, take her home and fuck her sideways.

Give a shit!

She stabbed her cigarette into the metal bench, let the butt fall to the ground. She glanced over at the street again, watching the cars whiz by, all those lives spinning about, and here was hers, for all it was worth, plopped on a bench in the wake of a miserable morning, hoping things got better from here. After all, she was with her angel, and it was still early on a Saturday. Lots could still—

A small yellow taxi came ripping up the street. Didn't see those very often, in this part of town. As she began to glance away, the taxi's tires screeched across the asphalt.

"*What the*—?" Lori mumbled.

Lori could just make out a woman's voice squealing. A face popped out of an open window.

"Lori? *Lori!*"

"You're kidding me," Lori said, standing. "*Jasmine?*"

Jasmine wrestled her way out of the taxi and bent over to pay the old brown driver. As the car took off, Jasmine—yeah, it was her, right there, in the flesh, *holy shit!*—came hurrying up the path toward her, barefoot, a Safeway grocery bag and a pair of heels swinging from her hand. Her friend drew closer, and Lori saw that she looked a little worse for wear—makeup faded and smeared, eyes bloodshot, hair a mess. She was wearing some kind of blue party dress, clearly from the shindig the night before. She came right up to Lori, glancing left and right.

"Sweet Jesus, girl, are you all right?" Lori said.

"Where's Jordy?"

"I don't know, but I know he's out of his fucking mind looking for you. Where have you *been*?"

Jasmine glanced over at the 'Vette, parked conspicuously against the curb. "He's not here?"

"Oh! No, he jumped out of the car while we were looking for you."

"What? You were looking for me?" Jasmine was obviously exhausted, and now all energy seemed to seep out of her. Her shoulders sagged, and she began to cry.

"What is it?" Lori said, taking her friend into an embrace. "What happened?"

"Lori, I think I fucked up."

Jasmine initiated a word dump—typical of her, except Lori usually experienced these from a happy Jasmine, an excited Jasmine, a giddily tipsy-with-life Jasmine. This Jasmine was hungover, wiped out, defeated, even a little fragrant. The words came spilling out of her on weary exhalations tinged with fear.

The two of them sat down, perched on the bench, holding hands, and Jasmine gushed on, mumbling one moment and almost pleading the next, about the party at Tommy's, creative substances passed around, the disorientation, the bleary drive west to In-N-Out Burger of all places, the cold sleep huddled up to the take-out window, and in the frigid morning the realization that she'd taken something from Tommy, but she hadn't thought *that* through *at all*, and *shit what was she gonna do?*

Lori felt a lurch in the pit of her stomach at that last point—particularly as Jasmine told her what the thing was that she'd stolen, and that she'd dumped it the first chance she got, on impulse.

"Oh, shit, sweetie."

"I know."

Jasmine looked as if she had more to say, was on the verge of it, but then bit her lip.

"Well, he knows you took it," Lori told her. "He's looking for you. He's not happy."

"How do you know *that?*"

"We followed him. We thought he took you."

"You talked to him?"

"No, we—we overheard him."

Jasmine stared at her, uncomprehending. Then, "Well, I'm gonna get the coins back, I'm gonna come clean, it's not worth it."

"I'm not sure he'll underst—"

"I have to find Jordy."

"He's got your purse, by the way. Your phone, everything."

"Oh thank Christ."

"So what now?"

"Oh my gosh, is that Sarah?" Jasmine wiped her eyes, finding her smile.

Sarah was sitting at the far end of the little playground now, listlessly sifting sand through her fingers. She glanced over at the mention of her name, then went back to her playtime.

Taken aback by Jasmine's interruption, Lori stuttered a bit, then said, "That's my girl."

Jasmine was already off the bench and stepping into the sand. She swayed herself over to the little girl and plunked herself directly in front of her, a big smile, eyes glittering post-tears—"Hey girlfriend, whatcha up to?"—and Lori marveled that she could turn it on like that. Jasmine began engaging Sarah in an animated conversation, and soon enough they were on the seesaw, Sarah giggling and squealing.

Lori glanced down at the grocery bag a couple of times before finally opening it and seeing for herself the modest bricks of cash. Ah, Jesus, she'd really done it.

For all Jordan's fears that his sister had been abducted or whatever, that she was in the hands of someone nefarious, and hideous things were being done to her—that all amounted to nothing. Jasmine had simply been swept away on a smack bender in the middle of the night, probably had just been hungry as hell and talked some poor schmuck into craving a midnight burger with her. All of which would be fine, and easily explained, were it not for the bag sitting next to her, and the knowledge of both Tommy and Jordan still out there, both of them with this crazy girl on their brains.

Lori watched Jasmine play with Sarah, and a knot began to form, way down deep.

"Jasmine?"

"Uh huh?" Laughing.

"Yeah, um, this is serious, I mean I think you have to take care of this. Like, now."

Jasmine gave her a long look.

"I know," she said.

"Can you call Tommy or something? You can use my phone."

The seesaw came to a stop, and Jasmine maneuvered it gently so that Sarah could climb off safely. She gave the girl a sad smile—"I gotta go talk to your momma"—and returned to the bench while Sarah skipped happily to the swings. She let out an enormous, almost comical sigh.

"I need a shower, and I need some sleep, and I need a Tylenol, and I just want this stupid day to be over," she said.

"OK, but let's take care of this. I'll help you." She swallowed hard, nearly biting off the last word.

"Jordy probably hates me."

"He's just worried about you."

Jasmine made a face, like *What else is new?*

"Can we go home?" Jasmine asked. "Maybe Jordy's there? Maybe he went back? Then I can get my phone and call Tommy."

"I'll drive."

In the car, Jasmine descended further into a funk as Sarah babbled from the tiny storage area behind the seats, happily crammed in there. The girl found it hilarious. Jasmine tried to engage with Sarah, but her heart seemed no longer in it. Lori watched the neighborhood flow by, feeling Jasmine's mood go further south by the moment. She'd never seen her friend this way. It was disconcerting, to say the least. Finally, as the 'Vette approached their apartment building, Jasmine broke off from Sarah and faced front, taking a big lungful of air, girding herself for what lay ahead.

"Jordy's gonna hate me," she said again.

"No he won't," Lori said. "Trust me, he'll be so happy to see you, he'll shit himself."

Jasmine shook her head. "We're gonna have to move again."

"What? Why?"

No response. Eyes averted.

Lori pulled into the rear parking lot—watching for any sign of Tommy's truck—and found Jordan's numbered space. Jasmine helped Sarah out of the car, and the girl danced around her like a kid sister. Lori locked the car and handed Jasmine the keys, and then they made their way into the building. They went quickly up the stairs, hoping against hope that Jordan had made his way back. Finding him was the first step to making everything right.

From a distance, from the end of the hall, Lori sensed something was wrong.

Sarah skipped on ahead, toward Jasmine's door. She'd been in there a couple times, knew exactly which one.

"Mommy, the door's open!"

She pushed at the door with her little hand, swinging it wide. She made no sound, just stood there staring.

"Sarah!" Lori shouted.

Everything stuttered to slow motion.

It was Jasmine who screamed first.

18
MARK

She'd come into the store like something out of a wet dream—yeah, he remembered that so well, it was like a hot knife to the dick. She'd walked right in with her calf-bouncy confidence and had started perusing the shelves without a care in the world, like she was feminine ideal personified. She wore faded yellow tennis shoes and mismatched ankle socks. Two lovely creamy legs reached up to fringed jeans short-shorts. There was potential in those legs, in so many ways. Didn't need no fancy gym, either—he already imagined helping her out in his garage, private coaching, calculating the lunges, the squats. Up above the legs, a funky purple blouse, looked secondhand but totally her. She had her dirty blonde hair up in a scrunchie that was the same yellow as her shoes. Her face looked fresh out of puberty, little ski-jump nose, a bit of wear to the skin as if she'd seen some weather or some psychological abuse, and he could tell at once that she preferred the light-makeup look, tried hard to make it look like she didn't wear any, or maybe she *wasn't* wearing any, like legitimately, and that might've been the thing that really did it for him.

He was a goner.

Right away, Mark Pellegro had known what the girl was at the store for—a kickstart, a new beginning, a rebirth—and it was as if God himself had placed him in her path. He was the man with the plan, the dude with the food. Food for the body, you know, and by extension, food for the soul.

Exactly what she needed.

His approach didn't work with a lot of girls. Even he would admit that. He wasn't blind to his flaws. It's not like he spent a lot of time admiring himself in the mirror. But there were some girls whose innocence allowed, at least, the approach. Those were the girls who were hypnotized enough by his best feature—his eyes, naturally—to fall into conversation. And once that was done, he could talk the talk. He could certainly do that, better than anyone else at the store.

That day, he'd made his approach, he'd initiated the conversation, and she had succumbed to his charms.

"Hey there," she'd said.

"Good morning, how you doing today?"

"Nice hat." Like she meant it!

"Thanks!"

"Looking for a fresh start?"

She'd given him a curiously pleased look. "As a matter of fact, I am."

He'd listened to her, all thoughtful, had digested her needs (which were exactly what he'd anticipated), and had smoothly laid out his recommendations for a regimen and then—

—and then Tommy had moseyed onto the floor from the back.

Turned out, Tommy knew the girl from way back. Name was Jasmine, must've had hippie folks. She and Tommy had gone to school together, over in Garden Grove or wherever, what were the odds? *Fuck!*

He'd wandered over to the register to brood and watch the two of them flirt and bat at each other, and …

Who cared now, right? The girl was a spewer, had fucked up his ride, had splattered her goop all over the Jetta's passenger seat and onto the fabric floor, and he wasn't gonna get that smell out no matter how many cleaning materials he used or how many times he went over the cloth with a steam vac. That had been his morning, not sleeping more than three winks, then back to scrubbing the seat with an array of Tuff Stuff, Chemical Guys, and Black Diamond cleaners and sucking it all up with an industrial vac at the self-service place on 3rd. And the vomit stench still radiated from the seat, goddammit! That shit wasn't coming out of his car without a replacement of the seat cushion itself, and what were the odds of salvaging a pristine cushion, considering the age of his prized VW?

"Yes! *Yes!* I can still smell it," Kayla said. "OK? Get over it, dude. Or at least shut up about it. I could give a shit about your car. I care about that girl. I care about *finding* that girl."

He shook his head as he made the turn out onto Main, heading for 17th. He adjusted his hat, glanced at her.

"It's been *hours*," he reminded her, as gently as his gritted teeth would let him.

He had to talk respectfully around Kayla, obviously. She was Tommy's arm candy—*well, more than that now, after, what, two years?*—and he acknowledged that. But sometimes she could be one of the dumbest bitches he knew, and that was saying something. It wasn't just because she stuck with Tommy despite his obvious assholery, or the fact that he'd probably plinked and dallied with twenty or thirty other women since he and Kayla had started; it was that her worldview was distinctly centered around Tommy, protecting him, doing anything in the world for him, everything else be damned. She'd become a forcefield around the guy, and very few people could get past her. And he couldn't see any possible benefit she could be deriving from it. They lived in near squalor, he treated her like creamed shit, she didn't have any real friends. She seemed to despise everyone she encountered, including Mark.

"The chances of us finding her like this are about a zillion to one," he said.

"Fuck you with your chances. She's on foot with no money. Ten bucks says she's still in that parking lot, begging for food."

Kayla was a mad mix of ingredients that all added up to an enigma whom he could barely interact with. He avoided her at parties, just watched her from afar. He didn't want to get entangled in all that, get on her bad side and therefore *Tommy's* bad side. He was a hands-off kind of guy. Which made it all the more sweatily weird that he suddenly had to ferry Kayla over to Westminster in his vomit-spattered once-primo '06 Jetta, five-speed manual. He sighed, recognizing that this kind of thing was his lot in life—spending his Saturday driving his boss's woman around in his ruined car, in search of sparkly vomit girl.

Like he was any better than Kayla, doing her bidding without question or complaint.

Mark let loose with an irritated growl.

"You say one more word about the puke," Kayla said, "I will twist your balls in a knot."

He shut his trap, scooted his ruined car along Westminster Boulevard. All the Jetta's windows were down, and that was helping, but the stomach-acid undervibe wouldn't soon leave his nostrils. It was psychological now, he knew—just knowing it had happened three feet away.

One traffic signal at a time, they got closer to the In-N-Out. He felt a hunger pang, despite everything. He could go for a burger.

"It's like Little Vietnam over here," Kayla said.

Mark looked at her. He couldn't recall a time when he'd shared more than pleasantries with Kayla.

"It's called Little Saigon." Stopped at a signal, he looked out on the sea of Asian businesses, pho shops, markets. "Part of it, anyway. You didn't know that?"

She shrugged, not really caring.

"Largest Vietnamese population outside Vietnam, actually. Kind of amazing."

"SoCal has changed so much." Spoken with an echo of regret.

"What are you, Republican?"

"*Fuuuuck* no." She gave him a snarl. "Jesus."

"Make America Hate Again?"

"I'm just saying ... it's different from when we were little, right?"

"Sure, I guess." He stepped on the gas. "More interesting, more diverse."

"Doesn't *bother* me."

He watched her. "I don't know, sounds like it maybe does a little."

"I mean, they could try to at least speak the language ... assimilate better."

"Ho-ly *shit*, you *are* a Republican. You're a closet Republican!"

"Shut the fuck up, dude." She stared hard at him from the passenger seat. "That shit ain't funny."

He laughed. "I'm just messin' with you."

"Can't you have a normal fuckin' conversation?"

He shook his head. "Nope."

They moved on past an old Stater Brothers, a couple apartment blocks, a seedy motel, then more strip malls full of beauty salons, donut shops, gun outlets, teeth-whitening shops, day spas, locksmiths. He had to admit, talking to Kayla—actually talking to her—was making him feel a little better about things. There was no denying that she was beautiful in her way, her chocolate skin, her flashing eyes, her quick mouth. Even though she'd never ever be his, it was fun to spend time with her. Sorta like test-driving a car, maybe, or wandering through a model home.

"So, this girl," he said, breaking the silence as they idled at the next stop.

Kayla side-eyed him. "Yeah?"

"Did she do something? I mean, before the vomit?"

"I don't know. Why?"

"Well, otherwise, why are you doing this? It ain't because of the puke."

"You tell me—why'd Tommy ask you to keep tabs on her?"

He started to shrug. "I don't—"

"Don't *even* do that, man," she said. "Tell me the fuckin' truth."

He paused, glancing to his left at a wine-colored Honda minivan idling next to him. It was filled with a family that appeared to be heading to the beach. The fat brunette mother in her stretched one-piece was gesticulating wildly about something, and the father sat mute behind the wheel, gazing straight ahead. The two kids in the back were zombified by something playing on a screen, their eyes dull. The boy had a thumb in his mouth.

"Maybe he had his eye on her, I don't know."

"Did he or didn't he?"

"Yeah, OK, yeah, he did, shit! He asked me to keep her away from her brother, I don't know why."

"He wanted in her pants."

"Hell if I know."

"Why else would—?"

Kayla's phone began to ring—a high-pitched jangle like one of those old landlines. She dug the phone out of her pocket and stared at the screen.

"Speak of the devil," she said, stabbing at the phone and bringing it to her ear. "Hey." Voice dead.

Mark could clearly hear Tommy over the tinny speaker, his voice a flinty growl. It was the voice Mark dreaded, the raised tone he'd never had directed at him specifically but had heard aimed at unfortunate others.

"I shit you not, I'm sitting on Bristol getting a fucking speeding ticket, and that asshole's Corvette is parked a couple blocks behind me."

"What, like now?"

"Yes, now. They're fucking following me. I think it's both of them."

"What do you mean, 'both of them'?"

"Both of them, the runt and the sister. I think she's even driving, that little bi—"

"They're both there? Are you sure?" Kayla glanced over at him.

Tommy said something he couldn't make out.

"And you're pulled over?" Kayla asked. "Like, there's a cop there?"

"Yeah."

"Well, Tommy—" Kayla glanced over at Mark, her expression going *Duh*. "—tell the cop what they did! They probably have the coins in the car!"

Mark thought, *Coins?*

"*Fuck that, I'm going after them,*" Tommy's voice warbled.

"Wait, why are they following you?"

Silence from the other end of the line, then, "*That's what I'm telling you, Kay, I have no fucking clue why.*"

"Are you sure it's them?"

"*Who else has a Corvette like that? Looks like a fucking DeWalt drill.*"

Mark motored forward when the light changed. The family in the van continued on toward the beach, and he lost sight of them.

"*Wait, someone got out of the car.*"

"Well, is it them? Is it one of them?"

"*I can't tell.*"

Mark envisioned Jasmine then, stepping out of the car behind Tommy. In his rearview. He tried to picture her fully. He remembered her from the night before, of course. His memory of the brother was more indistinct. When the two of them had walked in, Mark had initially experienced a flash of adrenaline, an inner *whooooop!*, because Jasmine had preceded her brother, and she'd been decked out in that fucking dress that showed off her legs and shoulders, all that potential, and her face young and innocent, and for a split second he thought the world had turned his way. But then the brother followed right behind, and Mark had turned back to his conversation with Derek, just wanting to lose himself, and Tommy had nearly crashed into him, and it was the second time his boss had neatly snipped away any chance Mark might have with the girl from the store. Tommy'd whispered at him, Derek too, his stupid plan, like something out of some high school party. *Derek, you make sure she gets the stuff, not right away, work up to it, OK? Pelly, you just keep an eye on the girl, keep her away from that runt brother, right? I've got Alicia taking care of Jordan.* Tommy's breath already had that metallic reek from Derek's gravel. So that was what it was gonna be: Mark was gonna help Tommy fuck the blue girl. Ultimately get her to Derek, get her smoothed out, get her pliant.

Jesus, his life.

But as he eavesdropped on Kayla and Tommy now, it became clear to him that this wasn't about all that. Something else had happened last night. Something beyond the pre-rapey drama he'd taken part in with Tommy. Had that girl or her brother actually had the titanium balls to steal something from Tommy Strafe? Mark had heard of his boss's fabled coin collection, handed down from his father. Bunch of old shit, apparently pretty valuable. Mark himself had never seen it. It wasn't like he and Tommy were close, thank Christ. He just worked for him. Whitham had been the one that told him about the collection, years back, and he always assumed it was a myth. All talk. Had dismissed it early on. Who cared about a bunch of old coins in the digital age?

"Pull over," Kayla said now, looking at him.

"Where?"

She didn't answer him, went on talking to Tommy. "You want us to go back home?"

Mark felt his insides seize.

He gestured wildly, shaking his head. He did *not* want Tommy to know he'd swept Jasmine away from his house last night, possibly with stolen coins or whatever. *Jesus Fuck, had he been Jasmine's getaway driver?*

"What?" Kayla said, frowning, covering her phone with her hand.

"Don't tell him you're with me," he whispered back.

"I'm with Pellegro," she said into the phone, smiling.

"You're with Pelly? What in the—"

"We were just out trying to find her. Mark took her out for a burger last night and left her there."

There was the briefest of silences before Tommy went apocalyptic with shouted questions. Kayla actually held the phone away from her ear. She watched Mark's reaction with a malicious twinkle in her eye. *Oh you fucking bitch.*

"Hold on," he heard Tommy say over the phone. *"They're on the move. Here they come. Lemme see."*

Silence.

Mark watched Kayla.

"Huh! It's not them. Shit. Some girl, never seen her before."

19
SARAH

When Sarah Holst pushed the cracked-open door and began to step across the threshold, she immediately saw Jasmine's weird brother Jordan sprawled on the floor, all crooked, next to the kitchen counter. Her first instinct was to giggle, as if he was teasing her, but then she saw all the red, and it looked like thick spilled paint, and for a long moment all she thought was that someone was going to be in trouble and at least she was far enough away to not be blamed. Nothing else registered. Sarah went blank, goggle-eyed, mouth slightly open.

Then she felt Jasmine and Mommy behind her, and Jasmine began to scream.

The sound of that scream—warbling, hysterical, hoarse—scared Sarah so badly that she felt her bladder nearly go loose. She dropped her stuffed bear, felt her limbs start to shake, then bent to pick up the bear and squeeze it to her. With her other hand, she reached out for Mommy's leg, but it wasn't there. Mommy was clutching at Jasmine, who was falling to the floor even as she surged forward. Mommy looked like she was trying to keep Jasmine standing.

"What happened?" Sarah asked, but no one heard her.

Mommy held on to Jasmine as she crawled toward Jordan. Jasmine was crying so hard that her voice was a hard, prolonged gasp, like a screaming whisper.

Abruptly, Sarah collided with the hallway wall behind her, making her bite her tongue, but she was half-numb and merely winced. She slid down the wall and stared at the scene in front of her. Jasmine had reached her brother and was holding on to his lower leg, begging him for something, like trying to wake him up. It was hard to understand her. Mommy kept saying, *"Oh my God."*

Without even realizing it, Sarah put her thumb in her mouth.

Motion to her right caught her attention, and her head swiveled that way. There were two older kids peeking out of a doorway across the hall, young teenagers staring at her. The kids had dark skin and big white eyes, a boy and a girl. Sarah gave them a small wave, but they didn't react.

"No!" Mommy cried now, and Sarah stared forward again. *"No, no, no—you can't touch him, Jasmine, you can't touch him! This is a crime scene, it's a crime scene!"*

"Jordy, Jordy, Jordy!" Jasmine bawled.

"Oh Jesus. We have to call the police."

Sarah watched Jasmine shake her head. *"No! No police!"*

"What? *Why?* We're calling the police."

"No police, Jordy said—" Jasmine started, then dissolved into horrible tears again.

"Jasmine, a murder happened here! Jordan was fucking *killed.* We're calling the police."

"Just wait—"

Sarah's eyes blurred with tears. She wanted to go back to the park and swing. It was one of her favorite things to do with Mommy. Or she could go home. She brought up her bear and started talking to it, murmuring about her room back at Daddy's where all her other dolls were. She was too old for tea parties, and anyway Brittany—that was Daddy's girlfriend—didn't like tea parties anyway, but Sarah suddenly had a pure, wonderful sensory longing to bury herself in her covers at home surrounded by all of her dolls and bears, where everything was calm and quiet.

"Mommy, I want to go home," she whispered, but Mommy didn't hear her.

"Jasmine! Just come over here! Get away from him!"

Mommy was straining, dragging Jasmine away from Jordan.

"Come on!"

"I have to—"

"Jasmine, don't—"

"He's my brother!"

"I know!"

Their voices began to jumble, and Sarah turned her head away from them. She got up on her feet and began to wander back down the hall the way they had come. Another door had opened, and Sarah stared at an old woman who was standing in her open doorway. The old woman wore a bright flowery green-and-yellow gown, and she had big round glasses that made her eyes look gigantic. Sarah quickened her step toward the stairs.

"Is everything all right down there?" came the old woman's creaking voice.

Sarah ignored her and started up the stairwell. She climbed them one at a time, and soon she couldn't even hear the voices behind her. She stepped onto Mommy's floor, one flight up, and walked slowly down the empty hallway toward the familiar door. She always knew Mommy's door because taped to it, below the peephole, was the little pink pig that Sarah had colored for her. The curling-paper pig had been fastened there for months.

Sarah tried the doorknob but found it locked.

She reinserted her thumb in her mouth and glanced around. This hallway was completely deserted. If she listened hard, she could hear television sets murmuring, and kids' voices coming from somewhere, and traffic outside, and a barking dog somewhere, and something buzzing. It was the light above her that was buzzing, she discovered. She stared at it while she wandered in a deliberate circle in front of Mommy's door.

Sarah decided she hated it here.

Mommy's apartment was like Daddy said—a "fucking crap hole." Sarah hated having to sleep with Mommy in her bed, and she despised all the noise, and she didn't have any friends in the whole building. The kitchen was a scuzzy mess all the time, like nothing had been cleaned in forever. There was none of the food she was used to at home, none of the gleaming surfaces or marble countertops, and there was no beach even close to here. She was only here every other week, for a single day, but she still didn't like it. There was nothing to do except drive to the park.

She wasn't supposed to tell Mommy all that, though. Every time Daddy said goodbye for the weekend, he reminded Sarah to be nice, to remember what happens when Mommy gets sad.

She'd been too young to remember when Mommy had what Daddy called her "freakout" in the supermarket—the episode that drove her parents into separate homes and meant that Sarah had to come to this smelly apartment building every other weekend. Apparently, Sarah's bruises from the freakout had lasted for almost three months (she'd heard Daddy shouting that on the phone several times over the years), but she didn't remember any of it. It was all like something out of a dream—the shouting and the crying and all that time in the car driving across Santa Ana, Sarah watching SpongeBob on Daddy's iPad, crisscrossing the city for reasons that baffled her.

Well, she did remember one time when Mommy got so mad that she slapped Sarah across the cheek. It had stunned her, because she didn't think she was doing anything wrong. Or at least anything *too* wrong. She had been eating dinner quietly next to Mommy, and she had scrunched her nose at the salad on the side of her plate because it was wilted and looked dirty and smelled funny. She knew Mommy was acting weird that night, and she hadn't wanted to make her sad, but there was no way that lettuce was going in her mouth. Mommy had already been weepy before dinner, something about her boyfriend, and the third time Sarah said *"Uh-uh,"* the slap had stung her and she had nearly tumbled from her chair. Sarah had righted herself quickly and stared at her mom with sudden tears in her eyes, and both of Mommy's hands were covering her mouth, and her eyes were as wide as she'd ever seen them. *"It's OK, Mommy,"* Sarah had said, holding her cheek—again, not wanting her mom to be sad. And it worked. For the rest of that weekend, Mommy had been super nice.

Something clattered at the end of the hall, making Sarah jump. She took her thumb out of her mouth.

Mommy was half-dragging Jasmine into the hallway.

Mommy was crying.

"—can't handle this right now, Jasmine," she said. *"I can't handle any of this. Get off your ass!"*

Jasmine flailed. She still had that grocery bag swinging from her left hand, but she also had a backpack now, like a real school backpack.

"I killed him!" Jasmine cried out.

"No, you didn't!" Mommy snapped.

"But I did!"

That was when Sarah first heard sirens. The sound was coming right up the stairwell, and it was a constant scream, right outside. The noise made Sarah clap her hands to her ears. She nearly dropped her bear to the grimy floor again; she squeezed it tight. The sound of the sirens reminded her of something deep in her memory, and it had to do with Mommy. She started singing a song, something mindless, to tune out the shrieking.

Turning in her tight circle, she glanced at Mommy and Jasmine again. Mommy had that look on her face like something was about to happen, as if all she wanted to do was lie down on a couch and put a pillow over her head and moan.

"Sarah!" she said now. "When did you come up here? Never mind." Shaking her head, pulling at Jasmine.

Jasmine was scary as she got closer, pale, her face streaked with tears, shaking, eyes unfocused, gone. Sarah liked Jasmine, but not this way. Sarah turned away, but then both women were hovering over her, and Mommy was digging for her keys in her purse while holding on to Jasmine.

"Let's get inside and talk, Jasmine" she said, flustered. "Come on, Sarah. Inside."

Mommy finally got the door open, and she pushed Jasmine inside. Sarah followed, and she heard the door click shut behind her as Jasmine bawled. Sarah moved past the women, went to Mommy's bedroom and fell onto the unkempt sheets and blankets. She kept humming lightly to herself, but it was hard to block the voices coming from the front room.

"Come here, come here, sit down, over here, come on."

"I killed him, I killed him, I killed my brother." Gasping, coughing.

"All right, try to calm down, sit down, over here on the couch, come on."

"Lori, he's dead, I killed him."

"That's the money, in the bag?"

"I killed my brother!"

"Jasmine, the bag, is that the—"

"Oh my God, Jordy's gone."

"What do you want to do?"

The sirens continued to scream, reaching a crescendo and then finally cutting off violently, right outside. Sarah heard Mommy making her way to the window.

"Well, someone called them."

"Oh God."

"We should be down there, Jasmine, we should be telling them exactly what happened."

"Just let me think, I need to—"

"What do we do?"

"It was Tommy, Lori, I know it, I FEEL it." More tears came from Jasmine, and gasping and wheezing, like she couldn't hold anything back.

"All the more reason to talk to the—"

"He'll KILL me, Lori, he'll kill ME! This money belongs to him! Tommy thinks Jordan took the coins, and he murdered him for it! Instead of me!"

Jasmine exploded into more tears.

"Then what do you want to do? What do you want to do, Jasmine?"

A pause.

"I don't know, what should I do?"

"You should go downstairs!"

A hot whisper: *"I STOLE this!"* There was the sound of a crinkling plastic bag. *"Don't you get it? I caused this. I'm not going down there!"*

"Well, I don't know what to—"

"You have to help me, Lori. PLEASE help me."

"I *am* helping you."

"Oh God, help me fix this, help me make this right! I don't want to die! I just want to make things right. I want my brother back! Nothing like this was supposed to happen."

All that was followed by footsteps, and Sarah envisioned Mommy walking back to Jasmine.

"I don't know what to do, though." Mommy's voice. "Are the cops gonna come up here?"

"Why would they—?"

"I'm sure someone saw us down there, right? The neighbors?"

"Oh Christ."

"Jasmine, what do we do?"

Mommy had the tone of voice now, the desperate emptiness, the pleading.

By instinct, Sarah sat up. She took her thumb out of her mouth and stepped off the bed. She walked into the front room, bear dangling from her fist, and saw Mommy and Jasmine. Jasmine was sitting cross-legged in the middle of the floor, holding the wrapped grocery bag against her chest. Her backpack lay next to her. Jasmine glanced over at Sarah when she came into the room.

"Oh baby," Jasmine said.

Sarah went over to Mommy and hugged her leg.

"It'll be OK, Mommy."

20
TOMMY

Tommy Strafe pulled into the big parking lot, and the gray warehouse loomed in front of him, *Mawk Construction* in big blue letters over the three delivery bays. He parked the truck crookedly in front of an expanse of corrugated metal and hopped out. He slammed the truck's door, still irritated by that fucking cop and the maddening Corvette. The whole episode had thrown him off his game.

He still wondered if it'd even been Jordan's 'Vette. It had sure *seemed* as if it was tailing him, but—really—why the fuck would Jordan be following him? Tommy couldn't think of any earthly reason for them to not only still be in the city but to actually tail him—and for what purpose? If it was true that Jordan and his sister had ripped him off, then they were probably in Arizona or Mexico by now.

Oh, the fucking *balls!*

He kept replaying the moment when the 'Vette had turned on to Bristol in his rearview. It had fallen in line, blocks behind him, and then suddenly it had veered over into the bike lane. Frowning, he'd had no choice but to pull over, too. That far ahead of the car, it was impossible to tell who was behind the wheel and who was riding shotgun, even when he twisted around to stare out the back of the cab, but it was definitely two people, and as far as he could tell, a woman was driving, and it was a man who finally stepped out of the 'Vette, slammed the door, and took off at a clip for the shopping center his right.

It had *looked* like that shitscrape Jordan, the way he'd slunk about (the same gait since fucking middle school), the way his clothes always seemed to succumb to gravity—but, goddammit, Tommy couldn't be sure.

He'd been about to flip a U and check it out when the 'Vette pulled away from the sidewalk and began a careless approach. Two blocks away, then a block away, he'd squinted through the mirror, then watched plainly as the car nonchalantly passed him by. A woman was driving, no doubt about it, and for a moment he was *sure* it was Jasmine, and he'd felt a snarl forming on his lips, but then suddenly it wasn't Jasmine at all. It was a perfect fucking stranger, and *what the fuck?*

It was some lady who'd probably just been dropping off her man for work or something. He'd watched open-mouthed as the 'Vette made a right on 1st. Fucking waste of time.

"Whatever," he'd mumbled, and hit the gas, ripping back onto Bristol.

Now, standing next to his truck and lighting up a Camel, he noticed Charlton in the shadow of the third delivery bay, against a leaning pile of black countertop granite, also smoking. The young man glanced up, expressionless, and Tommy began walking over that way.

"Hey," Charlton said as Tommy moved into the shade beside him.

"What's goin' on?"

"Waitin' on the man."

"You got a job?"

"Just a meeting. Home after this. I haven't slept in a couple days."

Charlton flicked his butt out into the parking lot. He'd grown into a steely throwback dude who reminded Tommy of some greaser from the '50s, straight out of one of those black-and-white movies. Greased-back hair, all squinty, always wearing a white tee shirt. Old-school tough guy in a young man's hard physique. He was Rennie's son, so that's where the lean, musculature shit came from. He was a hard worker, just like his pop, Tommy had to admit. It wasn't like he lifted weights at a gym or anything. Fuck that noise. He came by it all honestly.

And these days, unlike the old times, Charlton backed up his look. One time, couple years ago, a beefy bearded customer armed with a baseball bat had stalked straight into this very bay and tried to get the jump on Charlton, had come up from behind yelling something about cheating him, and Charlton had disarmed the guy midswing, taking the wood to the ribs without even a flinch and flinging the bat end-over-end across the cement floor. It was like he got that kind of crap every day. Cigarette didn't even fall from his lips. Tommy'd been begrudgingly impressed, watching Charlie choke out the big dude with one bicep. He'd helped him load the guy into his truck and drive him to a park, where they'd placed him barely conscious on a bench, kept his wallet and phone—a way of saying *We know where you live.* They never saw that guy again.

"What are you doing here?" Charlton asked.

"Rennie upstairs?"

"He'll be down eventually."

"I got a problem."

"Yeah?"

"Couple of motherfuckers stole from me."

"Stole what?"

"Coin collection, man, right outta my house."

"Break-in?"

"No."

"You collect fucking coins, man?" A smirk.

"They were my dad's, yeah. You knew how much they're worth, you'd shut the fuck up."

Asshole.

"You know who took 'em?"

"Yes. Yes, I do."

"I guess I know why you're here, then."

"You want in?"

"Shit, man, I just want to kick it with a sixer, watch some TV, and drift the fuck off. I don't even know why I'm here."

Door opened then, second level. Flinty voices echoed out from the doorway, and here came Rennie from on high, down the narrow wall-hugging stairs bow-legged, the way he always did. He was followed by a large dude in jeans and a white button-down, naturally bulging eyes, and no hair on his shiny head, not even a wisp. The two of them were forcing laughter and exchanging platitudes.

Tommy took a long drag off his Camel, flicked it out to join Charlton's, waited while Rennie and the visitor shook hands fake-warmly. The fellow gave Tommy and Charlton a long glance, then sauntered out to a black Mercedes parked in the shade on the far side of the lot. After a time, the rumbly vehicle eased out of the parking lot and was gone.

Only then did Rennie acknowledge Tommy.

"You trying to call me?"

"Yeah." Tommy shook his hand.

Rennie cocked his head toward the upstairs office. "Was in a meeting. That was Powell outta the Irvine job. He's the one with fucking Sanders? Total assholes, both of 'em. But I can out-asshole anybody, am I right?"

"Something up?"

"Nah, I knew they'd be trouble, they're like fucking Nazis over there."

"What is it? You need me for it?" Flashing a glance at Charlie.

"Oh, they're just watching every goddamn penny, they got a kid over there, some kind of idiot savant, every time I'm onsite she sidles up to me with her clipboard and walks me through line items. This Powell dude wanted to meet up and go over that shit. Job's not fucking worth it."

Rennie was a master of construction collusion in Orange County, had been engaged for decades behind the scenes with most of the big subcontractors, and those included Highline Builders, Porter Drywall, Nuance, Fountain Construction, others. Through a combination of Rennie's surprisingly winning outward personality and his long-time reputation (reaching back to Gordon Strafe's days), he'd found himself leading a backslappers' ring, all of the subs working smoothly together to fix prices and rig bids. It was no secret, really. It was the way of the world. Not even very illegal—well, it would never be the focus of any criminal investigation, anyway. Cops didn't give a shit. Didn't give a shit about *that* part, anyway. Mawk Construction dealt daily with labor inflation, bribes, kickbacks, bid rotation, bid *suppression*, and fake subcontractors—and occasionally the repercussions among pissed-off customers. It was a slick operation, and it could be brutal.

Rennie threw an arm around Tommy's shoulders. "Anyway, we'll deal with that Monday. What's up?"

"Need your help."

Tommy laid it out—spying Jasmine at the store, inviting her and her asswipe brother to the party, then making the even more moronic move of showing them his dad's coin collection, and finding it gone this morning. Then there was the news that Jasmine had high-tailed it out of there and was now missing, probably already looking for a way to hawk the coins.

The more Tommy talked, the more his voice sounded as if it was coming out of some fuckin' retard's face hole. Rennie and especially Charlton were giving him the goddamn looks. But Christ, man, he was talking about his *inheritance*. Some of those coins were *valuable*. His dad had whispered stories about them a hundred times—the double-die pennies, the silver Roosevelt dimes, the misprints and the misalignments and the incredible rarities. He'd *relished* the telling. There was probably better than a quarter of a million dollars wrapped up in those coins by now, better than any 401K or savings account, just good old-fashioned American metals gathering steady value right inside his home, safe inside the custom-made cabinet that Rennie himself had helped him design.

Rennie was nodding now, a bemused smile on his thin lips.

"You wanted to sniff this girl's panties, and you got careless."

Tommy stared at Rennie, glanced at Charlton, who also had a half-smirk on his face.

"Well—"

"How do you think I can help you, son?"

"Help me fuck them up, Rennie! Get my shit back, and make them wish—"

"Tom, that boy and girl are in the wind by now—if they're really the ones who did it."

Tommy didn't know what to say for a split-second. "I'm fucking *positive*—"

"Where do you expect to start?"

"I have the bitch's phone number, we use your guy to find her address, we go to their place, start from there."

"You don't think they cleared out?"

"They obviously don't know what the hell they're doing. Shit, they're probably holed up there right now, wondering what the fuck happens next. They're goddamn *kids*."

"You didn't go there first? Addresses are pretty easy to figure out."

Tommy Strafe had to consciously unclench his fists. Somehow, he was losing control of the conversation. His words had been echoing hollowly on the warehouse walls. There were usually scads of Mexicans streaming through here, scowling and single-minded, carrying loads to the flatbeds, nodding curtly at him, but now it was empty and everything felt foolish. He stood there on the dirty concrete, willing himself motionless in the middle of all the silence.

"All right, look, no, OK, this was my first stop—obviously. I always come to you, Ren. Shit happens, and I come straight here. That's what you taught me. But this is another level, too. This is about my dad. This is about Gordon. These are my dad's coins. I have to get those back. I have to." His teeth gritted almost helplessly, and he had to force the next words out on a hard whisper. "And then, when everything is back in my hands, I want that fucker dead. Jordan Frank. Maybe his sister too. *Dead.*"

Rennie was nodding, he appreciated that kind of talk, and now he glanced over at Charlton. "Give me one of those cigarettes, willya?"

"No way."

"Charlie, I swear to fuck, if you—"

"You told me to say no if you ever asked me—"

"I know what I told you, now give me a goddamn cigarette."

"Dad."

"What I say and what I mean are sometimes completely different things, that's one of the things I've strived to teach you for fuck-all-how-many years, now give me a fucking cigarette when I ask you for one, do you hear me?"

Tommy glanced at his part-time boss through the length of a pregnant pause, then moved his gaze to the stoic son, and then decided to give up one of his own cigarettes. *Fuck this nonsense.* He took the packet from his shirt pocket and shook out an unfiltered Camel for Rennie while Charlton stared down the side of his face. Tommy felt it like sunburn, didn't give a shit.

"Ahh, my boy." Rennie placed the cigarette between his lips and squinted while Tommy lit him up. "Son, with this tobacco-wrapped tube, you just bought my help. Charlie's too." He took a deep pull on the raw tobacco, blew it out. "We'll help you get the coins back, but then I need your help next week. Need the muscle. Deal?"

"What, for the Irvine deal?"

"Well, that eventually, probably, but I'm talking about the gig off Jamboree, the same one you took care of last month. That fucking cripple."

"Hey, man, I'm available for you whenever, you know that."

"I *don't* know that, actually. That fucking store sucks up your time more than I'd like."

Rennie flashed a dangerous smile behind the smoke. Tommy'd found himself on the receiving end of that smile only a handful of times in his life, and it stung. He knew Rennie would rather he cut ties with the store altogether, but Tommy didn't see that happening. He had a good thing, splitting his time between Rennie's outfit and the store. Working for Rennie had its benefits, it was mindless and it *definitely* paid well, but the store was simply more interesting. Made him feel better about himself—like, he actually made his own decisions, devised his own product, found success of his own making. He was his own boss over there, even though Derek owned the biggest share of the store.

Tommy didn't know how to answer, so he left it at a shrug.

"All right, give me the goddamn number."

As Tommy gave Rennie the girl's number, and as Rennie scrawled it on his palm, Charlton watched Tommy with casual contempt. There was no love lost between them, especially not since Charlton had botched the Van Nuys job earlier that summer and Tommy'd had to bail him out.

"All right, fuck, gimme a bit," Rennie said, and Tommy was left with Charlton as the boss shuffled away. "Not even sure Dick's taking calls. It's Saturday, and he usually sleeps late. I mean, *way* late. He hibernates on the weekend."

The two of them watched the old man climb the stairs as he went on about his cop buddy. Rennie was still wiry, almost feral in his movement. Simian, even. He was gonna live forever.

The door slammed up there.

"Thanks," Charlton whispered, deadpan. "This sounds fun."

"You got nothin' better to do."

Charlton could flash a smile just like his dad.

21
GEORGE

George Brenner watched the girl in the blue dress as she plodded across the parking lot and onto the sidewalk and headed east on foot. She had a fetching swing to her hips that was perky and young and effortlessly sensual, not one of those exaggerated swishes he'd see among the beach bimbos who frequented the tanning joint two doors down. Those plasticine girls were always flowing in and out of there, wearing practically nothing, reminding George of his early days when erections sprang unbidden and babes mattered.

Sigh.

This girl, this Kelly, now *she* was the kind of specimen who would've made an impression on the young George Brenner. Well, hey, he wouldn't lie: She'd made an impression on him mere moments ago. He wondered where she was from. Not from around here, that was for sure. It was like she *wanted* to fit in with the SoCal crowd, but her innocence shone through like a foglamp. This place would never totally mute her. A small, distant part of him regretted ripping her off—and ripping her off *big*—but the truth was, he'd been dreaming about this kind of shock payout for decades.

In the distance, the Safeway bag full of his stash money swung from Kelly's fist. He watched it go, felt like waving bye-bye, maybe giving it a big ol' wink. Talk about a sweet transaction!

He'd kept a give-or-take $10,000 stash hidden in a fireproof security pouch above the store's bathroom ceiling tiles for the past five years, doling out safe bits of cash for minor transactions here and there. After forty years, he had a sixth sense for what he could handle quietly in the store, in full sight of the cameras—the over-the-counter sleight of hand that fed him a tidy profit month to month. Sometimes the minor scores paid for his groceries, sometimes his rent. They were the pennies and the nickels and dimes with the little errors only he could spot, the adjustment problems and the double strikes and the denomination mistakes. He could throw down five bucks for a coin like that and flip it in another county for forty, no sweat. The customer was always happy to walk away with a bill in exchange for a coin, sometimes laughingly so. *You're kidding!*

Thanks man! Envisioning a quick stop for an ice cream cone while George padded his stash, biding his time for the next grab.

Hell, it kept him flush with insulin, at the very least.

George locked the door and flipped the OPEN sign to CLOSED. He swayed over to the counter, patted the brick of coins with one sausage-fingered hand, and dug out the WILL RETURN IN 30 MINUTES card, went back and hung it from its yellowed suction cup. He stared out the glass door one more time, watched the traffic flow. Practically no one in the parking lot.

Truth was, customers were rare these days. It was no longer the heyday of the '70s or '80s, when the flashy youngsters would flow through here, dollar signs in their eyes as they hauled in their family collections, looking to get a quick hit and go blow it on Reagan-era coke. George had lived through all that and made a living off it. Now, times were tighter than Nancy Reagan's asshole. He'd worked one Tuesday back in January when no one had come in the store—not a single soul. He'd sat on his stool all day like a fat fool, while life (for what it was worth) flowed along Westminster Boulevard, heading everywhere but here. He knew it going into this racket: Chances were miserably low that a lottery score would happen to him on any given day, and that was especially true in the new millennium. Everyone was too savvy, with the internet and all.

In the bathroom, he climbed laboriously atop the toilet, anchoring himself with thick arms against the close walls. He centered himself, then reached up to push at the ceiling tile above the mirror, the one with the crumbling corner. He angled it out of the way and took hold of the security bag's edge, sliding what was left of his stash toward him. There was an awful, sinking moment when he felt himself beginning to slip off the cheap toilet lid, and he imagined himself crumpling into the space between the filthy commode and the urine-splattered wall, and finding himself stuck, unable to move his old limbs. But he caught himself, breathing hard, and he closed his eyes to wait out the giddy panic.

Slow it down, George. You got this.

Whistling uneasily, he stepped heavily off the toilet, without incident.

He made his way to the back room, a tiny claustrophobic space that contained a microwave oven, a mini fridge beneath it, an old card table covered with chipped mugs and instant coffee and takeout menus and paper towels, a water heater, and a cramped storage area sectioned off by an orange curtain. His trusty old backpack hung from a peg. Inside the backpack was a weathered imitation-leather file folder in which he kept his mail and his lists and his occasional scribblings. Way in the back was a note he'd penned several years back when, one boring morning planted on his stool, he'd fantasized about the precise situation he found himself in at this very moment.

He slid out the note, scrawled on plain printer paper, and perused it. Addressed to Hank, it laid out a believable scenario that found George becoming suddenly ill with a stomach ailment (he'd laid down careful precedent over the years), closing the store reluctantly while unable to contact his boss, and determining to tough it out and drive directly to the closest ER. Obviously, it wouldn't do to actually *call* Hank with this story, as the old man would groan up off his ass and head to the store or—worse—to the closest ER to check on him.

He brought the note out to the counter and taped it to the cash register.

Feeling jittery, fingers dancing with anticipation, George took a moment to imagine Hank finding the note—Hank Woody being the mostly silent owner of Woody's Coins and Metals. Hank worked a couple hours a week in his old age. He was mostly confined to an easy chair planted in front of a gigantic Sony TV watching *Three Stooges* reruns while his sweet wife Belinda catered to his every need. George had been over to their place a few times over the years, but he'd always been careful to keep Hank at arm's length. Belinda, too. A real friendship might have developed there, but George never let it. How could he, with a secret stash hidden at the store, and a windfall escape plan mapped out for years?

He glanced out the front door again. No activity. The girl was gone.

This was remarkable timing, he mused. It was like it was meant to be. God was finally smiling down on him. As long as nothing happened the rest of the day—it was still early, after all—then George was safe Sunday and Monday, the two days of the week the store was closed. Hank would probably not find the note until Tuesday, late morning. The boss almost never called, simply let George handle the day-to-day operations and sales, for what they were worth. Hank was practically retired, only came in to get out of the house.

George stuffed the girl's brick of valuable coins into his backpack.

Jesus, he was holding probably a quarter of a million dollars.

How many years had he waited for something like this? Sitting on that stool, watching the specks of dust float, he calculated it in his head. After the twin scores in '79 and '84, there'd been the decades-long dry spell until that stupid kid in '07. He'd raked in low triple figures with the two early ones, without having to skip town—miraculously. The '07 swindle, now that was a time. It'd been only about thirty grand (ha, only), and he remembered the young man returning to the store to challenge the payout he'd received days earlier. George still got shivers, playing with the *what ifs*. What if the kid had returned to the store while Hank was manning the counter? What if the kid had gone to the police? Man, the shit life threw at you! The near misses and the hair's-breadth avoidance of catastrophe!

Anyway, the kid had done some research on his computer, apparently. George'd had to dig deep into his bullshit vault to explain away discrepancies, anxious the whole time because of the guy's furious expression and aggressive stance. George had even gambled, had offered to reverse the transaction because he himself was doubtful of the value—and he'd won the gamble. Dude had relented and finally walked out of his life. Never saw him again, and George had ultimately realized a $27,500 profit through his San Mateo buyer.

And now Kelly. Girl of his dreams. Dropped the motherlode in his ample lap.

This was it! This was the score.

George scanned the trashy innards of the goddamned store, knew he'd never be back. He barely saw the cases, the collections, the idiotic framed themes. His immediate future was stretched out before him, locked in place. He didn't even need to go back to his shithole month-to-month apartment. No pets, nothing of value there. He knew exactly where he'd park his Karmann Ghia at LAX, knew precisely the number of the cash flight he'd take to Aruba to begin his new life under the identity Mickey Dragone—a package of paper materials obtained in 1996 and minimally cultivated over the years. Long-term plans? Buy his way into a rum distillery and relax his way into a slow oblivion, that was all.

He unlocked the door and pushed his way out, locked it back up behind him. There was no one around, least of all Kelly.

He waddled across the asphalt parking lot to its edge. His Karmann Ghia sat facing Westminster Boulevard. Vehicles whisked by, not seeing him, not noticing the smile plastered across his silly mug. He fiddled with his keys and swung the creaky door wide. He flung the backpack into the passenger seat, then let gravity take his bulk into the squashed driver's seat. He closed the door and sat there panting, so excited that his limbs were tingling.

Deep breath, then he turned to the backpack. He rifled through it, removing the stash and the brick. Laboring, he leaned over to open the big glove compartment and shoved both items inside, using his key to lock the box.

"*OK,*" he breathed.

He stuck the key in the ignition. All he had to do was turn the key, and his new existence would begin. It was an easy reality to contemplate (he'd had decades of practice), but now that it was here, in his reach, he was almost too nervous to make it happen. He reached for the dangling keys, then drew his hand back, shaking it out. His fingers felt numb.

Adrenaline was making this difficult. His chest felt tighter than a drum. He had to calm down.

"*Easy,*" he mumbled.

If he had to sit here for an hour, he would do it. There was no hurry now. Just take it easy, get to the airport, absolutely no one had the faintest idea what he was about to do. The future lay ahead of him like a magic carpet, his alone, room only for his daft self, all he had to do was get onboard. But the tingling wasn't going away, and he found himself muttering laughter, and then outright giggling in the confines of his old Karmann Ghia, imagining a scenario in which he got *this* far, *this close,* only to be cut down at the precipice. Wouldn't *that* be a shitshow of karmic comeuppance?

"Oh for the love of Christ," he breathed.

He'd forgotten his shit. In his mind's eye, he envisioned his little medical packet in the bathroom, filled with vials and pills, his prescriptions.

George heaved his weight out of the car, locked the doors, checked them twice, and began the slow waddle back toward the store.

22
JASMINE

Jasmine Frank was numb. Her left arm felt as if it were loose in its socket, dangling roughly as Lori yanked at her. Flailing from her other arm was the plastic Safeway bag filled with cash, feeling like poison now, like something dirty and toxic. Her legs were thick and heavy, as if she were dragging swampy logs. Her skull felt stuffed with wet cotton. And she experienced it all as if she were lagging moments behind her body, sensing everything from outside herself.

Jordan's face, slack in his destroyed head, was locked in her vision—blunt, unbearable. Eyes flat and dead, nothing behind them except ravaged tissue, not even a ghost of what had been. She couldn't look away from his face, couldn't blink it savagely away no matter how hard she tried. It was there in front of her, always.

"*Come on, Jasmine!*" Lori whispered. "You want outta this, then *come on!*"

Jasmine blubbered out a sob, stumbled against a crack in the asphalt. The backpack slid off her shoulder, and she lifted it back dazedly.

Sarah tottered along next to her, occasionally looking up at her as if not understanding her tears.

"Why are we running, why are we—?" the girl cried, skipping helplessly and almost falling herself.

"*Quiet!*" Lori shushed. "Let's go!"

The apartment building receded behind them.

Lori yanked Jasmine into the narrow cinderblock alley behind the stinking trash area—just as Jasmine glimpsed a patrol car nosing into the apartment building's rear parking lot. The sight of the black-and-white filled her with a baseless terror, baseless because there was a small part of her that wouldn't mind at all if a patrolman found her and took care of her and laid her down in the back of his car and drove her somewhere where she could sleep, just a random cell somewhere, anywhere, and whispered to her that everything would be all right. That it was way past time to take care of the people who had wronged her, and that justice would be served, finally and fully. But then she recoiled at the thought as surely as if Jordan were there whisper-babbling into her ear his hatred and distrust of the police, like he did when he was alive.

When Jordy was alive.

She felt Lori pushing down on her head—*"Lower, lower!"*—and the three of them stumbled down behind the broken wall, to the ground, Sarah looking confused and now angry.

"Mommy!" the girl blurted.

Lori shushed her savagely, making her daughter cry. Jasmine felt for the little girl. They listened to the patrol car ease its way through the parking lot. Jasmine risked a look and watched the vehicle come to a stop directly behind Jordy's Corvette. As the cop opened his door, Jasmine shrank back behind the wall, deadened. She didn't understand anything, didn't *want* to understand anything. She was so glad for Lori, taking charge the way she did, because mostly she didn't want to think about *anything.*

The three of them huddled together, and Jasmine felt Lori's quick breaths on her forehead.

"OK, he didn't see us." Lori coaxed Jasmine forward. "This way."

They exited the short alley and entered into a quiet neighborhood populated by small bungalows, spread far apart, and mature landscaping. They hurried along the sidewalk, Jasmine's sweaty hand still trapped in Lori's determined grip.

"I'm sorry, Lori," Jasmine said, trudging along. "So sorry, so sorry."

"For what?" Voice hard.

"I didn't—I didn't mean to drag you into this."

"You didn't drag me into anything," Lori said shortly. "Come on, let's get a few streets over and I'll call Steve. I just hope to Christ he answers."

The name *Steve* clanged dully in the mush that was Jasmine's head. She'd met Steve exactly twice since Lori'd hooked up with him, and she hadn't been impressed. He was one of those guys that treat you like an afterthought, like he always had something better to do. If there was something in it for him, then yeah, he would be there for you, but otherwise, see ya. And it wasn't like he'd earned that kind of privilege: He was kinda pale, he was paunchy from restaurant food and no real exercise, and he walked weird, like this drag-shuffle with the toes of his feet pointed wide.

It was a long shot, Lori'd said as they fled down the back stairs moments ago, Jasmine barely hearing her. Steve worked weekends at the restaurant, and Saturdays usually went long, but it was all she could think of at the moment—this, after Lori had spent precious seconds in front of Jasmine's door whisper-screaming that she couldn't do this, couldn't drag her daughter into this, *are you insane?*, and she couldn't get involved with the police either, *I mean, imagine the world of shit that Daniel would dunk me in if he saw Sarah in the back of a cop car! Jesus Christ!*

"Oh what the fuck am I doing," Lori moaned now, monotone.

"Mommy, you keep saying bad words, you shouldn't say those, they're not ni—"

"I know, honey, come on."

Jasmine kept fogging out, lagging even farther behind her physical self, and before she realized it they had walked three blocks into the neighborhood. They took a turn onto a nondescript street and finally collapsed onto a shadowed curb. Immediately, Jasmine dropped her head into her hands, the sensation echoing into infinity.

Somewhere, Lori was already on her phone, muttering *"Come on, come on ..."*

"Where *are* we?" Sarah said with little-girl exasperation.

Jasmine glanced up, vaguely registering the tautness of her tear-streaked cheeks. The quiet, normal neighborhood, swaying from side to side, up and down, seemed to mock her. The day was now bright and warm, and the squat homes appeared colorful and even cheerful, paying no mind to the girl in the gutter. In one of the windows, she glimpsed a woman vacuuming her floor while dancing to music over headphones. Jasmine muttered a soft curse in her direction.

"Steve?" she heard Lori say somewhere, followed by a string of indecipherable entreaties.

When Jasmine glanced up again, she wasn't sure how much time had passed. Sarah was lodged against her, sweaty and silent, and then time passed weirdly and Lori was talking to her.

Reality stuttered.

"... morning shift. I guess Ray is a total douche, and Steve had to duck out without being seen. Don't be surprised if he's in a mood."

Quiet descended on the curb, and Jasmine couldn't physically stop herself from weeping, couldn't stop the image of Jordy's ruined face intruding over everything in the world. She felt Sarah's little hand on her forearm, and then Lori's arm around her shoulders from the other side.

"How could this happen?" Lori said in her ear.

Jasmine recognized fear in her friend's voice. She shook her thick head. Out of nowhere, she felt the sweaty weight of her backpack behind her. She shrugged out of it laboriously, a pulse of black anger thumping at her spine. She stared at the pack with loathing.

Next to her, Lori took in an audible breath. "Wait," she said. "That's your backpack. Jordan had it. Is the gun still in there?"

Jolted from her funk, Jasmine stared at Lori as if she were a complete stranger. "What? How do you know—?"

"It's your mom's, right?"

"How in the world do you know that?"

"Jordan found it, OK? When we were looking for you. He was trying everything and dug in there. But Christ, man, now that thing's haunting me. On the run from the cops, and carrying a gun, great."

"Well ..." Not knowing how to respond. "I wasn't gonna just leave it in the apartment."

She began fiddling with the zippers, and Lori clutched at her hand.

"Not in front of Sarah," Lori said severely.

"What did ... what did Jordy say about it?"

"I don't know."

Jasmine felt struck silent, as if she'd been hit in the stomach, as if she'd been cheated out of these impossible conversations Lori'd apparently shared with Jordy, conversations she'd never hear for herself. Conversations she *should* have had with him. About their mother, and about Karl. The aftermath of their escape, everything they'd left behind and everything they'd taken with them. Jasmine had never told him she'd taken the pistol. What had he thought when he found it in her backpack? Or had he known about it all along? It had been inside her pack all this time, in their tiny apartment; it wasn't as if she went to great lengths to hide it. She'd only wanted to keep it there, ready for the both of them if ... if things went bad again.

At the mere thought of Karl, she shivered, recalling her brief trip home earlier.

No, she thought. *Impossible.*

Jasmine looked at the backpack helplessly for long moments, the silence of the street beginning to wear on her. She felt as if she had to be doing something. Going somewhere. But at the same time, she wanted to disappear inside herself and never return.

That's when she heard the buzz of her phone.

Now she unzipped the pack with full force, rooting around for the device. She finally unearthed it and stared at it. *Her phone.* She powered it on—27 percent battery. Somehow it had gotten partially charged, and somehow she had it again.

As her chest hitched with emotion, she scrolled through her texts, just two, one from Rachel at the spa asking to switch shifts, and another from Jordy that made her breath catch.

Looking for u, hope your safe, call me!

She nearly dropped the phone, nearly threw it away from her, into the street. She felt a raw, angry desolation hollowing her out. She was about to stand and begin to pace when she noticed the icon for a missed call and a message. With trembling fingers, she accessed it, and immediately Tommy's voice was raging in her ear.

"Jasmine? Jasmine? Hello? Was it you? It wasn't you, right? Or was it your retard brother? Was it both of you? Hello? ... You took it, didn't you? Oh my fucking god, you bitch, you took it. You don't think I'll fucking find you? I will. I'll find both of you. And when I do, if you don't have it, I'll—Jesus Christ."

The message ended abruptly.

Oh my god.

Lori was now watching her from a dozen feet away, hands on hips. "What? What is it?"

Jasmine shook her head, didn't want to say anything, but then thought better of it.

"Message from Tommy."

"Oh. That."

"You heard that too?"

A pause. "Yeah."

"It was him, Lori. It was him. He killed Jordy." Trying to convince herself.

"You think?"

And it was my fault.

All Jasmine could do was sit there and nod slowly. She was out of words, out of shouted helpless questions. She had no earthly idea where to go from here. No idea how to absorb her own terrible culpability. She entered into a brutal denial, pocketing her phone and going silent.

She found herself petting Sarah's head. The little girl was practically asleep now, exhausted. When Jasmine bent to peer into her face, she saw that Sarah was sucking her thumb, a look of consternation on her face, a mix of peace and stress, as if beneath the surface she was churning in pre-nightmare.

"She still does that sometimes," Lori said, just to say something. "Sucks her thumb."

"I don't blame her," Jasmine whispered, then, to Sarah, "Shhhh."

Lori went back to pacing.

The grocery bag full of money felt hot and sweaty in Jasmine's grip, and she stared at it with self-hatred. She didn't even want to look at the disgusting thing. She wanted it as far away from her as possible.

"Sarah?"

The girl glanced up miserably, waking back up, letting her wet thumb fall out of her mouth. "Uh huh?"

"Can you do something for me? It's an important job."

"What."

"Can you keep this for me? Keep it safe in your backpack?" Jasmine held out the plastic bag.

"What about ... what about *your* backpack?"

"I think yours is safer."

Sarah watched her for half a minute, pondering. Then she made her decision.

"OK."

Sitting up straight for her task, Sarah shrugged off her backpack, pulled it in front of her, and unzipped the main pocket carefully. She gaped the pack open for Jasmine, offering the storage, but Jasmine told her to place the bag deep down at the bottom where it would be safe. Sarah did so, taking her time to situate the money deep down.

"Thanks, kiddo," she said, trying to evoke a smile.

"You're welcome."

And then they settled in to wait.

At one point, a Toyota van drove past them, and Jasmine glanced up to see a preteen boy staring curiously from the passenger seat. He was holding some kind of electronic gaming gadget. Kid was oblivious to Jasmine, but Jasmine suddenly envied him to no end, envied him and his normal Saturday afternoon. The van moved along into its future.

"I have to pee," Lori said after a while.

"I can kill him, Lori," Jasmine whispered.

She felt Lori's glare on the side of her face.

"You can't kill anybody, and you won't, so just shut up about that right now."

"I can do it, I can get close to him and I can do it, for Jordan."

"What are you even talking about? This isn't you, you don't do this kind of shit, it's like something out of the movies or something. This is already unreal, and you want to make it fucking preposterous? I can't even believe what you're saying to me."

"Then what?" Jasmine cried. "This can't be happening, Lori, it can't! What should I do?"

Lori let out a strangled cry. "How should I know? Shit, Jasmine, I just want to wipe my hands of all of this! I can't be involved! My life sucks as it is, I can't just stand by and—and—and be an accessory to this!"

"No, no, Lori, please, I need you, please don't leave."

Jasmine hugged Sarah closer, trying gently to block her ears from the screaming, but the girl seemed stubbornly intent on staying oblivious, remaining unaware of anything.

"Of course I'm not gonna kill anyone," Jasmine said. The word *kill* felt stupid on her tongue now. "I couldn't—" She broke off. "But I have to do *something*. Right?"

"What can you possibly do? Outside of the police?"

She shook her head, desolate. She didn't have an answer.

"Why did you *do* it, Jasmine?" Like she couldn't help asking the question, couldn't help putting it out there, and it made new tears squeeze out of Jasmine's eyes. "Why did you take those goddamn coins?"

She didn't have an answer for that, either. With something akin to disgust, Jasmine thought about the bag of money in Sarah's pack. It made her almost inconsolably remorseful. Empty, hollow, bereft. She felt her lip tremble. Why had she done this stupid thing? *Why?* She kept spiraling down through her emotions to the hard bit of grit at her center, that dot of anger. It burned, deep, abrasive, and she felt like it blinded her when she looked straight at it. It had to do with the blank spots from last night—the way the party began to stutter at a certain point until it almost completely dissolved, simply a void in her memory. She hadn't been in control, and Jordan had been inexplicably gone from her side, just gone, despite what she'd agreed to on the porch before they went in, and it wasn't her fault, was it? Please tell her it wasn't totally her fault, because Lori was right, none of this sounded like her.

"Here's Steve," Lori said, voice flat.

A little red Mini Cooper pulled tightly to the curb, off to the right. Jasmine could see Steve's head swiveling back toward them in the driver's seat. He waved superfluously, then the motor cut out. He pushed his unwieldy body out of the small vehicle and came around the rear. He still had a filthy white apron hanging from his waist.

"What happened?" he asked, immediately confused seeing Jasmine's face, Sarah's exhaustion, Lori's desperation.

"Hey babe," Lori said, going to him. "We're in trouble."

23
KAYLA

Kayla Jennings stared hard at Mark Pellegro as he chewed.

He glared back at her, all innocent.

"What?" he said, muffled around meat. "You really think I'm going to In-N-Out fucking Burger and not doin' some animal style?"

"How can you eat after driving around in upchuck-mobile all morning?"

He didn't answer, simply chewed exaggeratedly, open-mouthed, in her direction.

"Just hurry up, you fuckin' weirdo."

"Hey, I'm not really in a rush to see your boyfriend right now," he said. "Why'd you tell him I brought that girl here?"

"*Because you did.*" She felt her eyes go big and incredulous.

"You—you made it sound like I fucked him over! Like I was her getaway driver or something. I didn't know she *stole* something from him, Jesus Christ!"

"That's none of your business."

"The hell it is!" He took an angry bite of burger. "You made it my business when you practically sicced him on me. Now he's gonna be all up in my shit! Everything was going great before last night. He was giving me more hours, more responsibilities, running orders and shit, and now everything sucks! Thanks!" He mouthed a wad of fries, then punctuated his outburst with, "Fuck!"

Kayla practically never went to Tommy's stupid store, didn't want to be a part of all that sketchy shit, but the two of them would sometimes joke about how deeply into Tommy's colon Mark could reach. The dude was harmless enough, and according to Tommy there was no doubt he was the best salesman on the floor, but she'd always found him a little strange—the way he carried himself, the way he talked. Frankly, seeing him mad about the girl's spew spoiling his Jetta's interior was sorta refreshing. Like, she was really seeing him for the first time, rather than the insufferable suckup he usually was.

She watched him chew some more.

As she did so, she pondered her options. It'd been nearly twenty minutes since she'd launched herself from the vomit-mobile and rushed the In-N-Out order window to talk with three paper-hatted teens, asking after the blue-spangly girl, had they seen anyone like that in the parking lot, like early this morning, *way* early. The teenage buffoons had merely stared open-mouthed at one another. A few crew members on the morning shift had already left, they said, but no, huh-uh, they didn't remember anyone like that, nope. Fucking teens, man.

It was that quick, and now Kayla was back to having nothing.

She stared east down Westminster Boulevard, thinking. She'd been so *sure* about coming here. She'd had this grand vision of finding the girl, huddled up in front of the burger joint where Mark had left her, clutching Tommy's stupid coins to her tits. Grabbing hold of her and dragging her ass back to the house and making everything right again, making Tommy happy again. But shit, when did anything ever go easy in Kayla's life?

"We can still find that bitch," she said.

Mark shook his head. "Whatever."

"Where's she gonna go?" She turned to focus on him, stole one of his fries. "She's probably still walking home."

"It's like you have no idea how big Southern California is. She could be fucking *anywhere*."

"I don't agree. She has one path, and that's straight home with her tail between her legs. Straight down that street right there, same way you got here."

"Yeah, the street we just drove down." Mark grabbed another wad of fries. "There's nothing there."

"She's close, I'm telling you."

"Remember I told you she was babbling on about her mom? She could be on her way there, wherever the fuck that is. Could be around the corner, yeah, but she could also be in fucking Long Beach, I don't know. She could be in Mexico by now. Or Arizona." For some reason, he laughed.

Kayla was shaking her head.

"It's easy enough to borrow someone's phone," Mark went on, sucking on his Coke. "Or hitchhike. She found a ride, she's at her mom's house in fucking Santa Monica, and we're way out here twiddling our dicks."

"Hey!" Kayla said, "fuck you!"

But then she went quiet. She listened to the traffic, closed her eyes and faced the sun for a moment. Then, at length, she turned back to Mark.

"Why do you work at that store, anyway? Does it bring you great satisfaction? I mean, does it?"

He shrugged, continued speaking with his mouth full. "I'm good at it."

"Really? You don't mind working in that fucking drug-lab *front*?"

"Hey, that's not my thing, you know."

"The hell it isn't."

He finished a bite, slurped some more soda while shaking his head. "OK, fine, I do the skim now and then, make a drop, whatever, but that's all. I wipe my hands of it. I'm not taking any of that money, I'm not involved."

"Must be nice to be able to absolve yourself like that."

He frowned at her. "Not my store, Kayla. I just work there."

"Didn't the Nazis say something like that?"

He laughed out loud. "Oh, the Hitler analogy."

She glanced away, rolling her eyes. "I'm just saying, Mark …" But then she wasn't sure what she was saying.

"What?"

"I mean, you're not a bad person. You should get out from under that bullshit."

"Yeah, well, same to you."

They stared at each other for a while.

She looked away again. Finally, she said, "Hurry up."

A sweet little Hispanic girl was staring at her from two tables away. The girl was with her mother, a frumpy troll who sat miserably over a messy burger, staring dully at her phone. The daughter was staring at Kayla judgmentally, so Kayla gave her the finger without the mom seeing.

Truth was, Kayla wasn't in a hurry to go back to Tommy, either.

She clucked her tongue and watched the line of people ordering food. There was a group of more teenaged girls flipping their hair and making duck faces for Snapchat, and Kayla felt a deep loathing for the entire generation. In front of that group stood two older gray men chatting amiably, and in front of *them*, placing an order, was a father with his preteen son. Dad was joking with the employee. The mother stood off to the side, gazing at the menu. The family appeared utterly alien to Kayla. She couldn't even begin to imagine that kind of domestic scenario with Tommy, and a small part of her deflated at the thought.

She realized someone was staring at her from behind the counter window, some girl gesturing toward her. A boy next to her nodded, receded.

"Yo," Kayla said to Mark.

"What." Mouth full.

"We might have something." Nodding toward the window.

Kayla felt a spurt of hopeful energy inside her.

Mark craned his neck to see. After a moment, the boy came out the side entrance, armed with a broom and dustpan, and made his way over to them. He was incredibly young, baby-faced, probably sixteen, acne, awkward.

"Hi," he said, "Brianna said you were looking for that girl."

"She's my step-sister, yeah," Kayla said brightly, feeling Mark's gaze on the side of her face. "Blond hair, all made up? Blue dress? I just want to make sure she's safe. She left early this morning saying she was coming this way, and we haven't heard from her. I don't think she has her phone."

"Uh huh, I saw her. I talked to her."

"When?" Mark said, clearing his throat.

Kayla poked Mark's shin softly with her foot, a warning not to be too eager.

"Before we opened." The boy used his cute little broom and dustpan to sweep around their table, as if to appear busy for the boss. "Around nine-thirty, nine forty-five?"

"Did she look OK?" Kayla asked, playing the part.

"She looked tired. Cold. She was hungry and thirsty, but like I said we weren't open yet, so I gave her some water, and once we got the flat top going, I snuck her a burger."

"You did?"

"Yeah." He offered a modest smile.

"That was sweet of you." Yeah, Kayla knew the effect Jasmine had on the boys. She had to tamp down the urge to roll her eyes. "Did she have anything on her? Did you see her use a phone? Any phone?"

The boy was quiet for a moment. "She had a bag of something, like a grocery bag, but I didn't see any phone. I didn't see her talking to anyone."

Kayla gave Mark a glance, and he shrugged, biting into the last of his burger.

"We just want to get her back home," Kayla said again. "Did you see which direction she went?"

He nodded, almost bashfully, as if not wanting to admit his schoolboy crush. He gestured with his broom, straight east down Westminster.

"She went that way," he said. "She took off her shoes and headed that way barefoot."

"Yeah," Kayla said, "that's what I figured, straight toward home."

"She'll be OK, right?" the boy asked her, his gaze serious now.

"Of course, man," Mark put in. "We'll take care of her, we'll find her."

"Say hey from Tim, willya?"

"You bet we will, hey, we really appreciate the help." Kayla placed a hand strategically on the boy's forearm. "Can we pay you anything for the burger she ate?"

"Oh no no no," he said, like urgently. "Just, you know, tell her to come back some time."

Kayla couldn't help but laugh a little. "Sure, sure, I'll bring her back myself."

Shit, the testicles on the boys these days. Even the nerdy ones.

"See ya," he said, that same small smile on his lips.

As the boy scooted off, sweeping the patio, Kayla eyed Mark, who was wiping his face with a napkin. She began to nod smugly, and he caught the nod as he gathered his trash atop his red tray. He was already standing up.

"Fuck you, all right?" he said. "Let's go."

Kayla wasn't an *I told you so* kind of girl, but she gave Mark a shove anyway as he dumped his garbage. They hurried across the parking lot and piled into the Jetta, and their expressions soured at the vomit stench. In the heat of the moment, they'd forgotten.

"Son of a bitch!" Mark bellowed.

"Keep the windows open, for God's sake."

All four of the windows rolled down simultaneously. Mark pulled the Jetta out of its space, dispirited, and waited to join the traffic heading back east on Westminster.

"It's been even longer now, though," he said, making the turn. "Even if she took her time, she'd probably be home by now."

"Then that's where we'll end up." She would bet her right tit that Tommy had her address already. "Stick to the right lane, yeah? Shit, why didn't I get a shake or something?"

"Their strawberry shake is fucking radical."

"*Radical?* How old are you?"

It was easier on this side of the street, scanning the strip malls and the parking lots and the sidewalks. Kayla tried to think where Jasmine might have walked with her bare feet. She'd probably stuck to the pavement, avoided the asphalt that warmed up more quickly. As the morning heated up, she'd probably stuck to the shade, too, and that was tough to come by—bus stops, sparse palms, the ubiquitous cinder-block walls that ran the length of Orange County's streets.

They passed an endless array of sun-bleached storefronts and huge, busy signs and bland office buildings, and her eyes began to hurt. The sameness of it all, the patterned repetition like puzzle pieces that would never assemble into anything meaningful.

She watched for the blue dress, and she watched for that perky, carefree walk, in case it wasn't emblazoned in blue any longer. She'd know Jasmine when she saw her, even if she'd somehow discarded the dress in favor of something more anonymous. A thrift-store switcheroo wouldn't get by her.

After a couple miles, she started watching things more closely. They passed a restaurant with giant bay windows, the tables dotted with people—no Jasmine. Kayla watched the bus stops in case the girl needed a break from the sun. She scanned the storefronts in hopes of catching her window-shopping. But it felt wrong: Kayla knew Jasmine would be feeling some urgency as her sobriety returned. She'd be wanting to fix her mistakes. Otherwise, why would she be heading this way?

As they came to a stop at a light, Mark gestured with his chin.

"Check that out."

In the parking lot up ahead to the right, there was some kind of emergency situation. A firetruck and an ambulance sat askew in the middle of the lot, a couple of squad cars, too. Cops milled about, talking with people. All the attention was focused on a small blue-and-white tent that had been erected atop the asphalt, presumably to prevent prying eyes.

"Pull in there," Kayla said.

Mark made the turn and found an unobtrusive space away from the action. Without a word, they got out of the stinking car and began walking casually toward the scene. Kayla made her way over to a couple of languorous young women in short-shorts and bikini tops who were standing with their arms crossed, watching the cops.

"What happened?"

The taller one glanced sleepily at her and shrugged. "Some guy died."

"No shit," Mark said, sizing up the two girls.

This time, Kayla did roll her eyes at him. She turned to face the cops and tried to get a better sense of what had happened. The little tent had been constructed between an old orange Karmann Ghia and a riced-out Honda, stupid homemade spoiler screwed to its trunk. She couldn't see into the tent. She guessed a part of her imagined that it might be Jasmine lying there, for whatever reason. Like, the girl could hardly survive a few hours on the streets alone.

"Do you know how he died?" she asked the girls.

"Huh uh," said one of them. They were interchangeable except for their height. The other one was already swiping through nonsense on her phone, appearing impatient.

"Do you know anything about him, where he—?"

"I think he worked over there." Pointing.

"Where?"

Kayla followed a manicured finger and found herself staring at a cluttered, sun-bleached storefront called Woody's Coins and Metals.

24
TOMMY

Tommy Strafe watched the front of the apartment complex buzz with cops. He cursed, bit his lip.

What in the name of titty-fuck was going on in there?

He tried to play out the scenarios. Jordan returns home last night from the party, carrying Tommy's fucking coins *(gaaaah!!)*, drops them on the sofa or wherever before going to look for his sister, panicking, leaving in a huff, and—what?—the place is robbed by some miserable rando? *I mean, look at this neighborhood!* But no, that didn't add up, even that idiotic waste-of-space Jordan wouldn't call the cops if he were jacked of a fortune he'd stolen himself. OK, so it's Jasmine who goes home with the coins, driven by that fuckwit Mark Pellegro, and then she and Jordan stop just short of a vicious sibling murder-suicide that leaves Tommy's coins in the hands of the Santa Ana Police Department. But no, according to Kayla, Pelly drove Jasmine in the complete opposite direction, out toward godforsaken Westminster in the wee hours. And, plus, Jasmine had been out of her mind, leaving her purse and wallet and phone at Tommy's, for chrissakes, it's not like she'd been capable in her state of any devious plan—and he still gritted his teeth toward obliteration when he imagined Kayla just fucking *handing everything to Jordan* while Tommy slept.

Or all this drama at the apartments could have nothing at all to do with anything except everyday dismal strangers.

Right.

The way he saw it, there was a 50-50 chance his coins were in that building at this moment.

Next to Tommy, Charlton Mawk sat smoking, his arm flung out the truck's passenger window. He looked as if he could fall asleep to the old-school Rolling Stones pouring out of the premium speakers Tommy'd had installed in Fountain Valley last year. There was a subwoofer the size of a Doberman growling behind Charlie's seat.

Charlton said something under the music, sounded like *"sit here stewing."*

Tommy turned down the volume. "What?"

"I said what the fuck are we doing?"

"You wanna go over there and check it out?"

"Me?" Charlton looked at him squarely, mumbled, "Fuck you, this is your thing."

"Yeah, that's what I thought." He chewed on the insides of his cheek for a moment. "It's just, my name is in the girl's phone, they might know she was at my party …."

"You might think I give a shit, but in fact I don't."

"Then why are you even here?"

"Good fucking question."

Tommy knew this wasn't going to go like he'd hoped when Rennie bowed out of the hunt, letting Charlton be his proxy while he attended to business at the warehouse. The old man promised to lend his expertise once the Frank siblings were in hand, but there was no reason for him to get involved in the nitty-gritty so early. At his age, he didn't like getting dirty. That's what he'd said. *"You and Charlie are more than capable,"* he'd also said. *"I'll be right here when you've got 'em. I've got stuff to do."*

Rennie did get Jordan and Jasmine's address for him, faster than Tommy imagined possible, but then Tommy'd been left with Charlton riding shotgun, back in his own truck. A more-pissed-off-than-usual Charlton Mawk simmering over to his right, wanting to be anywhere else, apparently most pressingly on his couch in his shithole apartment, watching TV.

Yeah, perfect.

Tommy always remembered the time—*waaaaaaay* back near the beginning of everything—when he'd met young Charlton at a construction site in Irvine. (Tommy was positive Charlton recalled this, too, *oh yeah*, no doubt.) Rennie and Gordon happened to bring their sons to the site of a new block of apartments, what else were they supposed to do with 'em in the middle of summer, and they left the kids to their own devices while the dads slapped up two-by-fours—catchup work on a weekend. Tommy must have been twelve, Charlton eleven. Tommy'd had no interest in making new friends, preferring instead to wander the site alone and practice tagging. (His dad gave him freedom on most surfaces given they'd be covered by the drywall and finish teams in a matter of days.) But Charlton, lean and already sullen, had followed along silently and quickly become an annoyance. Tommy'd grinned and borne

Charlton's presence for an hour or so, but when the two of them encountered a trio of black teens smoking shitweed in one of the empty apartments, Charlton took the opportunity to try to prove himself. He'd casually tossed dismissive racist epithets toward the druggies, lobbing a hate grenade, and immediately the black boys were in both their faces, glowering, shouting, all gangly dark limbs and dangerous wide eyes and body odor. The most potent memory of that day was Charlton's panicked retreat from the black boys, sprawling behind Tommy on the ground, and obviously the tears that sprang into Charlie's eyes, the way he clearly despised himself in that moment of pure fear. Tommy, quiet until that moment, had surged forward and laid out the biggest of the black boys, and the other two had staggered backward in shock, watching their de facto leader writhe on the ground. After that, it had taken a single word from Tommy—*"Enough!"*—to bring closure to the incident, and the boys had skedaddled. Tommy could hear them bickering angrily amongst themselves as they stalked off the property, and Charlton had only stared at Tommy from the ground, not accepting a hand up as he wiped his eyes.

It wasn't as if Tommy ever brought up that grade-school shit, but it would forever be a part of them, and when Tommy thought of that, he couldn't resist a little squirt of glee accompanying the recollection. It was always there. Their genesis.

Tommy had the notion that the episode had been formative for Charlton, who'd evolved into a different person after that. You'd hardly recognize that kid now. Dude didn't back down these days. Tommy had to hand it to him. Plus, he was, you know, Rennie's son.

"Come on, man, I need you to get over there," Tommy said. "I honestly can't do it."

Charlton smoked and watched him talk.

"All I need is for you to ask around," Tommy went on. "You'd just be a fucking passerby."

Charlton was waiting.

Tommy relented. "Shit, man, fine, I'll get you some shit, OK? What do you want?"

"None of that gravel or flakka shit, I could use some good old-fashioned Vicodin."

"I can get Derek to cough up some 5g Norco tablets, he doesn't have a source for vikes right now."

"Yeah, his own recipe, right? Last time you dropped that 'norco' shit on me, I didn't feel right the whole night and into the next fucking day."

Tommy glanced at the ceiling of his truck, sighed, let some time slip by.

"Look, I can get you some morpho, but it's a one-time deal."

"Seriously?"

"Yeah, my own stash."

"How much of it?"

"Um ... how about ten 15mg tablets?"

"Twenty."

"Hell with that, man, I'm just asking you to take a quick walk, basically, ask a couple questions."

"All right, fine, a dozen." He flicked his butt out the window into a shrub. "What are their names again?"

"Jordan and Jasmine Frank."

"Frank's the last name?"

"Yeah." *Fucking idiot.*

Charlton stepped down from the truck and walked coolly to the intersection up ahead, hands stuffed in his pockets. He crossed the street at a diagonal and moseyed along the sidewalk toward the apartment building. There was a knot of people, maybe fifteen, facing the building's façade, all of them shlumpy, slouched. Couple of kids on bikes, just watching. All of them separate from the three or four uniformed cops who were standing near the entrance, crime tape and everything. Charlton walked straight into the group of bystanders and chummed it up with a couple of beefy guys who had their arms folded. They got all animated, pointing, nodding. Charlton joined into the nodding and pointing, folded his arms in solidarity.

Tommy's phone rang. He glanced at the screen. It was Kayla. While the phone buzzed, he dug out his last cigarette and lit it up, took a deep drag.

He answered. "You still with fuckin' Pelly?"

Yeah, Tommy was gonna have words with Mark at the store on Monday after all this shit blew over and the coins were back in his hands. He didn't know all the details yet, but it was possible that Pelly had single-handedly exploded the entire situation by providing a goddamn ride for that bitch Jasmine. And if that was the case, Tommy didn't even want to ponder Pelly's fate, didn't even want to *think* about that yet, he'd just get distracted and not see clearly. Besides, his gut was telling him it had to be Jordan, that gangly fuck, and not his sister. She'd been a cool kitten all along. That wasn't something you could fake, that girl was genuine.

"Really? That's how you answer my call?"

"I'm a little busy."

In the distance, Charlton had turned to a young woman in the small crowd and appeared to be deep in conversation with her.

Kayla's voice abruptly cut in and out. "I'm only out here on—uckin' Saturday because I—cou—help you out, you underst—."

"Look, I gotta go," Tommy said, irritated. "Something big is going on where those two brats live."

"So you're at their place? Are they there?"

"Don't know yet, but something's hit the fan."

"What are you doing right now?"

"Watching Charlie get information."

"Well, I might have something here, too."

"Yeah, what's that?"

"So we've been backtracking where Mark took the girl last night, up and down Westminster, and as we're driving along we see this big commotion, like, an emergency response. Apparently, someone died in the parking lot of one of these strip malls."

"So?"

"*Sooo,* the guy that died—get this—word is, he worked at a fucking coin shop. I'm looking at the shop as we speak."

Tommy's eyes went unfocused as he processed that. "Wait, *what?*"

"I know!"

Tommy didn't believe in coincidence. He saw existence as a series of straight-ahead narratives, one episode leading logically to the next. It was how he'd lived his whole life, and it had worked out pretty fucking great for him. Things didn't just happen, and living by that creed, he could say that nothing really surprised him. The universe had always been pretty straight with him. He supposed the philosophy came from his mom, who'd died of breast cancer when he was all of four years old. She'd whispered on her death bed to him about the beauty of mystery, the meaning, the destiny, the faith in something greater, and though he didn't ascribe to any of that fucking nonsense, the memory of her calm certainty had been contagious, had always nudged him forward to the next thing with confidence. She'd even seen meaning in her own inevitable death, had envisioned the trajectory of his future without her in it, and shit, man, she'd been right.

"But no sign of Jasmine?" he mumbled. "Or Jordan, for that matter?"

"Well, no, but isn't that weird?"

Charlton was walking easily back toward the truck, crossing the street at a stroll. He took a moment to stop at the window of a bakery and check out the goods. Then he was approaching.

"Keep an eye out, I'll call you right back," he said to Kayla and hung up before she could answer.

Charlton climbed aboard, made a show of sitting there for a minute, not saying anything. Tommy watched him, waiting. Then he couldn't take it any longer.

"Well?"

"Yeah, so that Jordan guy? He's dead."

25
STEVE

From a parking lot across the street from a raggedy strip mall, Steve Riordan scratched his itchy goatee and watched several muscular EMTs load a large bagged body into black coroner wagon. He had just rolled down all the windows and cut the engine, but now he regretted it. He didn't want to stay here any longer than was necessary. How the hell did he get here, anyway?

Next to him sat Lori's drop-dead gorgeous friend Jasmine—the girl he was really here for, if he was being totally honest—but she wasn't looking her best today. Her mouth was hanging open under a slack face, which was tear-stained and pale. She was mumbling a string of words.

"That's Tommy's girlfriend, I'm sure of it, *oh god oh god oh god!* Kayla or something, crap! How did she—oh, I'm dead, Lori, I'm dead too, just like Jordy, *no no no…*"

"Which one?" Steve asked.

"*That* one, the one on the phone!"

"Jasmine, will you calm down please?" Lori begged gently from the cramped back seat, "you're freaking Sarah out, and you're freaking *me* out, too!"

Steve checked the rearview. Lori was getting that alarming expression on her face where it seemed like she was going to implode. When things escalated and became too much for her, she'd start shaking a little, and then the shaking would get worse, and she'd get all sweaty and unresponsive, and then you just had to hang on for dear life. There were nights when Lori was so manic that he considered dumping her in front of a hospital somewhere and just going home to whack off. (Well, shit, OK, that wasn't true, he was exaggerating, but he'd be lying if said the impulse wasn't there.) One time, maybe two months ago, he'd dealt with the full brunt of her panic. Something involving her ex-husband Daniel, no doubt. Steve had dutifully held her for hours while she trembled and cried, and he'd come *that* close to leaving and never calling her again. He didn't need that in his life. But that would be cruel, right? *Fuck.*

He looked away from the rearview and continued watching the scene across the street.

"Mommy, it's OK," Sarah whispered from somewhere.

"I know, sweetie."

Steve nodded, cheering on the kid. Good for Sarah, knowing how to soothe her mom.

None of this was what he'd anticipated when Lori'd called him at the restaurant to tell him her hot friend Jasmine needed help.

A half-hour earlier, Steve had lurched his beloved Mini to a stop in that little neighborhood adjacent to Lori's building and had been abruptly thrust into an incredible bit of drama: Apparently, Jasmine's brother was dead, murdered, on the floor of their shared apartment a floor below Lori's place, the result of something asinine Jasmine had done the night before at a party. Stolen some money or something? It had something to do with the coin shop across the street, but Steve didn't have all the details on that, wasn't getting good answers to his questions; there was too much passion swamping everything. Too much crying, too many indecipherable words. What he *did* know was that he'd acted all knight-in-shining-armor and carried the emotional females swiftly away from their apartment—only to end up in a newly dicey situation.

Jasmine had insisted on returning something to this store, it was vital, it was essential, it was a matter of life or death, blah blah. And it was personal. All her talk only left Steve confused and inwardly shaking his head. He was down to a quarter tank and wasting it by criss-crossing Orange County, and at this point he could be convinced that it was all for nothing.

Something was happening across the street here, though. No denying it. If it was really true that Jasmine's brother had been murdered (incredibly difficult to believe), then it was *possible* this buzz of activity was directly related to his death. It had the hum of significance. She believed, fervently, that she was in deep, deep trouble that could potentially lead to a fate like her brother's. It all sounded outrageous, especially the way the story had poured out of both Lori and Jasmine (and Sarah, too). He'd been sure when he found them on that neighborhood curb that he could be some kind of instant hero, smooth things out, calm everybody down, get everybody a free lunch or something. He had that effect on people, thanks to long years in the restaurant business.

But his brow was becoming increasingly furrowed.

He didn't need to be involved with anything like this. Death? Revenge? Mayhem? Fuck that noise.

He'd hung out with Jasmine a few times, and, hell, one time she'd even kissed him on the cheek, laughing, careless, and he'd had flash-fantasies of a threesome happening, but that had turned to mealy shit. When he'd started making moves in that direction, Lori had scoffed and guffawed, and Steve had ended up watching a Lakers game on her little TV in the bedroom while she and Jasmine finished their wine in the front room, giggling, gossiping, bunch of girl crap.

He rested his hands on the wheel and contained several sighs.

Sure, he was hot for Jasmine—who wouldn't be?—but she wasn't worth this. It was time to start devising ways to extricate himself, drop this crew somewhere (like the police department, hello, I mean, come on!), and then go find a bar somewhere. A bar with as many TVs as possible.

For now, he tried to play along. He eyed this Kayla woman across the street as she pocketed her phone and spoke with the dude she was with, dude with the hat. The guy had a hangdog expression on his face, resigned about something, and also frustrated. He was gesticulating, shaking his head.

"So—" Trying to sound like he cared. "—who's the guy?"

Jasmine wasn't paying attention to him, just looking anxious. Steve watched her for a long moment while she fetchingly bit her lip. Fuck him, she was still hot even with her life destroyed. He almost let go with a little laugh—at himself, really. He pondered the inherent contradiction that described the two women in his Mini. Lori was a hot mess, as the kids said these days, and she also had a part-time daughter that he had to compete with, and sometimes, let's face it, that was all just a bit much. And then there was Jasmine, a clear diamond in a bed of zirconia. It was clear she'd never have anything to do with him, but that didn't mean he couldn't take any opportunity to hang with her, wear her down with sheer charm or, in this case, helpfulness.

Behind him, Lori was taking deep breaths. She met his eyes in the mirror.

"No idea who the guy is, but I know it's not Tommy." Voice flat. "I saw *that* creep earlier."

Next to him, Jasmine did a sudden double-take. "Wait, that's the guy that drove me last night, I'm sure of it! Yeah, that's his car, the Jetta." She brought a small hand to her face, fingers twisting at her mouth, then gave Steve the wide eyes. "They're looking for me."

"Take it easy," he said. "They can't see us over here. They have no idea."

"Can you turn the A/C on?" Lori said from the back. "Sarah's really hot."

"Help me with gas later?"

"Yes, yes, Jesus, fine, just please make it cooler in here."

He started up the Mini again and put the A/C on full blast while bringing the windows back up.

"Thank you."

The car gradually cooled down. Tempers cooled, too.

Steve Riordan was not above sneaking looks at Jasmine while she anguished. She had on a blue sparkly dress, way out of place on a Saturday afternoon, but even though she was kind of ripe and her hair looked sweaty, she had that model sheen about her. There was no denying she was kind of arousing. He admired her lower legs, her bare feet, her flat blue tummy.

"Wait," she said again, startling him from his reverie.

"What?" Lori croaked.

"That orange car."

"What car?"

"The funny-looking old one."

A couple parking spaces removed from all the commotion, an orange Karmann Ghia sat facing them with its silly bug eyes as if spying back at them. There was nothing really remarkable about it, but it did look sorta cool in an old-school way. Thirty years earlier, Steve might have had his eyes on a scooter like that. But today? Nah. He liked the modern features too much. He wasn't into antiques.

"What about it?" Steve put in.

Jasmine turned and faced Lori. "The man I talked to at the coin shop, I saw him get something out of that car this morning. His lunch."

"So?"

"Oh my gosh, do you think that was him? The dead guy? Do you think that guy is dead, too?"

"Don't jump to concl—"

"*He's dead, too?*" Jasmine's face went ugly with new tears. "*Lori, I don't think I can take Jordan and now this—*"

"Jazz, calm down, OK?" Lori said. "We don't know anything. It could be anybody."

"Maybe we *do* need to go to the police."

Steve perked up. "Good idea. I can take you there, for sure, I know where the department is."

"*No!*" Lori said savagely. "*I can't.*"

He met her eyes again in the rearview, and her expression was adamant.

"*You* can't? Why?"

"Steve," Lori mewled, and in the mirror, she gestured with her eyes toward Sarah, the history there.

Feeling a knot in his gut, Steve let his hands drop from the wheel. Let his head fall forward. He found himself staring at the apron he was still wearing. The stains, the wear-and-tear. He shook his head. Honestly, he'd rather have been back at the restaurant, working tables, raking in paltry tips. Ah, who was he kidding? He didn't want to go back there. At this moment, he hated the restaurant and everyone there. He lamented his myriad weaknesses, but mostly the ease with which he could be manipulated. By Tony at the restaurant, but the other staff, by customers. Lori always took advantage of him that way, too.

Maybe he could pretend to get a phone call.

He sighed, big and long. Lori gave him a dirty look in the mirror.

"What?" he said.

Jasmine squinted at him, confused, beneath a blast of light from the sunroof, then she looked away. Now that Steve took the time to really get a look at her, really look at her, she seemed to be getting worse. Her face was blasted and pale and sweaty and exhausted, possibly the worst he'd ever seen her.

Lori didn't answer him.

Jesus Christ, what was he doing here? He was tired from the long breakfast shift. He'd been up since three, had put off a shower because he'd snoozed his clock seven times and been late to kitchen prep. He'd felt slimy through his whole shift, and his disposition had been lackluster, and it showed in his gratuities. Customers had given him the stink-eye all morning, like *What's with this guy?* That happened at enough tables, it started to wear your spirit down to a nub, and then you were just blunt for the rest of the shift, and you didn't give a good goddamn. And if at that point you, say, received a weird phone call inviting you to be the hero for a hottie, which might ultimately lead to some kind of fascinating bedroom scenario, well, that could very well cheer the fuck out of you—until reality came crashing down and you were suddenly a potential accessory to crime involving murder.

Across the street, the coroner vehicle simply sat in the middle of the parking lot while everyone in the vicinity stared at it. The woman, Kayla, was back on the phone, and her companion was pacing.

Steve spent the next ten minutes devising a strategy to get the females out of his idling Mini. It was elegant. He'd fake a phone call from Andrew at the restaurant, an urgent plea to fill in for Tori or Deidre, the frizzy flakes who called in sick at the slightest provocation. He'd taken calls like that from Andrew before, so he felt he could easily fake his side of it. He'd even throw in some exhausted refusals until an offer of overtime came into play. And then he'd hang up angrily, in a huff, and pretend to think about the situation, and finally offer an Uber for the girls. They'd pile out of his car, he'd act all regretful, and they'd have their ride back home, where they could deal with their problem on their own. Best of all, he'd be free and clear to move on with his Saturday afternoon, fuck yes.

He hadn't taken any action beyond further sighing when he heard rustling behind him.

Lori began talking.

"Look," she said, "I have to get out of this car. I have to get *Sarah* out of this car. I mean, I hate that this is happening, Jasmine, but we have to go home, you know? I can't keep doing this to her. Plus, I really to to fucking pee, and I could use a cigarette!"

Jasmine began to weep quietly.

Steve felt the end was near. He probably wouldn't even need to fake the phone call.

A collective gasp filled the tight confines of the Mini. Next to him, Jasmine shoved herself down in her seat until she could just see over the dash. She stared straight ahead with wide, wet eyes.

"Oh my god," she said.

Jason Bovberg

Across the street, a black monster truck was making a turn into the strip mall parking lot. It angled over close to the woman, Kayla, who'd stowed her phone. She gave a small wave of acknowledgment to the truck's driver, and the dude she was with gave a tight, contrite wave, too. The truck came to a stop at the far end of the parking lot, away from the coroner, and two men hopped down.

"What, what?" Steve asked.

"It's Tommy," Jasmine whispered.

26
MARK

Mark Pellegro noticed the Mini Cooper pull in across the street for the simple reason that he'd always wanted one of those funky little rides. It was a spiffy red sporty looker, striped and UK-badged, and he immediately coveted it. Best he could afford was his old Jetta—yeah, that one over there, the one that was going to stink of Jasmine's vomit for months—but the Mini was his dream ride. Ever since he'd seen that crazy movie *The Italian Job* when he'd swindled free Cinemax for a year, he'd imagined himself behind the wheel of one of those cars, like Michael fucking Caine, tooling around Santa Ana like he owned Main Street.

Mark had stood there baking on the sidewalk, admiring the Mini while Kayla yammered away on the phone with Tommy, and then he'd about shat himself when the car settled into a spot facing him and he recognized Jasmine Frank herself in the passenger seat.

Holy shit! he screamed inwardly, but he kept calm, flipped a U-turn in his pacing, and went about his business, half-listening to Kayla.

"Where are you?" she was saying to Tommy. *"If you hit Del Taco, we're about two blocks past that. On the left."*

Mark practiced his breathing techniques. He'd been dreading Tommy's arrival for fifteen minutes now, trudging up and down the Westminster Boulevard sidewalk like a basket case while the commotion in front of the coin shop continued full-bore, but Jesus, this threw a wrench in the works. His heart was suddenly trip-hammering, like *rat-a-tat-tat-tat*, and he felt as if he'd start stuttering if he were forced to actually talk to anyone. There was still a loitering crowd spread out across the whole parking lot, maybe a couple dozen people, scattered, gossiping. The bikini bimbos, bored, had gone back inside the tanning salon not long after he and Kayla had spoken with them, like they wanted nothing to do with the likes of him. Most of the other looky-loos were store proprietors who'd walked lazily out of their businesses to feign concern. This would be the most exciting day of their year.

Mark moved away from the crowd, thinking.

If he had his facts right, if he'd overheard everything correctly, Tommy and Kayla were sure that Jasmine or her brother (Jordan?) had stolen Tommy's fabled coin collection right out of their shared bedroom, straight out of some kind of custom secure case. The story had instantly sounded suspect to Mark: Again, who on earth would have the balls to steal anything from *Tommy Strafe?* And, honestly, how could a bunch of old coins be worth more than, say, a couple hundred bucks? This was the age of Bitcoin and PayPal. No one cared about physical manifestations of *anything* anymore. So Jasmine or Jordan ran off with some questionable relics. Who cared?

Tommy and Kayla cared, that's who! The furious energy wafting out of the phone was enough to tell him that Jasmine was seriously in danger. Whatever those coins were actually worth, they were worth *a hell of a lot* to Tommy.

Because Tommy was rather upset. He was *very* upset.

The thought made Mark literally shiver.

He could only imagine what Tommy was truly capable of. Two or three times, he'd witnessed the man in the grips of his unique, fuming rage, whether resulting from an order shortage at the store or a supplier flaking out on him or even the tiniest of miscommunications. It was a sight to behold. Tommy's face would go red as a precursor, and then his voice would rise, and then he'd start barking through gritted jowls, and then it would *really* get ugly. One time, as Mark watched stupidly from the register, Tommy had grabbed one of their sellers by the lapels of his cheap sport coat, and the poor asshole's nose had started bleeding before anything had even happened! Mark had never seen anything like that, even in the movies. It was as if Tommy could melt your face with the sheer force of his fury. He did end up lifting the seller off his feet and pounding him bodily against a wall, and the fucker had added pissed pants to his phantom bloody nose, and the urine on the floor had only further enraged Tommy. The guy had left the store wounded and stained and humbled, and a nervous replacement seller came in his stead ever after.

After a few minutes, Kayla disconnected from Tommy with a kind of feline growl and approached Mark on the cracked sidewalk.

"Big guy's almost here."

"Awesome."

"Oh, take it easy, I'll let him know what's up."

"Yeah, you're right, Tommy has always been a guy who listens to reason."

Kayla slung her hip, all attitude. "What kind of pussy are you, anyway?"

"Kind that just wants a clean car and a normal Saturday."

"Ah, this is more fun than you've had in months. Years maybe."

Mark about-faced and continued pacing.

Fuuuuuck.

Maybe she's right.

Behind his sunglasses, he snuck glances across the street. It was harder to tell now—even though Jasmine was facing him, she was now a little farther away after turning in to the parking lot, and the constant traffic obscured her—but he was sure that was her hunkered down in shotgun. Same blue dress, same hair with the blonde highlights, now flat, unkempt. Same bare upper arms, tanned, polished. There was a guy in the driver's seat staring this way. He had a goatee and a plump face. There seemed to be someone else in the back seat, but Mark couldn't make out more than shadowed movement. Whoever was back there must be cramped up to all hell in that little Mini.

What did this *mean?*

His mind raced, trying to piece everything together.

Mark had left Jasmine alone and essentially penniless in the In-N-Out parking lot—yeah, OK, he'd been annoyed as fuck at upchuck girl, and maybe he wasn't great at making decisions just then. She'd been confused, drug-drowsy, three quarters of the way toward blackout, hungry, probably had to pee, but he didn't care: She was one of those gorgeous idiot girls who lived a charmed existence, failing upward on a daily basis, and when she'd let loose with her technicolor yawn, all over his fucking car, well, his disgust overrode everything. He knew she'd find a way home. Girls like that always did.

Mark had left the beautiful goof to her own devices and had spent the next nine hours cursing her name, scrubbing his floorboards, and finally worrying about her, and then—coming to terms with what he'd done—he'd spent another couple hours with Tommy's fucking woman searching for the suddenly conniving soul. And now here was Jasmine again, staring at this very parking lot, staring at him, from a distance, like three moves ahead of him in a chess match.

I mean, what in the holy fuck?

Mark turned to face the coin store, across the lot. He considered its bland façade—the spidery crack in the window to the right, the faded posters and signs advertising theme collections from the past decade or more. The shadowed interior of the unlit store. It was obviously closed. Five minutes ago, Mark had wandered closer and found a sign in the door that read WILL RETURN IN 30 MINUTES. He had no idea how long it had been there, could've been minutes, hours, or days.

Word was, the dead guy on the sidewalk had worked in this store. Mark had to assume, now, that the corpse's story aligned somewhere with Jasmine's. Right? And that had to involve the coins. Obviously.

Tommy would be here in minutes, possibly seconds.

Tell him or keep this to himself?

Jasmine and whoever she was with clearly had their eyes on whatever was happening over here. Where had she gotten the ride? Who was that behind the wheel? Maybe she was smarter than Mark gave her credit for—or she was exactly what he thought, successful once again because of her exalted genetic fortune. Which was nothing to sneeze at.

The question was why? Why was she back here—and apparently with a goddamn crew? Clearly, Jasmine had gotten away, had escaped her early-morning predicament, as he knew she would, and she'd proven plenty capable. But what was her game?

Oh man. He turned again, kept his stride casual. *Play it cool.*

Tommy pulled into the parking lot a minute later, his big-ass truck rolling in almost humbly. The man clearly didn't want to attract an inordinate amount of attention to himself, despite his vehicle. He took a space on the far side of the property, in front of a hair salon and a bakery outlet, then eased down to the pavement, essentially unnoticed. Someone else there, too, oh it was that greaser dude, what was his name? Like this day could get any worse. Charlie something, with the slicked-back hair, cigarette riding a sneer, good lord. The dude jumped down from the passenger side.

Mark felt a stab of anxiety.

Kayla was giving him a look, beckoning him with her shoulder. Mark offered a tight nod and started her way. He had no idea what he was about to do or say.

"Hey boss," he managed to Tommy, nice and easy, as he came up close.

"Why don't you fuck right off, Pelly?" Tommy rumbled, almost under his breath, and Mark's stomach fell away from him.

"Tommy—" Kayla put in, but Tommy shut her up with a hard glance.

"I told you to keep an eye on that girl," he said to Mark, "not help her rip me off."

Mark withered, didn't know how to respond. Tongue-tied. Mr. Rockabilly was over to his right, his back against a weathered post—vaguely ridiculous but somehow threatening. Mark waited for Kayla to say more in his defense, but she was quiet, looking away, off toward the coroner vehicle. He watched the side of her face for the briefest of moments, then glanced over at the Mini Cooper across the street. There was no movement over there, but he caught a flash of blue.

He decided to protect her.

He took his sunglasses off, even managing to keep his fingers from shaking.

"I had *no idea* what she did, man," Mark said. "I'm *still* not really clear on it. All I know is she puked in my fucking car. As far as her taking anything? No idea. But anyway, I'm here now trying to fix it."

That didn't mean much to Tommy. Mark half-expected his own nose to start bleeding.

"I don't get my shit back—like, *today*—Charlie over there is gonna break your arms."

Charlie frowned, gave Tommy a look, shook his head at Mark. *No I won't.*

"What the fuck, dude?" Tommy gestured, exasperated, glaring at Charlie.

Charlie raised his eyebrows and smoked. "I'm not your hired goon." The guy looked completely at ease with his place in the world, and for that he earned Mark's respect and even envy.

Tommy stalked away in a tight circle, scanning the strip mall. He was taking in the coin shop, the loose crowd in front of it, the lingering cops. He looked like he was about to have a stroke—red-faced, stiff, barely concealing something. Then he caught Kayla's eye and gestured for her to follow him.

The two of them moved off, some yards away, and dove into a whispered conversation, and Mark couldn't hear any of it over the traffic noise. He nodded at this Charlie character, who seemed to be evaluating Mark with something between amusement and contempt. *Yeah, feeling's mutual, asshole.* He put his sunglasses back on, turned away.

He wandered over to the tanning salon, looked at the posters of the skimpy girls, not sure what else to do.

At that moment, Kayla emitted a shocked exclamation—*"Dead?"*—and Tommy glowered at her, grabbed her forearm, and hauled her farther down the sidewalk. Mark watched them retreat.

Someone else was dead? *Jesus Christ.*

Well, it wasn't Jasmine. Fuck, it could be anybody. Right? Or was it someone involved in all this? The brother? Jordan?

He folded his arms and scanned the lot for the hundredth time. He visualized Jasmine walking here from the burger joint in her heels—what was it, two miles from the In-N-Out? Or maybe she'd already found her ride, this guy with the Mini. Either way, she'd been wiped out, still exhausted from the night before, drugs long worn off, running on empty, and the only thing that would save her from further misery was the bag in her hand, the grocery bag that apparently contained a fortune. Well, at least a value of a couple hundred bucks. Was Jasmine stupid enough to trade the stolen goods for a quick payout? Or was it possible that there *was* a true fortune in that bag?

And if so, where were those coins now?

He firmed up his decision. He wasn't going to tell Tommy he'd seen Jasmine. *Fuck him!* A shot of adrenaline coursed through him. *Christ*, it was a risk. But maybe it was an opportunity. *Imagine!* Striking it rich *and* getting the girl.

He snuck a glance across the street.

The Mini Cooper was gone.

27
JASMINE

Jasmine Frank jostled in her seat as Steve careened over potholes. It was as if the ground itself were attempting to shock her out of her numbness. But everything was muted, distant, a flagging blue kite in dull skies, as if she were no longer connected to reality.

Her brother was dead. And now her own life was in danger.

It was that simple, that awful.

She'd *thought* going back to the store was precisely the right thing to do. March right back into the coin shop, drop George's bag of money on the counter, tell him she'd made a horrible mistake. He was a nice guy, she was sure he'd understand. Hell, he'd seemed reluctant about the whole transaction to begin with. She'd felt her insides begin to decompress on the drive from the neighborhood where Steve picked them up, as if she were taking the first positive step since finding—

But then!

The moment the strip mall had come into view, her stomach had dropped. A big crowd, more police cars, an ambulance ... a fire truck! Something had happened, and she'd known it was something to do with her. She'd *known it!* Like, no question.

Tommy had somehow figured out what she'd done with the coins—like *everything!* How? Not a single soul had seen her go into that shop! Well, except for ol' George. She wanted to *scream*, felt it surging out of her, but she tamped it down. *No!* No more tears. She wasn't going to accomplish much of anything if nothing came out of her except emotion and snot.

Somewhere behind her, minutes after Tommy's truck had arrived across the street like a nightmare made corporeal, Sarah had started voicing little-kid alarm, something about her mom, and Steve's ridiculous little clown car had started rocking with noise and stress. Lori had begun shaking and whining and sweating, in the grips of some kind of panicked seizure, and Steve had started up the Mini and bounced them out of the lot, back onto Westminster Boulevard, heading east.

At least real air was coursing through the car now. Steve had put all the windows down again, and the breeze had to help.

"So what do we do?" Steve asked. "Where do you want me to go, Lori?

The hospital?"

There was no answer, just a high whine.

When they were out of view of Tommy, Jasmine sat up in her seat and twisted to face Lori and Sarah. It was like reverse religious iconography back there, the child caressing her mother's sweaty anxious head, and that more than anything jarred Jasmine from her detachment. She reached back to touch Sarah's knee.

"It's OK, sweet girl," she said.

Sarah nodded, face drawn, then glanced back down at Lori, whose face was clamped and flushed, the muscles of her cheeks twitching. She had her hands folded up against her chest as if to prevent something from bursting forth—a scream, a sob.

"This happens sometimes," Sarah whispered.

"I'm going to the hospital," Steve said, loud.

"No, wait," Jasmine said. She moved her hand to his forearm. "Just … keep driving. Take it easy. She'll be OK, right Sarah? She'll be OK."

She didn't know how to help her friend, but the sight of her was all too familiar. She'd seen this expression on her own mother's face in her childhood, when things got tough. Even when Jasmine was little and didn't understand a goddamn thing, her mom would get that way, would descend into hell, and Jasmine remembered she looked just like Lori did now. The echo came at her, hard, and so did the memories of Jordan—somehow—finding a way to help their mother. Soothing, confident, understanding. She still had no idea how he had managed that. She'd shared their mother's womb with him, and yet against all reason *he* was the one who could help their mom and she couldn't.

"Can you make your mom feel better?" she asked Sarah gently. "Can you just, like, pet her? Tell her you love her? Do your magic?"

Sarah nodded again, and Jasmine exhaled, grateful for the girl, because she couldn't even begin to *try* to deal with Lori at the moment. On top of everything.

She turned back around, took a deep breath, let it out shakily.

Steve was saying something, softer now, but whatever it was, it was buffeting her ears like wind, unintelligible.

It was so hard not to give in to despair, to let those old feelings come back. *What have I done?*

Everything was in ruins, and she knew it was her fault.

Or *not* her fault.

She couldn't completely remember what had happened last night at the party—the fateful blurry steps that had led inexorably to this terrible moment. She *did* remember the first moment Tommy had shown her the coins in that elaborate case in the bedroom. Getting all braggy, as if his collections meant anything to her. And as he'd gestured Jasmine and Jordan out of the room, she'd caught that glimpse of the elaborate lock on the inner drawer. In that tiny moment, she knew that Tommy had left it disengaged by mistake.

She recalled the feeling of being ganged up on in the tight hallway, the way she'd abruptly realized that Tommy and his friends were working in concert to separate her from Jordy, and she'd thought that was funny at first. Flattering? She'd even laughed with all of them, even as she'd understood what they were trying to do. And then the whole party had become sinister.

But she hadn't been able to stop laughing. Her cheeks had hurt.

And now look where she was.

Her eyes blurred again.

"—going?" Steve was saying.

"Huh?" Wiping at her face.

"Where are we going?"

"Um ..."

The back seat was quiet. Remarkably, Lori appeared to be asleep. Sarah was stroking her mom's cheek with her little hand. At the girl's feet was her colorful backpack, the one holding Jasmine's grocery bag full of cash. She considered taking the money back, putting it in her own pack, but she held off, letting Sarah continue petting her mom. She'd have to get the money back at some point, though. She'd have to take responsibility. Jasmine had taken Tommy's coins, and she had *sold* them. My *God!* Even that felt like a different reality, like she'd dreamed it. Taking all that money from friendly George.

George.

"Turn around," Jasmine whispered, her voice a rasp.

"What?"

"Can you drive by those stores again? Where we were watching? Just drive by?"

"What for?"

"Please?"

"Fine." Steve made a quiet strangled sound in his throat.

He made a left at the first opportunity, then reentered traffic going west.

The trunk, she thought.

It all went back to the trunk. The trunk of Karl's gasoline-reeking LeSabre, sleek and growly, that long gray hood, the grill shining like medieval armor. Its vast trunk. Jordy trapped inside it overnight without her even knowing. Awakened by voices, Jordy muffle-crying and Karl's voice shutting him up. She'd peered out her bedroom window to find Karl releasing her brother from the dark, shivery prison—beaten, humiliated, freezing. Karl untying him, removing the stained rag from his mouth.

That was when her family became dangerous. Life-threatening. The moment when it all became too much. At least, that's when they'd come to terms with the fact. Later in the perilous morning, she and Jordan had looked into each other's eyes, wordless, Jordy still shivering, and they knew that they were in it together, just the two of them, and that their future was elsewhere.

"What are we looking for?" Steve asked her.

"I don't know," she lied.

She knew exactly what she was looking for—another look at the dead man's car.

The trunk.

"OK, slow down here."

They moved past the strip mall doing thirty, and Jasmine took a good long look from shotgun through eastbound traffic, staying low. The orange Karmann Ghia was still sitting in the same spot, facing Westminster Boulevard, as if watching her as the Mini drove by. The cops weren't anywhere near it, and Tommy's crew were on the opposite side of the parking lot, oblivious to it. The funky little car had a long front end, nothing like the old Buick of her nightmares, and it had a squat trunk. She caught only a glimpse of it as they drifted past.

The scene around the coroner van—the lingering cops, the EMTs, the tent—all seemed to be getting smaller. People were dispersing. The crowd was thinning.

Chances were, Tommy's coins were still in the shop, in a safe somewhere, maybe already in a display case, or they were in police custody—either way, lost to her, beyond her control. But she couldn't take her eyes off the Karmann Ghia's trunk. She kept flashing on the sight of portly George swaying out to his old-school vehicle and bending in for his bag lunch. Eyeing her as she waited for him to come back and open the shop's cracked-glass door.

Considering the fact that the store was now locked up again, early, and the orange VW was still there in its space, and—well—just the fact of this consistently horrible day ... she was nearly positive that it was George whose body had been loaded into that van.

The man she'd sold Tommy's coins to was dead.

The thought sparked fear, dread—and now curiosity.

Was it possible he'd had time to put the coins in car? In his trunk? Had friendly George ripped her off? She recalled the way he'd insisted on doing their transaction outside. That all felt hinky now. Why else would he do that, if not to avoid detection? He'd made it about doing her a favor, but that was almost certainly a ruse. She thought about the blast of vindication, of freedom, she'd felt as she'd left the store, swinging that grocery bag of cash—and now she imagined him watching her go, just waiting for her to get out of sight so that he could run off somewhere. Go sell the coins at another coin joint, for the millions they were really worth.

She nodded to herself.

He ripped me off.

The strip mall receded behind them, and Jasmine sat up, faced forward. If she could get those coins back ...? She could get them back to Tommy. Or she could *really* start a new life.

Either way, she could fix everything.

She closed her eyes.

That wasn't entirely true, was it?

"I still have to pee," came a soft voice in the back. At first it sounded like Sarah, but then Jasmine realized it was Lori.

"Oh shit," Jasmine blurted, remembering that Lori'd had to pee an hour ago. She scanned the street, then gestured to Steve. "Hey, turn into that 7-11 over there."

Steve turned into the lot and swung tightly into a parking space facing a filthy stucco wall and a concrete trash can wrapped with dying vines. As soon as the vehicle came to a stop, Jasmine hopped out, pulling her seat forward to allow Lori and Sarah escape. Out in fresh air that smelled faintly of urine, Lori let out a great groan of relief, bending over as if to stop herself from fainting. Sarah followed her mom out, looking scared and wary. On the opposite side of the Mini, Steve was already standing, watching over the low roof. He looked helpless and exasperated.

"Are you all right?" he called.

Lori nodded, motionless, head still down. Jasmine could see her breathing, could see the inhalations getting gradually calmer, as if her friend had been on the verge of hyperventilating in that car. Her armpits were dark, and her hair looked greasy, and her skin looked pale, and all those things made Jasmine feel bad for her, almost more than anything. For her part, Sarah seemed to not want to deal with it. She was staring at the 7-11's windows, all the promises of sugar candy and soda.

"Better," Lori finally said, her breathing like meditation. "Bathroom."

Lori stood up straight. There were tear stains across her flushed face, crooked, both new and dry. She glanced around, hollow, defeated. Jasmine smiled at her, no response. Vehicles swished by them in a near-constant swirl of exhaust. Finally Lori made her way toward the glass doors, a little unsteady, and pushed through, disappearing inside. Sarah followed her closely.

Jasmine was left staring at Steve, who was smiling weakly. He still had his apron on from the restaurant where he worked, and he looked like a waiter at the end of a double shift. He looked like he didn't want to be here.

"Sorry to ... to drag you out here," Jasmine said.

"Hey, look, I'm happy to help out." A pause. "I'm sorry about—"

"It's OK."

There was no way she wanted to hear Jordy's name come out of Steve's mouth at the moment. She nodded vague thanks. There was no way to keep her eyes dry, but she kept the smile rock-steady.

Steve didn't appear to have anything more to say, so he stood there awkwardly, watching her.

She went to the sidewalk and stared off down the street. She could just make out the strip mall that contained the coin shop, about a quarter mile east, but she couldn't see the Karmann Ghia. She needed to get to it, but it could be an hour or two before the coast was clear.

She returned to Steve, who was still leaning over the car. "I'll make sure she's OK," she said. "Listen … it's my fault she's like this. She's fantastic, you know. Best thing in my life. Sarah, too. I love that kid. *Love* her."

Steve kept quiet, but something had changed in his eyes.

She walked into the 7-11.

28
TOMMY

The coin shop on the opposite end of the strip mall seemed to glare at Tommy Strafe like a pale, apathetic eye, its cracked glass a sneering wink, its bleached-out window art mocking him with its age, its worthlessness. The coroner crew had apparently loaded the fat employee of that store into a meat wagon, and Tommy's coins were probably already behind lock and key in an evidence room at the Westminster Police Department.

He found he could barely speak, his rage was so palpable, like a great cramp centered behind his eyes and spreading out across his face and jaw. When he did speak, the words came out in a hoarse bray, and even as he spoke them, he knew they didn't convey the calm force that he intended. He usually took great pride in the imposing figure he posed by sheer genetics, so when he did something that *betrayed* that sense of innate power ... he disappointed himself.

Yeah, he was self-aware. Sure he was. Kayla sometimes told him that he lacked that trait, but he didn't.

He sucked air in and out, helplessly watching the EMTs begin to deconstruct the scene and clear out.

Over on the sidewalk adjacent to Westminster Boulevard, Mark Pellegro was watching traffic flow by. He'd been sitting at the bus stop for a while, planted there like Rodin's Thinker, and now he was back up, pacing east. Shit, man, maybe Pelly was blameless. That's what Kayla had been about to say earlier. Tommy knew Mark was OK; the guy just rubbed him wrong at every opportunity. He was a goddamn yes man to the bitter end. Had even said yes to Jasmine when she'd asked him to be her getaway man.

And then there was Charlie—the opposite of a yes man. The dude was still standing in the shade of an overhang like some cowboy, squint-eyed, relaxed, waiting. When Charlie had returned from Jasmine's apartment building to inform him what he'd learned—that the greasily odious Jordan Frank had been ganked—Tommy had been fucking *shook*. Stunned between bafflement and admiration. Jasmine had stolen Tommy's coins, yes, and she'd used his own gullible yes man to escape, and apparently she'd *sold his fucking coins to the lowest bidder (!!)* ... and by the looks of it she had *killed her own brother* (directly? indirectly?) to erase him from her criminal equation. What had perhaps started as a spur-of-the-moment brother-sister flight con had become all her own.

One way or another, Jasmine Frank was responsible.

Oh yeah, she owned this.

Jesus Christ! Maybe she even offed this fucker right here!

Tommy'd arrived on the scene and smelled her like sweat, like girl piss. Her scent was everywhere. She'd *been* here. And whatever she'd done had been too much for the poor asshole who was now in the back of a coroner van. Talk about underestimating someone!

Well, she wasn't going to get the best of him.

Only thing was ... even back at the apartments, sitting there waiting for Charlie, he'd started to feel achy. He'd been restless, had been *this close* to hopping down from the cab and walking around, trying to shake some of it out. It almost always tricked him, feeling like stress or nerves or sleeplessness from his sleep apnea. He'd yawn and sniff, he'd feel anxious about whatever. It was when he started to sweat, that clammy kind of sweat—that's when he knew.

Withdrawal.

He figured he had about an hour before he started throwing up. Or worse.

He checked his watch, glanced around, stood watching the EMTs scurry about.

"I'm fucking hungry," he announced. "I haven't eaten all day."

Kayla came up close to him. "What do you want to do about the girl?"

"Not much we can do here, right? I mean, look around."

Tommy had no intention of losing his birthright to that duplicitous cunt. The way he saw it, the equation was simple. If the coins were with the police, he would deal with that later, with Rennie's help maybe. He could prove ownership, if it came to that—at least, he thought he could. He gave that possibility a thirty percent chance. Short of that, his collection was either still in Jasmine's hands, or it was in that store. And as Jasmine was gone with the wind at the moment, he had to bank on the store. That was the next thirty percent chance he chose to focus on now. Put all his chips there—at least at this moment. He liked to go with his gut, and his gut told him his coins were inside Woody's Coins and Metals.

And even if they weren't, hell, he'd find something in there that was equally worthy.

Not that doing so would absolve Jasmine of what she'd done. He still imagined strangling the life out of her, watching the capillaries burst in her eyes, listening to her hack for breath, feeling her body let go of its lifeforce beneath him.

His teeth began to grit again. He growled under his breath and turned away from the sight of the coin store.

"We're attracting attention," he said.

"No we're not," Charlton said. "No one cares."

Tommy glowered at him, then glanced away.

He felt Kayla watching him, judging him, and he resented the sensation. He itched to snap at her. If it weren't for Charlie standing right there, and Mark within earshot now, and the loose crowd, and—you know—the fucking police at the edge of the parking lot ... she'd bear the full brunt of his anger, oh yeah. Kayla had had goddamn Jordan *in their house,* while Tommy slept in the next room. She'd *talked* to the miscreant! She'd *handed over* the phone, the purse, everything! What kind of ignorant twat—

"*Fuck!*" he grumbled to no one in particular.

"Tommy, can I talk to you for a minute?" Kayla asked. "In private?"

He ignored her.

"We need to get out of here," he said. "If we haven't attracted attention by now, we will soon. There's nothing we can do anyway, with this crowd hanging around. We need them to see us leave—all casual-like. Let's regroup and come up with a plan, get some food."

"Where?" Kayla said, deflated.

"We go back to our place, we come back la—"

"*What? No.*"

"Listen to me! We get some tools, and we come back here in a few hours, maybe even after dark, you know, after everything has calmed down. And when we come back, we're prepared to do some business."

"I'm not going to your fucking hovel," Charlton said. "I'm tired, man. This is stupid. I'm done."

Tommy felt the first twinges of nausea stir in his bowels and knew he had to get home. Get on that road like now.

He was picturing his stash in his nightstand, beneath the drawer's false bottom, his little red leather case. Over the past seven or eight months, he'd narrowed in on that flocka shit that Derek had turned him on to. Christ, it made him feel like a teenager again—muscles bursting like goddamn Superman, a rippled throbbing cock that could go seven or eight times, god-like euphoria. He'd started vaping it early on, that's what Derek did, but Tommy had come to the conclusion that vaping was strictly for pussies. He preferred to snort the gravel or, even better, warm it up and inject it. Smelled like a boy's locker room when he put it to flame, that's what Kayla always said (and she was right on that count), but to hell with her. Right now, he was imagining shooting up a hot dose and feeling that bull-rush, that warm lightning strike, oh Jesus, he could already taste the metallic jolt.

"Tommy, come here." Kayla yanking at his bicep.

"What?" Annoyed, dragged along the narrow sidewalk.

In front of an empty Chinese laundry, a twelve-year-old kid stared out at them from the register. Tommy gave the kid a glare. Kayla stopped and came up into his face.

"Tommy, you're shaking, you're doing that thing."

"What thing? Hey, *fuck you*, all right?"

"Keep it quiet!" she hissed, glaring around. "Understand me? Keep it down. You told me to tell you—"

"Just—just whatever, why do you think I want to go home?"

Kayla made a noise in her throat. "So what's your plan, then? We go home so you can shoot up, and then you get all crazy and determined again, and we come back here after dark? Break into that store? That store that the police will probably be watching? That store whose—whose owner or manager or whatever is no doubt on his way to as we speak?"

"Listen, as far as I'm concerned, you're the reason we're fucking *here!*"

"Right, I called you—"

"If you hadn't given Jordan the purse, the phone, fucking *everything*, then we'd have her."

Kayla cocked a hip, gave him some attitude. "How do you figure that?"

"Never mind."

Tommy caught sight of Mark, who was perched against his Jetta facing Westminster Boulevard. He looked all squirrely. The asshole knew he'd fucked up and was avoiding Tommy—that was crystal clear. He looked like he was just waiting to get the hell out of here, desperate to fall into his sad little car and mope on home. Sit in a chair in his dumpy apartment, wherever that was, and stress all weekend about what he'd done, then finally arrive at work trembling on Monday, eager to find any way to get back in his boss's good graces. For Pelly, that was probably his *best-case* scenario. *Aaarrggh.*

But shit, maybe Tommy was too hard on the suck-up. Dude was a good salesman. Had a way with people, despite what he looked like.

Kayla surprised him by sidling up into him. "Let me take you home, baby. Let's get you fixed up. We'll talk about it in the truck."

"Charlie doesn't have wheels."

"Charlie can take care of himself." She was rubbing his pecs. "Or Mark can take him home." A smile in her voice.

Goddamn it, the nausea was ratcheting up. He yawned, then surreptitiously scanned the parking lot with watery eyes. EMTs were probably fifteen minutes from clearing out, coroner another ten past that, police who fucking knew. Could be another hour, especially if—like Kayla said—the coin shop owner showed up to talk to them. Yep, Tommy was probably looking at nighttime for returning to the shop. Probably needed Rennie to gather a quick, down-and-dirty crew, couldn't let this go past tonight.

Tommy turned away from Kayla and wandered over to Charlton, leaned against the wall. The shade felt good. Eased the anxiety a little.

"I still need you, man."

Charlton ground out another cigarette on the cement. "You're not dragging me around Orange County anymore."

"Look, we're talking about a lot of cash with this thing. I'm sure there's some of that can go your way."

"Keep talking."

"Thousand bucks."

"Fuck you, a thousand bucks. Like you're just gonna hand me a thousand bucks."

"That collection is worth at least a hundred grand. Probably more like a quarter mil."

Charlton laughed outright. "You're all talk, asshole, have been for years."

"Why do you think that man is dead over there? Why do you think Jordan is dead? I'm talking about a small fortune. I guarantee it."

"You're talking a grand only if you recover the thing." Stuffing his hands in his pockets.

"Either way."

"Uh-huh."

Tommy's gut twanged, and he couldn't hold back a wince. Charlie smirked in response, the fucker—he knew what was up.

"You always do this, man, you always get dunked in shit that doesn't have anything to do with me, and somehow I'm riding shotgun because you need help. Look at you, you're not even right in the head."

He looked off to the east, muscles in his jaw vibrating.

Tommy didn't have the stomach to fucking argue with him, so he kept the hard stare, waited until Charlie glanced back.

"Whatever, fine, I'm staying here." He gestured to the café on the corner. "I'm getting coffee. I could use a reprieve from you unbelievable idiots."

"We're looking at more than a couple hours, maybe even nightfall. Probably that."

"Fuck are you talking about?" He spat into an empty parking space. "Just get lost, huh? Call me when you have something figured out. I can find my way around."

"I'll stay in touch."

"Yeah, you do your thing." He laughed a little.

"We'll bring your dad in."

"Not likely, but whatever you say."

Tommy stepped out into the sun, gesturing with his chin at Kayla—*Let's go.* Charlton stayed right where he was, and that made Tommy even more shaky. An hour ago, Tommy had felt invincible, in charge—wronged and enraged. The solution had been in sight, the equivalent of stomping bugs on asphalt. But ever since that useless punk Jordan had had the *balls* to get snuffed, everything had fallen apart. He'd lost control. He had to take the reins back, and that started with his little red case.

Kayla fell in line behind him, walking toward the truck.

From his Jetta, Mark reacted to their movement.

"What do you want me to do?" he called.

"I got it from here," Tommy said bluntly. "We're gonna come back later. Go on home. I'll see you Monday."

29
LORI

In the cramped confines of a 7-11 bathroom stall, Lori Holst contemplated her face in her compact mirror. Beneath her stupid bangs *(what was she thinking?)*, her skin was splotchy, ugly, drawn. Her nose was red, the pores huge and enflamed. Stupid bright bathroom.

She was a monster. Sitting on a filthy 7-11 toilet miles from home.

She clapped the mirror shut, stowed it in her purse.

This wasn't the way her Saturday was supposed to go—no way, no how. The plan had been to show a strong face to Sarah's asshole dad Daniel at pickup, then show her baby a good time at the park, and lunch, and dessert, maybe some game time at the apartment, stay off the fucking TV. Try to recapture some of the mommy-daughter magic they'd had when her baby was little. Prove to her that she was the shining, brilliant parent in this ridiculous equation.

Wishful thinking, probably. It was the kind of fantastical belief she always had in the days preceding her Sarah time. She'd puff out her chest in front of Daniel, put on a good show for his acrobatic yoga-toned child bride Brittany, who'd be touching up her eyebrows or lipstick in the passenger seat of their massive Acura SUV, and march away hand-in-hand with Sarah for their weekend … and then her grand plans would dissolve beneath long hours in front of SpongeBob and Dora while Lori scrolled endlessly through Instagram and Snapchat, sipping her cheap wine, munching on microwave popcorn.

Shit, shit, shit, what a wretched soul I am!

"Mommy?"

Lori broke sharply from her thoughts. "Yeah?"

Sarah was in the stall next to hers, had been quiet and patient for a few minutes. Lori had almost forgotten she was there.

"Can I get some candy?"

"Of course you can, yes, sweetie."

Lori rooted around in her purse and found some crumpled dollar bills. She flapped them under the partition at Sarah, who grabbed them with her little fingers. Without another word, Sarah unlocked her stall's heavy door, got it open, and walked out of the tiled bathroom, which then fell silent.

The shit of it was that once Jordan left the 'Vette and Lori got to the park (in the nick of time), everything had started going miraculously in the right direction! The dropoff had been smooth and uneventful, actual smiles, and Sarah had leaped out of the SUV to hug her. Daniel had come alone, no Brittany, and he'd even sat relaxed on the bench for a bit, catching Lori up on how Sarah was doing at school and at home. For her part, Sarah had kept running over from the playground to hug both of her parents, together at that rare moment. And Daniel had been *(gasp!)* a human being. Who knew how the afternoon might have gone? Maybe things would have been better. Easier.

But then Jasmine had shown up.

No! She would *not* blame her friend for any of this.

She wouldn't even blame Jordan.

Lori sensed Jasmine still out there, though, at the sinks, waiting for her.

"Look, Jasmine—" she started.

She let the words hang there, not knowing exactly how to proceed.

Jasmine sniffled, waiting. Lori tried to interpret the sound and couldn't. Regardless, the sound made her insides compress. She was trying like hell not to let her frustration spill over. It was emotion that she *knew* was misplaced. Jasmine had been through the wringer, and as her friend—probably her best friend, she imagined, what a thought!—Lori had an obligation to help her, didn't she?

But it was so tricky! *Fuck!* She felt as if she were always playing behind the eight-ball, always at a disadvantage because of this lurking unpleasantness inside her, this thing that always managed to define her, had in fact orchestrated her deeds and misdeeds since *waaaaay* early on.

"You OK in there?" Jasmine asked her, voice low.

It was Lori's turn to sniffle.

"What are you gonna do?" Lori asked the stall door.

"I have an idea," Jasmine said.

That's all she said.

Lori heard the faucet turn on as Jasmine began washing her hands.

"Jasmine ..." she started again, her voice halting.

The faucet stopped. "Yeah?"

"I have to go home." She paused. Still quiet at the sinks. "*We* have to go home. I'm so sorry about your brother. So sorry. I want to be able to help you—I mean, I always want to be able to do that ... but ... I feel like if I don't get home, I'm gonna fall apart. I just—I just need Steve to take us home."

There was only the sound of Jasmine drying her hands.

"And I think you should come with us."

Lori stood up, fastened her jeans, and opened the door. She met Jasmine's gaze in the mirror, went over to her at the counter. Lori'd assumed her friend had fallen into new misery, anchored there at the sinks, but the girl was exhibiting concentration now. Lori marveled at her: Jasmine was so much tougher than she was. Dead brother and all. Lori felt as if she'd been wrong about Jasmine all along. The realization made her feel like a huge pile of weepy shit.

"You could stay with us, like, at his place. He's got a great apartment in Fountain Valley, it's got an extra room. We could crash there and figure this out. You'd be safe. Sarah would love it, and—"

Jasmine wasn't looking at her, but she said, "No, you're right."

She started busying herself with her backpack, as if searching for something inside.

"So you'll come?"

"No, I have to see this through, but you're right."

"See what—?"

"I don't want to involve you and Sarah anymore in my shit. I shouldn't have dragged you into this. That wasn't fair—"

"Jazz, stop that!" Lori touched Jasmine's wrist, stopped the restless movement. "It wasn't your fault, it's not like you did any of this intentionally. I mean, shit happens, right?"

"You have your own lives. You need to take care of her. Take care of *you*."

"Jasmine, I don't want—"

"No, I mean it, you shouldn't even be with me at this point. I don't want you to get hurt."

While Jasmine kept talking, Lori washed her own hands unsteadily, dried them with stiff paper towels.

"... I have my phone now, I have my pack, I've got money. I got myself into this mess, and I can get out of it. I can take an Uber where I need to go. I know I have to talk to the police. I can go do that, but I have to do it alone."

Lori knew Jasmine was just babbling. She'd directed Steve to the coin shop for a reason, and Lori didn't think she was done with that. She had a bad feeling about her friend's immediate future but had no idea how to keep helping. It all felt insurmountable, dangerous, criminal.

Lori hopped up onto the counter, facing her friend. Neither woman looked her best under the harsh bathroom lighting. It was hard to believe this was where they were, now, on top of everything that had happened today. The dingy, cracked tiles. The overflowing trash bin beneath the paper-towel dispenser. Most of the counter covered with puddles and soap scum.

"You know …" Lori sniffed. "… we haven't talked about this since it happened, and I don't know why, but I keep thinking about that time you found me in my bedroom."

"You don't have to—"

"That was last October, right? Around Halloween? I'd known you, what, a month? I wasn't answering my door, I didn't want to see anyone, and you came in anyway. I'd left the fucking front door unlocked. I'd just been sitting in my shower, getting wrinkly, not caring, and then the water went cold. I couldn't—fucking—get warm." She shivered, remembering. "Somehow I dried off and got out to the bedroom and buried myself in blankets, and I was—I was on my way down. I mean—really—down into the shit. I don't know how many pills I took, or how much wine I drank to get them swallowed, but …"

Now Jasmine looked up at her, innocent, pure. "What were you taking?"

The girl was so naïve, and Lori loved her for it.

But it was for that reason that Lori had difficulty getting the word out. "Oxy."

Embarrassment bloomed in her chest. Embarrassment because it's not like she'd ever stopped taking it. Maybe she'd gotten incrementally smarter about it, but that shit was still in her daily regimen. She took it with a multivitamin, for chrissakes, every night after dinner.

"It's just so fucking easy to get."

She wrapped her arms around her legs, careful to avoid puddles. She realized she'd been holding both hands in fists. She uncramped her fingers and kept talking.

"But that night … I kept hearing you call my name, and I was ignoring you. All I wanted to do was sleep. I was trying to tune you out. But you came in anyway. You knew what was up, you saw the bottles, you saw my face. You pulled me out of bed, and I was all blubbery and screaming, but you kept pulling me, you persistent little bitch! You got me upchucking and all that."

She laughed a little, more like a cough, and Jasmine did too.

"I think I'm alive because of that. No, I know it."

"That's not true."

"I hardly knew you then, but you saved my life. You hear so many stories now about mixing that crap, taking too much, drowning in puke, people just ... going to sleep and never waking up. Gone before they even knew they had a problem. I would've died that night."

"Oh come on."

"That's what I believe."

Jasmine was watching her now, not saying anything more.

"What I'm saying is—that's why I'm here. I'll never forget that. So when you're in trouble, I'll help. I'll do my best. I got you away from whatever happened back there. You're safe here, right now. But I have to protect my girl, too. You understand that, right?"

Jasmine was faintly nodding.

"I was supposed to protect Jordan," she whispered.

The small bathroom was silent, echoing her low voice hollowly.

"Jasmine—"

"Well, he always thought it was the other way around."

"I know."

"I might have killed him, Lori, I'm serious."

"And I'm serious: You can't blame yourself."

There was something in Jasmine's downcast eyes that Lori couldn't quite decipher. She knew an essential part of her friend, something deep, has been irrevocably destroyed, right along with her brother. She was defeated, slumped there against the counter, looking straight down as if unwilling to gaze upon her own reflection.

"He thought leaving would save both of us, but ..."

"Leaving?"

"Leaving home."

"Garden Grove," Lori said.

"Yeah." Jasmine backed away from the counter and anchored herself against the towel dispenser. "My mom used to tell me that, you know. Before everything went to shit. Before Karl came. Even when we were young, she knew I'd have to keep an eye on Jordy. Like a *little* brother, almost. But she also knew it was important that he needed to think *he* was protecting *me*. From, you know, whatever. Everything. The world."

A tragic smile came to her lips.

"But that's what I was doing for him." Jasmine looked at her. "At least, I was trying."

Lori hopped down from the counter and approached her friend. She took her into an embrace.

"I'm sorry," she whispered.

"Me too."

Lori felt a measure of relief course through her, and with it, the anxious knot at her core loosened a bit—enough to pull her from the brink she'd been edging toward earlier. The bathroom air was cold on her sweat.

"I have to get Sarah." She pulled at the fabric of Jasmine's dress affectionately. "But you're gonna be OK."

Jasmine stood up straight, finally looking at herself in the mirror. "You go ahead, I'll be right out. Need to fix my face."

Inside the market, a dozen people were wandering about or waiting in line to pay for gas and junk food. Lori caught sight of the top of Sarah's head, still near the candy. Outside the big windows, she spotted Steve leaning against his little car. He looked defeated. She felt bad for him, would have to make it up to him. The day could still be salvaged, right? Maybe after Sarah was asleep, she and Steve could end up naked and entwined. What was the saying about lemons and lemonade?

She made her way to the candy aisle and found three kids there—and none of them was Sarah.

Wait.

She'd made a mistake. She'd mistaken one of them for Sarah, same color hair, same kind of ponytail. She glanced wildly about, then jogged over to the soda machine. Just a happy Mexican kid messing with the plastic lids, touching all of them.

"Sarah?" she called lightly.

No one reacted.

She went to the window and glared out toward Steve again. Sarah wasn't there either.

"Sarah?" she said, louder. *"Sarah!"*

Now everyone in the 7-11 was staring at her. All voices had quieted, and Jasmine came banging out of the bathroom, concerned as hell.

"What is it?" she said.

"Sarah's gone."

As the words left her, Lori felt as if she might fall straight through the ground, screaming toward the center of the earth.

"Come on!" Jasmine yelled, taking her hand, rushing toward the doors.

30
CHARLTON

The girl didn't even make a sound.

It was surgical, precise, the way Charlton Mawk swept in at exactly the right moment—Jasmine with her friend in the mini-market's bathroom, the girl lingering just inside the store by the newspaper rack gnawing on some kind of multicolored sucker. The fat dude was leaning against his Mini Cooper rolling his eyes, peering into the smoggy distance like he wanted to be anywhere else. Charlton gently took the girl's hand and maneuvered her out the door and around the front of the 7-11 toward the Westminster Boulevard sidewalk. She'd glanced up at Charlton curiously as they approached Pellegro's Jetta, which was parked at the edge of the parking lot. It was only then that the girl he would come to know as Sarah found her voice, and that was to ask "Who are you?" in a sticky voice that was so innocent and meek that it made even Charlton's heart skip a beat.

"Hey!" Mark cried out as Charlton dumped the kid in back and followed her in.

"Shut your fucking mouth." Knife-edged. "Get going."

"What are you doing?" Spoken like a dullard.

"I swear to god," Charlton said, calm, "if this car is not moving in three seconds, I'm gonna choke you with your own hat."

Mark closed his mouth, started up the Jetta, and pulled out into traffic. Dude knew he was caught.

"Keep going west."

"Wait, what about Mommy?" The girl's squeaky little voice was just curious.

"We're gonna pick her up, don't worry. Daddy too."

"Are you Daddy's friend?"

"Yep, that's right, now quiet down. Eat your candy."

Charlton felt the girl's inquisitive gaze on the side of his face. Peripherally, he saw that she did indeed take another lick at her lollipop. Fine. He watched out the rear window. No one following. Wow. Pellegro crossed two intersections, without talking. Dude was poised to piss his pants. By the smell of it, he'd already done something else in this car. Jesus.

"Open the windows. Fucking stinks in here."

The windows eased down in tandem.

"What do you want?" Pellegro asked.

"I want you to turn right at the next opportunity and find a nice shady place to park."

"Why?"

"Because you're an asshole."

Dude risked a look back at Charlton. "Why am I an asshole?"

"You don't think you are?"

"No."

"Well, that makes one of you."

The girl giggled, slobbered her sucker some more. Pellegro made the turn and drove a hundred feet before pulling over to the curb.

"Now what?" Hiking his elbow over the corner of his seat.

Charlton stared hard at the arm, and Pellegro removed it.

"Now shut off the engine."

Pellegro did so, and the three of them sat quietly for a long moment. The engine ticked.

Sarah sat up and peered through the back window.

"Is Mommy coming?"

"She's on her way."

"No, she's not," Pellegro said, sweaty, nervous. "What the fuck are you doing, man? You need to think hard about—"

"Say another word, *Mark*, go ahead. Say another fucking word."

Dude went quiet, stared straight ahead into a neighborhood.

"Let me think."

Sarah, licking her sucker, said, "Um …"

"Hold on, now," Charlton said, calm. "I'm serious. I need to think for a second."

Charlton prided himself on his quick thinking. It was bred into him, he knew: Take the advantage the split-second you saw it. Make the move. Consider consequences next, and if they weren't in your favor, then reverse the action, make things right. Chances were, though, his instincts would throw the consequences in his favor, and he would be free to take the next step. His actions were like rapid-play chess, slapping the time clock, just him against fate. Taking the girl had been a bold move—say, an unexpected grab of a rook—and now he had to brace for retaliation. While he did, he had to think of the next move.

While Pellegro had lingered in the coin shop's parking lot, Charlton had noticed the man's glances west down Westminster Boulevard. No one else had paid any attention, but to Charlton, the glances were fucking obvious. Equally obvious? Who he'd spotted.

So Charlton had let that retarded ape Tommy Strafe go, let him take his whore away down the road, wherever, probably back to their shack off Bristol to shoot up more of the dangerous chemical soup they got from that tattooed, pierced miscreant, co-owner of the store. (He would fucking *never* buy any pills off that goon Derek that didn't have pharm-origined branding on them.) Charlton had ground a cigarette beneath his boot and walked over to the corner cafeteria, all the while watching Pellegro wander off toward his car. Dude was so obvious, pretending purposelessness. Charlton had circled around the cafeteria's walkway and stopped at the street-facing corner, watching Mark sit there in his old Jetta. Now that he thought he was alone, the asshole was staring intently at something down the street. Charlton had followed the gaze toward a 7-11 on the corner of the next block, saw the typical activity—vehicles coming in and out, humans with Big Gulps, cheap commerce. Finally, a few people had sprung from a red Mini Cooper, and Charlton had smiled.

Mark had started up his Jetta, and Charlton had jogged calmly across the street.

And now here he sat, Pellegro's stiff posture showing nerves, Sarah's wet smacking sounds telling Charlton the same thing.

After about a minute of silence, Pellegro glanced into the back seat.

"Who's the girl?"

"Right, fuck you," Charlton said. "Like you don't know."

"I'm Sarah." And back to licking.

"Hey Sarah," Charlton said, nice and easy. "So, your mom told me you—wait, what's her name again?"

"Mommy's name is Lori."

"Right, your mom—Lori—she told me you love candy."

"Mmm-hmm."

"And that was Jasmine she was with, right?"

"Yep." Lick.

"Sarah—" Mark began.

"Do you know Mark here?" Charlton cut in.

Sarah glanced over at Pellegro, considered him carefully. "Huh-uh."

"I didn't think so. He's not a very nice man, so you shouldn't listen to him. Not that he's gonna say anything." Charlton manufactured a smile. "Don't worry, I won't let him get too close to you."

Sarah's eyes flicked from Charlton to Mark and back again.

"Where's Mommy?"

"I'm gonna get you right back to her, I promise. We just have to wait a few minutes, OK? She needed to do something with Jasmine."

She twisted to peer out the back window, then turned back, nodded, licked her sucker.

Charlton liked to think he had a way with kids. He had a natural rapport with them, mostly because they almost always told the truth. You couldn't count on *any* adult to tell the truth as consistently as a little kid. You managed to instill even the tiniest hint of fear or dread or wariness into a child, it was like truth serum. One time, a scheming tile vendor had stupidly brought his kid to a meeting at a job site; this was in Laguna, if Charlton remembered it right. Blustery dude had marched into the temp admin office playing the dad card, like nothing would ever happen to a family man. Nobody would dare cross a father in front of his son. Well, a quick nod to Eduardo, and father and son were wordlessly separated— father conversing nervously with Charlton, son ushered into a supply room where he sat and watched Eduardo scowl and tinker with his fabled gas-injected wasp knife. After ten minutes, Charlton and Eduardo switched duties. Charlton learned from the by-now-weeping boy that his father was armed with his own blade and was prepared to bring in a friend at the local precinct if the situation (which he viewed as grossly unfavorable to his business prospects) wasn't resolved. Kid even knew the cop's name. By the time father and son were reunited, the dad had lost his concealed knife—a never-used ebony Brawler folding blade that Charlton still carried—along with any notion of involving local heat, and was suddenly a team player.

"Hey, by the way, is Jasmine OK?" he asked, mock-concerned, in Sarah's direction.

Big eyes, pondering. "She's crying a lot. Like, a lot."

"Poor girl."

Sarah stretched to look out the back window again, then settled back. "Why is she crying?"

"Because of Jordan!"

"What's wrong with Jordan?"

"He died! I saw him!"

"Oh no."

"I know!"

"How did Jordan die?"

Sarah shrugged. "He was bloody. He was on the floor."

"So then what did Jasmine do with the coins?"

"Coins?"

"She had a bunch of coins, right? A box of them maybe?"

"The money in the bag?"

"Yeah."

"Those aren't coins. They're, like, dollars."

"Where are those, then?"

"I have them. She gave them to me. They're right here." Patting her backpack.

You gotta be kidding me.

"Can I see the money?" Charlton asked, all friendly.

"Sarah ..." Pellegro said again.

Charlton flashed him a deadly look.

"I want you to keep it safe, mind," he told Sarah gently. "I just want to take a look, make sure it's all there."

Another shrug. She opened the big zipper and pulled out a wrinkled Safeway bag. Charlton bent over it, opened the bag, and saw two loose bricks of cash. He thumbed through the small bills, estimating a couple grand. Then he wrapped it back up and zipped the backpack closed, patting it.

"Excellent, the money is safe with you. You did good. Let's just wait for your mom now."

A nod.

Charlton let things rest for a solid minute, synapses firing. By grabbing the kid, he'd inadvertently nabbed the cash. OK. Fine. If what the girl was saying, Jasmine had already sold the coins. Unless this was different money.

He doubted it, though. What other source did she have? By all accounts, there *was* no other source. Not even a long shot. Jasmine was fucking broke, just like her brother had been before he was greased. So ... what was Jasmine doing back here if she'd already sold the coins? The answer was fairly obvious, if you worked at it a bit: She was trying to undo it.

Brother was dead, she was scared out of her mind the same thing was gonna happen to her, and she wanted to get the coins back, make everything right with Tommy. Which betrayed a potent misunderstanding about how not only Tommy worked, but how the world worked.

"Gimme your phone, hot shot," Charlton told Mark.

Mark didn't say anything.

"I said gimme your phone, asshole."

"I don't have—"

Charlton surged forward and grabbed Pellegro by the neck. Pellegro began to gag, and his phone went flying off his lap, landing on the passenger seat. The screen was illuminated. A call was in progress, volume down. The name Tommy was emblazoned across the screen.

"How long—?" Charlton began, staring at the phone.

His vision went red.

He wrenched Pellegro's head back between the front seats until he was staring into the fucker's wild gray eyes and began pounding at his nose and open mouth with his fist. The man gasped and gargled, his jaw going abruptly red. Behind Charlton, Sarah started screaming, kicking at him until she was cramming herself against the far door. Charlton kept pounding until Pellegro went quiet, staring at him vacantly as he lost his front teeth and his nose went askew. The sounds issuing from Mark's throat diminished into involuntary gurgles. Finally Charlton let go, knuckles burning, and Pellegro went slumping forward against the horn, which emitted a long high-pitched blast. Disgusted, Charlton pulled the unconscious body away and shoved it down toward the stinking floorboards.

Charlton was left staring at the phone, which had gone dark.

Call ended.

"*Fuck!*" he shouted in the closeness of the car. "*Fuck fuck fuck fuck fuck!*"

Then he whipped his head to the right.

The rear passenger door was open, and Sarah was gone.

31
KAYLA

Next to Kayla Jennings, riding shotgun in his own monster truck, Tommy was groaning in full withdrawal. His fists were anchored on his knees, as if he were trying to hold something inside his body by sheer concentration, something that wanted desperately to claw its way out. Kayla pressed the gas, boosted their speed to five over the limit. She wasn't about to get a ticket on top of Tommy's earlier, but she needed to get him home, get him taken care of.

She should've seen it coming, the way he'd stormed out this morning, full volume, on his way to deliver whatever brute vengeance he had in mind. He could get so intense, so single-minded, that everything else left his brain. But she wasn't privy to his every movement. She had no idea whether he'd taken care of his business before raging off to wherever.

At a red light, she slowed to a stop and glanced over at him. His eyes were closed.

Kayla liked to remain willfully ignorant of what Tommy put in his body. She never did any of that with him. It was a private thing, that little worn-out case he'd had since he was a teenager. She knew he kept that shit in his nightstand somewhere, but she'd never opened those drawers. That was his business, and he kept it secret. He always did his thing behind the locked door of the bathroom.

But it was all wrapped up in their origin story, the drugs and shit. She'd been half-drunk at Derek's insane party, where they'd met, and Tommy'd been high as the space shuttle on whatever his freak buddy had cooked up that night. Derek, thorn in her side, was directly responsible for her hookup with Tommy. That was the truth: She wouldn't be here if not for that tattooed, intricately pierced deviant. (Alicia once told her Derek had undergone multiple hafada piercings, right through his scrotum, as part of a frenum ladder. Alicia had seen that shit herself—like, stared directly at it, mid-blowjob, mesmerized.)

Kayla would probably still be in contact with her mom, too, had she not hooked up with Tommy.

She did a little double-take in her head. Where had *that* thought come from?

But it was true. Last time Kayla had seen her mom was when she'd introduced her to Tommy, actually. Things had always been rocky between her and her mom, but that day had been weird all around—like, some odd territorial thing between Tommy and Audrey Jennings. Kayla recalled the side-eye glare that her mom had shot her from the kitchen, washing their dishes while Tommy made a deal on the phone. Rude of Tommy, she knew, but what are you gonna do? *A mother has a sixth sense about guys like that*, Audrey Jennings had said as she'd sagged into her old Toyota at the end of the night. *Just sayin'*. Since then, Kayla hadn't really spoken to her mom except for when her aunt died.

The light turned, and Kayla hurled them forward along Westminster Boulevard. A few more miles to go.

Tommy groaned again. He was sweating now, more than the truck's warm cab called for.

"Almost there, baby."

"I'm fine." Voice sounding squeezed out of a cheese grater.

"Ha!"

Christ, what a day. She was exhausted, and it was only early afternoon. Didn't help that she'd had, at best, four hours sleep last night. That fucking house party, perfectly illustrative of what her life had become. Hysterical, loud, stressful for a few hours, but *fuuuuuck*, the aftermath.

They were halfway home when Tommy's phone—nestled in the cupholder—started buzzing. Kayla glanced at it, saw the name MARK PELLEGRO, and rolled her eyes. What was he calling for? Her hand reached over to press IGNORE, but then she reconsidered. Maybe he'd seen something after they left.

She snatched up the phone, pressed speakerphone, dropped it on the seat.

"What?"

No answer, just a buffeting sound. An indistinct voice. Was that a little girl? What the hell?

"Mark?" she said, loud, and she felt Tommy wince next to her.

Nothing. Butt dial.

She moved to disconnect, but Tommy grabbed her hand.

"Wait."

She continued driving as a cacophony of sound emitted from the phone's speaker. Then it was only distant voices.

"Who is that?" Tommy said.

"Turn it up," Kayla whispered. "And put us on mute."

Tommy fiddled with the phone, set it down between them. The voices were clear over a hissing fog of gray noise.

"... *Jordan die?*" A crackling male voice.

"*He was bloody,*" declared a small voice, farther away. "*He was on the floor.*"

Kayla drifted to another stop at a light, behind a long line of cars. She listened intently.

"Who is that?" she said. "It's not Mark."

Tommy shook his head. "Shut up."

The voices continued from the phone. The man's voice was familiar, but she couldn't place it.

"*So then what did Jasmine do with the coins?*" the man asked.

"*Coins?*"

Tommy glared up at her, and Kayla met his gaze.

The man went on: "*She had a bunch of coins, right? A box of them maybe?*"

"*The money in the bag?*"

"*Yeah.*"

"*Those aren't coins. They're, like, dollars.*"

The little girl's voice was halting, innocent, and Kayla felt a faint ache listening to her. She sensed trouble. Like, the girl was in distress—barely there, like she was hiding it.

"*Where are those, then?*"

"*I have them. She gave them to me. They're right here.*"

"*Can I see the money?*"

"*Sarah ...*" There was Mark's voice, like protective.

"*I want you to keep it safe, mind. I just want to take a look, make sure it's all there.*"

Tommy jerked in his seat, nearly apoplectic. "Holy shit, that's Charlie! What in fuck's name is going on? Charlie's going on about my coins with a fucking kid? What in the—?"

"Quiet!" Kayla shushed him.

"*Gimme your phone, hot shot.*"

Kayla heard *hot shot*, and knew it was Charlton Mawk's voice. No doubt.

"I said gimme your phone, asshole."

Yep, Charlie.

"I don't have—"

There was a buffeting sound again, a struggle, a gagging sound. Kayla had to assume it was just the three of them in the car—Charlie, a little girl, and Mark. How were those three together? She and Tommy had left that parking lot all of ten minutes ago, maybe fifteen, and now the world had gone and flipped itself over. Again!

"How long—?" came Charlton's panicked voice.

Kayla reacted with panic, quickly stabbing the phone to end the call. Tommy shouted an obscenity at her, nearly backhanded her. The cab filled with his voice.

"Why'd you do that?! Why'd you hang up?!"

"Stop yelling!" she said, pulling forward with traffic. "He was gonna— Charlie was gonna see that it was you on the phone!"

"Who cares?"

"Don't you see what just happened?" Kayla scrambled for words. "Mark did that on purpose, called you so you could hear that. If Charlie sees that Mark called you—"

Tommy squeezed his eyes shut, clenched his jaw. Kayla tensed for an outburst, but he remained relatively in control.

"Turn around," he gritted through his teeth.

"We have to go home, Tommy, or you're just gonna lose your shit, you won't be able to do anything, you'll—"

"Turn this truck around, Kay." He hadn't opened his eyes. "Right fucking now."

"Baby, you need your stuff, otherwise you're gonna—"

That's when Tommy let loose. *"IF YOU DON'T TURN THIS TRUCK AROUND, I WILL DROWN YOU IN THE FUCKING OCEAN, DO YOU UNDERSTAND? I WILL HOLD YOU UNDER THE WATER UNTIL YOU ARE EXTINCT! JESUS FUCKING CHRIST!"*

Kayla felt her innards fall off a cliff.

She had taken Tommy within three miles of home, and that's as close as they would get to having a chance. Everything would turn to shit now—it was beyond doubt. She'd seen Tommy dopesick before, usually when he'd underestimated his supply. She knew the signs, knew what kind of behavior to expect, knew how to encourage him to do what he needed.

Tears spilled helplessly down her cheeks as she found a left turn lane and waited to make the U.

She thought of her mother again, felt a real ache for her, and she thought of all the friends she'd given up, and she thought of who she used to be, before Tommy—it all flashed at her in a strobe. The life she could have had. The life she *still* could have. She could have a kid of her own, a daughter, someone like the mystery girl on the phone, someone to take care of and love like that. Why did she always deny herself that? A nice house where she never had parties, a house with a porch and a pool. Laughter and good food, and candles and potted plants that she watered every day, and yeah, a little girl, so sue her for thinking all Norman Rockwell.

She wanted to call her mom, and she would've, too, if fucking *Tommy* wasn't *right here*, the blustery buffoon. Tommy and his stupid fucking coins from his stupid fucking dad that were probably worthless anyway. This was just another one of his stupid ridiculous quests that would lead to pain and anger and hard feelings, and look at her! She was the one at the wheel of this absurd truck!

She made the turn, crying openly, anger and shame burning inside her.

She realized she hated Tommy.

It wasn't the first time she'd come to this realization.

And with the realization came the equally certain understanding, the resignation, the humiliation, that she would still be sharing his bed tonight, would still open herself to him when it was all over and when he'd had his fix. It could still work out. Tommy had surprised her before. When his collection was secure, and their future was bright. She tried to control her breathing, but it came out in hacking gasps for a full minute.

"I'm going to fucking kill him," Tommy said, ignoring her. He was rubbing his knees with his big, large-knuckled hands.

Kayla didn't answer. She drove past the endless neighborhoods and banks and strip malls and restaurants and office buildings and parking lots and palm trees, weaving through traffic in a daze. Her tears dried on her cheeks.

32
JASMINE

When Lori screamed, it was a hoarse, ugly, bleating sound, almost like an injured animal, and at least a dozen people in and around the 7-11 parking lot stopped to gawk at her. Didn't move to help her or anything, just gawked, then pretended not to hear her. She doubled over, inconsolable, and the scream turned to sobs.

Someone took Sarah!

Jasmine Frank and Lori had combed the entire store, Lori becoming increasingly distressed. They'd even forced a harried, complaining employee to take them into the back—Sarah was nowhere. *Jesus, how could they have left her alone?*

Tommy.

Tommy had taken Sarah. Jasmine felt that truth in her gut, deep and heavy and immoveable.

She'd made the mistake of voicing it, and that's when Lori screamed.

In the parking lot now, having clanged through the glass doors, Jasmine held Lori clumsily, grasped at her limbs, shell-shocked. She was trying to keep her upright. She kept holding her friend close as she dragged her the final steps to Steve's Mini Cooper. Steve was running back toward the car from the north end of the property, having scoured the parking lot on Jasmine's screamed instructions.

"Nothing!" he yelled.

"She's gone!" Jasmine yelled back at him over the top of the squat car. "Someone took her."

"How do you know?"

"I just know. Get in and drive!"

"But where?"

"*JUST—*"

"OK, OK!"

Jasmine flung the front seat forward and crammed Lori into the back, struggling with the tight confines. Lori was crying so hard that she couldn't function. No help there.

"Goddamn clown car!" Jasmine yelled.

Lori submitted weakly, her sobs almost soundless now, and Jasmine wrenched the seat back and rooted herself in shotgun.

Steve hopped into the driver's seat, and the motor thrummed to life. *"Go!"*

"Where?"

"I don't know, just drive!" She had no earthly idea what she was doing. She let panic guide her, gesturing frantically forward. "They have to be close!"

Steve reversed out of the spot, wheels screeching like a bat out of hell. Jasmine and Lori *ooofed* forward, and then the little car leaped to the edge of Westminster Boulevard, pressing them back into their seats.

Lori was groaning *"No no no no no ...!"*

"Which way?" Steve shouted.

Jasmine tried to give it a quick calculation. "Right! Go right!"

Whoever took Sarah wouldn't have waited for the busy left turn. Traffic was a constant maelstrom.

Steve swung right immediately into the street, eliciting a blast from someone's horn. Vehicles streamed past them as the car got up to speed. Jasmine's eyes were wide, scanning, desperate. She didn't even exactly know what she was looking for, but she was watching for Tommy's truck, which would stick out like a sore thumb. She didn't see anything like it.

They passed an anonymous neighborhood street, then another. She saw zero activity down either one.

Her head swiveled about.

Anything, anything!

Despair clutched at her.

Jasmine couldn't stop herself from shivering. Her teeth chattered as if she were freezing, and yet she knew the day—especially inside this cramped car—had become hot and humid. She didn't know what to do. She was abruptly aware that some kind of low whine was coming out of her mouth, so she shut it. Her eyes were dry, glaring about.

She looked left down the next street. Nothing. But whoever had taken Sarah, they wouldn't have gone left, she just knew it. Where then?

"You watch the left!" she ordered Steve. "I'll watch the right!"

Some kind of activity—anything! Please!

The farther they got from the 7-11, the more seconds that passed, the more wildly futile the search became. She was staring down suburban streets that stretched out into interminable distances, dotted with parked cars, empty sidewalks, and everything looked the same. Empty. Futile. Shit! Behind her, Lori was sobbing louder again, sensing doom maybe, and she wouldn't stop. Jasmine wanted to tell her to shut up, she couldn't concentrate, all she could do was wince under the onslaught of noise. But she couldn't do that, not ever, not anymore.

Fuck! What if they couldn't find her—?

Nope, shut up, not going there.

They'd gone five blocks when Jasmine let out a helpless yowl of frustration—

Then something clicked, something faint and faraway.

"Wait, turn around!" she said.

"What? Where?" Steve cried.

"I said turn around! It's back there!"

"I can't just—"

"Just go back, goddammit!"

Something had lodged in her forebrain's periphery, something she couldn't name. She felt a spurt of insight, didn't even know why, but she followed its directive.

"Hold on!"

Steve jerked the car to the left lane and made an illegal U-turn, causing oncoming traffic to skid into collective outrage. Jasmine braced for impact, but none came. The zippy little Mini righted itself and sped forward, now headed east. Jasmine stared into the neighborhoods again, each one, searching.

"There!"

Oh god, it was the white Jetta. Wasn't it? Was that it? The guy from last night? Mark was his name. Jesus, that was his Jetta—the Jetta she'd thrown up in last night, the Jetta she'd *just seen* in the coin shop parking lot. Beyond a blue van and some kind of black sedan, the Jetta sat crookedly against the curb, and its passenger door appeared to have been flung open.

Lori was hunched forward, across her own lap, braying into her knees, but now she lurched up, staring out the window, her face a wreck of tears.

"Where?" she cried. "What's happening?"

"Turn here!" Jasmine shouted.

"I can't, there's no fucking turn lane!"

"Just do it!"

Jasmine was practically clawing at the window, staring at the Jetta. She was sure that was it—Mark's Jetta. But why in the hell would Mark take Sarah?

Steve slammed on the brakes, waited for traffic to clear. A chorus of honks bombarded them again.

"I swear, if I crash this thing—"

Vehicles came at them endlessly, and Steve inched forward, anxious, until he pushed through onto the narrow street, breezing past a taqueria and an Asian market on the corners. Everything quieted.

"Motherfucker!" Steve shouted with relief.

He took his foot off the gas and drifted onto the side street. A row of bungalows fronted a '70s-era neighborhood off to the right, and bland office space occupied the long block to the left. Jasmine stared at the parked Jetta, coming up on the right, situated in front of one of the bungalows. Someone was slumped in the driver's seat, but otherwise the car was empty, and it was the rear passenger door that was standing open.

Steve drew alongside the Jetta and stopped.

It was Mark, all right. *What in the world?* He was in the driver's seat, bloodied and seemingly unconscious. Jasmine stumbled out of the Mini Cooper, looking all around, and rapped hard on the door metal. Mark jerked awake and stared at her through the open window. He was a disaster—lower lip burst, nose bent and bleeding, looked like at least one tooth was gone. He was holding part of his shirt to the right side of his mouth.

"Jesus!" Jasmine said. "What happened to you?"

Lori scrambled out of the back of Steve's car. *"Where's my baby?"* she cried.

Mark appeared confused, glancing from Lori to Jasmine and then to the Mini Cooper, which his eyes lingered on. His head fell back to the headrest, and he seemed to try to say something. Nothing came out.

"Was she here?" Lori was at the Jetta's window, screaming. *"Did you take her?"*

Mark shook his head, wincing.

"What?" Lori begged.

Jasmine wrenched open Mark's door, got in close to him. He watched her with bleary, unfocused eyes. He was barely conscious. Her mind raced. Nothing made sense. Had Mark taken Sarah? Wildly, Jasmine imagined him taking her on Tommy's orders—and then Sarah doing this to him with her little fists. For a hot second, she almost burst out with nervous laughter. But the fact remained that Sarah was still gone, and Jasmine knew she'd been here, in this car, and the clock was ticking.

Jasmine grabbed Mark by the shoulders. "I need you to wake up! I need you to tell me what happened to the girl!"

He squinted at her, tried to focus on her. Then, "You ruined my car."

What? Was that what this was about?

"Did you take her?"

Mark's eyes rolled. "No." He swallowed painfully. "She ..."

"Oh my god," Lori whined, impatient.

"Guy with Tommy," Mark mumbled with grimacing effort. "He took her ... Charlie."

Guy with Tommy?

There *had* been a guy with Tommy, across the street, the one that climbed down from that stupid-ass truck. Jasmine had got a look at him but hadn't paid a lot of attention. She couldn't come up with any details about the guy. But if what Mark said was true, then Tommy had been aware of Jasmine across the street. *Impossible!*

"Where'd they go?" Lori begged.

Mark shook his head minutely. "Dunno."

"But she was here?" Jasmine said, placing a palm on Lori's shoulder to keep her calm.

"Uh huh," Mark managed. "Got away."

"Got away?" Jasmine stared at him. "What does that mean? She ran?"

Mark closed his eyes, squeezed them shut. "I don't know." His breathing was horribly congested. "He took her. Ran with her." He snuffled back a glob of bloodsnot, and the effort looked insanely painful. "Went that way."

He gestured, and Jasmine stared into the neighborhood desperately. "Let's go."

"Where?" Lori cried.

"Get back in the car." Pointing at the Mini Cooper. *"Go!"*

She heard Lori running.

Jasmine felt as if she were vibrating. Her mundane minute-to-minute reality had turned to pure instinct. She was letting adrenaline guide her. She took a second to gauge Mark, make sure he was OK sitting there. His head was already sprawled back against the seat again, and his mouth was making wet snoring sounds.

"He needs a hospital," Jasmine called back.

"*Fuck him!*" Lori cried from the open window of the Mini. "*He probably took her in the first place!*"

Jasmine froze, considering that, and decided that it wasn't true. He wouldn't have done that. Jordan probably would've said she was naïve for thinking that, that she always saw the best in people even when they didn't deserve it, or even when all evidence suggested otherwise. Too often, he'd say, she'd go with her heart instead of her head.

She leaned in close.

"Did you?" she asked him, in his ear. "Did you take her?"

He shook his head miserably. "Fuck no."

"You OK here for a bit?"

He looked at her with the one eye that hadn't become swollen, then whispered, "I'm sorry. I tried to help her."

"We'll be back."

"Hey," he said, a gargled whisper.

"What?"

"Be careful." Staring at her meaningful through one eye. "Be careful of that guy."

Jasmine hurried to the Mini and fell into the low passenger seat without buckling. Steve was watching Mark, aghast. She gestured with her hand, north into the neighborhood.

"She's in there somewhere."

A quick nod from Steve, and the little car launched forward with a chirp of rubber. The quiet neighborhood came at them in a rush as he took the corners tight, trying every street. It was a suburban maze, every short street looking the same. Jasmine kept her eyes on everything at once—windows, shrubs, corners, hiding places, open doors. Nothing! She leaned in and out of the corners, barking frustration while Lori wept. A moving Honda Accord saw them coming and moved to the side of the road defensively, and Jasmine watched the outraged driver, an older bespectacled man, stare at them as they passed.

"We have to find them!" Lori cried.

"I'm working on it!"

At her feet, Jasmine wrestled with her backpack, Steve's turns jostling her about. She found what she needed, made sure it was loaded.

Steve took the turn onto the first major connecting street, and they all scanned the area.

Jasmine saw the truck before she saw Sarah in the grip of a hard-looking man.

The truck she knew all too well.

"There's Tommy!" Jasmine shouted.

Then the claustrophobic interior of the Mini Cooper went crazy, as all three of them saw Sarah at once. The car leapt forward nimbly.

Jasmine held on for dear life.

33
TOMMY

There was one time, maybe five years ago—not long before Tommy Strafe's dad died behind the wheel of his Camaro on a stretch of the 55 freeway—when Rennie and Charlton were over at the house, some kind of impromptu dinner to celebrate finishing a job. Tommy was fuzzy on the details of that night. He'd still been a teenager then, girls on his mind, weightlifting, riced-up Hondas. Probably had just met Derek, and an entirely new world was opening up to him. Anyway, the four of them were at the old house, the nice spread in the hills now lost to time and his dad's financial misfortunes. Tommy recalled Sinatra flowing from his dad's giant wood-grain stereo credenza in the living room, built-in turntable, face-up controls. They'd ordered pizza or something, and while the men spoke of meetings and plans, Tommy had sized up Charlton ... and found him wanting. Charlton was still a nervous kid back then, hadn't yet found his rhythm. Face enflamed with acne, hunched a little, squirrely, but always watching with those glinting eyes. He'd been quiet, standoffish, insolent. What Tommy remembered most about that night was later, the quiet aftermath, after the Mawks had left. His dad had remained in the darkness of the living room, brooding. Out of nowhere, Gordon Strafe had said, "That kid's a useless runt, but he won't always be. You can tell. Careful of that one."

Over the years since, Tommy *had* kept his eye on Charlton. Of course he had. As Charlton had grown from teen to man, he'd always, always seemed on the verge of some kind of betrayal. He seemed to harbor an existential mistrust of Tommy, and in his better moments, Tommy got that. He dug it. Rennie sometimes chose Tommy over Charlton for an intimidation gig, still did, and it probably rankled Charlie every fucking time. Shit, Rennie seemed to find it easier to even *talk* to Tommy. Some nights, Tommy laughed about that with Kayla while Charlton no doubt *broiled.*

Of *course* Charlton would double-cross Tommy.

Tommy was the son Rennie'd always wanted.

A pothole jostled him from his thoughts.

He opened his eyes, blinked hard. His jaw ached. He could handle it.

Tommy realized Kayla hadn't spoken since she'd turned around. He sensed her angry frustration like waves of heat. He didn't care. Tuned her out.

He was sweating despite the blast of the A/C. He'd stabbed off the music a while ago—that auto-tuned girl-power pop that Kayla loved—and the silence in the cab was itself like a wall of sound. His head was full of shifting lava, and he was concentrating on focusing it into a laser dot that he would eventually train on Charlton's forehead.

Even though it was unsurprising that Charlton Mawk would betray him, the thought still left him dazed and disoriented. He wanted to call Rennie, but instinct held him back. What he *really* wanted to do was grab Rennie's fucking greaser-wannabe son by his oily hair and crank-snap his neck like a chicken.

"Where am I going?" Kayla asked, flat.

"Just get me back over there, that parking lot."

She sighed, all dramatic. "At least drink some water. There's some in that bottle."

At that moment, his phone rang. It was still resting between them on the bench seat. Tommy stared at it. The name on the display was CHARLTON MAWK.

"*Seriously?*" he spat. He grabbed the phone and answered it, putting Charlton on speaker. "I'm talking to a fucking dead ma—"

"You there?" came Charlton's voice, out of breath. "Tommy?"

"What?" Tommy said, disoriented.

"I think I've got that girl for you," Charlton said over a hissing and crackling line. "That Jasmine."

Tommy and Kayla exchanged uncomprehending stares.

"Say that shit again."

"I mean, I don't have her yet, but I got the next best thing."

"Which is?"

"I've got something she *really* wants back." More crackling. "And I've got a backpack full of money, money she got for your coins, looks like."

Tommy sat there stunned while the road came at him, urgent, cars everywhere, too loud. He felt as if he couldn't trust any sensory input. His mouth worked silently, and he felt Kayla watching him.

"You there?" Charlton said.

"Where are you?" Kayla said haltingly. "We're already headed back to the store."

"Go a few blocks past that, I'm in a neighborhood off to the right. There's a big white sign that says Auto Repair, turn right there." He broke off. "Shit, girl, let go, *ow!* Turn there at that sign, got it? You'll see me."

"Who's with you?" Kayla said.

"That's the surprise."

The line went dead.

"That son of a bitch!" he muttered.

"But he says he got her."

"Just go!"

Kayla stomped on the gas, got over into the right lane. Tommy was left staring forward, watching for the strip mall, watching for the sign. They passed an interminable number of same-looking stores and bland office buildings, and finally they were close—and then a goddamn red light stalled them at an intersection.

"*Fuck!*" he roared, and Kayla flinched.

Tommy's entire body was shaking, and with the realization came a great twisting cramp in his bowels. A cold sweat overcame him. He was going to shit his pants. He was as sure about that as he'd been about anything in his life. He clenched his asshole shut and prayed with unprecedented fervency. *Stop stop stop stop …*

"What is it?" Kayla asked, suddenly alarmed.

"Kay, I'm gonna shit my pants, I swear to Christ."

"You are *not* going to shit your pants," she responded like some kind of Jedi master.

"*I am, here it comes, oh fuck me.*"

He thrust his abdomen forward and held the pose, clenching hard. He looked like a goddamn spider in full death spasm, or like that poor schmuck in *Alien* when that little fucking thing burst out of his guts. Mercifully, the cramp eased. *Oh thank Jesus!* He fell back to the seat, but the shakes remained. He locked his hands on his thighs, tightened his jaw, determined.

"Damn, man," Kayla breathed, staring at him.

The light turned green, and the truck eased forward. After a few blocks, the strip mall with the coin store came into view on the left—there were still a few cops milling about—and in the distance Tommy thought he spotted the Auto Repair sign. Yes, that's what it was.

"There," he gestured for Kayla.

He wiped his eyes of inadvertent tears, staying focused.

Kayla barely missed the signal at the next intersection, pressing the brakes, and Tommy felt himself go helplessly ballistic, yelling profanity at her while she sat there calmly like a stone-faced mongoloid. Any other sentient being would have motored through the hard yellow, and they'd be turning onto street with the auto repair shop and finding fucking Charlton. *Christ … women!* No, not just women, *this* woman! He knew he was keeping his anger consciously cranked to eleven, because it helped with the worst of the pain, and he knew *Kayla* knew that too, but *fuck!*

The light turned, and Kayla lurched the truck forward. The big white sign came up, towering over them, and Kayla made the turn. The street looked like a long, empty road to suburban nowhere. His eyes scanned the length of it eagerly.

"Got him," Kayla announced, and hit the gas.

"Where?"

"Right there!"

Two figures were half-crouched behind a weathered white van, as if hiding. They were a hundred feet off to the left. One was unmistakably Charlton, who emerged fully from behind the van when he saw Tommy's truck approaching. Charlton fucking Mawk, man—right there in the flesh. The black jeans and the button shirt, the slick hair, the boots. Dude had come through. Whereas earlier Tommy had dwelt on that thing his dad had once said—*"Careful of that one"*—now he had to admit that Charlie was genuinely standup. He'd come through. And with that came a further measure of relief in his bowels.

The other figure was a little girl with a backpack hanging from her shoulders. Charlton had the backpack's strap in his fist and was basically marching her in front of him.

Tommy stared at the girl in confusion.

"Who the fuck is that?"

"Jasmine have a kid?" Kayla said.

"No," Tommy scoffed.

Fifty feet away, his eyes were still locked on the girl, trying to figure her out, when a little red striped Mini Cooper swept in from a side street and cut off the truck. Kayla skidded to a stop, yelping, and Tommy braced himself on the dash. The Mini's driver was staring directly at him. At first, Tommy's instincts told him that some anonymous asshole driver had just made a dumb mistake, but the look in the man's eyes insisted otherwise.

He was a bulky fellow with long sideburns and a goatee. His mouth was open like a halfwit, and he seemed to be wearing an apron. He looked like a goddamn waiter. Tommy'd never seen the man before in his life.

"Who the hell are you?" he asked the windshield, to zero effect.

But then the Mini's passenger door opened, and out popped Jasmine Frank.

Tommy froze. Stopped breathing.

Jasmine fucking *Frank!*

She was still in her spangly blue dress, looking sweaty, agitated, nervous as hell. She tripped a little on the asphalt, held her right hand up, palm out—*wait wait wait!*—turning from Tommy to Charlton and back again.

Jasmine settled her gaze on Charlton and the girl, said something in their direction that Tommy couldn't hear. Charlton smiled at her—cold, calculating—and nodded in Tommy's direction. Jasmine turned toward Tommy, and her hand came down. She watched him with something like fear, yeah, more like terror, and then it gradually morphed into something else, and he realized it was a sort of sadness.

"What?" he mouthed at her.

As if by afterthought, Jasmine brought up the hand again, and this time in its grip was a little pistol, purple and girlie. Tommy did a double-take, figured he must be living a frickin' cartoon, the way she brandished it, limp-wristed and uncertain, trying and spectacularly failing to look tough. It stopped Charlton, though. On the sidewalk, he jerked to a halt, maneuvered the little girl in front of him, wrapped a lean forearm around her little shoulders.

Tommy opened his door, guts twisting a little, and stepped out onto the running board. Kayla reached for his arm—*"Hey!"*—but he shrugged her off.

"Stop!" Jasmine shouted, her voice shaky. "Enough! That's enough! Stop moving."

He stared at her in outright, comical confusion.

Jason Bovberg

"Did you take my fucking coins?" he asked her, reasonably, but also still in a state of disbelief. "I mean, did you actually *do that?*"

There was a long pause.

Jasmine seemed to gulp multiple times before she could speak. She kept glancing between Tommy and Charlton. Then, unbelievably, she started to cry. She was obviously trying to control the tears, but they came, and they came hard. She choked back hacking breaths, and the gun wobbled in her grip.

"What the hell are you *doing*, Jasmine?" he called down to her. "This isn't *you*."

"You ... you killed ... you killed my brother, you ... you *asshole*."

Tommy stared at her uncomprehending. The street was quiet around him, Westminster Boulevard's traffic noise distant and meaningless like white noise. His head felt thick and dizzy at the same time, and he knew worse was coming until he could finally score that hit, but Jasmine's statement was unreal, almost dreamlike—out of some other crazy reality. What was going on here? Was she trying to frame him? Was that it? Or did she really think he'd killed Jordan?

"I didn't touch your fucking retard brother."

"You're a liar!" came some woman's sobbing voice.

Tommy looked down in that direction. It was some hollow-eyed brunette in the back seat of the Mini, staring up at him through an open window. He hadn't even noticed her. Tommy felt as if he were going batshit.

"That's my daughter!" the woman yelled, pointing. *"Let her go!"*

"I'm taking her!" Jasmine announced, still teary but becoming more sure of herself. She stabilized the pistol in her grip. "OK? I'm taking her. Just stay there. Don't move. I'm taking that girl. That's all there is to it."

Tommy watched the purple pistol, wondering if it was actually loaded.

"You're not gonna do anything with that popgun."

Jasmine pointed the pistol into the air, as if afraid of the thing, and pulled the trigger. The gun emitted a sharp report, and Tommy flinched despite himself. Jasmine lowered the pistol until it was pointed right at him, and fury boiled out of him.

34
STEVE

"Where are my fucking coins?" the flat-faced thug shrieked from atop his preposterously jacked truck.

So this was Tommy, the asshole they'd seen pull into the coin shop's parking lot earlier. Up close, the big man was a sweating, glaring mess, as if he'd been sprinting frantically toward this moment and now couldn't fully catch his breath. He looked like a pot about to boil over.

From the confines of his Mini Cooper, Steve Riordan watched the spectacle play out with an anxious intensity he'd never felt before—not once in his entire life. He was involved in some *shit*. It was all really happening. It was all true, everything Jasmine had told him. It was like a goddamn movie, as if this was *finally* what he'd bought this car for. The past ten minutes had made him feel like a kid again, on the edge, adrenaline-fueled, ready to take on the world. And to think he'd been about to abandon this little group!

"I don't have them, OK?" Jasmine called. "They're not here."

Jasmine was in some kind of warrior stance now, aiming her little purple gun straight at Tommy's cliff-wall face. In her skintight blue dress, Jasmine was fucking *badass*. Who knew? Yeah, she'd broken down into tears a moment ago, but could you blame her? The girl had just lost her brother. But now she'd found some reservoir of strength and was standing there confronting this big goon in his big truck, and Steve couldn't fucking get over it. He didn't think he'd been more attracted to a woman, ever. When Jasmine had pulled out that gun, he was in love, like a stab to the heart. Way more smitten than before. Lori had lost all semblance of control behind him, but Jasmine—god*damn!*

"But you *did* have them, didn't you?" Tommy said.

Jasmine's mouth worked a little. "You're going to jail, Tommy!"

Tommy appeared incredulous. "For *what?*"

Steve glanced over at Sarah. *How about kidnapping?* he thought. Lori's poor little girl was wrapped up in the strong-armed grip of a throwback-looking dude straight out of *West Side Story*. The man had a Clint Eastwood stare, you couldn't tell where he was looking, but you felt like he was gazing into your soul, judging you, anyway. Underneath his steel grip, Sarah was clearly trying to be brave under her calm exterior, and—looking into her innocent eyes—Steve abruptly felt for her. Normally, on the weekends Lori had her, the girl was more in the way than not, but seeing her in danger ... well, that changed things, didn't it?

Steve leaned over to the right so Jasmine could hear him. "Watch that guy with Sarah," he said. "I don't trust him. Might be armed."

Jasmine swiveled that way, but kept the gun pointed at Tommy. Clearly didn't want to endanger Sarah. Man, she was smart, too. Nervous, yeah, but smart. Where was *that* coming from?

"Don't do anything!" she told the greaser, her voice cracking. "Just let her go. Take your hands off her and let her mom take her."

Steve glanced into the back seat at Lori, who was still sniveling but now poised with the door open to run get Sarah. She looked at him uncertainly, then at Jasmine.

"Go!" Jasmine told her.

Steve gave her an encouraging nod, and Lori took off with a small whimper.

"This is so fucking stupid," Tommy said above them, watching Lori scamper over to the sidewalk. He was clenching and unclenching his right fist. "I had nothing to do with your brother, Jasmine. I swear to God. All I know is, you stole my fucking coin collection straight out of my house, straight out of my *bedroom. You* did that. And now you're telling me *I'm* the one going to jail?"

Lori approached the greaser warily, with a halting motion. Steve felt his heart slamming underneath his ribs. But finally she snatched Sarah away, yanking at her little arm and pulling her close.

"Charlie ..." Tommy started, but his voice died out.

The whole thing happened without incident. Lori practically dragged the girl back to the Mini. Steve watched the greaser stand up straight, watching, resigned, a snarl on his lips as if he'd been personally affronted.

The little car rocked as Lori and Sarah dove into the back seat.

"Hi," Sarah said to Steve, as if nothing had happened. She still had a lollipop in her little hand, for chrissakes, but her eyes were red-rimmed. She grabbed for her little bear, which was squished into the seat cushion.

"Hey kid." He smiled at her, tried to ease her mind. "Everything cool?"

"Uh huh."

Lori was slobbering all over her. *"Oh my God you're safe, I love you, I'll never let you go again …"*

And then something happened in the periphery of Steve's vision.

There was a jerking motion, followed by a grunt. When Steve turned his head that way, he saw Tommy bent over, hanging precariously from one hand, which was latched to the truck's door jamb. A perfect jet of vomit was arcing from his locked-open mouth, spattering on the pavement. The stuff was mostly clear, tinged with yellow, like bile, and Steve felt his own jolt of nausea, like that time a kid had thrown up all over a table at the restaurant a couple years back, the vomit spreading across the polished wood like a sewage tide, toxic and frothy.

Everyone on the street paused.

Steve thought: *What just happened?*

Tommy spat a curse, then spat for real, cleaning out his mouth with exaggerated tongue wipes. He rose back up and stared blearily about. Dude was sick with something, Steve *knew* it! Asshole was pale all of a sudden, blinking his eyes as if bothered by all the brightness flooding the street. He looked down at the vomit puddled in spattered disarray across the asphalt, clearly shocked by what he'd just done. Then he seemed to nearly lose his grip on the truck, but he caught himself at the last millisecond and fell back to the edge of his seat, glaring out at the street through the door's open window. Inside the truck, the driver, an exotic-looking woman, said something, concerned, reaching out for him, but he ignored her.

"Look, Jasmine," Tommy said, angrily queasy, "I don't even know what the fuck is going on here."

Jasmine shifted, gun subtly trembling in her grip, her other hand braced on the top of the Mini.

Tommy burped in his throat, winced, tried to cough up a bitter laugh. He looked and sounded defeated now.

"This day has gone from bad to fucking worse," he called, spitting again with distaste. "I woke up to find out someone had stolen my shit, and later I found out the person who took them was you. You! Yeah, I mean, sure, I *wanted* to kill you. I *wanted* to kill your fucking brother. But I *didn't*. I didn't kill your fucking loser brother, Jasmine."

Steve flicked his gaze from this wounded ape of a man to the woman in the truck's driver's seat, who looked confused and out of place, like she'd been in the midst of a pleasant drive to the beach and had suddenly become involved in a criminal shitshow.

Tommy gestured limply. "And I didn't take that girl, either. It was that asshole over there."

The greaser stood anchored on the crumbling sidewalk, under shade. At some point, he had receded into shadows, as if not wanting anyone to get a good look at him. But Steve could see the man's flinty eyes now, the way they regarded Tommy after that remark.

"Now are you gonna give me back my coins, or what?" Tommy asked, his voice barely making it the distance to the Mini.

For her part, Jasmine was listening calmly to Tommy, and her mind seemed to be working at something, trying to put everything together. Steve watched her face for a moment, then couldn't help glancing down at the muscles in her lower thighs as they twitched minutely below the hem of the riding-up dress. The skin was damp, vibrant in the sunlight. At that moment, he realized that he would do just about anything for this young woman.

"I sold the coins," she told the thug, "but I guess you know that."

Tommy shook his head as if in disbelief. Steve saw that he was also wincing under the sway of the sickness inside him. Dude was in pain.

"I'm guessing you have a plan to get them back?" Tommy swallowed hard, like he was holding down more puke. "Because even if you drive away right now, I don't see how this ends in sunrises and rainbows for you. You see that, right?" Now he made an audible groan and closed his eyes momentarily. "One way or another, I'm getting them back. And it won't end well for you."

"I have the money I got for them. I have—"

Tommy raised himself from his seat again, staring down. *"I don't want the fucking money! I want the coins!"* He was sweating visibly, raging. *"Don't you get it?"*

"You don't even know how much I got for them."

"It doesn't matter! It doesn't matter! Whatever you sold my fucking coin collection for, it doesn't matter! They weren't yours to sell! Jesus Christ!" His whole face squeezed into a mockery of agony, but he pushed through it. "I don't even want you to say the number out loud, because that would

piss me off even more and make this fucking charade more true! I mean, come on Jasmine, get a fucking clue!"

Jasmine watched Tommy the whole time he was yelling, more like half-whining, and finally she dropped her arm, pointing the pistol loosely at the ground. A tragic frown overtook her features. She opened her mouth to say something, but then closed it. When she finally did speak, her voice was deadened—sad, almost.

"You drugged me, Tommy."

"Oh, *fuck* you, I did not *drug* you—"

"You drugged *both* of us, and you know it." She stared at him, sorrowful and yet defiant. "And now ... all this has happened, and Jordan is—"

"I told you, *Jasmine*, I didn't have anything to do—I didn't fucking *drug* you! That's ridiculous."

"You were sweet to me once, you know. A long time ago. Do you remember that time when I first came to the school, to Alamitos I mean, and your friend was the one they picked to show me around?"

Tommy only watched her. His face was a mask of torment, and he was clutching his belly as if to contain his entrails. The woman next to him was reaching over to him again, almost tentatively, second thoughts, still shocked by what was happening.

"I don't even remember that boy's name, but he did hate dragging the new kid around." She was watching him, waiting him to remember. "I just, like, jogged along behind him trying to catch up. But we ran into you in the hallway, and ... and you were sweet to me. I mean, you were a good guy. You were a *good guy*. You helped me. You walked around with us, and you talked to me, unlike that other guy."

Tommy seemed to be hyperventilating. He was all antsy and sweaty. He didn't say anything.

"What *happened* to you?" Jasmine said.

Tommy dropped his head for a moment, wincing hard, waiting for something to pass.

Finally, he said, "I just want my coins. OK, Jasmine? I just want my fucking coins."

Jasmine ducked her head into the car and looked directly at Steve. Her eyes were filled with hard tears.

"You ready to go?" she said.

"Whenever you are."

"You'll have to get us out of here fast."

"I'm on it." Steve re-shifted into first, felt the pull of the clutch, readied himself.

Jasmine gave him a half-smile, then rose up again.

"Tommy?"

The thug raised his gaze and looked at her. Dude was in deep shit. Steve was surprised he was conscious.

"What?"

"Look, I think I know where the coins are."

Tommy nodded as if his head weighed a hundred pounds.

"I just need you to—"

Steve heard the sound of a racing motor before he saw anything. Then he noticed a blur of movement to his right. The white Jetta from earlier—the one with the bloodied-up driver—came barreling onto the street and crashed headlong into the greaser, crushing him against a wooden fence.

"*Jesus!*" Steve shouted.

Jasmine fell into the passenger seat beside him.

"Go, I guess."

35
MARK

In the distance—somewhere ahead of him in the neighborhood, if his ears were still working—there was the sound of a gunshot. It woke Mark Pellegro from a short, chaotic dream full of shifting imagery, barely glimpsed faces, shouting mouths, anger.

The street lay quiet in front of him, and he was in more pain than he'd ever thought possible. It had started—immediately following his beatdown—as a shocked, numb ache, but that had gradually given way to stunning torment, pinpointed somewhere between his mouth and nose and spreading across his face in a series of spikes. The peak point of that pain was nowhere in sight, still on its way.

He let out a low groan. One of his eyes was completely out of focus and throbbing, two teeth were missing, and his shirt was getting bloodier by the moment from wounds he couldn't even see. Or maybe it was still his nose that wouldn't stop gushing. First Jasmine's vomit, and now his own blood staining up his car? What was next? He was lucky he hadn't pissed his pants. Or maybe he had.

He'd barely gotten a glimpse of the asshole who'd dragged the little girl into his Jetta. It was Charlton Mawk, yep, the squinty-eyed hoodlum who'd been right there in coin shop's parking lot with Tommy. Mark could picture him hopping down from the hulking truck and then receding into the shadows of the strip mall. He hadn't paid much attention to him after that. Admittedly, Mark was confused at the moment, probably concussed, but he hadn't the faintest idea how Charlton had followed him from there to here. It had been like a magic trick. Had the freak known all along what Mark had been thinking? *Did Tommy know?* Impossible!

He shook his head, trying to dislodge some of the damp, cramping thickness, but something clanked in there like a piece of metal, and Mark went still, terrified. Jesus, he was going to kill himself just by turning his head.

That *fucker!*

He concentrated on breathing, on merely staying awake. He was abruptly conscious of the steering wheel in front of him. It was his lifeboat.

He grabbed onto it and held on, loosening and tightening his grip. He white-knuckled it for a full minute, willing himself awake and aware. He felt that if he were to fall asleep, he might never wake up, or he'd wake up in the middle of the night, robbed, his Jetta stripped of its wheels, everything he owned—gone.

His mind drifted back to what had just happened.

The girl had seemed to come out of nowhere.

When he'd lost sight of the Mini Cooper from the parking lot, he'd casually wandered over to the edge of Westminster Boulevard and glanced east then west—immediately sighting the little red car turning into the 7-11 parking lot. It had pulled partially out of sight and parked, and he'd seen the doors open, but he hadn't seen any little girl. He guessed it was possible a girl had been inside, but what the fuck, man? Even if the kid *had* been in the car, who kidnapped a goddamned toddler in broad daylight?

He couldn't concentrate.

He tried to sit up further in his seat and was rewarded with dazzling pain at the center of his head. The laser beam of misery at least woke him up a little more. He opened his eyes wider and stared out the window through skewed vision, hands still locked on the wheel.

The neighborhood lay quiet, deserted. He could still visualize the rear of the Mini as it careened around that closest corner, the tires squealing a little. How long ago was that now? Seconds, minutes, hours? Had the position of the sun changed? He thought it might have. He blinked.

Mark felt his throat tightening with some kind of emotion bubbling up in his chest, and he had to tamp it down because he could not afford snot and tears on top of the wreck his skull had become.

He sat there, alone, staring.

It was just like at the vitamin store, solitary figure behind the counter on a desolate weekday, kegs of overpriced protein powder and big vitamin bottles gathering dust, laughter in the back room. Mark consciously trying to maintain the store's veneer, and often getting mocked for it. At least, that's what it felt like. He was the best salesman at the store, by far, no one would doubt that. Was he supposed to feel guilty for that? Lesser? Was he supposed to endure the smirks as the others passed by him on their way through the double-locked door? If not for him, Jake and

Martin, Kelsey, Derek—hell, even Tommy himself—they wouldn't have a back room to gather in and laugh it up while they concocted their mixes. Twice the little button under the register had saved the store, and twice it had been Mark who'd pressed it.

Shit, even his flippant invite to the party last night had been an afterthought, hadn't it? Tommy had asked all the others long before he'd invited Mark. Mark paid attention to these things. And when Tommy *did* finally invite him, it was the day before the party—that windy Thursday morning—when Tommy had been heading out to his truck and paused reluctantly at the vestibule, like, oh yeah, party tomorrow night, can you make it? As if he were simply *reminding* Mark, and sure, Mark knew about it, the others hadn't exactly been discreet about their plans for the weekend, but it was the first time Tommy had mentioned it himself. And Mark had dutifully said *Of course I'll be there*, and he'd caught the glint of resignation in Tommy's eyes as he'd nodded and left the store. He hadn't even tried to hide it.

And then, at the party, "Keep an eye on the girl," Tommy'd told him, long after Jasmine and her brother had arrived. He'd told him that, then drifted abruptly away, like Mark was his employee all the time, every waking hour.

The hell of it was—*Mark had done it!* Without question! Yes boss!

This morning, he'd awakened with fire in his blood, livid about the goddamn puke in his car. Livid at *her*. The universe had seemed to align, and Mark had rushed over to Tommy's, eager to supplicate himself, yearning to please his boss—what *was* that? He'd fallen in line with Kayla, and it had felt right. He and Tommy's woman had gotten along for the first time, he'd thought, had established an almost-friendship. At least a kinship. And the moment Tommy had shown up at the parking lot, everything reverted back to normal, and Mark had been demoted to the periphery.

That's when Mark had made his decision to go after those fucking coins—and then of course that greaser cretin had been on to him the whole time.

Look at him, stunned and pummeled in the driver's seat of his own car.

Forever the laughingstock. Forever the loser.

"No more," Mark whispered.

He raised himself fully in his seat, enduring another spike of agony in his head, then reached for the key in the ignition. He twisted it, listened to the motor start. He hocked back a huge bloody knot of phlegm and spat it out his open window.

Then he crept the Jetta forward, following the path of the Mini from who-knew-how-long-ago. The little car had turned right here, but he wasn't sure where it had gone after that. He kept his breathing steady, focused on staying awake, *staying awake*, and followed the streets around an almost predetermined path. Most of the side streets were cul de sacs and dead ends. He doubled back on himself twice, and finally faced a stop sign leading to a larger artery leading back to Westminster Boulevard, and then he saw a corner of that red Mini, parked crookedly in the middle of that street, and when he got closer, there was the front of Tommy's dick-compensation truck, and Tommy himself was hanging off of it, and suddenly Mark hated him. Hated him for everything he stood for, for every asinine thing he'd ever done in his life.

Jasmine was standing adjacent to the Mini, brandishing a pistol, of all things. For a few seconds, Mark took his foot off the gas, coasted the Jetta, and marveled at the image. It was like something out of a comic book. It couldn't be real. She was a superhero.

Then he saw the hoodlum, partially hidden in shadows against a fence, just fucking standing there, all his attention directed toward Jasmine and Tommy and whatever they were shouting at each other.

It *was* real.

Without even a wisp of a thought, Mark pressed the pedal deliberately to the floor—avoiding gunning the engine, wanted to stay quiet—and launched the Jetta toward the man in the shadows. Fuck this car anyway, this old car he'd settled on years ago, fuck it with its puke stench and his blood in the fabric and its cheap after-market alterations. Fuck this fucking guy and his greased-back stupid hair and his fists, and fuck the damage he'd done to Mark's teeth and his nose and his face and—

The impact threw Mark forward into the wheel and filled the world with the sound of clanking metal.

He couldn't breathe.

He sucked at the air repeatedly and was only able to huff in tiny gasps—*not enough!*—and a black wave of panic began to consume him as something ticked loudly in the Jetta's crumpled front end. Something was steaming, voices were shouting. There was the sound of multiple tires screeching, then silence broken only by the sounds of the Jetta dying with a clatter.

The tiny gasps of breath got gradually bigger, and then he could breathe, but there was a new deep ache at his sternum. He sat back and stared through the cracked windshield, straight into Charlton's eyes. Guy was leaning over, pinned at stomach level against the fence, which was now caved in on itself. The man was staring back at Mark, a single line of blood from his nose to his chin. He was wrestling with something out of sight below the fender.

Mark figured it was probably a gun, but that was the least of his worries.

Or he simply didn't care.

"Fucker!" Mark tried shouting through the windshield, but it came out a whisper.

The hoodlum watched Mark impassively and brought up his trembling right hand, which held a phone. After laborious effort, he managed to reach its screen with his left arm, which appeared close to immobile. The man's face betrayed no indication of pain or struggle. He brought the phone to his ear after a couple fits and starts, and listened. He said something that Mark couldn't hear, speaking for close to a minute. Then the hand holding the phone went lip, falling to the Jetta's crumpled hood, and Charlton continued staring at Mark.

Mark tried starting the Jetta, but the ignition would only give him a series of useless clicks. He tried it repeatedly, still not really caring, and finally let his hand fall.

His thoughts drifted to Jasmine, for some reason.

The memory of her in the store that first time, just browsing. Before Tommy came onto the floor from the back room. He recalled the young and innocent way she'd looked at him. Mark had helped a thousand people like her.

No, Jasmine had been different.

He could see that now. He forgave her for puking in his car. He couldn't believe he'd held that against her. He was ashamed of himself. He couldn't even smell it at the moment. Besides, who cared about this fucking Jetta now, anyway?

Like he ever had a shot at a girl like Jasmine! As if someone like Jasmine could ever love a guy like him. Maybe he'd helped her just now. It was possible. Maybe he was her hero. That was something.

Or even Kayla. He didn't deserve someone like her, either. Could never have her. Just thinking about her, he laughed, frowning at the pain it caused. They'd had a time, hadn't they? Who would've guessed he'd share a day like this with her?

He heard sirens from faraway, and they grew inexorably closer. He watched the hoodlum, who was still staring at him. The man's eyes were still fierce, but something was draining from him. Or was he projecting? He wanted to laugh some more but was afraid something might bust open further.

He waited.

36
JASMINE

The Mini bounced recklessly onto Westminster Boulevard, threading the needle and turning westbound traffic into a perpendicular, snarling, horn-blaring mess. Jasmine Frank didn't even brace herself for collision. She was twisted in her seat, unbuckled, staring back through the vehicle's small rear window, waiting for Tommy's truck to come barreling out of that side street. But it never came. Even as Steve rocked them east, the open maw of that little street remained empty of activity.

"Is he back there?" Steve asked her. "I don't see him."

"Huh-uh," she said, unable to believe what was happening.

If Tommy was anything, that thing was *persistent*. She knew he would do anything, *anything*—especially now that she'd *held a gun on him*—to get back at her. To get back what was his.

"That guy in the Jetta, that's the one who drove you last night?"

Jasmine nodded. "Yeah, I know him."

"Why did he ... I mean, what the fuck was *that* all about? I think he probably *killed* that guy."

She didn't answer. Her gaze moved to Lori and Sarah in the back seat. They were still intertwined in an embrace, and Lori had gone mercifully quiet. She was breathing evenly now. Jasmine watched the two of them for a long moment, and she realized that she'd never seen Lori hug her daughter so fiercely.

Jasmine's gaze lingered on the little girl's backpack. It was still zipped up, still on her back. She hoped to all that was holy that it still contained the money. Either that, or it didn't matter at all.

But checking the girl's pack could wait.

She turned back around, feeling the handgun still in her sweaty grip. She looked down at it as if it were an alien thing. She had actually fired it. In the jostling, claustrophobic confines of the Mini Cooper, she wondered where that bullet was now. She thought about the projectile's trajectory into the sky, its rainbow arc, the endpoint somewhere in the direction of the beach. Had it traveled a mile? More? Less? Had it shattered someone's window somewhere, or had it fallen harmlessly on a rooftop, or had it lodged in someone's arm? What were the chances? She hoped it hadn't hurt anybody.

By sheer muscle memory—distant recollection of accompanying her mom to the range, out in the desert, learning early against her will—she released the magazine from the pistol, caught it in her hand. She carefully placed the mag at the bottom of her own backpack at her feet. She checked the pistol's open chamber, then dropped the gun into the pack, zipped it back up, took a breath.

She felt Steve staring at her.

"That was awesome," he said. "Like, all of it."

She could tell he wanted to say more, but in her peripheral vision he seemed to bite his tongue and leave it at that.

Jasmine faced forward, letting his words hang there. The Mini had found its fourth-gear groove, and the road came at them relentlessly in its OC whitewashed sameness. Abruptly she felt all the energy drop out of her, and she gave in to despondency.

You know what it all comes down to? she thought. *I just wanted to have fun. Shit, man, I just wanted to have fun at Tommy's party.*

She'd known that running into him at the vitamin store was a ludicrous fluke that Jordan would flip out about, and she'd known even as she'd accepted the invite that she should've *sprinted* out of that store the moment she'd seen Tommy. But—dammit—Tommy was a familiar face, and they'd been young and stupid back in the day, and it was time to let the past be the past, and it was an opportunity to let loose after doing nothing for too long.

There'd been so many lost weeks, months, holing up in the crappy little stinking apartment, worried that they were still in danger. Never going out, never having fun. Jordan had found the way to escape from Garden Grove, had engineered the whole thing, new identities and all, and then they'd spent the next bulk of a year imagining Karl's retaliation. So often, she'd insist to Jordan they were safe. So much time had gone by. Nobody cared anymore. But Jordan was so paranoid. He said they'd never be safe from that sociopath, and that it was stupid to even be so close to him still. His eyes would go all red and wet just *talking* about it. They were less than fifteen miles from the old place, from their mom. Jordan wanted to increase that distance a hundred times or more.

Jasmine wouldn't have it.

She just wanted to have fun. To live a life.

After everything they'd been through, all those years … she didn't think it was too much to ask.

A sign caught Jasmine's eye.

Woody's Coins and Metals, coming up quickly on the right.

"Turn in there," she said.

"But that's where—"

"Make like we're going to that restaurant."

"First place he'll look."

"Yeah, I know."

Steve braked for the turn and made it, gliding into the far side of the parking lot and finding a space. Jasmine watched the area warily. There were only two policemen left, and they were talking casually with one of the store owners near the corner. The older woman was gesticulating despite swaying arm flab, and one of the cops was taking her statement. The other just watched.

Jasmine surveyed the outer parking spaces, her eyes landing on the Karmann Ghia. It didn't appear to have been touched.

She turned again to Lori and Sarah. Lori had unclenched from her daughter and was petting her hair. There was a look of sweaty serenity on her face. Jasmine reached back and took her hand, glancing from mother to daughter.

"I need you to leave me here now," she said.

Stunned silence.

"I need you to be safe."

Steve turned to her. "But … how will you …?"

"Don't worry about me," she said to him. "I just need you to get them home. It feels like—like we've got a second chance right now, and those don't come around very often. I'm so grateful for your help—all of you. But I need to take it from here."

"Just …" Lori said, "… just leave you here?"

Crammed into the back seat, her friend stared at her meaningfully. Jasmine felt something pass between them, and she knew they would never forget this moment—this moment right here—for as long as they lived. Like, they'd survived something, and this decision right now was going to determine what the future held.

"Yes, and we need to do this quickly. He's probably coming here first."

Jasmine grabbed the straps of her pack and lifted it to her knees, then spoke more softly. "I love you guys. I'll try to make this up to you, I mean as long as I live." She looked at Steve. "You too."

She thought he might've actually blushed at that. He was a good guy—no denying it. Sometimes you had to push people out of their comfort zone to see what they were really like. He'd come through for them, for all of them. She pushed the door open and stepped out into the sun.

"Wait!" Sarah cried.

There was a scramble in the rear of the car, and the passenger seat sprung forward, allowing Sarah to squeeze out on the asphalt. The little girl slammed into her, embracing her fiercely. Jasmine held on to the girl's diminutive shoulder tightly for a quiet half-minute, eventually feeling Lori's hand on her back.

"You'll be OK?" her friend asked her, urgently, at her ear. "I mean, really OK?"

Jasmine brought Lori into her hug with Sarah.

"Thanks for everything," she whispered.

Then she dropped to one knee in front of Sarah while keeping a watch on the cops at the far end of the lot.

"Now, Sarah, I need that bag from your pack."

"Oh yeah," said the girl.

She shrugged off the pack and let it fall to the ground. She unzipped the large pocket and pulled out the rumpled Safeway bag. She handed it over, and Jasmine stuffed the cash into her own pack.

"You did great today, Sarah. I don't think I'd be alive without your help, I really don't. So, I mean, you saved my life, kiddo."

Sarah was nodding. So innocent, that girl.

"OK, now, get in that car. Take care of your mom."

As they climbed back in, Jasmine walked around to Steve's window.

"Call if you need help," he said. "I mean it. I hear from you, I'll be here as quick as I can."

She managed a short laugh. "This car sticks out like a sore thumb. You need to go put it in a garage for a year."

"No doubt."

Impulsively, she bent down and kissed his cheek. "Thanks."

More blushing. He had a face for it.

"Any time."

"All right, get out of here."

Sarah's little hand was pressed against the glass of the side window as the Mini scooted away, and then both her little face and Lori's face were visible through the rear, dwindling away as Steve took them to the edge of the parking lot and then back out into the maelstrom of Westminster Boulevard. Then they were gone, and Jasmine was alone.

She moved to the shade of an elaborate overhang in front of the now-closed donut shop. The store was situated near the corner of the strip mall, where she would have a good vantage point. She sat on the lone metal bench beneath the window, trying to breathe steadily. This day was going to go down in the annals of stupid-crazy days, and she'd withstood a few of those in her time on the planet. Why did she immediately think of Jordan when she thought of all the crazy days she'd lived? She found herself opening and closing her hands into tight fists. She stopped, shook out her fingers. Every time she thought of Jordan, she started down the road toward hyperventilating disbelief. It simply couldn't be.

She dug out her phone, turned it on. Battery was getting low—thirteen percent.

She found Tommy's number and called it. When the connection was made, there was a fumbling racket on the other end, and then his voice.

"What?" His voice sounded high, confused, almost desperate.

"I'm at the coin shop."

"Do you have my fu—"

She hung up.

Her heart was hammering. She lay her phone on the bench next to her, then rocked in position for a few moments, humming to herself off-key. The cops at the other end of the plaza had finished up with the store owner and were standing next to their cruiser, waiting for something. She was glad for that. She didn't particularly want them to leave. Not that it really mattered. Wherever Jasmine went, whatever she did now, Tommy would find her. He had the tenacity, and he had the resources, and he had the experience. She knew all that. Just look at how quickly he'd found the coin shop. Even if she went to Thailand or New Zealand or Antarctica, he'd be on the next plane out of LAX.

Or, at least, that would be her fear. She'd forever be looking over her shoulder.

She closed her eyes and focused on her brother's face.

"I'm sorry Jordy," she whispered. *"I didn't mean to do this. I didn't mean any of it."*

And she knew it wasn't Tommy who killed her brother.

Maybe she'd known it all along—since the moment she'd stood next to her mother's drunk-slumbered body and swiped through her phone. Even then, she'd felt the trill of dark dread, deep inside. Reading her own drugged words, recognizing her own stupidity.

Or maybe she'd left her address on purpose.

It was horrible to think that.

But everything in the aftermath of their escape from Garden Grove had been abstract, the ravings of Jordan's fear, and she never consciously bought it. Her brother had become hysterical, almost mad with paranoia. She'd thought him unrealistic and suspicious, herself carefree and optimistic—or at least *trying* to be. He'd been unrelentingly careful, and she'd always encouraged him to lighten up, enjoy life. He'd become an albatross. She'd come close, many times, to making a mistake—for the sake of making it. Tempting fate.

And when she did finally make that mistake ...

Everything was different now.

It was like she'd always been Jordy's kid sister, the impulsive one, the careless one. The one needing big bro's protection. But it would never be the same now. She would always be older than her brother, from now on, if only she could get past this and stay alive. She felt it like a monumental responsibility. Is this what it took to grow up? She set her jaw and waited.

It was five minutes later when Tommy finally pulled into the parking lot in his big black truck.

He was alone, and he was wild-eyed, and he was shirtless.

37
TOMMY

From his perch at the truck's flung-wide passenger door, Tommy Strafe watched the girl in the blue dress. She had a gun in her hand. He wasn't even sure what he was supposed to feel about her anymore. Hatred lingered inside his shivering chest, but there was also the memory of a coiled tightness somewhere lower.

This was not going to end well. Chills had consumed him, and he felt a cold glaze of perspiration across every inch of his body. His bowels were undergoing a prolonged compression. He could barely see Jasmine through his blurred vision, let alone Charlton over there in the shadows.

"What?" Tommy said. His voice felt made of meat, stuffing his skull and leaking out his ears in wet chunks. Then he wasn't even sure why he'd said, "What?"

"Look," came Jasmine's voice, like through liquid. "I think I know where the coins are."

Coins? he thought. *Oh yeah.*

His thoughts kept breaking into shards.

"I just need you to—" Jasmine began.

At first, Tommy heard the sound of the racing motor through the filter of his own sickness—a revving up of fever through his veins, or of puke up his esophagus. Hissing in his head. Then the sound went outside of him, and his head jerked up and to the right. A white Jetta—some distant part of his brain *knew* that car—blew past a stop sign at musta-been 50 miles per hour and careened across the street, dead-straight at Charlton, who barely had time to move a centimeter. The Jetta crushed him against the wood fence beneath a fat hackberry tree, and the weathered slats folded around him.

"Oh my *GOD!*" Kayla cried out next to him.

Someone shouted, *"Jesus!"*

And then the little red car, the one with Jasmine tucked inside it, took off with a chirp of rubber on pavement.

Kayla made a helpless screaming noise somewhere in the distance. *"Tommy?"*

He blinked his eyes, trying to align himself with whatever was happening.

Before he could register her opening the driver's door, Kayla was climbing down off the truck.

Then the world was somersaulting, a kaleidoscope of glints and glimmers.

The air *whoofed* out of him, and a thudding pain took sudden hold of his shoulder and hip and head. He was on the ground with no real memory of falling. He was staring up at the underside of his truck, and he smelled vomit. *Oh shit.* Yeah, he felt it in his hair. His own puke was in his goddamn hair, it was sticky on his shirt. New nausea grabbed him like a glove of mucus around his throat, and he spewed again, whiplashing his head to the left just in time to spray bile toward his rear tire.

He scrambled to his feet, retching.

He should've gone home. He should've listened to Kay. He hadn't had a hit since last night, *early* last night, and now it was afternoon the next day. Why didn't he keep a small stash in the truck? Yeah, sure, and what if that cop earlier had decided to search him, what then? It paid to be careful, but it was also stupid to be careful, because this sucked, man, this feeling like chemo or something, like wildfire through his nerves. It had to be more than just withdrawal, though, it *had* to be.

He heard sirens, wasn't sure how long they'd been blaring. They were on their way here, no doubt about it.

Kayla, staggering toward the crash site, did a comical pirouette when she heard him fall, and then ran to him.

"Holy shit, Tommy, what are you—?"

"I'm fine."

"You're not *fine*, your arm is crooked."

Tommy glanced down at his shoulder, saw that it was slumped low, dislocated. His arm hung, bent and rigid, numb. He grabbed the useless wrist and shoved downward, twisting his upper body, and felt the shoulder pop back into place.

"Tommy!" Kayla cried, hands flying to her mouth.

"We gotta get outta here," he said, testing his shoulder and finding it sore but functional.

"I'm staying."

"Get—*what?*—get back in the truck!"

Kayla stood indecisive in the middle of the street, glancing off toward the crash. Hearing the sirens blare louder, she made one step toward Tommy, then reversed course and moved away from him.

"Kay!"

She didn't say anything, just rushed to the Jetta. To Pellegro! Not to Charlie, no, she was going straight to Pellegro, *I mean what the fuck?* Christ, Tommy's eyes were gummy now and he couldn't seem to maintain focus, but he swore he could see blood on Charlton's face, and yet Kayla had gone directly to the asshole that caused the wreck!

"Kay!"

She was ignoring him now, bent into the Jetta's front window, her curvy butt mocking him. After a few seconds, she poked her head back out.

"Just go! Go get that silly girl! I don't care!"

"Get back here!"

"No!"

"Kayla, I swear to fucking Christ, if you—"

"Fuck off!"

Tommy realized he was clutching his abdomen, his whole arm wrapped around his midsection. The smell of vomit was about to make him puke again. It was all in his fucking hair. Jesus! He pulled off his tee shirt and, wincing under constant cramping, used a clean section to wipe puke from his hair as best he could. His hands were shaking.

Well, fuck her then!

He spat a glob of vomit-speckled phlegm in Kayla's direction and hobbled over to the driver's side of the truck, then climbed laboriously to the cab. Goddamn, man, he could barely do it. He felt like some hopelessly heavy nerd kid clambering up a jungle gym. But he made it, even though his arms felt as if they were made of aluminum foil. What was the matter with him? He'd been hours off the shit before, and it was never this bad. He tossed his shirt onto the floorboards.

He cranked the ignition and pulled away from the scene, careful to avoid making tire marks, although that probably mattered for shit at this point. He caught a final glimpse of Kayla as she leaned over Mark, and he threw several curses in her direction, and then he was facing Westminster Boulevard. He pulled up to the stop and glanced both ways at the ocean of traffic.

It was hopeless, Jasmine was gone.

"Fuuuuuck!" he yelled.

Which way?

He sat hunkered over the wheel as the sirens grew louder, and he felt as if every muscle in his body was twitching. He couldn't wait any longer. He squeezed into a tight gap in traffic headed west, and moments later in his rearview two cop cruisers swung into the side street he'd just pulled out of. The sirens dwindled to a stop after he'd driven another block.

Restlessly, he reached for his phone, then immediately dropped it to the seat. Where the fuck was he going? This felt wrong. His teeth were chattering as he jerked into the left lane and then finally into a turn lane. He waited with shallow breaths for an opening and finally made the U, heading back the way he'd come. There was no way around it: He had to go home. He had to dig into his stash. That would fix at least part of this problem.

He pressed the gas, steadfastly heading toward east Santa Ana. He was imagining his nightstand, and with that came the whole bedroom, the collector case—the sight of it broken, the little drawer empty. It was the reason he was here, right now, on this road, with fucking *murder* on his mind even as his body was betraying him, this shaking, fevered mess. Minutes passed by, and the farther he got—past Beach Boulevard, past Brookhurst—the more he could taste relief. Muscles trembling, eyes emitting helpless tears, he imagined the injection, the enveloping heat of it. For Tommy, it was always like drifting on a warm sea, a long slow continuous release, like God holding him in his splayed palms and smiling at him forever.

His phone rang, jarring him from his anticipation. Against all reason, it was Jasmine's name that blurted off his screen, staring at him, daring him to answer. Tommy felt a surge of something, but he no longer knew what that was, it was a mishmash of wrath, of confusion, of old fiery need.

"What?" he answered, feeling his voice rasp in his throat.

There was an eternal pause.

"I'm at the coin shop."

What the—coin shop?—the—coins, right—right, it was the coins that this was all about, the coins …

A surge of wild anger thrummed up inside him, and he let it find his voice.

"Do you have my fucking coins or not, you bitch? I swear, I'm gonna—"

The line had gone dead.

Tommy hissed frustration and slapped his phone to the bench seat repeatedly, then flipped a dangerous U back westbound. The hiss whistling through his teeth became a raw screech. Through sheer force of will, he pushed past his fevered delirium and nausea and forged ahead, pushing everything else out, everything except Jasmine. The road tunneled out ahead of him, narrowing to a cruel point in the distance. He realized he was practically roaring now, pounding the dash with his bruised fist, and he didn't care, in fact he needed it, needed the distracting pain as he spiraled into a vortex of shit.

The strip mall loomed on the left, and he turned in abruptly, jerking crookedly into the first spot he found.

The cab went silent as he studied the bright parking lot, squinting. He was breathing too quickly. He felt a lurch of panic. Jesus, he had to get home.

Then there she was, over in the corner by the donut shop. The blue dress, the sheen, the glow.

He watched her for a teeth-grinding moment—and it was like time travel. It was like the first time he'd seen her, back at Alamitos, the gangly girl with the innocent eyes, so different from the other bitches with the jaded stares and the goth-slumped shoulders, the ethnic closed-off sullenness, the vapid gigglers, the shy mousy girls. There was that spark, that shine. She'd kicked something inside him, and if not for her irritating brother he would've outright fallen for her. Why'd she have to be saddled with that? Jordan as her twin fucking brother diminished her, hell yeah it did, *uggghhh*, but god*damn* she made him feel something, something new, just looking at her. Like you wanted to have her, you wanted her to be yours, but you had to be careful with her, too. You had to protect her; she was fragile.

Sweating, trembling, he knew that's where he'd failed.

He hadn't done that, he hadn't protected her.

Tommy climbed out of the truck, feeling as if he might fall. He swayed for a second, then walked over to her, keeping his eyes on her.

He sat heavily on the bench next to her.

He wasn't shaking anymore, at least not as much. It was as if being near her relieved his symptoms a little.

"Hey," was all she said.

He turned his head to face her, saw her faded makeup, the exhaustion in her eyes. He didn't know what to say to her.

"I didn't even know I *took* those coins," she said, almost a whisper. "Then I just … I just *had* them … in a plastic bag. And then I was mad at you. For what you did to me. Don't deny it, OK? I'm not stupid." She looked at him earnestly. "And then I remembered. I remembered why I took them. And when I saw that, that store, and I—I took them in there. I didn't know what I was doing."

There was a long silence, just traffic noise.

He felt better in the shade, in the quiet, sitting next to her with her soft voice.

"I'm sorry," she said, and then a frown creased her expression. "Or maybe I'm *not* sorry. You hurt me, Tommy, and … and … I know you didn't do it, but—but—Jordan's gone, my brother is dead." An involuntary gasp of emotion escaped her. "He's gone, *he's gone*, and it's because of last night, it's because of this awful day, and I don't even know what to do about it. I don't know what to do now."

Tommy stared at the ground, his body abuzz.

"I just wanted to have a good time," Jasmine went on. "That's what you said, you know. You said the party would be a good time. We'd have fun. But look at everything that's happened."

She sniffed, went quiet. Then she bent to her backpack and unzipped it. She drew out a grocery bag that held out a brick of something.

"Here's the cash I got."

Tommy didn't even look at it.

"I think the coins are still here," she said in that quiet voice, and now he looked at her. "I think they're either in the store, or they might be in that car over there, that orange one. I saw the man from the store getting something from that car earlier. I think he might've bought the coins for himself, you know, to sell. We did the whole thing outside the store, so it—it felt off the record. Like he took them to his car right away for himself. Maybe. I don't know."

Tommy glanced off toward the Karmann Ghia, thought about his coins. His father's coins. For some reason, they didn't mean much to him at the moment. They'd been cooped up in a locked drawer for years, out of sight, part of his past, dusty and forgotten. Always there, yeah, but unseen. Why'd he been so careless with them, anyway? He'd shown the fucking things to *everyone*, some kind of misplaced pride, memory of his dad, maybe, his dad who he liked to prop up but sometimes wasn't the greatest. He never liked to acknowledge that shit, but it was there, simmering.

After a while, he let out a shaking breath.

Everything seemed to fall away from him.

He felt a measure of clarity, as if finally opening his eyes to something that he'd been steadfastly shielding himself from.

"Fuck those coins," he said, voice flat. "I mean, I can get 'em back. Somehow. Rennie knows someone on the force, I can file a report. I don't even have to mention you."

Jasmine watched him, still holding out the grocery bag.

"You can keep that," he said.

She dropped the brick of cash to her lap, stared out at the traffic. They sat there for a while, not talking.

38
KAYLA

The sirens were getting closer.

Any second now.

Tommy's truck had just rumbled away, and Kayla Jennings hadn't even cast a glance in his direction. She was *disgusted* with him—his sickness in plain view like that, spewed onto the asphalt, embarrassing as all hell. Everything she hated about him, wrapped up in a stinking bow, a gift to the fucking world.

Mark was stunned and battered behind the wheel of his crumpled Jetta. Through the open window, she was trying to engage him, keep him awake.

"Mark! Mark! Stay awake! Can you hear me?"

His eyes flickered with intermittent awareness, but mostly he was staring dully straight ahead.

She glanced over at Charlton, who was smashed against the shattered fence and bent over the Jetta's front end. He was broken below the waist, caved in. He appeared to be conscious—but barely. She noticed he had a phone in his loosening fist. As she watched, it fell to the Jetta's hood, then slid soundlessly to the weedy ground. His face went gray.

Good riddance.

At that moment, she heard a cop car race onto the street. Ignoring instinct, she straightened up and faced the approaching vehicle, acknowledged it, kept her hands in view. The cruiser, lights flashing, came to a professional angled stop, and two officers hurried out and went straight to her.

"What happened here?" asked the driver, a serious-looking black cop with piercing eyes, one hand at his weapon.

"I only heard it," she said. "I came running from over there. I think that man is dead, but the driver is alive."

As if replying to her, an ambulance blared onto the street from the south, gliding to a stop. The scene was immediately busy with responders, wordlessly attending to both Mark and Charlton. The cop asked her to step to the sidewalk but stay close for any questions.

Kayla stepped backward, tripping a little on the curb. She chewed on her lower lip, caught between impulses to flee or stay. She could easily slip beyond this patchwork fence right now and be gone, undetected, forgotten. Catch an Uber back home, explain herself to Tommy, get back to living her life. She hadn't yet given her name, and both cops were occupied.

But there was Mark, still stunned in the front seat of the Jetta in which he'd driven her around this morning on their weird adventure along Westminster Boulevard. Even from her vantage point on the sidewalk, she could see the line of blood on his face; he'd probably banged his head on the steering wheel with the impact. Apparently no airbag in that old Jetta, which still had the faint aroma of princess vomit.

Why did Mark Pellegro matter, anyway? Mark with the stupid hat.

He'd plowed straight into Charlton Mawk, that's why he mattered. Out of nowhere, he'd deliberately slammed his Jetta into Charlton fucking Mawk—one of the many banes of Kayla's existence—and it looked like he'd actually rid the world of the toxic asshole for good. Beyond everything, beyond their little journey and their burger and their bickering, there was that.

Plus the fact that he'd helped save a little girl.

Mark Pellegro!

She decided to stay.

Oh Jesus, Tommy would exact his revenge. He'd find a way to get back at her. But this time … she didn't care. Even as that thought twanged inside her, she endured a cold shiver.

She *had* to know what had driven Mark to do this! She *had* to. Because right now, it didn't make any goddamn sense. Last she'd seen Mark, he'd been wandering aimlessly back and forth across the strip mall's parking lot, kicking at parking-space curbs, looking bored, seemingly ready to bug off home and try to forget everything that had happened earlier. Get on with his silly life. Then, not a half hour later, he'd gone all Mad Max on a vicious, remorseless hoodlum, apparently killing him, and now he looked like the victim of a prison beating, dazed and confused in the driver's seat of his Jetta.

She was so eager to talk to Mark again, she could barely contain herself. She'd backed up a little, and as the cops tended to him she thought she could see his eyes opening a little wider, thought he was becoming more responsive. Could she ask the cops if she could talk to him? That was weird, right? She'd already presented herself as a stranger. But she *had* to ask him how it all had come to pass. Charlton Mawk—*dead!*

She knew he was going to catch hell for it, one way or another, and—god help her—she wanted to help him. As dorky as he was, as desperate for coolness as he was, he was a good guy. She always laughed at the poor dude, but dammit if he hadn't shown his colors. That had to count for something.

Kayla lit a cigarette and folded her arms, watching the scene.

When she saw the sleek black Lincoln turn onto the street, she felt her soul plummet to the ground. It was a like a gut punch. She couldn't breathe.

Oh Jesus shit.

The phone. In Charlton's dying hand, falling from the Jetta to the weeds.

The Lincoln glided to a stop on the other side of the street, and Rennie Mawk was staring at her from the driver's seat. She could not look away from his face. She knew him, and he knew her—all too well. He accepted her gagging distaste for him; in fact, he always seemed to relish it, roving her body with his lecherous eyes, and always with the suggestive comments. Tommy aware of it, too, forgiving of this horrible old crook, probable murderer, because of family history, *blah blah blah*, those predatory eyes, that repellent smirk.

Her breath was still caught in her throat. She felt her hand toss her cigarette as if dissociated from her body. She felt faint. Rennie's gaze moved methodically to the wreck. She knew he couldn't see much from his angle, and she wondered with real terror if at this moment *she* knew a truth that *he* didn't: His son was dead.

Rennie pushed the Lincoln's big door open and stepped out onto the street, and he was so real standing there, larger than life, surveying the wreckage with a stoic wariness. He swung the door shut behind him like an afterthought and screwed up his mouth in an uncharacteristic way, as if uncertain.

Then he started toward Kayla.

Aw fuck, she murmured under her breath.

"Where's Tommy?" he called, halfway over.

"He left."

Rennie kept his eye on the wreckage, and now—Kayla knew—he could see his son's body against the fence. He stopped and stared at the EMTs surrounding Charlton. A couple of burly ambulance personnel had already carefully removed Mark from the Jetta, and they appeared to be preparing a stretcher for him a few yard from the car. A cop was about to back the car away from the fence. Charlton was limp, clearly dead.

Rennie cleared his throat.

After a long tortuous moment, he repeated what she'd said. "He left?" His voice was strained, as if he'd taken a gut punch and was trying to save face. "So he was here."

She watched Rennie warily. "He was here."

"Where'd he go?"

Kayla said the first thing that came to her head. "He went after his coins."

She supposed she wanted to punish Tommy, and that was why those particular words came out. She was prepared to explain to Rennie what had happened over the past hour, but to her surprise he nodded, clearly knowing what she was talking about. And then it made sense: Tommy had already spilled everything to Rennie when he picked up Charlton. Of course he had.

But at that moment, Kayla realized something: She'd consciously *not* mentioned Jasmine.

She was *protecting* her.

The little girl in the blue dress, the party girl. Kayla had started this day hating that girl, no question. But, hell, she had to admit Jasmine had been fuckin' *groovy* coming out of that little Mini Cooper, totally unexpected, armed and righteous, snatching that little girl from Charlton. Because Charlton Mawk was never on the right side of anything in this world. But more because … because it was as if Kayla had seen Jasmine for the first time, like really seen her, and if she'd seen even a hint of herself in Jasmine, well, it was infinitesimal, and that had fucking ached, man, it had *ached*.

Rennie was walking over to the scene.

A cop immediately broke from his task and met him.

"Sir, I need to ask you to keep clear of—"

"That's my son." Gesturing.

"Which is why I have to ask you to step back." Palms up, holding Rennie back. "We're taking care of him, and we'll let you know what to do when the time comes, OK?"

Rennie kept walking. "Back off. I'm gonna see my son."

"Sir—"

"You got a problem with me, you can bring it up with my friend Lieutenant James W. Powell at the sheriff's department. You got me, son?"

The cop grimaced and nearly rolled his eyes, stepped aside, arms still up, now defensively.

Rennie moved forward into the fray, not having even glanced at the cop, and Kayla watched him with contempt. He went straight to the Jetta's left front fender and stared at his son's gray face while EMTs flashed glares at Rennie. They said things Kayla couldn't hear, gesturing, pointing. Rennie ignored them. Finally, he turned away and studied Mark, surrounded by technicians on the ground. Mark had been stabilized with some kind of neck gear. His eyes appeared to be closed.

Kayla heard someone yell, *"Get him outta here!"* Referring to Rennie.

But Rennie was already walking away. He took out his phone, went around to the back of the Jetta, and snapped a photo of the license plate. He then pocketed the phone, standing like a statue about ten feet from the vehicle. The expression on his face was one of cold concentration. Kayla didn't see any outward grief there, any emotion at all, really, and it felt like she wasn't even looking at a human being.

Then he was walking back toward her.

She steeled herself.

"What happened?" Chilly, hard gaze.

"I'm—I'm trying to piece it together myself." She spoke as quickly as her synapses could fire. "Tommy figured out it was this kid named Jordan who took his coins from our bedroom last night, and so he was after him with Charlton, I guess. They were in his truck. They followed Jordan here. I think Jordan wanted to sell the coins somewhere." She took a final drag of her cigarette and flicked it away. "Well, they got the kid, Jordan, away from his Corvette over at the coin store, and then Jordan got into the Jetta here and took off. That's our friend Mark over there—" She gestured. "—he works with Tommy at the store. They'd—Tommy and Charlie cornered Jordan, and Mark was just trying to get his car back when Jordan ran down Charlton. I saw that happen. Mark was trying to push Charlie out of the way, but he was too late."

Fuck, I'm stuttering too much.

Kayla tried to decipher the look in Rennie's eyes as he stared at her. She couldn't do it.

She cleared her throat, crossed her arms.

She pictured Mark at In-N-Out Burger, that goofy smile on his face, his stupid jokes. Before all this.

"So the driver, this Jordan," Rennie said. "Where is he?"

"I don't know, he ran off, like immediately. That way, over the fence. He had a gun, man, that's how he got us out of the car. The fucker."

"You were in the car?"

"Before that Jordan guy took it, yeah. He spotted us tailing him and ordered us out."

Rennie was watching her almost passively now. Kayla was hoping to Christ the cop wouldn't come over and start asking his own questions.

"And Tommy followed Jordan?"

She thought about it. "Yes."

I think that story'll check out, she thought.

There was a long silence while they stood staring at the scene. Kayla noticed some people emerging from the homes across the street to watch.

"I'm sorry about Charlton," Kayla whispered, not sorry at all.

"Me too."

And Rennie left. Simply turned heel, glided across the street, seated himself behind the wheel of his big Lincoln, and drove the behemoth quietly away.

Kayla started shivering and couldn't stop.

39
KARL

The street lay calm and sweaty, lined with a row of neglected '40s-era minimalist traditional homes common to this scuzzy, broken-down part of Santa Ana. Karl Granger was parked against a cracked curb in his custom gray Buick LeSabre. Obviously, Jasmine would recognize the car, so he'd parked it one street east of the apartment building with an angled view of the entrance, where a few cops still mingled.

In retrospect, it was obvious Gloria's worthless kids would end up at a place like this—low-rent, not terribly far from home, and barely tenable.

Walking over to that apartment building earlier—the address of which Jasmine had revealed in her drunken voice message—had been uneventful. He'd also had no trouble entering the structure (in his black ballcap, his sunglasses) and speaking with a couple of neighbors to ferret out the unit number, and then, Jesus, the fucking kids had left their door unlocked, so he'd donned his gloves and walked right in, making himself at home in the squalor. First, he'd gone to the refrigerator and withdrew a bottle of water from the door, hydrating himself. Then he'd made his way through the sleazy domicile, absorbing everything. Under an empty Rice Krispies cereal box, he found several pieces of mail addressed to the kids' real goddamn names, care of a P.O. box in Orange. One was a cell phone bill. Another envelope appeared to hold a paycheck from a salon.

There'd been a single bed in the bedroom, and Karl stared at it with revulsion for a long moment. The mattress was covered by a single thin sheet in disarray. There were clothes flung to the ground, piled in the corner, dirty in an overflowing box under the window. These were a teenaged boy's clothes—jeans, tees, old athletic shoes. The closet contained the well-kept clothes of a young woman. He sniffed dresses and blouses and skirts and could detect Jasmine's scent, even though the bedroom smelled like perfumed feet.

Even as he'd inhaled her essence, he'd felt a sneer take hold of his lips.

He remembered reading once that olfactory memories were the strongest, and this one had certainly taken him back. Back to the beginning, really, when he'd taken the Franks into his home. That was years ago, after Gloria had lost her worthless previous husband, and her whole life had melted away into a ghastly pool of ennui. Back then, she had a body well beyond expectation for her age. He'd assumed she was a good ten years younger than her real age of thirty-two. At the bar on Katella, they'd magnetized, and they'd hooked up in the women's can. He'd been shocked later to find that she'd pushed out not one but two kids—at the same time! Twins. As he'd increasingly brought Gloria into his life, he'd paid her children little attention at first, but over time they'd become a necessary evil. After he helped Gloria through the legal aspects of her meager estate, securing her dead hubby's investments, he brought the abruptly adrift family into his own home in Garden Grove.

The kids had been all of eight or nine years old at that time, suspicious but innocuous little entitled burdens, but time had delivered puberty, and puberty had delivered odors. And disobedience. In his home.

His home.

Karl Granger had rules—simple as that.

On the sidewalk to his right, a couple of slovenly young women strode giggling past his Buick, jolting him from his thoughts. One of them casting a long gaze in his direction as her ample ass swayed. They were probably on their way to pick up their laundry somewhere. They were dressed horrendously in what appeared to be pajama bottoms, stretched-out sweatshirts and flip-flops. What the fuck was wrong with this generation? Karl challenged the woman's gaze until she finally looked away with a glint of unease.

That's right.

He settled back into his seat, watching the tenement where a crew had—about an hour ago—removed the body of Jordan Frank. The boy had a single entry wound to the back of the skull, exit wound roughly in the area of the left eye, pattern of blood spray and mist in the general direction of the fridge, spots of gray matter near the chair leg. Backspatter like subtle abstract art. Oh, the image against the back of Karl's eyelids delighted him.

He recalled making his way through the dim apartment, to the kitchen from the bedroom. He'd sat waiting on one of the uneven chairs at the young Franks' filthy kitchen table, letting his eyes wander, and he'd thought, *This is what becomes of no rules.* Near the sink, ants had formed a line to some glorious destination in one of the cabinets. Something in there smelled sticky-sweet. He hadn't wanted to touch anything in this place, so he'd challenged himself to remain utterly still as he counted the minutes in increments of ten in his head. He'd heard a clock ticking minutely somewhere, but it had been bothersome. His mind was like a metronome.

Karl Granger was a patient man.

Almost ten years with the fucking Frank family proved that. He'd even acquiesced to the three of them retaining the Frank surname, despite his own prominence in their new life. (His new wife had objected to alliteration.) He'd demonstrated his patience with his new brood, growing into the role of father and doing his part to mold them. He'd successfully controlled Gloria through a careful regimen of opioids and isolation, and he'd done the same to the children through sheer force of will. And it had worked for years. And then ...

Last year, September fucking thirteenth, near midnight. The Garden Grove police pounding on his door, a defensively postured unit of five responding to an apparently screaming 911 call delivered by one Mr. Jordan Frank. Karl had stood in the doorway finishing his Scotch, glaring into a flashlight. Cops yelling at him. He'd complied, had invited them in. Fucking apes had cranked his arms behind him, and that's when Jordan had come stomping downstairs crying, a bleating mess, yelling something unintelligible, all snotty. His sister watching from upstairs in her underwear. And then Gloria, herself hysterical, flowed down and attached herself to her son, fervently pleading *misunderstanding, mistake, PLEASE officers ...*

At that point, it hadn't taken much for Jordan to recant, to apologize, to go with the flow of his mother's excuses: *Her son suffered from nightmares in his psychosis, he was under a doctor's care but sometimes he still had episodes.* Jordan had watched the Garden Grove police unit depart, one by one, watching the boy with pity as he cowered in his mother's arms.

And then both of them, gone, that very night, while Karl slept and dreamed of seething retribution.

Nothing but gritted teeth for months.

And now ...

The gift of an address, straight from Jasmine's little whore mouth.

After letting precisely an hour go by, sitting without moving in that chair, Karl had removed his 9mm Sig Sauer from his shoulder holster and contemplatively attached its black-market suppressor. He'd had the weapon and its illegal accompaniment since his time in San Francisco, Christ, twenty years earlier. He'd placed the weapon atop a pile of napkins that seemed to have come from a fast-food establishment. Thirty-five minutes later, he had delivered a full metal jacket 9mm round into Jordan Frank's brain, as quiet as a soft sneeze, and had then taken a full minute to bask in the sense of satisfaction, watching the kid's body settle imperceptibly to the grimy floor. He'd known he could spare that minute; he'd known how long he had. And then he'd disassembled his weapon, pocketed the components, and walked out of the apartment building as unobtrusively as he'd entered.

Really, the Frank children had been aligned against him from the start. He'd never had a chance with the twins. Perhaps he'd misunderstood the potency of the bond, which had been revealed to him in glimpses over time. Curled in the closet together, asleep, embracing. Bathing together. Whispering at night, colluding, petting. Disgusting.

The Frank children never adjusted to his methodologies. Neither of them had the character to do so. Karl felt as though he'd come close with Jordan before his ill-advised midnight call. Jasmine was the tougher case. Jasmine'd had the halo about her, that steel halo. It had been vital to keep the children under his control, and yet she resisted the most—almost effortlessly. That's what got under his skin.

He wasn't even sure what he might do when he encountered her today. Jordan was simple—the easiest comeuppance imaginable. Jasmine was a different question altogether. There was something about her that resisted easy answers. Karl saw a young Gloria in her, that was one thing. Gloria long before her descent. An ideal. Hell, he'd seen that when Jasmine was a girl. Had tried to get to her then, but Gloria was just strong enough then to intervene.

He didn't want to kill Jasmine, even though when he thought about her his mind scribbled into an angry scrawl. He wanted to control her. Reestablish his rules. Take her back.

And *ooohhh*, he'd almost had his chance, had been this close, a couple hours ago—not long after he'd snuffed out Jordan. The girl had swept into the building with another young woman and a child, he was sure that had been her! Karl had been on the verge of stepping out of the Buick once more and taking care of all three of them if necessary—but then the cops had swept in, a full squadron. Karl had cursed to himself and then settled in for the long haul. Perhaps the cops would take her to the station, question her for a while. If he was lucky, they'd only talk to her inside one of the parked squad cars and let her go. He knew she'd be busy for a while, though.

Sooo, he'd motored away for a relaxing lunch on Main at a seafood joint. Waited it out.

Did a little window-shopping.

She'd be back to the apartment at some point. No worries. He had her.

It was mid-afternoon when he returned to find just a couple cops remaining on the scene. He'd settled in at the same parking spot, watching. No light at Jasmine's window yet.

At one point, a Mexican family walked by, along the sidewalk across the street, carrying groceries. Four fucking kids toddling along behind the parents. Jesus Christ. None of them noticed Karl sitting in his Buick. Karl imagined himself as perfectly camouflaged as a desert dragon, inhuman, hyper-conscious and yet utterly still, nourished by his Buick shell. Vehicles rumbled past, north and south, unaware of the predator in their midst. He chuckled dryly at the metaphor he'd conjured.

An hour later, the police had cleared away from the apartment building, and activity surrounding the place returned to the almost banal—at least from this angle. But for Karl, this seemed prime time for Jasmine to try to finally return to her little hovel, perhaps having stayed away from the scene but eager to return for clothing, for food, before taking the next step in her newly desperate existence. Because, oh yes, she knew what had gone down here. Somehow, she knew. That sense that twins have, that shit was real. Or she'd been tipped off by a neighbor, a friend, whatever—she knew. And this was when Karl would swoop her up with words of faux forgiveness, promising to return her to a sane life where she would be taken care of, where she could right herself.

Where she could be with her mother again.

He watched a young man striding toward him along the sidewalk on the right, immersed in his phone, oblivious of his surroundings. Large-headed simian, low-class rube, wearing a disgusting crusty tee-shirt, about to trudge on past, didn't even give Karl a glance. But just as the man came abreast of the Buick, he paused, searching his surroundings as if lost. That's when he caught Karl's eye.

"Hey, man," the young man said, "is this the right way to Bristol?"

Karl took a closer look at him. The thug's eyes were jittery, a bit nervous—he saw that clearly as the man jumped down from the curb and curled around the Buick's front end, and Karl had a split-second impulse to start the Buick's ignition, but his hands didn't even lift from his lap. Then the young man was right at the window, stinking of puke.

"Bristol that way?" he said.

Karl rumbled out his most threatening voice: "Get the fuck away from my—"

Out of nowhere, the thug had a small silver blade in his large grip, and it flashed in a quick movement, and Karl felt a sharp iciness at his neck, and only then did his arms fling uselessly up, buffeting against the bottom of the steering wheel, and then there was nothing.

40
JASMINE

The streets came at Jasmine Frank like a hot-liquid dream, denouement of an endless nightmare but no end in sight. Her body felt as if it wanted to cry, but she was empty of tears. Her head was heavy, zoned. She thought distantly of Lori, poor Lori, and little Sarah, and yeah even Steve, that would-be family, and she hoped they were OK, hoped desperately for that, because she—Jasmine—would be the one to blame for any repercussions. She'd managed to dip all three of them into a sudden vat of liquid shit, and then, miraculously, pull them out. She felt good about that last part, and not so good about the first part, so she focused on the last part.

She glanced over at Tommy. He'd put his filthy shirt back on and was now hunched over the wheel, single-minded, quiet.

He'd immediately wanted to break into that Karman Ghia at the edge of the parking lot, but when she wandered near it to check it out, she found evidence that it had already been searched. She'd gotten close enough to get a glimpse of the interior and found the glove box flung open, innocuous papers and manuals and old maps spread out on the passenger seat. Who knew what had been taken out of there? The trunk was slightly ajar, too. There was even a length of crime tape affixed to the driver's door. When she'd reported this back to Tommy, he'd nodded with shivery resignation. She got the sense that he was going to go back to the store that night, after he was feeling better.

"Come on," he said, voice barely short of a groan. "I'll take you home."

The thought of *home*—wherever that was now—filled her with a foggy anxiety. She wanted desperately to *go home*, to the quiet humid stillness of the apartment, lose herself to unconsciousness in her bed ... but at the same time, she never wanted to step foot in there again. But at least it was a starting point for the rest of her life—if only to deal with what had happened there, gather her meager things, and leave.

In the truck, Tommy settled in to a focused, seething posture, bent forward a little as if to help them get to his own home that much more quickly. He was still sweating more than he should've been, and his eyes looked hyper-alert, but cast inward on whatever was happening to his body. He looked beyond sick.

They'd driven in silence for a few miserable minutes before Tommy, in a cramped voice, said, "Sorry about your brother."

The words startled her. She didn't say anything.

"I didn't kill him, Jasmine, I swear to Christ." Squinting under apparent abdominal anguish.

"I know."

He glanced over at her, not saying anything.

"But ..." she began. "What did ... what did he ever do to you?"

"*I told you, I didn't—*" he squeezed out painfully.

"I know you didn't kill him, Tommy! OK? I've just—I've always wondered why you ... hated him so much."

He was quiet.

"He never did anything to you," she said.

He shrugged. "Just something about him, I guess."

"*What* about him?"

"I don't know! *Fuck!* Weak, maybe. He was weak."

The truck moved erratically in the lane, and she touched Tommy tentatively on his rigid forearm.

"All right, all right," she said. "Be careful."

He came to a jerking stop at an intersection, his thick fingers drumming the wheel with no rhythm at all.

"I have to get home."

"I know."

As they sat there quietly, she tentatively scooted herself closer. He watched her warily out of the corner of his eye. She moved still closer, staring at his sweaty cheek. She brought up her hand cautiously. He didn't object, so she placed the backs of her fingers against his forehead. The fever there seemed to lick flame at her, and she actually flinched.

"I think you need a doctor."

"What I need is at home."

She moved back across the bench.

"You can drop me wherever. I can Uber."

"No, it's all right."

The light turned green, and Tommy emitted a grunt of relief. They passed banks and Mexican grocers, used car lots and hobby stores. Office parks, Asian markets, bodegas, endless tire outlets. And then more of the same. Vehicles moving like a great collective, a teeming ant hive, in and out of parking lots, racing around endlessly.

At the next intersection, Jasmine glanced idly at the corner bus stop, where a late-teen girl was pacing and talking and laughing and gesturing in front of a stern-looking dude in a wife-beater and a bomber jacket who was perched on the metal bench, staring off into the distance, eyes obscured by huge sunglasses. The girl had track bruises on the backs of her legs, beneath her short purple skirt. Her hair was periwinkle blue, but Jasmine could see a half-inch of brown unhealthy roots. When she saw Jasmine looking at her, the girl stopped moving and gave her the finger.

Jasmine turned back to Tommy.

"I always thought you and I could be friends," she said, and she let that hang there in the silent cab for a few seconds. "Back in school, you know, I thought I could find the right way to do that."

Apparently Tommy didn't want to talk about that.

"How'd you end up in Santa Ana, anyway?" Tommy grunted.

It was a subject Jasmine assumed they'd get into at the party last night. How quickly optimism could turn to excrement! She could already barely recall or even imagine her spirits as she and Jordan had arrived at Tommy's house—her first real night out in months. Getting her first look at the people already inside, the thump of the assaultive music, the drinks just waiting, the dopey laughter. The prospect of talking to real people. But they'd never really gotten there, had they? Things had started going all sideways after only an hour. Conversations edgy with mean-spiritedness and teasing.

She still resented Tommy for all that, but she decided to be honest with him. The rawness of what had happened to Jordan left her splayed open.

"We ran away."

"From what?" Ending the question on a note of pain.

"Everything." Pause. "Doesn't matter."

She waited for him to say something, but he didn't. He rumbled them forward for a while, but another red light stopped them at the next intersection, and he glanced over at her as if waiting for her to go on. So she did.

"Things were bad at home, so we had to get out of there. We were old enough. Jordy had a friend who he worked with back then at an ice cream place, and she moved over here. But she kept in touch with him. She knew what was going on with us, and she knew a landlord that would take us in. She helped us take that step, you know? Never would have left Garden Grove if not for her. We had to get away and leave no trace. She helped us do that."

Tommy was nodding, sweating. He looked as if, beyond his obvious physical turmoil, he was thinking of something. But Jasmine couldn't decipher it. Tommy could be thinking of anything from devious and mean to curious, contemplative. She'd always recognized that dichotomy in him, had always had this odd desire to push him toward the latter, to help him do right.

"How about you?" she said.

"How about me what?"

"How'd you end up here?" She realized she was asking the question just as they were entering Santa Ana.

Tommy stared resolutely forward. "My dad moved us here after my mom died."

"Oh." The word came out a little constricted in her throat.

"That's OK, she was a—" He glanced over at Jasmine. "She didn't ...."

She waited for him to say more, but he only gritted his teeth. She watched his jawline as it flexed.

"How did she die?"

Small shake of the head, then he said, echoing her own words, "Doesn't matter."

"Well ... Tommy ... of course it does."

She saw his eyes flicker, and then he was focusing on the road again, features tight as he underwent his inner turmoil.

"Cancer," he croaked finally.

She nodded. "I'm sorry. That's terrible."

He drove on.

"I miss my mom, too," she said.

"She died?"

Tommy stopped at the Bristol intersection, and looked over at her, waiting. She felt his eyes on her, and this time it was in a good way, the way she liked to be looked at—one human being to another. Like, a connection. She felt a sadness, though, that it was a day like today, and Tommy feeling the way he did, that made it possible.

"No, she didn't," Jasmine said, and she felt her brow furrow with past regrets, past shame, past pain. "I saw her this morning, actually."

"What? When?"

"In Garden Grove. I took a taxi. Early."

She wondered if he would put it together that she'd used some of his coin money for that taxi. She saw something working behind his eyes, maybe even anger working there, anger about what she'd done to him in the wee hours, but he let it go, confused, face damp with perspiration.

She looked down at her lap.

"I used to love my mom." The moment she said it, her throat constricted. Thoughts of her mom were almost completely wrapped up with Jordan. She closed her eyes and got through it. "She was alone for a long time after my dad died. She raised us by ourselves and did a good job. As good as she could. Not a lot of money, you know. But she sacrificed for us when we were little."

The truck started rolling again.

"You know what I remember most about her?" She smiled wistfully. "All those times in this little corner of Mile Square Park, that little island in there, in the trees—you know the place?" Tommy didn't. "Well, we'd walk out onto the little island in the lake there and set up a picnic spot and just laze around. Read our books, tell jokes, whatever. Away from the traffic noise, not many people, just ducks and the sounds of the trees. It was like our oasis. She'd run her fingers through my hair while I ate my bologna sandwich. That's what I remember most about my mom, those perfect moments with her on the weekends."

"What happened to her?" Tommy squeezed out.

Jasmine shrugged. "She wasn't a strong person. She gave in to this asshole years ago. A fucking monster. I mean, he hit her, demeaned her, got her hooked on some shit, and she changed. Forever. It was like he enslaved her, kept her curled up in their bed. He was gonna do the same to me and Jordan—like, we were halfway there. But we got away."

At the next stop, Tommy gave her a long look, and Jasmine couldn't read it. He looked as if he might open his door at any moment and ralph again.

"Anyway," she said.

"But you saw her this morning?" Tommy managed.

"Oh. Yeah, she was asleep. Or unconscious, anyway."

He turned back to the road when the light changed.

"So that guy is still—?"

"Uh huh."

"Wait, so you think he's the one who—?"

"Uh huh."

He frowned and shook his big head as if he couldn't make sense of anything. He looked like he had a hundred questions, but they'd all just jammed together in his forebrain like jumbled wires.

Outside the truck, things were getting more familiar. A couple blocks south of here was the salon where she worked. And a block from there was the pizza joint that sold cheap slices and soda. In the distance was the 7-11 that marked Flower and 17th, and on the other side of the street, the old Spanish-style medical center that always looked so out of place to her.

"Turn right up there at Flower."

She let the surroundings flow by.

Jasmine supposed she'd begun to feel a sense of foreboding way back in Westminster when she'd climbed up into Tommy's passenger seat. It was probably why she'd opened up to Tommy just now—that dark knowledge of what was ahead, and the need to pull armor around herself. Gather ammunition. She'd probably examine this weird premonition for years to come. But the fact was, when Tommy turned on to Flower and the apartment building was minutes away, she felt Karl in the vicinity as powerfully as she'd felt anything in her life. Approaching her street, it was like seeing a glow in the distance—except in negative, a dark blot. She felt her breathing go uneasy, felt her heartbeat quicken.

They got closer.

"Turn here—wait, can you go kind of roundabout? I want to see what's going on there first."

"OK."

She instructed him around the back way, and she watched the streets, eyed the cars. They'd taken only four or five turns before she spotted the gray Buick, otherwise nondescript but now throbbing with darkness, a pulsing black hole in the middle of her new life. She jerked in her seat as all the pain and horror came flooding back.

He'd gotten Jordan. It was true. Karl had killed him.

She felt rage and she felt terror.

"What's the matter?"

"That's him, Tommy." She was crying. *"That's him, in the gray LeSabre. Jesus Christ, that's him."*

She watched as fury took hold of Tommy like a drug.

41
MARK

The ambulance rattled over a pothole, jarring Mark Pellegro into a semblance of consciousness. He rolled his eyes, caught blurry glimpses of faces, of tubes and white machinery, a small window through which he could make out blue sky and the tops of occasional palms. Muted pain rippled across his face and down his right shoulder.

Oh yeah, he thought sleepily. *I'm in trouble.*

He blinked further into wakefulness, not sure he wanted to.

The details of what he'd done trickled back to him, one at a time, and he felt an odd mixture of accomplishment and dread. Charlton Mawk's face hovered over everything—that expressionless façade. Shit, Mark wasn't going to soon forget the way Mawk had stared at him through the cracked windshield, pinned against that weathered fence. Was he still alive? What kind of black retribution was Mark going to face, whether the guy had died or not?

What had gotten *into* him? He wasn't *that guy*.

He heard muffled voices inside the ambulance, but their meaning was lost on him. He didn't care.

Mawk's face, his clenched jaw, his piercing steel gaze, earlier, as his right fist pistoned down on him in the car. The little girl behind them, cowering.

He felt the swell of full-body rage again, even as he lay there half-conscious. The tightening of the muscles, the high keen of his blood through his veins, the compulsion to act. The same fury that had propelled him toward Charlton as he stood there on the sidewalk. Mark had felt no remorse at that moment, no holding back, foot pressed firmly to the floor, as if his anger had occupied him wholly. He'd had no choice. And he would do the same thing again, right now.

But goddamn, man, *Charlton Mawk*. If he was dead, then good riddance to the evil motherfucker.

Tommy'd brought the vile asshole into the store a few times when Mark had been on shift, and each time the guy'd looked as if he'd rather be anywhere else, as if everything were beneath him. Not even giving Mark the time of day, barely concealing his contempt for the place. Picking up items off the shelf, rolling his eyes, tossing them back. Mark would make a show of returning the items to their proper place, and he'd hate himself for doing it, for letting the asswipe get the best of him. One time, Mawk had said, *"Nice fuckin' hat,"* under his breath, but Mark had heard it. He tried to ignore the guy, but Mawk was just one of those people that got under your skin like a needle. He'd always demean Mark somehow, whether with words or just a glance, before following Tommy into the back, where the more interesting stuff was going on, with Derek and Trey and those other freaks. Mark would hear him belittling even those guys sometimes, he didn't care, dude was fearless. Everything was transactional to him, just a deal to make, always in his favor, and everything else was just in the way.

He felt himself growl and wake a little further, and pain gripped him like a giant fist around his midsection, and then he heard a young man's voice.

"… all right, you're all right, let me give you a little more …"

Metal things jangled, and he felt the warmth of someone's small hand on his arm, and he turned his head slightly to find Kayla Jennings looking into his eyes with uncharacteristic kindness, and gradually the warmth of her hand expanded as if it were caressing his entire body, skull to toes, and he fell headlong into the warmth and was gone—

—and immediately he was waking, greasy-eyed, but now he was in a hospital bed. Some part of him acknowledged a male nurse bending over him and calling out, *"Wake-up time, Mark!"* Mark brought up his right hand to wipe at his eyes, partially clearing them, and he found that whatever wounds he had were professionally bound with gauze and tape.

He started to drift, and the man was back immediately: *"How you doin', Mark?"* Then he was gone again. Mark wanted to tell him to shut up. He reached up to touch his scalp and felt bandages there. They were also wrapped tightly around his left hand and cinched around his abdomen. He had some kind of lubrication in his eyes; he even tasted something medicinal. He'd been treated. How long had he been out? He drifted again, and then—

"Hey," came a woman's voice.

Startled, he jerked his head left and winced with the echoing, subdued pain of the movement. But there was Kayla, reclined in a plastic chair next to the bed, her phone frozen in her hand. Her gaze had flicked over to him.

"You're awake." She sat up straighter and stowed her phone.

Disoriented, Mark didn't answer at first. He closed his eyes, lay back, tried to get his bearings.

Finally, he said, "I guess so."

"How do you feel?"

Pause.

"Weird."

After another pause, Kayla asked him, "Want me to make an In-N-Out run?"

Despite himself, he laughed. "I don't think so."

"Good, because—no car."

"Bummer," he whispered.

"Gonna have to get those teeth fixed before your next burger, too."

He glanced at her out of the corner of his eye. Somehow, she looked better than she'd ever looked before. A little drawn, a bit tired, but relaxed in a way he'd never seen her. He'd always been a little bewitched by Kayla's skin—that coffee color, the sensuousness of it, clear and clean, the sarcastic pout of her full lips. But again, hey, she was Tommy's, so there was a brick wall between such observations and any heart-twitch or genital-yank. He could acknowledge her beauty privately, platonically, and then turn away, find other pursuits. It helped that Kayla herself had never, ever betrayed the slightest interest in *him*.

He blinked a dozen times, trying to get his focus right, and stared hard at her.

"What are you doing here?"

"We need to get our stories straight."

He tried like hell to wake himself further from the anesthesia. "Huh?"

"Oh, wake up, you idiot." Smiling.

He watched her face. "Why are you being nice?"

"I just called you an idiot."

"I know, but you were nice about it."

"I've got my reasons."

"OK."

"But, listen," she said, pitching her voice lower, "you're gonna get some cops visiting you, pretty damn soon, and if you don't, Charlton's daddy will surely do the trick, so if you want to stay free and, you know, alive, you're gonna wanna listen to me, like right now. So, are you awake?"

Mark looked around the room, took in the drawn white ICU curtain, the white cabinets, the medical machinery surrounding him, the IV stand, the beeps and clicks.

"All right—go."

"It was the brother, Jordan, who took the coins. Not Jasmine. Tommy and Charlie were after Jordan. They wanted to get to him before he sold the coins. Got it?"

He nodded. He wasn't sure where she was going with that, but ....

"They caught up to him at the coin store—remember, that parking lot?"

"Uh huh."

"Jordan had a gun, OK, and he used that gun to carjack you, you got it? He took your car."

Mark looked at her dubiously.

"Go with it, dude, trust me—I'm trying to save your ass."

He kept looking at her, curiously now, wondering why on god's green earth she was doing this.

"You tried to push Charlton out of the way of the Jetta, which *Jordan was driving*, but you were too late. He was killed, and you were injured. Is that *totally clear?*"

"Charlton is dead, then?"

"Yeah, he's dead."

"You're sure?"

"Abso-fucking-lutely."

He took a deep breath, let it out slowly.

"Fucking *good.*"

A small, almost reluctant smile took hold of her lips. "Yeah, well." Something flickered behind her eyes. "So, after that, Jordan ran off over the fence, and Tommy followed him. That's all you know."

She asked him to repeat the story back to him, and she corrected one detail he got wrong. Together, they added little details here and there. Then he had it. He played it over and over in his head, made it real.

He turned to her again. "OK, I got it. Backwards and forwards. But, Kayla ... seriously, why are you here? You get me? Why are you doing this?"

She fell back into her chair.

"I'll tell you something, Mark," she said. "I'm done."

He waited.

"I'm done with Tommy. I'm done with that life." She sat up straight again, fidgeting as if nervous, as if she'd just now decided all this. "There used to be something good there. You might find that hard to believe, but it's true. He was a good man. At least, I saw a good man inside him. A good *person*—you know, with morals and values and humor and a … a brightness. He liked music. Art. I mean, he had … empathy."

Mark did find that hard to believe.

"You're looking at me like I'm crazy," Kayla said. "And, sure, maybe it was all in my head, maybe it was everything I *wanted* to see in him. But I saw it. And I kept telling myself it was there, like, for years. I was fooling myself." She looked down. "And, yeah, I know what you're thinking, you could've told me that, that I was kidding myself."

He shook his head. "I'm not thinking that."

She looked up then, shrugged in a fetching way. "What are you thinking?"

I'm thinking Tommy's gonna fucking murder me, he thought. *One way or another. I've killed his main boy, I've let that girl Jasmine get away AGAIN, and his woman is sitting here at my hospital bedside, confessing to me that she's leaving him.*

He opened his mouth to say something—he didn't know what—but he was saved by a new nurse who abruptly swept aside the white curtain. The jaunty young woman had blue hair and tattoos up and down her arms.

"Well, you look wide awake now, how you feelin'?"

"Pretty good."

And he did feel pretty good. He was aware of pain in his ribs and somewhere inside his skull, but there was a warm thickness distracting him from it.

"Can you rank the pain on a one-to-ten scale?"

"Um … three?"

"All right, we'll get you up to your room in a bit, then pump you with some more good stuff. I think they're cleaning a room for you right now, OK?"

"Thanks."

She went about checking his vitals, looking at his bandages.

"Lookin' good, Mark," she said happily. "Can I get you anything? Ice water?"

"Oh, that would be fantastic."

"You got it. Give me a few minutes."

The nurse yanked the curtain back, leaving him alone with Kayla again. She was watching him thoughtfully, this suddenly adrift woman who'd risked her own well-being to come to Mark's aid. He wasn't sure exactly what time it was, but he marveled how everything in his life had changed in the space of about eight hours. The world had flipped over on its axis, and he wasn't sure what to say to her.

"I'm gonna stay with you for a while," she said. "I hope you don't mind."

He laughed a little. "Surely you have better things to do than—"

"Shut up, man," she admonished. "Have a little self-respect."

He just watched her.

"Did you know that little girl on the street today?" she asked. "The one that Charlie grabbed?"

He considered the question.

"No."

"You helped save her, you know. You maybe even saved her life."

He shrugged, feeling pain in his shoulders. "I guess."

"Not many people would do that."

She stood and approached the bed, smiled at him, and leaned over to kiss him on an unbandaged section of his forehead.

"You look good without the hat."

The skin of his forehead tingled.

42
TOMMY

The gravel simmered in the contact solution, and Tommy Strafe felt so braced and anxious that he could barely maneuver his fingers. Fever roared loud in his brain, and his bowels were in a state of now-constant cramp. He let the lighter drop to the ground and cursed at himself as his gnarled hand struggled with the wad of cotton and then the syringe. He located a vein—*miracle!*—and finally delivered the goosed payload. Instantly his body relaxed, and it was like settling into the warmest, most sublime zero-gravity, enveloping orgasm he'd ever experienced. A full-body hard-on fat-gushing its release and relaxing into bliss.

A smile took hold of his entire head, wrapped around it, all teeth, and cleaved off the top of his skull. He luxuriated into the sensation, laughing with relief.

"Jesus Christ!" he screamed at the top of his lungs, radiating pure pleasure.

He barely recalled the rollercoaster drive from Jasmine's place that he'd just endured, but it itched at him down deep. Fact was, Jasmine made him feel good, it was as simple as that—fuck everything else. Just being with her in his truck, in the midst of a withdrawal meltdown and whatever else his body was going through … it had calmed his shit. He remembered that from when they were young, the two of them. The way she'd flash that innocent smile. Just proximity, man, that was all it took. The smell of her. What was that?

He fell back into the comfortable warmth of the sofa, breathing evenly, enjoying a warm and squishy eternity.

After a while, his neural pathways began to open up again.

Wait ….

Sweet Jesus, had he just killed a man? Had he just murdered a stranger for *Jasmine?* For piece-of-shit *Jordan*, for fuck's sake? He shook his heavy head, focused on his exhalations. And the coins? What about the goddamn coins? He'd had these grand plans this morning when he'd discovered them missing. This morning, jarred from sleep by the garbage disposal, he'd bleared into consciousness to find his day mapped out in front of him like a Thomas Brothers Book of Revenge. In short order, everything had turned to steaming crapola.

If there was one thing Tommy hated, it was showing weakness.

There'd been times his dad had shown weakness with his mom, and Tommy remembered the hot embarrassment he'd felt—even as a little kid—watching Gordon submit to his wife. Tommy couldn't even recall the exact circumstances, but his mind always flashed on that single afternoon in the blazing sun of their front yard, Helen Strafe berating her husband as he stood there, statue-still, cowed in the dusty grass. It didn't even matter what her beef had been. His gambling? Had that been when she'd found out about the waitress in Long Beach his dad had hooked up with? Had it been about Gordon's lifelong reluctance to secure a reliable, long-term job? (Oh, Helen Strafe had complained about that one—to her dying day.) What had mattered was the way Gordon had stood there, face down, shoulders slumped ... beaten. By a woman.

Tommy had fallen asleep that night, feeling abject humiliation, as deeply as if the reaming had happened to himself. He'd never looked at his dad the same way after that. Not even after Helen was dead from late-diagnosed breast cancer, in wrenching agony, delirious or screaming, or sometimes both, depending on the quality and dosage of painkillers Gordon could bother to secure. After her death, Gordon had sat slumped in their bedroom watching her corpse into the wee hours before he even called someone.

Tommy woke from the memory, feeling more alert.

Functional.

But, fuck, man, he'd done just *that*, he'd been *weak*, right there in front of the big wide world. In spades. He'd barfed all over the goddamn street, he'd been out of control. Flailing. In front of Kayla, in front of Mark. In front of fucking Charlton. *Jasmine*. Had he actually driven her home—the girl who'd taken his coins—and *killed* a man for her? What in the name of fuckballs?

Tommy hated himself sometimes. It was *weak* to set himself up for failure the way he'd done this morning, it was *weak* to fly off the handle and race off toward kneejerk revenge, it was *weak* of him to blindly do Jasmine's bidding—even if she hadn't asked him for anything. There was just some part of him that lost all control when fury enshrouded his vision. He couldn't help it. He knew he had to be methodical about these things, but too often he let the heat of the moment get the better of him.

It's what Rennie always warned him about, even way back—the importance of being able to rein it in, to be in control of your power. Exactly once had Tommy lost his cool in front of Rennie, and that had been in the aftermath of Gordon's death out on the highway. Rennie had been there. The *only* one there. Rennie'd taught him how to be tough, how to be a man. That hadn't come from his own father, that had come from Rennie.

Oh Christ, Rennie.

He lurched forward off the sofa, looking for his phone. He patted his pockets—nothing.

He realized he still felt feverish. He'd swayed a bit, standing up so suddenly. Spots darted in front of his eyes. He'd caught something. A bug. Goddamn it. From the party? Too recent. From the store, probably.

He floated out to his truck, climbed up as if weightless, found the phone still in the cupholder. He yanked it out, drifted to the ground, and made his way back into the house. He let himself fall into the couch again and closed his eyes, finding his happy place again. Then he brought his phone in front of his face and stared at it with wide, all-seeing eyes.

Rennie had already called him twice. No message.

Shiiiiiit.

Somewhere deep, he registered a kind of alarm. He wasn't thinking right. All fucking *day* he hadn't been thinking right, and he still wasn't thinking right.

He stopped just short of calling Rennie. *Wait, wait, wait …*

He backed out of Rennie's contact screen and went to Kayla's. He called her, and she answered right away. Her voice sounded tired and resigned.

"Tommy?"

"Kay, what's up, where are you?"

"I'm at the hospital."

"What? Why?"

"I went with Mark in the ambulance, I guess he's got a concussion and some broken ribs. Face is messed up. But he'll be all right."

"You're with Pelly?"

"Well … yeah."

Jason Bovberg

Tommy closed his eyes and tried to steady the sea-sawing ripple in his forebrain. Despite the warmth and general well-being that he'd introduced into his vascular system, there was this goddamn fever, getting hotter over the dope-warmth, and now the slightest undercurrent of nausea. It was as if the couch were shifting under his bowels like tectonic plates.

"What about Charlie?"

"Charlie's dead, Tommy."

His breath stopped.

"Fuck you, he's dead."

"I'm serious, he actually fucking *died*, Tommy." Her voice broke up into glitchy stutters, then came back clear. "You took off after that silly girl, and then he died, like, right in front of me."

"Tell me you're lying."

"I'm not lying! I'm hanging up now. I'm in a hospital. You know, like, sick people everywhere. I'm in the—I'm in the middle of a waiting room, there's like fifty people all around me, and it stinks in here like a locker room. I have no ride, and I'm here for Mark. They're moving him from ICU to a room, and when they do that, I'm gonna sit with him. OK? As far as I'm concerned, Mark did a fucking noble thing, and so—yeah—that's why I'm here." Her voice went shaky, less confident. "Deal with it."

Tommy took the phone away from his ear and stared at it, feeling a kind of angry confusion. Then he brought it back to his ear.

"What did you—?"

"I'm hanging up, Tommy."

"Wait, did you see Rennie?"

Kayla's voice went quiet, and the line shivered. "Yes."

"How is he?"

"I don't know, Tommy, I don't know how he is, I don't know the first thing about him, how should I know about that creepy fuck?"

"Did he ask where I was?"

Tommy heard a tiny sound over the line, a snick of the lips.

"Of course he did."

"What'd you tell him?"

"I didn't tell him anything, OK?"

"What does that mean?"

"I'm hanging up now, Tommy."

"*Wait—*"

The phone went dead.

Tommy bounced up to his feet again, and the fever complained anew, made him light-headed under the sway of the gravel. With mildly shaking hands, he pocketed the phone and then clutched his skull. He bent over, curled his shoulders like an animal, and let loose with a tremendous howl. The sound ended raggedly, and he shut his eyes tight, riding out the exhalation until he felt as if he might squeeze between the rotting floorboards and leak into the earth. Then he stood up straight and inhaled voluminously.

After a while, he was pacing across the room, back and forth a dozen times, chewing the insides of his cheeks. He felt a great hollow power in his chest, expansive and grasping. He altered his course and stalked the dim hallway all the way down to his bedroom, flinging open the door and pounding in with his big black steel-toed boots. The custom cabinet stood in the corner, damaged and impotent, the small drawer open on the bottom, contents gone.

"*I am a fucking idiot,*" he whispered.

Weak.

That's what he was. A weak fucking idiot—with no control over his life.

He strode across the room to the cabinet where he kept his stupid collections, and he swung his boot at it. The sturdy wood cracked but held. He delivered another blow, and this time a long corner piece on the right side popped askew. Encouraged, he rained kicks upon the cabinet until it broke apart completely. Mostly fastened to the wall, the cabinet stood in place like a pilloried and broken skeleton, large pieces hanging crookedly. The few shards of glass fell and bounced away, and he made a point to stomp them and pulverize them. He saw a shelf fixed in place still, as if defying gravity, and he aimed a higher kick at it, and it jerked to the left, spilling eight or nine paperback books, all of them sealed in tight plastic bags. As he mashed these into pulp under his boot, baseball cards fluttered down from the case like an afterthought ... Steve Garvey's infuriatingly prim pose, Ron Cey's stupid mustache, Don Sutton's frizzy goddamn hair—why had any of this shit *mattered* to Tommy? Fuck ol' Gil Jones, that scrawny bastard he'd got the cards from, back in another age. They were all just stupid things, and he'd built a fucking *altar* to them. *Jesus Christ!* He wanted to fall to his knees and rip them to shreds, but instead he merely stomped them, and after a moment he realized there were tears flowing down his cheeks.

"*Fuuuuuuuuuck!*" he screeched inside his drugged fever.

He didn't know what to do.

He wanted to leave, but he also wanted to fall onto the bed and go unconscious. He wanted to call Rennie, but it was also the very last thing he wanted to do. What the fuck would he even say?

He pulled his phone from his pocket, then put it back, then pulled it out again and put it back, and then he repeated that motion three more times.

Twenty minutes later, he was on the couch and chills were making his arms and legs shake even harder. His head was wet and heavy, as if immersed in chocolate milk, but he couldn't get the fever under control. He'd grabbed Kayla's red blanket from the corner and was shivering underneath it. He'd ignored one more call from Rennie.

When a knock came at the door, Tommy had just drifted off into a doze.

43
LORI

"Mommy, you're squishing me."

Lori Holst eased up. She watched Sarah settle back into the seat. The kid had just endured a fucking *kidnapping,* and she was sitting there watching the scenery go by as if they'd all just enjoyed a day in the Newport sand—a little sweaty and frazzled, tired under the eyes, but eyes open, even a half-smile on her lips. She'd finished her lollipop, and the wet, destroyed stick lay near her sandaled feet, forgotten.

"Are we going home?" Sarah asked.

Lori felt a small smile take hold of her mouth, which was aching with the effort of holding back something, she wasn't sure what it was. Her lips trembled.

She nodded.

"Back to your place?" Steve said, looking at her in the rearview mirror. "You sure? It's safe?"

"Yeah." She wasn't sure, no.

"Would you rather go to my place?"

"I want to, thank you, Steve, but right now I need to go home."

"You got it."

Lori reached out to touch Sarah's shoulder or the side of her face or her hair, but she pulled back, tentative. She placed the hand back in her lap. She couldn't trust herself to avoid doing too much, making a wrong move—that's what she always seemed to do, from the beginning.

It was the knot in her, the narrow channel where things always plugged up like a clogged toilet. There'd been a therapist named Jenn, early on, who'd put it that way one time, back when Lori was young. The trick, Jenn had said, was to do everything in her power to keep that narrow tube wide open. To find ways to do that. Whether that was medication or therapy or meditation or exercise or all of that. Keep everything moving, keep everything healthy and functional. The problem was, there were some sufferers who wanted to *keep* that tube choked, who kept flushing all *kinds* of horrible shit down there. It was a self-defeating spiral sometimes, Jenn would say, this crazy thing about wounded people. They *wanted* to be wounded. Of *course* Lori'd known Jenn was talking directly about her, or at least she'd come to realize that over time, but Lori liked to keep the obviousness of it apart from her, separate from her, five feet away from her. A shadow that would always be connected to her but away from her at the same time. Like, she knew this about herself, she was conscious of it, it wasn't even worth talking about. It was simply her reality, something to come to terms with, and fuck you if you couldn't deal with it, and especially fuck you if you *wanted* to deal with it because this wasn't *about* you. And there'd always been a muted whisper, always behind her somewhere, this whisper that spoke to her like a forbidden lover and reminded her that she coveted the choke. She clung to the anguish, the tears. Always would. Sometimes the voice was *waaaaay* back there in the distance, so far back there that it seemed there was no way it would ever get close to her again, and other times it was right at her ear and she could feel the hot breath of encouragement. Sometimes the voice was enraged, and sometimes it cried with her all night.

She didn't feel the voice or the choke at the moment. Both of them were as far away as they'd ever been. Watching Sarah, she reveled in that, but she also felt as if she had to be extremely careful not to provoke them.

So she simply watched her daughter.

"Can I watch *Iron Giant* when we get home?"

The DVD they'd found at the garage sale last summer. She'd watched it a hundred times.

"Of course you can, sweetie."

The next time Lori glanced out at the passing scenery, they were already back in Santa Ana, familiar territory. She started to recognize the trees and the cross-streets, the stores and the homes, and she felt a creeping relief that she didn't even resist. There was still a residual quake to her limbs, left over from the past ridiculous hour, but the farther the Mini moved away from all that, the better she felt. It was like a tearing away of something. No, not the clog, that was always there to some degree—but something else, something equally consequential.

There were no cops anymore at the apartment. Steve circled around the place warily, watching for them. An abundance of caution, just in case. (Would the police really be looking for her? Was there a way to connect her with Jordan and Jasmine?) But there was nothing going on.

Steve pulled up to the curb in front of the main entrance, and the three of them looked over at the building, its face full of windows, most of them adorned with crooked blinds or sloppy curtains, some of them neat and tidy. Lori could see Jasmine's window, second floor, the cheap curtains pulled aside onto the room where they'd found Jordan. She wondered if the horror that had occurred in there would scar Sarah. She hoped not. But then ...

We all have scars.

"Looks OK," Steve said quietly as he pulled the seat forward to let her and Sarah out of the back. "Pretty quiet."

Lori nodded, taking Sarah's little hand, and the three of them trudged up the short walk to the building, wound their way through the familiar vestibule, up the familiar staircase, down the familiar hallway. At the door, Lori dug her little keyring out of her jeans pocket and unlocked the door, let it swing open. Sarah let go of her hand and danced in, not a care in the world.

Lori felt Steve's hand on her back.

"You sure know how to show a guy a good time."

The words didn't register for a long moment while she watched Sarah plop on the couch.

Then they did.

She turned to Steve and stared up into his eyes. He gave her that grin, the one that she'd first responded to at the restaurant, and she crashed into him, embracing him tightly. It felt like need. She hugged him till her muscles ached. She thought he might recoil like he sometimes did, but she felt him reciprocating, and she leaned into it, inhaling him.

"Thank you," she whispered.

"It was fun," he murmured.

"Ha!" She smiled into his chest, and then the smile went away. "It was more than that."

"It was my pleasure," he said, like he always told people, hollowly, at the restaurant.

She could hear his smile, the old joke. But this time it sounded like he meant it.

"Think Jasmine'll be all right?" he asked.

Lori thought about that. The afternoon had been filled with the kind of horror that never really touched Lori's life, and Jasmine—her doe-eyed friend from downstairs—was, against all odds, at the center of it. Lori felt a lingering jitter about her friend, at this moment back at that strip mall with the cash and the gun … but she had a feeling Jasmine would be fine. She would work it out. Hell, if Lori and her little girl could come out the other side of the episode relatively unscathed, Jasmine certainly could. She was the kind of girl who found a way to the light.

"I do."

Lori and Steve stood in the open doorway, looking at each other. At some point, the soundtrack of *The Iron Giant* came spilling out of the little room next to the kitchen.

"You busy later?" Steve asked.

"I want to spend some time with Sarah, but … later sounds good." Mischievous smile.

"Want me to bring some food over? We can all hang out."

"I'd love that."

Lori tried to read his face, because there was something new there.

But then he was heading back down the hallway, a little jaunt in his step. He was tossing his car keys, as if what they'd gone through was just another day at work for him. Made her smile, despite herself.

She knew he'd be back. It was nice to be certain about that.

While Sarah watched her movie, Lori locked the front door and engaged the chain, then excused herself to her bedroom, where she stripped down and took a scalding shower. She scrubbed and exfoliated and shampooed, and she thought about Jasmine and Jordan. She cried for both of them, but mostly, in all actuality, for Jasmine. She realized that as much as she thought of herself as Jasmine's friend, she didn't really know her at all. It was as if Lori had, after months of casual, everyday conversations, walked in on Jasmine snorting a line or giving some homeless dude a slobbery blow. Like, *what the fuck?* Who *are* you?

At the image she'd just conjured, Lori laughed under the spray of the shower, eyes closed under the hot water.

She knew she should probably be enraged about what had happened today—what had happened to *Sarah*—but with her girl happily watching TV in the next room, safe, content, she couldn't bring herself to feel that emotion. And damn, man, her head felt good, it felt right. At least, for the moment, it was like she'd taken some kind of delirious drug.

Jasmine was a genuinely good person. She knew that in her heart. She fervently wished the best for her. And Lori knew she'd be there for her again, once this all settled down.

After the movie ended, Lori managed to coax Sarah from the TV and enlist her help with a jigsaw puzzle they'd found at the same garage sale as the DVD. When they finished it ninety minutes later, they found it was missing three pieces. After that, Lori wanted to move on to a more involving game like Monopoly or Clue—two of the four old games she had wedged high in her little hall closet—but Sarah wanted to play a card game, and Lori didn't know any. Lori proceeded to listen to Sarah babble on about a game she'd learned from her friend Sofia, some simple shouting-and-card-slapping thing that Sarah found endlessly hilarious.

Lori relaxed into it, laughing right along with her daughter.

In moments like this, when the whisper that lived behind her head felt far away indeed, Lori could reflect with almost cold detachment on everything that had brought her to this precise moment. They were rare moments, but this one was powerful. She sat watching Sarah. Watched her play, watched her squeal. Watched her eyes flash with humor and mischief. They were so like her daddy's eyes, back when Lori met him on the beach, reflecting bonfire in the cold night. The whirlwind of their romance played behind her own eyes—the Vegas marriage, the midnight roar across the desert in his Firebird, the languorous morning sex (*god she loved his cock,* nothing else compared before or since!), the five months of diminishing bliss—and then the discovery of the sexting with "Christine" on his discarded, older-generation iPhone. She'd been eight and a half months pregnant. Earlier in the day, she'd spent an hour preparing their kit for the hospital, for the inevitable, weeks-away drive to Hoag that was supposed to be full of happy terror. Instead, there'd been all the screaming, the disbelief—like a thunderous blot in her head, all the old shit surging forward until she'd had her episode in the middle of Von's grocery, her first episode in at least ten years, and the others after that, and Christ, none of that mattered anymore, did it? Couldn't she just leave that crap in the past? It was all history.

It was time to look forward now.

"Mommy?"

Lori snapped to attention. "Uh huh?"

"It's your turn." Laughing.

Lori's smile faltered, then relaxed.

The voice and the choke would always be there, but she knew she could try harder at moments like these. Take her meds, stay active, eat right—all that shit she'd been told repeatedly—and fucking just try harder at every opportunity. Why had that been so difficult to stick to? And even though she could see all this now from a point of understanding, and could ask that question of herself right now at this moment ... would she stick to it? Would she even be *able* to have that kind of self-awareness tomorrow?

Lori started dealing the ridiculous cards face-side up, and Sarah screeched with joy.

"You're silly!" Sarah cried.

When Steve returned later that night, he was all cleaned up, too, and they shared knowing glances about it from the start. He'd brought a crapload of mac and cheese from the restaurant, and some salad, some meatballs, and they all dove into the feast with gusto, reliving the day as if it had been an awesome TV show. Sarah and Lori both went on about how Steve had acted like some kind of action hero, and he laughed it off, obviously enjoying it. And after Sarah crashed to sleep, utterly exhausted, Lori took Steve to bed and they snickered about how the day had been like a goddamn aphrodisiac, and she treated him to an expansive array of delights—and vice versa.

In the wee hours, her usual dreams came, edgy with shivery blackness, but whenever they started, she was able to shudder out of them and think about Sarah, and sure, even Steve, and calm her heartbeat, and try slumber again. The shadow would always be there, she wasn't stupid, but—despite everything, and despite her terror and her screams while it was happening—it had been a good fucking day.

44
RENNIE

The sea had a moderate chop to it.

The bowrider took the swells almost violently—Rennie Mawk's one complaint about the runabout boat, the rough ride. He'd owned the vessel for almost ten years now, bought it new from a dealer in Laguna, all above board, he had all the papers, the proper licenses, everything. He'd motored the waters between Huntington and Catalina so many times that he felt as if he could map the waves, but sure, he dreamed of a smoother ride, maybe a deluxe closed-cabin job, but, hell, that was probably three times the cash. More.

Seawater misted his determined face and blurred the reach of the navigation lights. He estimated he was a mile, mile and a half out from the piers. The lights on the shore to his left rose and fell like sped-up film. He kept going, liking the way he had to brace himself.

Rennie had known for a long time that Charlton would never make it to a ripe old age. He knew he'd outlive his wild son. The kid was just too trigger-happy, too fly-by-the-seat-of-his-pants. He'd always been that way, or at least since he came of age. Rennie'd tried to teach his son the ways of the world by example. Apparently, that was an ineffective prospect. He guessed ol' long-gone Sally, Charlie's bitch mother, had been right: Rennie wasn't much of a dad. He'd never been one to pal around with the kid, had never played catch with Charlton. He was the kind of father who threw his kid into the deep end to teach him how to swim. Damn right. He'd done that exact thing, and it'd worked, by god. But it was probably inevitable that Charlton had turned out the way he had—lacking in the social graces but goddamned effective in behind-closed-doors negotiations. Theirs had gradually become a mutually beneficial relationship, if not a traditional father-son thing.

Charlton could be vicious, determined, and convincing. There wasn't much room for anything else. So perhaps it was only a matter of time before something like this had happened. Crushed by the front end of an errant foreign heap in the midst of some frivolous chase. Buncha kids, fuckin' around.

Tommy shoulda known better.

The boat took a few thick swells and then settled into a groove on a calmer stretch. He could see probably a dozen vessels off in the scattered distance, their lights bouncing like EKGs. His own heartbeat remained slow and steady.

He thought about Tommy's whore. Kayla. She might've been lying about what had gone down. It was possible. But why would she lie? Who might she have been protecting, if not Tommy? Rennie had no clue, and he didn't care to have one. What Rennie fixated on was the coins.

Gordon Strafe's fucking coins.

As the seawater sprayed him, Rennie shook his head in disbelief.

Karma has a way of biting you in the ass.

That's what Gordon himself would've said, and he would've said it completely without irony.

Almost to his dying day, Gordon was unaware of the fact that Rennie and Helen Strafe had humped like rabbits for years. Shit, close to half a decade, before she kicked. Helen had a wild horny streak that was exposed through consumption of a very particular drink: the whiskey sour. Get a few of those in her, and her twat achieved a magnetic core that was drawn inexorably to Rennie's prick. Never failed. For about a year, Rennie kept himself armed with Wild Turkey, sugar, and lemons.

They hadn't even been quiet about it. Gordon had just been one of those oblivious souls, too naïve to believe it even possible that a close friend was capable of that kind of epic betrayal. Rennie couldn't begin to count the number of times Helen had sucked him off in Gordon's kitchen or garage or bathroom or back yard while Gordon watched a game in the TV room, or how often Helen had met Rennie at job sites to christen in-progress construction operations—office buildings, recreation centers, hell, even a cavernous new senior center. Over one glorious period of three months or so, they'd managed to break in every single apartment in a small complex in Laguna before the units were available to the public. Rennie still laughed about that stretch sometimes late at night.

It was Helen, unsatisfied gorgeous housewife Helen, who'd first illuminated Rennie about the true value of Gordon's coin collection. Of course, Gordon had casually mentioned his hobby over the years, but Rennie had dismissed it all as old man talk, ridiculous in a way, like collecting stamps. Gordon had never really talked about value. The man was modest, to a fault. No, it was Helen who'd keyed Rennie in on dollar amounts. At first, her insistence that the coins had amassed a value in the hundreds of thousands of dollars was equally dismissible, but one afternoon, with Gordon out on a job and little Tommy at school, Helen had risen from bed, lithe and naked and shining, and had dug the coins from their hiding place in the closet for him, the actual coins wrapped up in little paper envelopes, pristine like treasure.

It was a month later that Rennie'd found the opportunity to secret the collection away to his waiting associate in Fullerton, Ivan Little, who Rennie knew had been connected to a steel counterfeiting outfit half a decade earlier. Ivan—by sheer chance—had recently come into contact with an old Chinese coin counterfeiter who'd once headed up a metals ring in Taipei. So, long story short, Rennie had paid out a measly couple grand for a Mr. Li Jie to document the collection, procure cheap similar coins, and use his intricate skills to alter those coins' dates, add mint marks, and recreate flaws such as toning and wear so that Rennie ended up with a duplicate and near-worthless collection. The quality was astounding. He'd switched out the collections for good later that summer between sessions of sweaty lovemaking with supple Helen Strafe atop Gordon's marital bed.

And he'd sold off the real coins over a period of two years, for a grand total of one hundred and seventy-two thousand dollars. That was in 2003 dollars. With that seed money, he'd started a business and opened several high-yield investment accounts at various banks. Those investments were still paying off. He earned enough later to purchase a Porsche 964 Turbo, and—oh—this very bowrider!

About six miles from shore, Rennie found calmer seas and pulled back on the throttle, settled into neutral. He walked fully around the cabin, checking the dark sea for lights. Everything was at least three miles away. He went to the cargo area and hauled out the weighted bags, one by one. There were four of them, and each weighed seventy pounds, give or take. Grunting, he shoved them overboard, and they sank instantly under the waves.

Poof, gone.

Two minutes later, he was turning the boat back around and heading back toward the docks.

God, he hadn't thought this much about Helen in years. Despite the cold, stinging salt spray, Rennie actually felt himself achieving an erection as he recalled their misadventures. The mouth on her, the twisting limbs, the eager hands!

So long ago.

It had been Tommy who'd wrecked it. The little fucktard. And he didn't even realize it.

Rennie had been embedded in Helen's magnificent rear, right there on the white couch in the middle of her living room. He'd felt like some glorious and ferocious animal. Gordon was away in Phoenix organizing some shipments for Rennie's blossoming construction outfit, and Rennie was feeling like the fucking king of the jungle. Tommy, all of six years old, was sound asleep down the hall. At least, that was the assumption. Maybe Rennie and Helen had been cocky, too confident in their crazy fling after months and months of shamelessly cuckolding Gordon.

At some point, Helen had gasped in horror and pulled away from Rennie, covering herself with a blanket. Leaning against the hall corner was little Tommy, watching the two adults curiously. Rennie had simply stood there with his wet dick out like a divining rod, while Helen scurried over to the boy and guided him back to bed.

It's over, Helen told him later, crying softly.

Not that it mattered much. Helen got abruptly sick a few years later and died a year after that. But, dammit, she and Rennie could've had a *ton* more illicit time in the sack. The fucking kid had been *sleepwalking*. He wouldn't remember a goddamn thing about that night, would never mention it to anyone in his life, and yet he'd gone and wrecked the whole thing.

Rennie might not have cared a *whole* lot—women came, and women went—but much later, years after her death, Gordon had unearthed a fucking confession from Helen and had confronted Rennie about it. The bitch had laid out all the details on tear-stained pages. And then there came Gordon, drunk on Rennie's porch one night, tears in his eyes. A grown man, crying. Was there anything worse than that?

Rennie'd been forced to arrange Gordon's car accident a week later, with the help of some Mexicans off the Long Beach crew. Out of a sense of almost family obligation, Rennie'd taken on Tommy after that, but now he was gone, too. Husband had followed wife into the grave, and the son had followed the father.

Those fucking coins! Had it been worth it, copying those coins way back then? How could he foresee that the collection would come back to haunt him like this?

Take his only son from him.

"Fuck it!" he shouted into the wet maelstrom as the bowrider skiffed over the waves. The sea was an enveloping roar.

He mourned none of them.

Hell, maybe it was time to go it alone.

That was the thought that occupied him the rest of the way to shore.

He docked the boat and then found a towel in the cabin, wiped himself down. After locking up, he hopped over onto the dock, strode the ramps, passed the deserted fuel pumps, and fell into his Lincoln in the parking lot. He found his way to Pacific Coast Highway, top down, hair whipping about. Rennie Mawk was feeling the winds of change.

After all, the only constant in life was change. He'd gotten that from some ancient Greek dude, read it in a book somewhere along the way. Give the guy some fucking credit: He was spot on.

Truth was, Rennie's life and business had stagnated. He hadn't felt the passion for it in years. Maybe all this had happened for a reason. Get those impulsive boys out of the picture, start fresh with a new outlook, a new mission statement. Kids these days, with the drugs and all—they were changing the business for the worse. It was time to reverse course. The way Rennie saw it, this was an opportunity for a return to the old philosophies. Hand-shake deals. Community. Brotherhood. None of this intimidation and violence.

Sometimes in life, you had to wade through some serious shit to get to the other side. Rennie had gone through some shit. Losing all those people. And through that kind of hardship came an appreciation for what you had. Not only that, but a renewed understanding of your potential. Adversity tested your mettle, no doubt about it.

He knew he was up for it.

He parked in his garage and locked the doors behind him as he entered his home. He punched in the security codes and locked the place down. After getting himself comfortable in his robe and slippers, he poured a whiskey sour on ice for old time's sake and sat down in his darkened living room, on his cold leather sofa. The house was so quiet that he could hear the hum and clatter of the city beyond the thick walls, the endless frothing surge toward the next thing.

"What's next?" he shouted, his words echoing across bare walls.

45
JASMINE

On her 18th birthday—or, rather, as her impressively fraudulent ID maintained, her 21st birthday—Jasmine Frank sat on the edge of the Huntington Beach pier, her legs dangling beyond the metal bars. Next to her was a big black purse, and inside the purse was a plain white box, and inside that box was a plump, sturdy plastic bag, and inside that plump, sturdy plastic bag were Jordy's ashes. The sunset made the expansive sky look like some kind of exotic candy display.

Muted laughter floated from Ruby's Diner, the large octagonal red-and-white structure planted at the end of the pier, and Jasmine smelled grilled burgers on the slight breeze. It was a Sunday, and traffic on the pier was light. There was that feeling of humanity letting out a sigh, squeezing the last out of the weekend, preparing for the week ahead.

Jasmine herself would be reporting tomorrow for her first day at a midscale salon in Garden Grove, and she was actually looking forward to it. She'd met the owner last Tuesday, an old beauty queen of a woman named Lydia—to whom Jasmine had been referred by Rhonda at the joint in Santa Ana—and she and Jasmine had hit it off immediately, chatting about the job in a way that made Jasmine feel much older than she was. An old pro. The job offer had come the next day, in a delighted phone call from Lydia herself. Jasmine could still feel the high of that phone call running through her veins.

"Do you want to say anything?" Jasmine said over her shoulder.

The forty-three-year-old woman seated on the stone bench behind Jasmine was quiet. Bundled up against the sea breeze, she had been watching the horizon with unblinking eyes. When the woman didn't reply to her question, Jasmine twisted around and repeated it.

Gloria Frank's eyes flickered with life, and after a long moment she sat up from her slouch against the structure. With visible effort, she stood up, got her bearings, and came over to the edge, grasping the top metal bar. Jasmine could hear her ragged breathing. Gloria wasn't an old woman, but she sounded like one. Jasmine was already helping her mother fix that. They were starting gradually on a fitness and nutrition regimen. There was no reason why the two of them couldn't find their way again to the kind of relationship they'd once had.

Gloria Frank was slowly acclimating herself to a reclaimed life.

Very slowly.

But, hey, she was here.

Watching her mother's face glow with the fiery light of a SoCal sunset, Jasmine saw the same buried regret that had been there since she'd gone back to the house to find her mother, the day after that crazy Saturday. Three weeks ago exactly. Jasmine had found her in the kitchen, asleep at the table, and when she'd awakened her, her mother had stared at her uncomprehending for a full minute, as if disoriented from anesthesia or from a long, deep sleep. Bleary-eyed, chin slightly trembling. Then, coming to awareness, her eyes had darted around, wary of *him*.

"*He's dead, Mom,*" Jasmine had told her, grasping her shoulders hard. "*Karl is dead.*"

Gloria hadn't been able to fully comprehend that fact for close to a week, and she was still dealing with the PTSD of the past six or seven years—would probably be dealing with it for the rest of her life.

It had taken Jasmine a little longer to open up with her mom about Jordy. She was all too willing to break the news about Karl, but Jordy—that was different. Jasmine herself still had trouble with that. She'd been the one who'd had to deal with the OC sheriff's department and all their questions. She'd been the one to arrange his cremation with the cash left over from Tommy's coins. Till now, the few halting words she'd tried to exchange with Gloria about Jordy had been met with silence, but increasingly Jasmine could see the turmoil working behind her mother's eyes.

Last week, needing to talk to someone about everything else that had gone down, Jasmine had spent a rainy afternoon with Lori and Sarah at Steve's condo in Fountain Valley. As relentless showers had battered the clay tiles above their heads, Jasmine had found a place to shed her tears and express everything she had felt since that Saturday. Lori and Steve provided sympathetic ears, and Sarah had been all huggy, not wanting her friend to be sad. If Sarah had any scars from that day, they were buried deep. She was a friggin' happy girl, according to Lori. She whispered later that Steve had really stepped up and was looking like fantastic stepdad material. Sarah adored him now, considered him some kind of superhero in that car of his. Lori did too.

That had been the first time, in the aftermath of that crazy Saturday, when Jasmine had begun to feel normal again. After Sarah had gone to bed, she'd hung out with her friends into the wee hours, taking little sip-like puffs of truly primo weed, honest-to-god *laughing*, and she'd felt a comfort and warmth with them that could only result from a powerful shared experience. It was as if they could survive anything now. More than that—they'd survived this thing *together*, as a unit. They were connected forever because of it and had come out stronger on the other side. All three of them. But Lori in particular. Lori had overcome some personal obstacles of her own, and her pride at doing so was evident in the way she held herself now—and the attention she devoted to her little girl. Lori loved that goddamn kid, and just watching the two of them horse around made Jasmine all gooey inside.

But that was also the day Jasmine had first heard about what happened to Tommy, whose name she'd never uttered to the police officers who questioned her. That same weekend, apparently, Tommy had disappeared and was now presumed dead. Jasmine's hand had flown to her mouth when Lori had told her that, had shown her the *Orange County Register* article, and she'd let out an involuntary gasp, wondering if it was possible that she'd been the last person to see him alive. In a flash, she remembered his sweaty desperation in the cab of his truck, and then—conversely—the calm efficiency with which he'd dispatched Karl, as if the act of murder were like a drug to him. She remembered the final look he'd given her after he'd dropped her off near her apartment building, that grim look on his face that told her he was sparing her somehow, that he was on his way to an unknown future that he wanted her to have no part of.

Jasmine shivered as a colder breeze buffeted her on the pier.

Some older couples were wandering around the octagonal restaurant, but there were no fishermen over here, no kids, no giggling teens. A uniformed security guard had moseyed along the pier twenty minutes ago, but he was way over on the boardwalk now. Online earlier, Jasmine had found that it was illegal to dump ashes off the pier, but yeah, like that was gonna stop her.

Gloria was still quiet, so Jasmine spoke up when the area was empty.

"I miss you, Jordy, I really do." Glancing around, she removed the white box from the big purse and cradled her brother's ashes in her arms. "I hate that you're gone, and I hate … I hate that it was my fault that—"

She stopped there, shutting her eyes.

She'd blamed herself enough already.

"I wish I could do that day over again. I wish the three of us could be together right now, on this side of it. You'd be sitting right here, and we'd be talking in a way that we haven't talked in, like, forever." She looked out onto the sea. "Free, you know? I almost can't even imagine it—what you'd talk about, and *how* you'd talk about it. To see you smile again …."

A young man and woman came wandering around the building, chatting lovingly. They stopped at the railing for a moment to admire the dwindling sunset, then moved away because the woman was cold. As they went out of view, the man was placing his jacket around her shoulders, like a scene from a romance movie.

Jasmine went on, "You're the one who deserves this moment, Jordy, right here, right now." She held the box firmly in her grip. "Love you, bro."

Gloria was watching her, and now she glanced sadly at the box, then out to sea again.

"Happy birthday," Jasmine's mother whispered, startling her. A long moment passed, her breath sounding like a wheeze, and then she said, softly, "I'm sorry."

She noticed that her mom's eyes were glistening.

It was a start.

Jasmine stood up and took another look around. She believed she was in a security-cam dead zone in the precise area where she was standing, and the security guard was still nowhere to be seen. She took the bag of ashes from its box and quickly snicked open the pocketknife she'd stowed in her front jeans pocket. She sliced the bag open at the top and dumped the ashes out over the railing. They scattered down and to the west on a slight breeze, settling on the rocking waves. A single curious gull fell on a patch of ash, tested it, left it alone. Jasmine smiled, absently crumpling the bag and returning it to its box and into the purse.

Done.

She placed her arm around her mom's shoulders.

"Come on," Jasmine said, and guided her back to the bench.

Jasmine and Gloria Frank sat there for another hour or so, until the horizon was merely a purple glow. Then they walked slowly back down the pier and found the blue Camry that Jasmine had bought with the money they'd earned from the sale of the Buick—this after they'd gotten the deep-cleaned vehicle back from the police department, Karl's blood removed completely from the upholstery.

Jasmine drove them silently back to the house, twenty minutes with no words, just thoughts. They went inside and got on with their evening ritual of board games and smoothies. They were getting to the point (nearing a month since that fateful Saturday) where it was becoming easier.

The early days of Gloria's withdrawal had been characterized by a lot more screaming and crying, more visiting health practitioners—and now all that had just about dried up, and they were going it alone. Jasmine was by her mom's side almost constantly, and she actually felt love coming back. Not necessarily understanding, but love. Maybe forgiveness would follow.

That night, after softly singing her mother to sleep, Jasmine settled herself into the couch in the dark living room and stared out the front window onto the quiet street.

It was what she did almost every night.

Her ritual.

But tonight was a little different.

Next to her lay a cardboard sheet full of state quarters. Few days earlier, she'd gone back to Woody's Coins and Metals to buy the sheet of minty coins. A miserable old man sold them to her, hardly exchanging any words with her at all. She guessed he was Woody himself. The owner. Didn't matter.

She'd brought the coins home and shown them to her mom, asked her which was her favorite, and her mom said it didn't matter—that Jasmine should choose.

She picked up the sheet now and placed it on her lap. She studied it for a while, admiring the design of each quarter in turn. Then she poised a finger above the sheet, closed her eyes, and let her hand fall. Her finger had landed directly on one of the quarters, and she smiled at the shiny coin. Drew it from its slot, rubbed it between her fingers.

There had been monsters in her life. Sometimes she'd cowered from them, and sometimes she'd faced them down. Sometimes the monsters had gone away on their own. Maybe monsters would always be out there. Jasmine knew she'd always have to be wary of them.

But she felt more prepared now than she'd ever been to give them hell.

Acknowledgments

To the ever-enthusiastic cheerleaders among my family and friends—you know who you are!

Thanks especially to my sister Missy for a groovy day wandering Santa Ana, gathering sights and sounds. Big-time gratitude to Gary Phillips, Kirk Whitham, Sally Sanders, Mike Parish, Shannon Lacey Cavanaugh, Nikki Jackson, and—of course—Barb Bovberg for their sharp observations during the early reading phase, and to Michael Morris and Kirk Whitham for the cover art, design, and layout. And finally, cheers to the authors who took precious time from their own writing schedules to read this book and provide excellent cover blurbs: Scott Phillips, Gary Phillips, and Kirk Whitham.

About the Author

Jason Bovberg is the author of the *Blood* trilogy—*Blood Red*, *Draw Blood*, and *Blood Dawn*—as well as *The Naked Dame*, a throwback pulp noir novel. His forthcoming books include *Tessa Goes Down*, a border noir, and *A Small Poisonous Act*, a suburban crime novel. He is editor/publisher of Dark Highway Press, which published the controversial, erotic fairy tale *Santa Steps Out* and the weird western anthology *Skull Full of Spurs*. He lives in Fort Collins, Colorado, with his wife Barb, his daughters Harper and Sophie, and his canines Rocky and Rango. You can find him online at www.jasonbovberg.com.

CPSIA information can be obtained
at www.ICGtesting.com
Printed in the USA
LVHW031129130721
692557LV00012B/1185

9 780966 262988